PACIFIC NOCTURNE

Pacific Nocturne
by Don Denevi
Published by Creative Texts Publishers
PO Box 50
Barto, PA 19504
www.creativetexts.com

ISBN: 978-0-578-49015-1

PACIFIC NOCTURNE

CREATIVE TEXTS PUBLISHERS
Barto, Pennsylvania

TABLE OF CONTENTS

"No one, absolutely no one, is who he or she seems to be. All humans, without exception, wear the mask of the actor to hide the true face. If evil exists beneath the face, hidden in the deep unknowable clefts and crevasses of the unconscious mind, it must be engaged and pondered for the world at large. We need more understanding of evil's existence, and potential for murder, in human nature, because the only real danger that exists is man himself."

"If in his abysmal darkness he has acquired a nauseating taste for blood, murder further kindles murder. The natural man, with all his wholeness, is in great danger, and we are pitifully unaware of it. We know nothing of the evil murdering man. Far too little. His poisoned mind must be studied, because we, too, on the borderline of madness, are the origins of all coming evil."

C. G. Jung 1977: 436
"What Is the Source of Evil?"
in "Jung On Evil", selected writings,
Introduced by Murray Stein,
Princeton. University Press, 1995

INTRODUCTION

In a nationwide broadcast to the American people on V-J Day (Victory Over Japan), September 2, 1945, the day of formal surrender on board the U.S.S. Missouri, Douglas MacArthur, General of the Army, a vanquisher with sincere compassion for the fallen foe, began,

"Today, the guns are silent. A great tragedy has ended. A great victory has been won. The skies no longer rain death—the seas bear only commerce—men everywhere walk upright in the sunlight. The entire world is quietly at peace . . . I speak for the thousands of silent lips, forever stilled among the jungles and the beaches and in the deep waters of the Pacific . . . a new era is upon us . . . the survival of civilization . . ."

Admiral Chester Nimitz, Commander-in-Chief, Pacific Fleet and Pacific Ocean Areas, also a kind man a with strong feelings of empathy and mercy, and fully aware millions of lives were doomed because an ambitious, reckless military clique forced a good people into war throughout Asia in the 1930's and Pearl Harbor in 1941, followed with,

"On Guam is a military cemetery in a green valley not far from my headquarters. The ordered rows of white crosses stand as reminders of the heavy cost we have paid for victory. On these crosses are the names of American soldiers, sailors and Marines— Culpepper, Tomaino, Sweeny, Bromberg, Depew, Melloy, Ponziani - - - names that are a cross-section of Democracy. They fought together as brothers in arms; they died together and now they sleep side by side. To them we have a solemn obligation - - - the obligation to ensure that their sacrifice will help to make this a better and safer world in which to live."

With the long and bitter struggle at an end, and a spiritual recrudescence underway for all that is virtuous, moral, and exemplary in Man, who would remember, let alone believe, the inexplicable, unfathomable deaths of nine Marine privates and nurses at the hands of a multiple-murdering fellow Marine? With Armageddon averted, the fear of world destruction superseded by the dream and hope of a new emancipation for the enslaved, who was to flash a glance at rumors of a deadly terrorizing week-long killing spree on a far-off islet in the South Pacific basin? Granted, murders of defenseless Marines by a fellow Marine in an orderly, systematic manner are so horrifying a betrayal of brothers-in-arms, combat chums, and fellow Americans that they defy belief. Few soldiers, sailors, airmen, or Marines of all the world's armed forces can fathom killing one of their own.

No, best to allow the intelligent mind, both individual and the official collective, complete its conscious work of focusing upon the utter destructiveness of an ocean war to blot away a series of unsubstantiated nocturnal episodes trifling in the loss of life, especially in a ridiculed, now abandoned airbase, depot, staging and rest area.

Although based upon several actual unresolved mystifying incidents stealthily insinuating serial murder, the following pages are full of unadulterated fiction. This "whodunit" detective story challenges the reader not only to determine who the imaginary sanguinary slayer is, but also to decide if the Mad Ghoul, or Charlie the Choker, even existed.

In the December 1947 issue of the USMC "Leatherneck Magazine", a letter appeared in the column, "Sound Off", edited by Sgt. Harry Polete, written by Mike Nelson of Minneapolis. It was entitled, "Choker vs. the Ghoul", and read,

"Sirs:

In the August issue there was an article called 'Pavuvu Nocturne'. If my memory serves me right, I believe this creature was called the 'Mad Ghoul' and not 'Charlie the Choker'. I may be wrong, but in the old 1st Battalion, First Marine Area, it was called 'The Mad Ghoul'.

Otherwise, the story is absolutely true and I'm sure many of the fellows from the old First can substantiate this."

Sgt. Harry Polete responded, "Charlie the Choker and the Mad Ghoul are but half a dozen names used by Marines to describe their nocturnal visitor. 'Leatherneck' used Charlie the Choker more for its dramatic sound than anything else and did not intend to imply that it was the only name Charlie was known by. Some of the men, especially those who felt his fingers about their throat, probably had some names that we would not be allowed to print."

Fourteen years later, Russell Davis, in his memoir, "Marine At War" (1961), devoted 19 pages to a chapter entitled "Rumor and The Mad Ghoul" which described how the "creature" was "born" and "walked by night among the men of the First Marine Division" then "confirmed" by having been seen on several occasions, chased and shot at. According to the reports of sightings by sentries and others, "the Ghoul loped like an animal, his hands almost touching the ground". The PFC then concluded his chapter with an appraisal of the Ghoul's "demise". He wrote,

"There was no proof that such a creature as the Ghoul ever existed. But I believed in him at the time, and so did most of the Marines. Loneliness and a life in which rumor served as a morning newspaper could have created the Ghoul, spread his fame, and killed him. No one will ever really know… But in time one character will always stand out in my memory—the Mad Ghoul. He was the dark spirit that was in all of us then."

That island of Pavuvu in the Russells during mid-year, 1944, is now a vanished world. No crossing, no number of words or photographs, except imagination can carry us back to the months the fighting men of the 1st Division experienced it as little more than a rat's nest. Palm trees with their forest-green fronds are still there, as well as well-groomed coconut plantations and wide coral-crusted asphalt roads. Cobalt-blue white-crested ocean waves still crash the rugged coasts and there has been no letup in the daily torrential rains pounding the islands, just as they have for thousands of years. Today, tourists line up to sightsee the rusting World War II ocean and land wrecks, both American and

Japanese. Visitors house in prestige apartments, waterfront villas and bed and breakfast flats. Although not exactly a Pacific jetsetter's playground or exclusive island of costly resorts, it is nonetheless an island featuring a plethora of land and water sports; peace and tranquility are its major attraction. The major caution: falling coconuts capable of causing serious concussions.

Pavuvu of the Pacific War almost three-quarters of a century ago will never come again. It resides and breathes in a historical yesterday. Time has erased much, and virtually obliterated the handful of references to the Mad Ghoul and Charlie the Choker.

As this is a work of historical fiction attempting to follow historical fact, it is necessary to remind the reader that it is within the purview of the novelist the task of portraying in detail what might have happened if the full story unfolded to its natural conclusion. Storyline and personality are subordinated to setting—in this case, the small island of Pavuvu deep in the Ocean of the Southwestern Pacific.

CHAPTER ONE

-

Pavuvu Island

"Since the last war many mysterious tales have come of the Pacific Islands. One of the weirdest of these accounts found its origin on Pavuvu Island in the Russell's Group.

Marines of the First Division, stationed there during the spring of 1944, called it 'the island the good Lord forgot'. And, not without good reason. The continual rain and sweltering heat were almost unbearable, but these seemed to be minor plagues when compared to an elusive creature which stalked the night."

So wrote Corpsman Donald H. Edgemon in one of his monthly columns, the August 1947 issue of USMC "Leatherneck Magazine".

For the first time in public print, mention was made of a series of nocturnal visits in which several battle-worn veterans of the 1st Marines from the Guadalcanal campaign who swore someone had cut through the mosquito nets in their pyramidal tents and tried to stab them while they were asleep. Each suddenly-awakened rifleman in various areas of the 600-acre Tent City pledged that he had observed a face and a shiny butcher knife over him. Two insisted they felt fingers on their throats with attempts to strangle them.

While guards were posted throughout the Regimental areas during the late Spring, of 1944, most of the officers of the 1st Division were somewhat skeptical. Some openly accused the victims of hallucinating, delusional dreaming, and concocting "frightening demons" in order to be shipped stateside to mental hospitals. Most officers shouted the same insults at the hapless, according to Corp. Edgemon,

"Who ever heard of big Marines complaining of something as silly as this? Get your assess back to your tents and stay away from the raisin jack or bug juice or whatever else you knotheads have been belting at."

Within days, an uneasiness spread among the 16,000 recuperating, relaxing, refitting Marines on Pavuvu, and an additional 5,000 serviceman on Banika across the narrow channel. Few slept peacefully. Some were angrily agitated, others quietly anxious. Not until several weeks had passed without a further incident did the officers and troops begin to relax.

"See, you dumb sons-of-bitches," shouted sergeants throughout the training and rest-camps, "Not a scratch, let alone a wound."

By mid-June 1944, however, with everyone relaxed and at ease, "that thing" resumed prowling the arteries, byways, lanes and shortcuts of Tent City and its adjacent tent camps, searching in the soaking midnight showers for a defenseless victim.

Over the span of a week, four more assaults occurred. Two of the victims were alone, while the other two were asleep with as many as five tentmates. More impudent than brave, insolent than audacious, the offender seemed mindless, suggesting a harmless, asocial, battle-scarred Marine with a severe mental disorder. Eye-witnesses observing the culprit fleeing could only identify him as either a savage jungle "tree-hanger", a wild "two-legged animal", a drunken Polynesian from Banika. One who had his throat fondled insisted it was the revered

Youza, the Fuzzy-Wuzzie native of Guadalcanal who served as scout for the 5th Marines captured by the Japanese during the final stages of battle at Cape Gloucester; he was nearly beaten to death and severely bayonetted by a Japanese Naval Officer proud of his shiny antique sword. Refusing to point out Marine positions, Youza was left for dead. Marine advanced pointmen found him bleeding profusely and managed to save his life. Later, in a small ceremony, riflemen unofficially promoted him to Major General Youza. Corpsman Donald H. Edgemon commented,

"A few of the ever-present sea lawyers, however, maintained that it was a time the creature had been named 'Charlie the Choker.'"

Apparently, the 1st Division officers of high rank grew less and less skeptical. With continuing complaints, most were convinced. Then, one night, the Choker truly attempted to end the life of his latest victim. Deep, long scratches around the unfortunate Marine's neck and throat convinced the brass to issue orders tripling the guard. "If there are any Jap or Marine sleepwalkers, stragglers, or assassins on this godforsaken island, shoot to kill."

According to those who were most involved in the matter, its verity and veracity, no number of precautions restrained the prowler from his nocturnal greetings, or as Edgemon phrased it, "sack-time visitations." Dashing and darting through the usual rain-drenching nights, he was fired upon, rifle bullets whizzing around and past him.

"The bastard has some mighty moves, all right. Can't really recognize who or what he is," said one night duty sentry.

"For sure, it's not our Youza. He's so riddled with wounds and in so much pain, he can't even walk."

Whether it was Youza, the Mad Ghoul, or Charlie the Choker, no one cared. At the expense of fellow Marines, someone was enjoying the fears and anxieties of the 1st Division personnel, and, as staff officers argued, only a personality formed by the island of Pavuvu could be so mean.

CHAPTER TWO

-

A Stench of Death

Poor Pavuvu.

Promoted as a panoramic "rest camp paradise playground" by the staff officers of Major General Roy S. Geiger's USMC III Amphibious Corps for the First Division's 16,000 officers and enlisted men after their fierce fighting for Guadalcanal, the tiny fabled island proved upon the first moments of arrival everything but.

The selection had been made during a flight over the Russell Group when someone noted Pavuvu's graceful shoreline and prewar symmetrical rows of palm trees suggesting prim and trim tidiness as the groundwork for rehabilitation, relaxation, and refitting. After the Guadalcanal campaign, and that of Cape Gloucester which immediately followed, the Marines were combat-spent, fatigued, and lethargic. By December of 1943, having set sail from San Francisco in June of 1942, the Division's losses were 621 killed in action, 1,517 wounded, and 5,601 stricken with malaria.

As the First Division boarded the troop ships for departure from Cape Gloucester, rumors were rampant their destination was Melbourne, Australia. Officers who supposedly had the straight scoop were quoted that the Marines were headed stateside. When at sea in the Coral Islands, men were informed they were headed for reposeful play and soothing tranquility at an unheard of isle amid more than 50, each smaller than the other centered around the two largest, Banika and

Pavuvu; the former approximately eight by two miles, the latter, eight by seven.

Allied strategists planned the Russells, Banika and Pavuvu, in particular, as forward operating bases and staging areas for invasion throughout the northwestern Pacific, the New Georgia Islands and the drive on Rabaul, first in a series of successions eastward. Banika was projected as a primary supply base with a 6,300-foot-long runway servicing both F4U Corsair fighters and torpedo and dive bombers, while suitable as a PT boat base, was seen as a training center.

No fewer than 16,000 service personnel were on the Russells at one time or another after April of 1944. By August of that year, the number had reached more than 60,000.

And, every single one of them assigned to Pavuvu felt the same way; it was the most God-awful, inhospitable environment they endured outside of combat itself.

At first glance, Pavuvu appeared to be a tropical picturesque isle, with lush foliage, large groves of coconut palms, coral-covered copra plantation roads, battle-surviving cattle roaming freely, dense tropical rain forests yielding logging, rugged coral coastlines, and beautiful blue ocean waves. On a clear day, one could see the crests and peaks of the Guadalcanal Mountains without binoculars. To the 1st Division officer corps gazing from the railings of their troop transports sailing but 30 miles W by N of Cape Esperance, the resting, recuperating troops would soon be proud to call the forever muddy, rain-soaked Pavuvu the "Home of the 1st Division".

Hidden deep among the southeastern Solomon Islands less than 125 miles directly east of the New Georgias, Pavuvu's locale and bearings were ideal for safety and security from both the Japanese naval bombardments and air force bombings.

In fact, air raids and attacks upon ships anchored off Pavuvu, the nearby storage facilities, and aviation-gasoline tank farms of eight 1,000-barrel tanks, barge landings and landing docks diminished considerably by late June. By the first of July, the air raids ceased after the last attack, which resulted in only three hits on American ships, with little damage and no casualties.

Upon disembarking by filing down the troop ships' gangplanks, the 16,000 Marines with their 550 plus officers, as well as medical support personnel and Seabees, found that Pavuvu, the supposed "most exclusive playground in the Pacific", was so insufferable many vomited.

What the island-selection committee and 1st Division officials didn't investigate and ponder was why in the 1920's the 350 Polynesian Lavukal natives fled Pavuvu to resettle on Tikopia. Only after the buildup on the island, and the arrival of the 1st Division, did anyone bother to question the refugees. Through translators, the Lavukaleves said that not only did the land crabs hate the island so much they began eating each other and the rugged coral coastline, but also insisted the coconuts were prematurely ripening so they could fall heavier on the heads of humans.

Once assembled on the landing platforms, the debilitated 1st began to smother in the hot, humid mugginess accentuated by the horrible smell of putrid milk from rotting coconuts and decaying land crabs, guaranteeing few stomachs would settle until before departure. The fresh Marine replacements from Melbourne who followed the Cape Gloucester—Guadalcanal veterans were heavily burdened with gear and weapons waiting to board buses for their bivouacs. "Tent City" could not escape the shower of rotting coconuts thrown at them by giggling earlier Marine arrivals hiding atop the roofs of the pier facilities. Despite sitting comfortably aboard the buses, and observing the well-groomed lanes of recently planted coconut saplings and rows of smart, green Quonset-hut warehouses, no one was impressed or amused with rancid, smelly milk all over their uniforms.

In a matter of minutes, the arriving 1st Division, followed by the contingent of replacements, would learn the true horridness of life on Pavuvu—the swamps, smell, repulsive, sordid waters of malaria-breeding mosquitos. When entering the nearby jungles, steamy and virulent, or terrain, shaggy and arduous, all, no exceptions, were warned to take their regularly-issued, bitter, bright-yellow Atabrine tablets that restrained the chills and fever of infectious malaria sooner or later, claimed by the N.C.O.'s and other officers, "Everyone in the 1st Division, from the Major General to the private, will contract the disease which in more than half the cases will last for years. Don't forget: everyone is susceptible."

Slightly less loathing but nonetheless abhorrent was the body odor of the island everyone carried with him. No one knew where it came from, or what to call it, not even the staff officers of the 1st Division. But, the smell was evident whenever someone approached another. Within the pitched pyramidal tents, with six to eight Marines on cots or hammocks, the smell was intensified, leading a Marine to chuckle, "It's not the smell of dysentery or burned-out flesh. If anything, it's the smell of unharvested coconuts that because of the war have been in a state of putrescence for more than two years."

Compounding everyone's misery was how soft and deep and mushy the topsoil was. Composed of decomposing non-integrating, workable coral, most of the men chose to walk shoeless since much of the island was a few inches or feet under water. After the heavy downpours, flooding was common.

Hardly had the 1st Division and equipment arrived on shore, and realized Pavuvu was not the promised playground of unlimited land and water sports including scuba diving and exploration, nicknames for it began to crop up: "Hell Hole", "Ringworm Rental", "Rupertus' Punishment", "Jungle Rot", "Bliss and Piss Cellulitis Center", "Morale Lost", "C and K Rations, Plus Insects", etc.

Such pet names lasted as long as they were audibly uttered, then forgotten as new ones were uttered, then forgotten. One name, however, overrode all others. Even the officers, employed its use: "This f---ing birdshit island."

The chow was tolerated because "There ain't any restaurants around here". Heated Spam, coupled with dehydrated everything, was served on tin plates every day, for lunch and dinner. Only the Spam, the main course, occasionally changed. Most Marines felt the Spam tasted worse than the drinking water which some believed the Japanese had somehow poisoned.

Hatred increased for the loathsome mosquitos and detested land crabs which nightly overran the base and Tent City usually to settle next to the cot or hammocks foot lockers. Particularly bothersome was the lack of bathing facilities and proper toilets. Bathing was accomplished during the frequent cloudbursts, the muddy open roads in front of the rows of tents serving as shower stalls. Bodily infections were common, especially in the feet of the tired Marines. The island's high humidity prolonged the healing process, especially in those areas around the toes and toenails. Pavuvu's remoteness, isolation, desolation, and boredom led to several sentry suicides while on duty with their Garand M-1 rifles.

One newly-arrived Marine replacement feeling the fever and sweat, the first symptoms of malaria, was overheard asking a battle-worn Guadalcanal veteran rehabilitating on the hospital sun porch. "Do you think that any evil was forgotten by God when he formed this place?"

Without hesitation, the veteran responded.

"Only one, a week-long murder spree."

CHAPTER THREE

-

"A Jap straggler or infiltrator, you think?"

Tuesday, August 1, 1944

Minutes past midnight, in the earliest morning hour of that tragic Tuesday, the typical tropical shower, violently teeming while lasting less than a moment, abruptly ceased. A billion sparkling stars shone through long rifts in the swiftly moving clouds, basking the entire Russell Island Group in illuminating moonlight. For a Pacific equatorial summer, the night air seemed unusually fragrant, lighter, and certainly cooler.

By 1:00am, the weather changed. Brusquely, the prevailing high winds of the Coral Sea began to howl down through the narrow slot in a southeasterly direction and sweep over Pavuvu, the largest of the Russell's two main islands toward Guadalcanal 65 miles away. For a murderer looming in the shadows of several open tarpaulin posts and platforms, the ferocity of the gusts and blusters was commensurable with his intense urge to slaughter.

Although Pavuvu was uninhabitable, rugged, rocky, and swamp-riddled, its coral terrain allowed enough solidity to accommodate a thousand tents for the 1st Marine Division combat veterans and stateside replacements recently arrived from Guadalcanal to relax and refit for the pending invasion of Guam.

Now, silhouetted against the shadow of a rolled up tarpaulin cover, a killer, dressed in officer clothing, was poised for an onslaught upon a randomly selected victim within a medically-modified, mosquito-netted canvas tent in the middle of the last row of more than 75 amply-spaced tents lined in a row in some 180 rows.

Within the targeted tent, stretched out under warm, soft navy hospital blankets were PFC Johnny C. Houser, a rifleman from the Fourth Marines, 5th Division; PFC Leo Cass, infantryman, 10th Defense Battalion, 1st Division; and, PFC Richard Mosequeda, 1st Raider Battalion, 1st Division. Lame and in pain, all three were recovering from wounds inflicted by shell bursts from the dreaded Japanese 150mm gun hidden in a protected hill emplacement during the final phase of fighting for Cape Gloucester, New Britain, months earlier. Under each of their cots was a Garand M1 rifle. Mosequeda, a 1st Raider Battalion Purple Heart recipient, also possessed a M1928 Thompson. All four weapons, the three Garands and Thompson, were fully loaded and cocked for firing.

Drowsily aware of strange steps outside the back of his tent, then a barely audible ripping sound of canvas overhead, PFC Houser, recuperating from numerous deep lacerations over his entire body, breathed quietly and listened lazily.

With the high winds partially muffling the cadence of the slow tearing sounds by some sort of sharp instrument, he grew increasingly puzzled, then concerned. Opening his eyes, he was shocked the pitch-black tent was suddenly lit by moonlight. A large flap was cut open and was hanging loosely at one corner less than a foot above his face. Silver rays of moonlight illumined a human head enshrouded by a tan scarf gazing down upon him. The object's brown hood over the tan scarf wrapped about his neck and face couldn't conceal huge, penetrating eyes staring straight down on him.

Stiffly, Houser struggled to rise, frightened beyond physical pain or even belief, especially when in the bright moonlight he glimpsed the glint of a shiny, wide-blade butcher knife rising in a slow, grim mechanical manner to engage in murderous work.

In one swift motion, without a single decibel of sound stirring the two tentmates slumbering soundly, a USMC-issued burnished razor-sharp Ka-Bar fighting knife cut out the large flap on the tent over Houser's head, and, in full force, plunged into the hapless PFC's abdomen, penetrating deep to the lumber vertebra. One poignant, piercing shriek in the fright and pain of a death throe was uttered by Houser as he feebly clutched his stomach and keeled over onto the floor's wooden plank, tumbling the cot on its side, tangling Houser amid the blankets and mosquito netting. Cutting the rest of the flap open to allow himself in, the killer entered, then pounced upon the enmeshed, dying PFC, repeatedly thrusting the bloodied blade into all of Houser's abdomen organs. The dull thudding of stabbing sounds on the soft surface of the tragic victim's stomach, blending with spattering and splashing of blood throughout the middle of the tent interior, finally stirred the other two sleepers into realization that something horrific was happening.

Awakening, Cass and Mosequeda threw their blankets off, struggling for their firearms, or own fighting knives, recklessly placed atop their small lockers at the foot of their cots. Believing Japanese infiltrators, or stragglers, had penetrated the camp's perimeters and were now attacking the bivouac of slumbering Marines; they were up in a flash, seeing the assassin leap off dead Houser, and dash through the open canvas' swinging flap. Within a moment, he was past the rolled up tarpaulin covering, scurrying over plywood floors, and vanishing into an area of jumbled warehouses tents, Quonsets, and other small facilities. Mosqueda, upon grasping the full carnage, angrily fired off a full burst from the Thompson, with no thought of aiming.

Turning on the light within the tent, the two PFCs were the first to observe the full extent of the butchery, hearing a final, barely discernable deflating gasping hiss from the victim who was believed dead. With all four quadrants of Houser's mid-section punctured and oozing bloodily, all the two Marines could do was feel for a hint of life, which they did so until sickened. Only the hideously contorted facial express and its gaping mouth confirmed the tragedy.

CHAPTER FOUR

-

" . . . no beast so fierce knows but some touch of pity... "
Tuesday, August 1, 1944

Gloomily, PFC Leo Cass, in his underwear clutching his Garand M1, and PFC Richard Mosequeda, now in combat fatigues holding his MI928 Thompson, both numb and bewildered, turned their backs upon the bloody corpse of PFC Houser and stepped outside the tent. All they could do was wait in pensive thought.

Outside, in the light of the full bright moon, with the heavy winds slacking, thick, black clouds could be seen swarming swiftly across the northern Coral Sea toward them on desolate Pavuvu. The air was much colder than earlier, stinging all human flesh it touched. A ferocious storm was on its way and, although Tent City and the base seemed deserted in the early morning hour, all hell was breaking loose.

With the loud burst from the Thompson erupting the island into chaos, sirens sounding, and search lights turned on, every available M. P. scoured the base, especially the deep shadows cast by tents, tarpaulin coverings, posts, from the warehouses, docking, and storage areas, including vehicle and garage ports, to the darkest corners of the tent rows. Meanwhile, armed sentries and guards raced to and fro, lit fires, formed search parties and dispersed with heavy-duty flashlights, everyone shouting and issuing orders. All this as the sirens continued to blare harshly, nonstop.

At the murder scene, two military police officers were the first to arrive, one a captain, the other a lieutenant. They were followed by cautious Marines from neighboring tents, fully armed and combat-ready, some jokingly demanding of the PFCs, "Bad dreams, boys?", or "No time for sex-crazy nightmares, men! We're Marines!"Cass would then hold the tent entrance flap open and motion for the loudmouths to glance inside. Turning away, some vowed openly to kill every "…goddamn Jap in the universe."

As PFC's Cass and Mosqueda stood outside the front of the gruesome scene with the first contingent of MPs to arrive, a second jeep loaded with MP investigators and medical personnel pulled up.

Upon hearing the sudden spurt of shots from the Thompson in the middle of the night, several Marines recovering from malaria at the nearby newly Seabee-constructed Pavuvu Station Hospital arrived in several jeeps. Quietly resting prior to embarkation later that afternoon on board the hospital ship, USS General Robert L Howze, for departure to San Francisco hospitals, some still in pajamas, took up positions behind the murder tent, all gleefully armed with recently issued Reising submachine guns.

Cass, leaning against the tent post, rifle still in hand, turned around to see a stout, heavy-set military police officer climb out of the jeep's front passenger seat.

"Holy Moley, it'll be Captain Marvel, himself!" Cass exclaimed, referring to the popular comic book hero. "None other than Captain 'Slim', himself!"

Before Mosqueda could respond, the huge man was upon them.

"Gentlemen," he beamed, chuckling. "We were just radioed there was a little sprinkling of blood this way. You boys fighting? No need for a gun barrage to excite."

"Yes, Captain Oscar 'Slim' Del Barbra. I know you from Copperoplis, California. Known you on 'Canal', too. We've both seen a lot of blood, but nothing like this."

"You from Copperoplis, too? Don't know you," asked the captain, quizzically.

"Galt, sir. Right down the road form Copperopolis. Knew your younger brother, Louie. We played hardball for the Sego Milk Company team, the Horny Cows, in the 'Central Valley Baseball League for Stupid Boys', as my dad used to say."

Oscar 'Slim' roared with laughter, then responded hoarsely,

"Yup, that's the name our dad gave that league, too, private. Right now, show me what the commotion is all about."

Both Cass and Mosequeda knew of "Slim's" reputation. He was one of the heaviest men in the whole 1st Marine Division, and everyone still called him 'Slim'. According to Corps veterans who served with him, the middle-aged captain had broken more than his share of bones, arms, legs, and heads, while arresting Marine 'jack-offs' and criminals galore, shooting three, killing one. Bred along the low, hot hills of the eastern San Joaquin Valley, he boasted to anyone who would listen his sole purpose on this 'Godforsaken earth' was to anger bad people so they would assault him and he, in turn, could "break them into little pieces." Friends and victims alike claimed he was a "smoldering volcano."

Cass insisted "Holy Moley, Captain Marvel, himself, the Biggest Fist the American Military Police Has" was the type of man you either loved dearly or wanted to kill violently. Others said Slim was a passionate man who inspired passion in others. With a resounding belly laugh, a devil-may-care snickering defiance that filled the entirety of his round face to the jowls, the captain feared no one, especially anyone who wore medals or decorations, referring to anyone with a medal hanging from his chest as an "asshole wasting cloth."

"He's a queer one, alright," Cass whispered to Mosequeda, as the captain pulled the front flap of the tent open and entered the now well-lit enclosure. "He brags that he is neither of the body nor senses, but of the intellect and spirit. I heard he likes his sex very much and is the first to the whorehouses, regardless of the city, or in what country. So goes one of the legends that abound about him," the PFC concluded.

There was little question this more than 300-pound man, slouchy, was one of the most baffling, well-respected officers in the entire United States Marine Corps.

Leaping from the jeep's driver seat was Second Lieutenant Leo Guidi. As a commissioned officer of the lowest rank, he catered well to Captain Del Barbra, always two or three steps behind him, and, if possible, in his shadow. Guidi was his opposite -- quiet, bland, mild-mannered, and radiating a general air of sincerity. In short, the military police officer was a casual, unhurried, perpetually smiling man who spoke easily with a quiet dignity. If called upon in an emergency, however, he was no nonsense, deadly serious, and capable of shooting any Marine malcontent of any rank, if deserved.

Entering the murder scene behind his captain who was stone silent from the shock of what lay before him, the second lieutenant recoiled in horror.

For a long quiet moment, neither spoke. Then, the captain asked softly,

"So, lieutenant?"

"Jap infiltrator, or straggler?"

"Neither, not from what I'm seeing"

"But who . . .? Can't believe..."

"I can't either…", responded Del Barbra. Then, after a pause, he chuckled,

"Never thought one of our boys would go off the deep end because he hated the island's smell of rotten coconuts and land crabs."

Guidi, shocked, turned to stare at his captain in anger, then bit his tongue lest his thought, if spoken, be instantly regretted, "Why you shallow, stupid, pallid ton of sickening fat flesh, how dare you find humor in the merciless, sadistic mutilation of one of our men who survived being shot at crawling in the steaming jungles and slogging the muddy mountains trails on that hell island of death over there called, 'F - - - - - - Canal!'

"Well, what say you, second lieutenant?" insisted the captain. "You're supposed to be the veritable mountain of high intelligence around here. I wait, you homely, bow-legged vociferous little peewee?" Roaring with laughter, he added, "You ready to ballet through blood."

Guidi, continuing to gaze upon the death scene, angrily remained silent.

Then, he quietly mumbled words Captain Del Barbra didn't grasp, words whispered so hoarsely they were meant more to himself than his superior.

"What's that you say, youngster?"

"Not for your ears, sir. Actually nothing. Only a few sentences from Shakespeare."

"Test this ancient 'wop', this Italian family that arrived in America without passports. Get it? 'Wop', 'without passport', that's me."

"I quoted Lady Anne's fierce denunciation of Richard. She says in Act I, Scene II of 'Richard III', 'Villain, thou know'st no law of God nor Man. No beast so fierce but knows some touch of pity.' And,

Richard, in cruelty, answers, '. . . but I know none, and therefore am no beast!"

After a reflective pause, the captain asked,

"What the hell does that mean?"

"That Richard says he is a murderous man, a human being who can commit heinous crimes no beast, even the most killing kind, the most poisonous, can ever equal. A monster-man can murder. No animal on earth can murder like this," Guidi slowly responded.

"Ok, you win. I'll read him someday, this Shakespeare. But I still don't get it."

The lieutenant added, "Captain, this murder defies description, it's so horrendous."

"And, committed by a Marine using his Ka-Bar fighting knife. Only a swinging ax, or Ka-bar, or hatchet could create such mayhem," added the captain.

"Later this morning we'll examine the body to see if there are any bite marks around the head, or if the killer is anthropophagy," Guidi concluded.

"Someone who consumes the victim's blood? Yes, possibly. But he had no time."

"In this case, no, he didn't have time. He had two sleeping tentmates."

"No, but he might have wanted to," said the captain. After a long thought he added, "O.K, cowboy, I'm leaving everything to you. Seal off the tent. Assign the MPs who are arriving for specific duties. Then, write up the initial investigative report. Have it ready within four hours for our 0600 meeting. I'll contact the chain of command. You see to it the body is removed carefully. See to the photographs. Coordinate everything with the medical examiner-coroner. Tell him he is to report to the 0600 meeting. I'll let him know where. Search for footprints outside the tent. Search the surrounding areas. Just make sure to safeguard the body 100%. Come directly to the meeting at 0600, probably next door of headquarters. Once the body has been removed and placed in cold storage, leave two sentries to guard the entrance to the tent.

"And, sir, with all due respect, what are you going to do in the next four hours?"

"Why, you silly ass, I'm going ballroom dancing, then to sleep, of course. What a dumb question, second lieutenant."

CHAPTER FIVE

-

"We probably won't see any more killings... "

All day, Tuesday, August 1

An air of anxiety pervaded Pavuvu the rest of that day. After the brazen, horrifying murder in the earliest morning hour, and the uproar that followed during the hectic predawn, few of the 16,000 resting or recuperating Marines were capable of resuming their sleep, or even drowsiness for that matter, let along breakfasting with an appetite.

One of their own had been slaughtered, nay massacred, and there was no plausible explanation for such an atrocious act, especially after their officers had returned from the hour-long briefing shaking, and unnerved. Staring straight ahead, and in deep thought, all they could offer was "Charlie the Choker" or the Mad Ghoul, has crossed the line from severe psychoneuroses into the sheer insanity of murder and no one had a clue to his identity.

With a cup of hot coffee in one hand, a pencil behind the ear, and clipboards in the other, Captain Oscar "Slim" Del Barbra and second Lieutenant Leo Guidi were in a frenzy organizing work parties, drawing up assignments and sentry duties, quietly selecting the Division's best marksmen and scribbling time sequence intervals for posting as lookouts with binoculars among the tops of the palm trees at varied strategic distances throughout Tent City. In addition, large drums of oil, gasoline, and aviation fuel had to be "borrowed" from the small, destroyer class naval vessels in the Pavuvu-Banika channel and the outer harbor, where the larger ships were anchored. Arriving by barge and light craft, the drums and men had to be supervised for disbursement to several strategic points within the base for unsealing and pouring. The smaller containers then had to be directed to the crossroads, alleys, avenues, and intersections of Tent City for igniting at twilight.

"Are we gonna be famous!" chuckled Del Barbra to his second Lieutenant. "No one in the history of the Corps has lit up an entire base in the middle of a war, lighting up every shadow in every nook and cranny, establishing a whole new level and standard in the art of military illumination."

"All this effort," grumbled Guidi, joining him from across the road, "without a single clue, or shred of evidence, of who's doing what to whom or why."

"I'm starting to think the whole thing was just between two malcontents who hated each other. We probably won't see any more murders. The killer wants us to put it on old Charlie, or the poor Ghoul. Good idea, when you think about it. But he doesn't fool an old professional like me."

As Army and USMC trucks, as well as other vehicles, rolled stocked with oil drums toward their designated depots, the Captain reflected, "I never told you, little one, but I was a cop in crime-ridden South Sacramento before signing up two years ago for the Military Police of the Corps. Between 15 years there, and two here, I must have taken off the street at least a thousand, and thrown them in one hoosegow or another, maybe two hundred of our boys included. I've had sons-of-bitches pull knives and hatchets on me, shoot at me, and pummel me with rocks and fists to baseball bats, with me enjoying every second of it, from case to capture. And, believe me when I say maybe three got away, and even they were hurt or wounded. I had a reputation then, and even now, as being 'fearless'. I hate crime and criminals, even the petty thieves. You get smart with me, and I'll show you. But, for me, it comes down to the sensation; the adrenaline rush. The medals and decorations were nice, but the excitement was the key, and that came from beating the bad guys up. I've seen the unimaginable all around me. And, because I didn't cause any of it, I could sleep without a thought and eat without a care. In 15 years, I saw more body parts than most cops in small towns, like old Copperopolis. Heads, arms, legs, hands, feet, and other body parts severed. Ghastly. But I know the feeling of having a wacko, or sophisticated assassin, lunge a butcher knife at you. As hardened as I am, it shook me up. But, after cheating death so many times, I'm softer now, but very anxious to catch up with, and clutch the throat of that killer."

That entire day witnessed not a single drop of rain. Cool night winds mingled with incoming Coral Sea breezes. The work parties hastily poured the inflammable gas, aviation gasoline, and oil upon the rocks and open sand-packed containers and lit them. Soon the bonfires were sufficient to light up the faces of the Marine work parties on the ground and snipers in the palms.

"All that's missing, Captain, are dirge songs of death being sung."

Second Lieutenant Leo Guidi would never know the number of songs needed to be sung by all the choirs of the world to prevent the two murders that would occur in the next few hours.

A little after 1:00am, a sentry in his early 20's was struck so hard from behind with a carefully sharpened screwdriver that his M1 bayoneted rifle flew more than 15 feet in front of him. Instantly deceased, not a sound was uttered as he collapsed from the weapon entering his temple on the right side of his head. The murderer paused long enough to bite the victim's face hard, drawing blood to ensure his teeth pattern could not be easily identified. Apparently, he had no concern his saliva was left in place since he knew full well Captain Del Barbra would have no idea what to do with it.

It was possible the unfortunate sentry faced the murderer moments before, being killed, recognizing and engaging him in a brief, amicable conversation. When the sentry turned his back to continue his designated pacing duty, the killer struck in one extremely violent blow, easily penetrating the victim's temporal scalp to the temporal bone above the ear canal. The murderer did not wait to see how much blood was released by the deepness of the swift thrust. He quickly raised up from the superficial biting and walked casually into one of the well-lit roads. There was no blackness of night on Pavuvu that evening. The murderer simply strolled, then disappeared, into the heart of Tent City.

The second death occurred within a half hour of the first. A lone PFC sentry patrolling the back area of headquarters was murdered in the same way. He, too, recognized the perpetrator, engaged him in a brief conversation without once raising his bayoneted rifle, then as he turned to resume his march, was struck violently in his frontal stomach area, penetrating his liver and spleen, while severing the young man's splenic artery. The death weapon was an icepick, and like the screwdriver, was left unabashedly at the side of the victim in his large pool of blood.

Captain De Barbra would later determine the murderer stood less than 18" from the victim in order to achieve three rapid plunges. Again, not a sound was uttered.

"His wielding of the icepick is surprisingly professional. A butcher or surgeon, perhaps?" asked the Captain at the post examination of the violent crime and its scene. "Also, note the subacute bite mark on the cheek. Two different weapons for puncturing; not cutting, not sawing, not slicing, plunging thrusting, punctuating yes. Deaths in all three cases were caused by hemorrhaging, massive perforating, penetrating as many arteries as possible; neck, heart, lungs, and aorta. My God how the Ghoul loves blood!"

CHAPTER SIX

-

"The Mad Ghoul? Charlie the Choker?"

Evening, Tuesday, August 1

With his thick, grayish hair tousled, and a facial expression mired in what appeared to be a stormy somberness, Captain Oscar "Slim" Del Barbra of Company A, 1st Motor Transportation, Military Police, climbed into the jeep's driver seat and drove himself the two miles back to the 1st Division's Command Post.

As he sped past sentries and bonfires through the occasional low island fog, he noted the rain showers and high moaning winds of both the Solomon Sea and the Coral Seas had ceased, as had the wild shrieks and shrills from the nearby Pavuvu jungles. With the blinking stars soon to fade into a near all-black gray, predawn hinted the last of the moving shower clouds would yield at daybreak a bright blue Pacific sky.

Parking before the new Division Headquarters facility, still in the final stages of construction by the 19th Naval Construction Battalion, an attached unit known as the "Seabees", Del Barbra walked rapidly past the armed sentinels of the temporary command post. A small pagoda-like temple built in the form of a two-story pyramid, the fully armored structure served as an aviation observation tower for light singled-engined reconnaissance aircraft. Hastily, he trotted up the steps and into his office.

There were more than 25 phone calls he felt he should personally make, if he was to meet his designed 6:00am conference time. This, of course, meant postponing his sleep for an additional 10 to 15 hours, at least.

Before anyone else, the captain chose to inform his own supervisor, Unit Commander, 1st Motor Transportation, Major Kimber H. Boyer, he worked closely with when the fledgling Military Police unit of the 1st Division was assigned to the 1st Motor Transportation in the recent Cope Gloucester "Backhander" Operation.

Then, over the often-malfunctioning telephone wires, he alerted the Assistant Division Commander, Brigadier General Lemuel C. Shepherd, of the murder and forthcoming meeting. After his third phone call, a lengthy talk with 1st Medical Battalion Commodore Everett B. Keck, USN, he phoned in less than 90 minutes 13 unit commanders, 5 group colonels, 5 battalion majors, and 18 company lieutenants.

In less than three hours, Del Barbra needed to conduct an informational meeting with all the major safety and security personnel on the island. With as many as 45 officers requested to attend the conference, the site for such a large gathering would have to be the open air dining patio of the recently completed sick bay adjacent to the Pavuvu Station Hospital. General USMC hospitals were large fixed installations that provided comprehensive care for severe wounds throughout a theater of battle. Station hospitals served a single post such as Pavuvu. Field hospitals were mobile, accompanying the troops.

Attached to a partially destroyed Japanese-built warehouse, the 200-bed prefabricated station hospital was neither a tarpaulin tent with a sizeable Red Cross sign above the entrance flap, nor the traditional brick building type, the trademark of hospitals found at such military installations as Camp Lejeune. The large ward, located in between the Division Command Post of the pagoda-like temple and the original regimental Pavuvu sick-bay and dispensary, was established the year before. Despite the primitive environmental, technical, and utility conditions of the terrain, the tiny medical facility, per the traditional USMC manner, provided the best possible medicines, first-aid treatments, and relief from the variety of small wounds, illnesses, pains and suffering associated with the Russell Island Group. Its once-demolished roof was repaired with palm thatch in less than a day by a boatload of Guadalcanal natives nicknamed "Fuzzy-Wuzzies" because of their meticulously coiffured curly black hairdos.

Nearing dawn and the 6:00am meeting, the attendees began arriving at the recently completed sick bay's open air dining patio by jeep at approximately the same time. On the Division Command Post steps, Captain Del Barbra greeted each arrival and directed him to the sick bay adjacent the Pavuvu Station hospital fewer than 25 yards away, where hot coffee and freshly baked rolls awaited them.

"Gentlemen, the meeting will be delayed until 0800 in the patio. The chairs are in a circle. If there's a cloudburst, we'll move into the facility. Enjoy the two hours with all the coffee and rolls you want."

The order had come down directly from 1st Division Commander Major General William H. Rupertus through his assistant, Brigadier General Lemuel Shepherd, that he wanted Chief of Staff Colonel Amor LeRoy Sims, as well as every psychiatrist on both Pavuvu and Banika to attend. The Banikin Island officers would be flown to Pavuvu, a flight time of fewer than 20 minutes.

By 0745, everyone summoned was assembled and seated quietly in a large circle in the open dining area patio. The hoped-for bright sunlight that morning hadn't materialized. Instead, a typical summer overcast, low with stiff breezes, brought comfortable cooling. As the minutes ticked down to the formal call for attention by whomever was chairing the session, top 1st Division commanders were seated next to company platoon leaders, and first Lieutenants next to unit, battalion, and group chiefs, all of whom were whispering, chuckling softly, and murmuring or muttering.

Within seconds of precisely 0800, Captain Del Barbra, with several binders under his arm, stepped from the corridor of the sick bay onto the patio and edged himself through the seated participants into the center of the circle.

"Gentlemen, I begin this call to order by calling your attention to four binder sets of murder scene photographs just received from the headquarters lab. Look carefully, officers of the realm, at three of our slaughtered boys who fought valiantly at Guadalcanal and survived, only to come to this homely, squalid, civilized-forsaken, eternally miserable sand hellhole islet 'rest camp' of rotted coconuts."

As the four binders were passed about the circle, the captain gazed upon the shocked facial expressions of the USMC officers. For a long moment, no one uttered as the death scene photos were passed from one to another. Then, Del Barbra said,

"All of you who have been mustered and mobilized here this morning have heard, the rumors of the 'Mad Ghoul' and 'Charlie the Choker' from almost the first moment our old 1st Battalion, First Marine Area, arrived."

One of his officers raised his hand, adding, "Those are only two of at least a dozen of such names used to label our nocturnal visitor."

"I know. I know. The more the creature appears, the greater the dramatic name given. Some of our Marines who felt his fingers around their throats had more obscene, unprintable names thrown at him. I was on duty that night the first call came in that a rifleman in the Fourth Marines, 5th Division ripped off his mosquito net and dashed shrieking and screeching down the company street. I was the one who interviewed him at headquarters. He wasn't intoxicated. We didn't think at the time he had a dream or nightmare. He claimed someone attempted to stab him while he slept. He insisted he saw a face and a knife over him. He screamed over and over he wasn't hallucinating. I had search teams scrambled and on grounds within minutes. I had my MPs posted around his tent. All regimental areas were scoured by as many as a hundred armed men. Nothing turned up. Nothing. But, then the same story happened again, and again. We all know that nothing happened, fingers around the neck, fingers on the face. But whomever it was doing these insane jokes, and trust me when I say I hope they were jokes, and nothing but jokes, and not something more sinister, whomever was doing those acts, has now suddenly carried the acts to a new level and we now have a multiple slayer on our hands, a lust murderer who enjoys killing."

"Well," a battalion commander said, raising his hand and standing up, "What's happening is that the whole Division, more than 16,000 troops are upset, uneasy, agitated. And, this slaughter of three fellow Marines is going to really discompose them."

"Well," confirmed Del Barbra, "We've learned just recently on the Eastern Front in Russian, the most stealth in the Soviet armies were taught to slinking across the lines in the darkest hours before dawn when soldiers were more apt to be sound asleep. They find the foxhole pinpointed earlier in the day, then cut the throat of one of the four or five occupants in deep slumber. Just one, not all! The assassin would sneak back across the lines to his side. That one act of slaughter, without the others waking up, would terrify a whole army!"

"So," interjected Brigadier General William H. Rupertus, "this Mad Ghoul, or Charlie the Choker, has to be a Jap straggler hiding out there in the jungle."

"Or," added Chief of Staff Colonel Amor LeRoy Sims, "a Jap or two or three infiltrators."

"Impossible!" responded Del Barbra. "We have the island secure. No one can get through or across our beaches or dry areas without being noticed. Can't be a Jap. And, there are no natives on Pavuvu. They abhor this real estate more than we do. They have all retreated across to the more livable Banika Island."

"You say a Marine did this?" demanded Rupertus. "I don't believe it, Captain!"

"Maybe, sir, maybe you're right. Up to last night, not a single prick or scratch occurred on a sleeping man. I, too, refused to believe it's one of our boys committing such a heinous act. But the three events this last night will certainly disquiet everyone. I've already given the orders for more guards to be posted, formed into patrols, for the island, both islands, all the islands of the Russells to be searched again for any clues whatsoever."

After a brief pause, Captain Del Barbra continued, "Let Lieutenant Guidi, my immediate subordinate, talk about the crime scene. He knows more about conducting malicious, wanton murder investigations than anyone else in our Military Police out here. He's all business when it comes to systematic, brutal, senseless butchery." Del Barbara concluded with finality, "Listen carefully, men, listen carefully."

"Yes, sir," said second Lieutenant Guidi, as he rose from the circle and walked into its center. "If I know so much about solving homicide, how come I failed the five murder investigations I was assigned to stateside?"

Everyone chuckled, as the Captain turned and glanced at him with an affectionate smile.

"Gentleman, as we all know, there are no Jap straggler or infiltrators on the island. The island is too small and too populated with too much movement for so obvious an enemy to hide out. And, the Rising Sun's Navy is not stupid enough to allow one of their prized submersibles to ground itself in order to allow one or two infiltrators to sneak ashore and seek out a single Marine, especially when that submarine can attack a carrier. No, neither Jap nor native from our neighbor islands did these killings you're looking at in the photos being passed around."

"And," he continued, "We're together, I'm certain, that none of us can think of a greater treachery, disloyalty, faithlessness, indeed, personal treason, than a fellow member of our armed forces murdering a buddy, a tent mate, one of his company or battalion or division member, in short, one of his own."

"But, it is my opinion that's exactly the case here. The killer is one of us who has gone over the edge. Just being here makes you nuts. All of us have our own name for this abyss. Mine is, 'The Island that the Good Lord forgot'. And with good reason. The daily summer of '44 downpours followed by long bouts of sweltering, steamy heat make our rest and relaxation and refitting odious. But regardless of how unendurable the torrid temperature or drenching water and suffocating mud, strong minds adapt and tough it out. The fragile mind can't, in my opinion. He breaks down and turns into a murdering elusive creature who stalks at night. Choker or Ghoul, he's one of us. And, now, with his first murder, he'll strike again. Just look around in your units, your companies, your battalion, and use your intuitions to identify anyone you suspect as eerie, mysterious, strange, bizarre," continued Guidi, gravely.

"Why, Lieutenant, you've just described every private, senior NCO, sergeant, lieutenant unit commander, and every officer at Division Headquarters, including old Commander Major General Vandegrift," someone couldn't resist interrupting and blurting out. After the loud laughter diminished, the interloper added, "But not our beloved Major General William Rupertus and Brigadier General Lemuel Shepherd sitting yonder!"

After the second volume of laughs simmered down, someone asked, "Is there anything else you can tell us?"

"Yes. It's not much, but here it is. In my opinion, the Ghoul or Choker began his insanity out here in the Russells, not on Canal. He began by just thrilling, pretending to be a strangler, enjoying watching everyone scurry after touching their throats. As he dashed about hither and thither, he enjoyed that too. We've seen men like that, throwing them into our brigs, they being proud of even that. No, he started imitating strangling here on Pavuvu as he was slowly going over the edge. We know he simply walked into the tents and fondled the nearest throat to the entrance. When someone woke up, he ran like hell, enjoying every moment."

After a pause, Guidi continued. "The three killings last night probably made him feel like he bagged a trophy of some sort; animal, human, who knows? He may have enjoyed the puncturing of a man so much he's decided he's going to do it again. He'll act out his joys, growing stronger with every murder gratifying his fantasies that'll continue until he's caught or killed. We can call each death a lust murder, and him a lust blood-splatterer. It has to be all about excitement. In the planning, in the doing, in the pretended 'killing', in the getting away, and in the chase. He is unique and distinguished from the sadistic murderer. He doesn't mutilate. He is methodical and cunning. He is smart. He committed each slaughter in a frenzied attack. The planning was methodical, but the killing was not. He's among us now, premeditating the next murder of one of our men based on some obsessive fantasy. Then, his desire will build up and sometime soon, he'll act on an urge, triggered by a stimulus of who knows what."

"What about when he killed Japs?" someone shouted.

"Whole different thing. No hate, no vengeance, no enemy, there. Just a job to be done, efficiently, business-like. We never heard of his odd behavior on Guadalcanal. No, it didn't start until he got here, and it'll extend until we leave. Then, it will follow him to whenever else we land, rest or occupy. That's all I know, gentlemen, and I have no idea whether I'm right or wrong. Hell, for all I know, the Ghoul could well be Alexander Vandegrift or Bill Rupertus. Or, Lemuel Shepherd. For that matter, the way he behaves at times, it could be Captain Oscar 'Slim' Del Barbara."

With everyone laughing, the second lieutenant noticed the raised hand of Navy Commander Everett Keck of the 1st Medical Battalion.

Guidi smiled, and asked, "Yes, sir. If anyone can help us solve this, it'll be the Navy. What have you to say?"

"Just a question, Lieutenant. I commend you for your effort at offering a psychological autopsy of a murderer. But it's just a beginning, as you acknowledge. No one can identify a specific perpetrator, or suspect. But some conjectures and mind games are better than other conjectures and mind games. Being able to look at a murder scene and say what the killer is like is uncanny. You just offered us a side view of a full face. But it's a wholesome start, an outline, a contour. But a contour or outline will never specifically identify. All it can do is direct you to a clue to the behavior he left behind. Can a criminal hide the clues to his behavior of murder? I don't think so because it's harder to do than wiping fingerprints off a murder knife, or remembering not to leave behind a hair or spot of blood that can be analyzed somewhat to yield a clue. The mind of the murderer is not only the cause of his killing, but how we determine who he is. I've been thinking a lot about this concept. After the war, I'd like to propose it to the homicide divisions of state and police departments across the nation. Maybe even the FBI, the Federal Bureau of Investigations. If anyone can turn the murderer's own mind, own personality, own body, against him, revealing who he is by combining science, art and intuition, it's the FBI. So, lieutenant, you are to be commended for touching the frontier of criminal investigation in the future."

"Why, thank you, Dr. Keck. Coming from you, that's a supreme compliment. As you all know, Everett runs the 1st Division's Medical Battalion, which is the first our unit ever received. Navy Captain Bruce Logue is his division surgeon. Everett is from Wisconsin and has already seen considerable action on Guadalcanal."

"The thinking I just introduced you to isn't mine, Lieutenant Guidi. It's a vague consonance of thoughts from the likes of commander Stanley Wollin, Commander Emil Napp, and the surgeons and doctors of 'C' Medical Company which established a field hospital shortly after landing here as an expanded clearing station. These fellows would all sit around at night and try to understand the minds of our battle-exhausted men, and how to help them through their pains. But not one figured on a murderer of fellow Marines. But all these thoughts have to be pulled together, chronicled, then tested, researched, and debated."

"Is there anyone on your staff, Commander, to lead such an inquiry, as to who might have committed such an heinous killings? What contours we should aim for? What clues these contours may yield? In short, can you lend us one of your psychiatrists until we catch this monster?"

"I'll lend you three—three of the finest minds we have in the medical services in our war against Japan. All of you know Colonel Franklin Hallam, in my office; Nurse Helen Weant of the 13th AAF 801st Medical Evacuation Squadron, assigned to the 17th field hospital, and a comer from stateside on board a troopship scheduled for arrival in three days. They will find your killer for you, trust me."

"How soon can we assemble?"

"I'll have Colonel Hallam and Nurse Weant in the jeep, then pick up Lieutenant Toscanini and come right over."

"Meanwhile," interrupted Division Commander Major General William Rupertus, standing up, "We'll put more additional work parties out this morning gathering every empty 100-gallon drum and large cylindrical box, tub, can or the like, anything for packing or storing good and fill then pack each item with sand like you did the oil drums. We'll place one every 10 or 15 yards throughout the base in Tent City half that distance, and at dusk, saturate each one with gasoline and set it afire. Three hundred to five hundred, plus what you're doing now, should light up the place. Lemuel, you handle this. Put a thousand men on work details now. LeRoy Sims, as chief of staff, have your D-1, Major Meyers, check with Naval Intelligence in Pearl if there are any elements of the Japanese Navy or Airforce anywhere in the vicinity. If so, all is postponed. Pavuvu is too exposed when approached by the Western Coral Sea. Unit Commanders, post sentries every five tents by four. No one, not even a shadow, will penetrate the area without being seen."

After a short pause, the 1st Division Commander sat down. Captain Del Barbra stepped into the middle of the circle and said, "Well, gentlemen, unless there are any questions, or anything anyone wants to say, we're concluded. You must inform everyone what photographs you saw and heard here this morning. We have a vicious murderer on the loose. The Mad Ghoul, or Charlie the Choker, is now pure evil. He'll undoubtedly kill again. Major General, will you issue an order to shoot to kill?"

"Within a minute of returning to headquarters."

"We should meet again within a few days, whether there are any killings or not."

What no one foresaw was two additional murders would take place late that night.

CHAPTER SEVEN

-

Three Friends

Tuesday, August 1

"My God, how stunningly beautiful," reflected Lieutenant Peter Albioni Toscanini.

Standing alone in the fading twilight near the long rugged coral coastline at Renard Sound on Banika Island across from Loun Island, the young naval medical officer steadily gazed upon the calm waters of Masquitti Bay, then past Pavuvu to the eastern mountains of New Guinea.

"Sunset on the South Pacific! How much more colorful can the sea and her countless islands be despite all the death and destruction?"

A humid fog began to stealth its way in from the southern Solomons, gracefully settling over the Russells, engulfing the 50 smaller islands, gripping the two larger ones. Increasing its density by the hour, it soon enveloped Pavuvu's coconut plantation groves, then crept slowly over the gloomy dense jungles, to the rolling barren hills and sharp mountain slopes, before proceeding across Sunlight Channel to the Banika airfield, hospital and various medical facilities and sick bays, tank farms, advanced base construction depot, piers, docks, wharves, piers and the all-important floating pontoon bridges connecting the two main islands.

"Nothing like a gloaming Coral Sea evening fog after all afternoon teeming, torrential showers," Peter concluded.

Just then, Lt. Toscanini turned behind him, clutching his .45. Rapidly approaching from a low coral ridge along a fringe of palms was Private William Lundigan, a Reising submarine gun strapped around his back.

"There you are! They said you came this way to waste your time watching the sun go down!" he said jokingly, a twinkle in one eye.

Lundigan walked past several squads of riflemen setting up the ordered bonfires along the beach, 100-gallon drums torched-cut in half for sand doused with gasoline and lit afire. The gray sand was littered with the relics and remnants of invasion, i.e. rusted weapons, machinery of sorts, light vehicles, palm tree splinters, strands of barbed wire, and abandoned gear and equipment; all the debris left over from both the 1942 Japanese and the mid-February 1943 seizure of the Russell archipelago as a forward operating base. Instantly, he lifted his cocked Reising, with the clip fully loaded, until he saw it was his closest friend, his "buddy", in the Division.

"Was told you were out here staring at the clouds again, dreaming of Joan. Glad to see you with a submachine gun. Sure it's loaded? And quit dangling it near your foot," PFC Lundigan teased. "The Mad Ghoul may have paddled over to this side tonight searching for a fourth victim."

"You should talk," chuckled Peter. "Glad to see you fully armed. With a Tommy, no less! Are its magazines large enough?"

"Would rather be carrying a Browning Automatic Rifle. Either way, just let him try to place his fingers on this nice-looking throat of mine! If he crosses the channel and surfaces over here, he'll feel an uncomfortable sting."

"And, to accompany your grand entrance as our South Pacific sun disappears below the western horizon, the OP's speaker over there is blaring 'Mairzy Doats'."

"Much rather have those guys with binoculars in the observation post play 'Maori Love Song' and pay attention to any Jap battleships sneaking up to shell us."

Peter grinned from ear to ear, nodding in full agreement.

Now, as squads of the Marine riflemen were igniting their night fires, total darkness enveloped all the Russells, the refrains of the most popular song of America's Hit Parade of 1944 wafting lightly over the northeastern shores of Banika. The two friends, sitting quietly gazing at the bonfires, relished each other's company while deep in thought about the events on Pavuvu across the narrow channel.

"Still unloading the latest transport arrivals down at the dock, I see," Lundigan said quietly.

"Yes, 24 new Amtracs, from the troop ships to the barges, then lifted up to the pier and lined up in two rows on the warehouse lot. And, the hospital ship out there. What a beauty. Never saw one so large, so white, with such a huge red cross. Think the Japs will honor the Red Cross or eventually sink her," asked Peter.

"Of course, they won't sink her. If they did, every ounce of energy we have as a nation would be unleashed so that the whole nation would evaporate."

"I agree. Weren't those amphibious tractors used on Guadalcanal?"

"Getting new paint and refurbishing for our new assault, I bet," Lundigan explained.

"Look, you can still see the cardboard signs of boat numbers, and assault wave letters our boys were assigned to on the sides of the

Amtracs. Those numbers meant life or death when approaching the beach," responded Toscanini.

"How so?" queried Lundigan.

"Russell Davis, you know him, he's part of the Second Battalion of the First Regiment. He said in our chow line a few weeks back that as an old veteran in the 1st Division he was taught in basic training before Pearl that if you're in the first wave of an invasion, you just might make it to, and beyond, the beach because of the shock of the Japs to see tanks, amphibious or not, coming right at them. But God help the unfortunate Marines in the second, third, and fourth waves. By then, the Japanese had pulled themselves together, regained their bearings, and easily fired their beach artilleries and mortars right at you."

"Damnable enemy," muttered Lundigan.

After a long, quiet pause, and a dwindling of the popular homefront tunes of 1943 and 1944 from the nearby Observation Post, Lundigan suddenly burst out, nodding toward the sand dunes near the pontoon bridge to Pavuvu, "Look who's coming to join us! Oh, sweet, pretty, fresh, south Pacific purple flower of three red-blue hued petals!"

"Why, it's Ellen," smiled Peter. "Poor thing looks so disheveled from nursing."

"Yeah, but darned if her beauty, brilliant, so full of color, doesn't match the most breathtaking of all the ocean's orchids," responded Lundigan slowly, softly, as if weighing every one of his words.

"My goodness, Bill. I didn't realize until this very moment, you're way beyond just liking her. You're crazy in love with her!".

"Oh, gosh, I confess. But not a word about it, or our friendship ends, unless I shoot you first. She's not to know. My problem, what I fear more than a Jap bayonet, is that she's crazy in love with you!

Homely, plain you, a nobody with nothing to offer. You're in love with, and will marry, a Nisei 4,000 to 5,000 miles away in an internment camp and care for nothing except your Joan, and me, every time I stand before Ellen, I pee all over myself. . .!'""

"Shhhh, here she is," whispered Peter.

"One last word: Doesn't that beat all?" uttered Lundigan. "My situation is the same damn exact situation as in my favorite comic strip, 'Krazy Kat' by cartoonist George Herriman, who just died a few years ago. The mouse, 'Ignatz mouse-fool' hates Krazy who's in love with him. He rewards her love by throwing a brick at her head every chance he gets. Meanwhile, Offisa Pupp, the dog cop, tries to prevent this because he loves Krazy, who won't have anything to do with him. But the mouse hates the cat, who loves him. She hates the dog who loves her, and the dog hates the mouse who loves him! What a crazy world they live in, that Coconino County. And, that's what my situation with Ellen is all about! Crazy!"

Suddenly upon them, Ellen smiled broadly.

"I could hear the two of you mumbling about something way up there on the dune. About what, who can say?" she asked, grinning from ear to ear, hand on her hips, legs slightly spread apart as she stood before them, demanding an answer.

Neither, Peter nor Bill, frozen in loving warmth for her, could conjure a fib.

Finally, Peter, to save his friend from further embarrassment, told one of the very, very few lies of his lifetime.

"How price of almonds in Galt, near the Lodi-Wood bridge area south of Sacramento, in the San Joaquin Valley went up 2 cents per pound since 1939."

Bill, meanwhile, regaining his composure, said thoughtfully,

"You come this way without a weapon? Not even a .45?"

Ellen sat down on the sand between them, the illumination from the nearest beach bonfires providing sufficient light to silhouette the three against the darkness of the dunes beyond.

"The OP's Marines were watching me all the way from the Pavuvu hospital."

"What good are they if the Ghoul hides along the path that edges the mushy swamp, slices your throat, and gets away in the murky waters?"

"Oh, Bill, you know as tired as I am from today's 12 hour shift I'd still give him a swift kick."

"Huh?"

"Besides, I'm far too pretty to have my head detached from a beautiful body."

"I'll drink to that!" Peter exclaimed, struggling to refrain from outright laughter.

"Oh, the reasoning of a diminutive, dazzling sweetheart!" acknowledged Lundigan.

"And, oh, oh, you're giving yourself away, movie-star friend of mine."

Ellen blushed, then managed to say,

"How picturesque we must appear from that high tower over there. And, with moonlight for the first time in weeks!"

"Ellen, dear, you must, must promise me, us, Peter and me, never, ever again to walk along ANYWHERE, even to the potty, without a .45, which I doubt you know how to use. Not until we catch the Ghoul. Promise us, Ellen, or I'll put the muzzle of this Tommy gun to my chin."

"Oh, you silly man. All right, I promise." Ellen responded, sensing the deadly seriousness of the moment.

"Shake on it!"

Ellen shook Peter's hand longer than she should have, then Bill's, no longer than necessary.

Peter realized it at the moment her eyes dropped while shaking his hand. Bill, of course, knew it weeks before, when the two first encountered the lovely young nurse in the lobby of the 1st Division headquarters.

"Well, kids," yawned Peter. "I'm headed back to quarters and my cot. Been summoned to General Headquarters, SWPA, Southwest Pacific Area, 0600 for a special order. May mean another redirected change of assignment. Join me, Bill, then I'll take you, a lowly private combat photographer, to an elegant ham and eggs breakfast with real coffee in the doctors' mess next door."

"Can't turn that down," responded Lundigan. "I'll bring my 16mm Bell & Howell for a few takes within the Banika officer's first-class New York City restaurant. Meet you at the flag pole in front of GHQ at 0530."

"See you soon, Ellen. You have a full-fledged Reising machine gun with loaded clip escorting you back to the nurses' quarters. Try to join us, if you can."

"I hope so. But who knows if we'll ever meet again, knowing the Medical Administrative Corps. We're so short of staff, surgeons, general practitioners, corpsmen, psychiatrists, rehabbers, and nurses; they may put you on a plane for England to follow the troops breaking out across France. I doubt if they'll hold the plane so you two can leisurely enjoy ham and sunny-side-up eggs and coffee," Ellen said, hesitantly and without humor.

"Oh, I doubt that, Nurse Ellen. If that was the case, a Special Order, an SO, would indicate it's from the G-3 Operations Officer, Division of Higher Staff. The one I received a few hours ago was from the Medical Corps Office of the Chief Surgeon in San Diego."

Bill intervened, "Ellen, Dr. Kildare, you know, the movie hero doctor starring actor Lew Ayres, belongs to the 1st Division, USMC, the Navy Office of Intelligence, and the U.S. Medical Corps. There's nothing he can't do, and the kid is only 26 years old!"

"I know, Bill, I know."

"Frankly, I would rather be a movie star," Peter laughed.

With that, Peter waved, adding over his back, "If you meet the Mad Ghoul, Bill, please raise your Reising, not the Bell & Howell, and aim. You must have the heart to pull the trigger."

"And you," retorted Bill, "don't depend on your good looks to barter your way past him!"

Escorting Ellen back to the Nurses' Quarters in Wing A of the Banika 1,300-bed portable surgical hospital MOB 10, an adjunctant of the Navy's Fleet Hospital 108 back on Guadalcanal, Bill, in all fairness to his wartime buddy, and partly to appease Ellen's loving curiosity, defined Lieutenant Peter Albioni Toscanini, USMC-USN.

"I have to admit, Ellen," Bill smiled, as the two walked slowly up the trail to the hospital adjacent CHP, "he really is more handsome, more intelligent, more serious about this damn war, than I."

Ellen laughed, "I agree. But go on."

"Thanks," he returned glumly, as they slowly walked on. "Well, first and foremost, you should know he's a Toscanini, an authentic, blue-blood relation to Arturo Toscanini, the world-renowned Italian maestro of classical music. My parents, who enjoyed the opera, ballet, and symphony on the radio, loved the conductor as no other—not only because of his genius, but also because he hated Mussolini as much as they did. In fact, most Americans of international understanding felt the same way, especially when the maestro refused to direct any form of classical music in Italy since 1931. Imagine, he told the dictator to go to hell. No operas, no symphonies, no ballets. He detested fascism and Nazism."

"What a brave man," Ellen said quietly, "That Arturo Toscanini."

"Hitler wanted Toscanini to conduct Wagner's compositions in Germany, especially those glorifying war, and he told him to go to hell. Instead, the Italian conductor formed, in the face of both those monsters, an orchestra of Jewish refugee players."

"Peter's mother's maiden name is Firpo. Her father was Antonio Firpo. But Peter's father is a Toscanini. So, you see the origin of the Peter Toscanini name. The village of Peter's grandfather, his father's father, was Suzzi, north of Genoa in Northern Italy." All the Toscaninis came from Suzzi.

"Such noble blood…"

"Yes, the noblest."

"You know Peter well, don't you?"

"We've been together since basic training in boot camp at Camp Elliott. I enlisted in the Marine Corps during the last day of May 1944, straight out of the Warner Brothers Lot in Hollywood. Peter joined two weeks or so later out of the Stockton's College of Pacific. We wound up in Elliott almost to the same exact day."

"How'd you meet? Who initiated the friendship and on what premise?"

"Well, like you ladies, when you enter a strange new program, a new way of life and existence; you want a 'girl friend', a 'buddy', too. You naturally start looking around for a 'buddy', a girl 'buddy' to pal around with. Each of us seized the other up. 'Do I want him?' Then, I arranged to have a mutual friend introduce us. It was a good, warm handshake, and he said then that he thought he recognized me. I asked if he was a 'movie-goer'. He said, 'No', but that maybe he remembered me as a San Joaquin Valley boy."

"That's funny," Ellen chuckled.

"A lot of fellas in the 1st Division were already calling me 'Dennis O'Keefe', not knowing there was such a person as Bill Lundigan. So, I finally asked if he had seen the three films out of the more than 50 I played minor roles in since I began acting in 1937: 'The Case of the Black Parrot', in 1941; 'A Shot in the Dark', also, in 1941; and, the last picture I made, 'A Salute to the Marines', early 1943, with co-star Wallace Beery."

"What did he say?"

"None of them because now that he was older, he wasn't going to waste money going to the Rialto Theatre anymore where all the cowboy, Bowery Boys, gangster film serials, and cheap comedies were playing. No, sir. When he went to the movies, he went to the Fox Theatre down the block on Main Street in Stockton to watch the real Hollywood stuff, not the cheap comedies steered over to the Rialto closer to the city's 'Skid Row'.

"Was he kidding? I hope so," Ellen offered.

"Of course, he was. He knew who I was, but pretended not to. He was testing to see if I could be teased, then laughing about it, because best friends tease and joke with each other all the time. If he teased me, I was entitled to tease him, as I do daily. No, Ellen, he was very respectful that during the past seven years I was under contract with Universal, Warner Brothers, and MGM. He's very proud of me being a combat photographer, knowing how dangerous it is when we have to go forward for the real footage of battle."

"You really like him, don't you?"

"If we survive this war, we will be friends for the rest of our lives. Do you know he's an inbred animal lover? Dogs, cats, and horses, especially. But I've seen him so angry when he caught a cocky Marine about to torture a stray dog. He would have killed the man, hadn't three of us, his friends, intervened. Every time he sees him in camp or Tent City, he'll approach him, even if he's with his buddies to ask point blank if he's tortured any other animals. No, not only is he a nice man, but a man of animal warmth, always smiling or grinning, which of course add to his fine looks."

"I know," Ellen said softly, "I know."

Bill cast a quick glance at her. Her somberness told him again how much she loved Peter.

"Well, we're here, Ellen, safe and sound. Would you like to hear the conclusion of how we became fast friends? You know most of it anyway."

"Yes, go on."

"After boot camp, in which we were always together, I was ordered to the Marine base on the east coast at Quantico, about 35 miles south of Washington, D.C. I was to be trained by the best documentary filmmakers in America on how to use the handheld 16mm camera under severe, dangerous combat conditions. I loved it. Meanwhile, Peter was preparing to be an advances corpsman, specializing in NP issues, neuropsychiatric conditions; primarily the criminal man. From the first moment we met, he told me his whole life was focused upon the labyrinth of the neurotic personality's mind; its sick structure and all its winding passages that lead to criminal behavior. And, of all the crimes possible, murder is the most baffling. We wrote to each other all the time, realizing that in the unpredictability of war, we might never see or hear from each other again."

"Did he have a girlfriend, a sweetheart?"

"Oh, yeah, big time. Joan is a Japanese-American girl currently interned in Arkansas."

"Really. A sad, sad story, that horrible interment of American citizens in concentration camps."

"I'll ask him about her when I see him next. And, you, what about a sweetheart for you?" Ellen looked up, quizzically.

"No one. But the last week in Washington D.C., before flying out here, I met a young woman I'm now corresponding with. Her name is Rena, Rena Morgan. I don't know if anything will come of it, but we write to each other every few days—going on eight months now."

Ellen remained silent, her eyes downcast. Bill continued,

"To conclude, Peter and I reunited just a few weeks ago, about the time you entered our lives as Nurse Ellen. As you know, I flew in from San Francisco to the airfield here on Banika. Crossing the channel between us and Pavuvu, I was loaded down with camera, film, and other accessories, as well as my own personal gear, searching for my tent number. Preoccupied, I wasn't paying attention to two medical lieutenants, walking in the opposite direction from the mobile surgical unit, one of whom was staring me down, wide-eyed, mouth agape. He had spotted me! I dropped everything I was carrying in the middle of the Tent City road, vehicles dodging it all, men in khakis enjoying our shouting and hugging. But the reunion was brief. Within the hour, I was to participate in documenting in film the 1st Marine Division amphibious landing operations for the invasion of New Georgia, the next assault. I'm still waiting for the order."

"But, what I don't understand, what's he do? He's certainly no ordinary PFC rifleman, machine gunner, or administrative clerk," Ellen said, turning her back to the hospital ward entrance, and leaning on the rail of the steps.

"Well, Ellen, as of this moment, I'm not exactly sure myself. Tomorrow morning, he'll learn where he's been reassigned to from the 11th Regiment of the 1st Division to G Company, 2nd Battalion, 5th Regiment. He has been summoned from this rest area to an office next door in the GHQ, SWPA. He's to receive yet another reassignment. It's in an SO, a special order, from USAF WesPac, U.S. Armed Forces, Western Pacific."

After a pause, Bill smiled and continued,

"I'm sure proud of that boy. As a young lieutenant, his reputation for intelligent investigative work. All the services would like to have him, especially our Marines and the Navy. You don't know this, but Peter received a wire a few weeks ago before we encountered each other on the road in Pavuvu's Tent City to be available for departure to Camp Elliott in San Diego, stateside. It seems he was to begin some type of inquiry, some sort of undercover probe, of how Marine inmate prisoners were being treated. That call came directly from a major officer in Washington D.C., superseding all other assignments. He's excited about the challenge, whatever it is. Now, this, tomorrow's SO."

"That may be the one to redirect him to California?" Ellen interjected, with a sad expression all over her face.

"He doesn't think so. This SO is from Honolulu, but he's not sure what office."

"Well, I'll be anxious to hear all about it, if he's free to tell us. But, one more question before I leave you."

"Of course, Ellen. We both feel you're one of us and we love you as such, even in the short time we've known you."

"That's all very nice, Bill. But you could help me now. I need to know this, and I need to know it now. Does he love this interned girl, the Nisei, the Japanese American? Does he love her a lot?"

CHAPTER EIGHT

-

Joan, An Interned Japanese-American

Despite the nurses' quarters and the First Division's General Headquarters serving as beehives of activity, the tropical night was unusually cold and still. Under the moon and stars the circular driveway entrances appeared cast in a gloomy dimness.

"Well, let's sit on the steps. If the Ghoul comes after us here, Ellen, he'll get a stomach full. O.K., nurse, let me tell you what I know about Peter's Joan—God only knows I had to listen to him day in and day out ennoble her."

Ellen smiled.

"What angers him the most, almost as much as seeing an animal put upon, is why all Japanese-Americans in our United States had to report to assembly relocation centers within weeks of December 7th, from which they were shipped to internment camps. Their Stockton, California, was one center of about 15 on the Pacific West Coast. From there, Joan and her family were sent to Rohwer, Arkansas, the easternmost of America's war internment camps. She was only 19 years old in 1942. Here it is, more than two years later, and Peter writes to her behind the barbed wire fences every, single day—can you believe it? Who cares for a woman that much?" Bill chucked, well aware of the answer.

"Why did they have to go? They are Americans like me and you, weren't they?"

"Of course, they are Americans! According to Peter, they were removed for their own so-called 'safety' from the 'other' Americans, and there was a fear there might be some spies and saboteurs and certainly subversion tendencies among them. Peter said he would swear on his life that no Japanese-American would turn on his own country. He felt, as his Italian-American parents, and most good Californians, that other farmers and ranchers in the state coveted their well-groomed, carefully-maintained lands and their crops. Without exception, their ranches and farms were the best, most profitable. If the owners were sent to camp, they would have to sell or entrust them, to friends. Most, unsure if they would ever return, simply sold, and cheaply."

"President Roosevelt was wrong listening to his advisers who were somewhat sympathetic of more than 125,000 good Americans having to read on cheap copy paper nailed to telephone posts that by the end of the week, in March, 1942, they were to assemble on a corner nearest them to board a bus for the Santa Fe or Southern Pacific train stations to take them to camps in almost all the western and mid-western states, as far away as Mississippi."

"Peter says Roosevelt's Executive Order 9066 was terribly, terribly wrong. Eleanor Roosevelt fought him on that order, and, I think, defied her husband by not only visiting several internment camps to make sure fellow Americans were being treated fairly, but also showing America which side she was on. Furthermore, and I didn't know this, but according to Peter, a whole regiment of Japanese-American troops were formed from the young men in the camps. They volunteered with their lives to show and prove they were as American as you and me. Peter, knows some, including his Joan's cousins, and keeps in touch with them. They write to each other all the time. He says they are mostly in the 442nd Regimental Combat Team and they were recently in North Africa, Sicily, and now are in Italy. A few from the camps are interpreters out here in the Pacific and a small number are in the 100th Infantry Battalion. The best fighting men we have, Peter insists. His hatred of the Army's Lieutenant General John Dewitt knowns no bounds. Thank goodness Dewitt was not a Marine."

"Why did Peter dislike him so much?"

"'A Jap is a Jap', he claimed in all the newspapers. He could not distinguish between a loyal Japanese-American and a Japanese homeland warrior, and the bastard was the Commanding General of the Western America Defense Command. Oh, I shouldn't curse him. He was an old World War I veteran from the east sent out west who never knew, understood, or cared for a good people who for decades felt a lot of prejudice and discrimination since the first arrivals from Japan, long before the turn of the century."

"I never knew any of this, being from the eastern seaboard. But it's Joan I want you to tell me about."

"Well, I was getting to her. Of course, I never met her. He's got four photos of her in his wallet. Four! Ask to see them. He'll be delighted!"

"Go on, please."

"Well, whenever Peter shows his photos of Joan, he always begins his dissertation of her personality by saying, 'She has an outer and inner beauty that will last a lifetime.' He says that by the time he saw her in Honor E, the honor Edison High School club for outstanding academic achievers, half the 9th grade boys, Nisei as well as white, Hispanic, etc. were already in love with her. Now, to understand who she is, Ellen, you should understand the Japanese generations in America. For example, 'Issei is a person of Japanese ancestry, born in Japan, moved to, say, California, as Joan's parents did, and therefore, were first generation. Nisei is someone like Joan, born in the USA, and considered second generation; Sansei, third generation, will be her and Peter's children someday; and Yonsei will be her grandchildren, fourth generation."

Bill paused, smiling, lost in thought. Then he continued,

"Peter says he was entranced with her the moment he laid eyes on her wonderful, dispassionate eyes, dark and large, studying him without the slightest hint of embarrassment. Then, he told me, he saw the rest of her amazing raven-black hair cut rather short, a somewhat pale, exquisite face, slimness and beauty of an elegant figure even at the age of 15 or 16. He had never seen anything quite like her physical beauty. He swears his face flushed red when their eyes locked together, and for a split moment, he thought he wet himself."

"Peter, as an Italian-American, says that there is an ancient Italian saying that if each of you, Peter and Joan, are struck simultaneously, at the same exact moment, by a flash of lightning followed by a shocking loud clash, you are destined to love each other through eternity, no, infinity, never to falter or waver. He says he was hit by such sudden streak, and now, just as soon as possible, they will marry and have a child."

Bill said, softly.

"Ellen, you should ask him about all this. I never heard of such crazy concepts. He insists his is the highest of the highest form of love there is. Never happened before in a man."

After a reflective pause, during which Ellen remained quietly gazing at the clear, bright, full moon, Bill asked,

"Do you want me to go on? I have more to tell you why Peter loves her so much. Doesn't this bore you?"

"Please tell me, Bill."

"Well, Joan's mother, according to Peter, the warm, loving, kind, patient, good mother every child should have, got up before there was light on Monday morning, December 8th, the day after Pearl Harbor, and baked a large chocolate cake. Joan said that when she, her sisters, and brother entered the kitchen at dawn, they thought the cake was for them later that evening. When asked, Mrs. Ikeda simply smiled and said nothing. There was little talk about Japan's sneak attack on our fleet anchored in Hawaii, and almost no real facts. The same for the Japanese communities in south Stockton and other towns. The elders certainly understood there would be repercussions for the Japanese-Americans, although few of them had any legal, familial, or emotional ties to Japan."

"Well, Joan, in the 12th grade, her younger sister in the 10th grade, and her older sister, two years older, at College of the Pacific and younger brother in the 9th grade, went to school as usual. Edison High School was only five blocks away. For Joan, whose first class was Latin 4, who was sickened America was now at war with the country of her parents' origin, was suddenly avoided by all the kids with whom she normally talked. Glumly, she went to her 8:00am class and took her regular seat in the first row as the other 28 students filed in and took theirs. Miss Youngblood, an ancient relic of a teacher from the 19th century, a 'battle-ax used by the Vikings', a woman certainly in her 60s who never married, and, Joan heard other teachers whisper, an old ox who hated men, began promptly taking roll at 8:05am to start her advanced Latin lessons. Well, as roll was being called, the classroom door suddenly jiggled with difficulty and finally pushed open with Mrs. Ikeda, Joan's mother, walking in with the large chocolate cake. Mrs. Ikeda, barely able to handle the large, beautiful cake, smiled at her stunned daughter, and then walked up to the desk of Mrs. Youngblood, smiling and bowing. Joan's fine, loving American parents had no idea how to handle the surprise 'dastardly attack' of the day before, 'a day which will live in infamy'. They had been shocked like all good Americans. What could they do to help? To show allegiance to their democracy in their United States of America, to demonstrate how sorry her family was for something they and the rest of the Japanese-Americans were for something they had nothing to do with."

"All Mrs. Ikeda, in all her wondrous humanity, could think of doing was baking a large cake for Joan's class."

"And now, bowing repeatedly, smiling graciously, she stepped up the one step Miss Youngblood's desk was on and placed it on the nearest corner where there were no papers or books. She then stood back a step, and with her arms at her sides, bowed several times."

"Not a sound could be heard in the classroom. Joan was horrified beyond belief. Neither was there movement of a single muscle among the 30 students.Joan leaned back in her seat as far as possible to escape what she was certain would happen next. And no amount of fear, anxious anticipation, or embarrassment could forestall Joan's pain and crippling grief of what happened next."

"Miss Youngblood, all 60 plus years of her fat ass sitting comfortable in her wide chair, swung it slightly around to face Mrs. Ikeda, then lifted her heavy right leg and kicked the large cake to the classroom floor. For a long moment, everyone was paralyzed, in utter silence."

"We want no apologies from the likes of you!" the teacher shouted loudly.

"Mrs. Ikeda, head down, struggling not to stumble, shaking while maintaining composure despite the worst humiliation the entire Ikeda family has ever suffered, quickly knelt and began placing the chunks and fragments of the chocolate cake, and the shattered glass dish, in the lap of her dress, having no towel to do so. Joan then leaped forward, and with fire in her eyes and fists clenched, faced her teacher, who stepped back. Joan turned and knelt next to her mother, fighting desperately to control her sobs, and with bare hands, struggled to clean up the mess. Instantly, several of Joan's closest friends were out of their seats reaching for paper towels, watering them in the restrooms of the main hallway, returning to sponge the mess up. Joan helped her mother place the remains of the cake in several lunch bags the students offered. Joan walked her mother home, and then returned to Edison for her next class. Not a word was ever said about the incident again, at school or home."

"How shameful," Ellen offered. "How utterly shameful. The Ikeda family didn't plan the attack on Pearl Harbor. The United States was not intending to declare war on Joan's family. How so, so despicable enough so I not only want to shed a tear or two, but also I want Peter to have Joan instead of me."

With that, she turned and walked up the few steps to the hospital entrance and her shared bedroom and cot.

CHAPTER NINE

-

Stalking the Patient Wards

Friday, August 5

After reporting promptly at 0600 to GHQ, SWPA, General Headquarters, Southwest Pacific Area, to receive his Special Order of "redirection" written in the form of "a memorandum" for the record from USAFWESTPAC, Peter was directed by the sergeant at the entrance desk, guarded by two fully-armed sentries next door to the new quarters of the Operations Officer of PBC's, Central Pacific Base Command, combined G-2 and G-3 departments.

Then, with Bill in tow, the two walked briskly back down the steps and across the 24 yards of corral gravel to the entrance of the new Russell Islands 1,300-bed hospital for MOB 10. Peter explained to Bill that an additional 1,400 beds were to be added in the adjacent facility under construction.In June of the year before, the current site consisted of only four 35-patient wards built as a naval dispensary, completely screened and equipped with emergency battle dressing stations that could be blacked out for the severely wounded from Guadalcanal. Since then, four operation rooms were added as an annex. Within the past month, construction began on a dental laboratory, administrative wing, two additional wards, and officer barracks and mess. Peter pointed out that personnel from the 15th Battalion were assisting the 93rd by working on the plumbing and electrical installations, and doctors and hospital corpsmen were aiding in the erection of the prefabricated-steel building, 20 feet wide and 250 feet long. Two of

Banika's twelve 20-mm guns were well-positioned around the annex. Next door to the annex was a small, prefabricated unit housing the operations officer for the joint G-2 and G-3 sections.

Opening the sealed envelope a naval captain handed him, Peter read on simple stationary with the letter CPBC in the left corner; Central Pacific Base Command,

"Lieutenant Peter Albioni Toscanini—

Henceforth, 'Operation Turncoat Mariner' is suspended, as is 'Operation Brigand', until further notice. Of utmost importance is your presence on Pavuvu to lead the murder investigations in coordination with Captain Oscar Del Barbra of the 1st Division's Military Police. Within the hours to come, the Joint Chiefs of Staff, in preparing for the final phase of the Pacific War, is establishing a new headquarters; The United States Forces, Pacific (USAFPAC) under the command of General MacArthur. He has been ordered to develop plans for the invasion and occupation of Japan. The USAFPAC's Chief Surgeon will be Brig. Gen. Guy B. Denit, Medical Corps. Brig. Gen. Percy J. Carroll, whom he replaced as Chief Surgeon, USAFFE and USA SO, has recommended you because of your work and interests in neuropsychological disorders and the work you began under Major Peter Kempf (MC) with the 1st Division. You are assigned temporarily to the latter, fully aware that your secondary is Captain Oscar Del Barbra of the Division's Military Police. As subordinate to both, you are called upon for the duration of the investigation to. . ."

Just then, the inter-island telephone rang loudly, startling Peter reading his SO, and Bill, fully absorbed and genuinely concerned about Peter's care approached Peter standing next to the desk.

"Yes, sir!" answered the desk sergeant.

"He's standing right here. I'll tell him, sir. Yes, sir. Less than a five-minute walk through the annex and past the warrior ward. He's on his way, sir."

The sergeant hung up, stood up, and pointed toward the annex.

"Lieutenant, you are to leave immediately for the meeting that began a few minutes ago in the mess of the ward and sickbay. That was Commander Everett B. Keck (MC) USN at the 1st Medical Battalion, 1st Division and, as you undoubtedly know, his is a higher law than God himself. Go!"

"Bill, you have to leave. I'll walk you part way to the entrance since it's on my way. Follow me."

As they made their way back through the hospital sickbays, Peter filled Bill in on what he knew about the "Mad Ghoul", or "Charlie the Choker".

"That's what this meeting is all about. I'm late. So, unless they've planned something special for me immediately, I'll be on the beach where I was last night. Try to get there earlier, say, before 7:00PM, just as supper is served at the battalion mess. The USS Comfort is coming in, the largest elaborate hospital ship ever built. Crewed and commanded by the Navy, it's supposedly the most modern of all our hospital ships. I'm anxious for a tour of it, when medical personnel will be allowed aboard."

"I'll grab something to eat and we'll watch her anchor. Can I bring Ellen?"

"Of course. But come armed," Peter said with a grin as they departed.

"After watching the Comfort anchor, you'll tell us about your first investigative assignment before it was just now rescinded, that Lieutenant Minoro Wada, the Jap in the 100th Division on Mindonao who wants to fly one of their advanced Zeros over to our side, then lead us on air strikes against his own troops!"

"Will do, Bill, nothing secret about Wada and his intent," Peter said, walking rapidly down the path and hurrying past the outdoor terrace off the hospital.

As he entered, Peter saw the meeting was just about to begin. Walking past Captain Del Barbra, who was just then stepping up to the podium, he realized that all the 'shiny new brass' must have been flown over to the island during the night from either Guadalcanal or New Britain's Cape Gloucester. He had not seen such a variety of freshly-pressed khaki uniforms with highly polished buttons and medals since Camp Elliott.

Peter, wending his way toward a seat in the back through the small assemblage waiting quietly and relaxed for the meeting to begin, was startled to hear over the microphone,

"Lieutenant Toscanini, please take a seat adjacent the podium."

Slightly embarrassed, Peter returned to the front and took a seat, a bit nervously, in the makeshift conference area. The cavernous dining area of the patients had been appropriated for the conference. Arranged around him were numerous older officers, virtually all of the gray-haired USMC luminaries in the Solomon Sea areas. Not a one knew what to expect, although most knew of the Houser killing, and assumed the session would focus upon their combined knowledge and expertise in fashioning a hasty, coordinated action to prevent the outrage from occurring again. The older officers, a few veterans of World War I, understood the urgency of their night flying onto the Pavuvu airstrip in order to be on time meant something far more serious was afoot.

Now, with the wall clock ticking toward 7:30AM, more than an hour's delay and the roar of heavy Pacific Ocean waves, no longer muffled by the high sand bluffs, pounding the nearby beach area, everyone, running out of small talk and chatter, suddenly fell silent. Part of the reason was noticing Del Barbra's dark, anxious face boding trouble as he pawed a small stack of papers on the podium. Everyone froze as the captain cupped the microphone close to himself.

"Gentlemen, a memorandum from the Marine Garrison Forces, Pacific, in Melbourne, is expected momentarily. Its Force Special Troops is arriving later this evening for deployment throughout Banika and Pavuvu by 0600 tomorrow. The MGFP was activated as a new Military Police Department under General Headquarters, Southwest Pacific Area, SWPA, replacing and coordinating all unnumbered military police companies in the Pacific North Africa, and Italy. For those of you new to the Order of Battle in this Theater of Operations, all our service battalions within the 1st Division, and others, possessed organic, unnumbered MP companies. We've all had our own personal experiences with MPs, especially stateside. Here, before this new organization, our 10th, 12th, 17th, and 18th Service Battalions provided the manpower whose sole duty was to guard Jap prisoners of war captured by all the services at the Iroquois Point Stockade at Pearl. I'm assigned to MP Company, 1st Provisional Marine Brigade formed April 18, four months ago. As of this moment, we can say that provisional military police companies, detachments, and platoons are on every one of our military bases in the world."

As Del Barbra paused, his head lowered, and eyes focused on the small stack of papers on the podium, everyone in the partially enclosed patio who personally knew the captain began to sense the enormity of a tragedy. A grave wickedness seemed to weigh upon the jovial captain. Deep facial lines now erased and supplanted his renowned ear-to-ear grins and resonant laughter. All traces of his rebounding paunch, and carefree, rolling head were gone; replaced by a reserved, awkward stiffness. Not a muscle in his entire body flinched. Usually vain and showy, he stood before the podium as a man murdered himself.

"Now, gentlemen," the captain continued, "You all may wonder what has all this to do with you? Well, when called upon, you and the specialists you supervise will be subordinated to my office and…"

Suddenly hearing loud, rapid footsteps behind him, the captain abruptly turned and saw Lt.Guidi, who everyone assembled in the large room knew as his chief assistant and second in command of the military police in the Russell Island Group, walking toward him with a sealed envelope in his hand. Equally sullen, he handed it to the captain without comment.

Unsealing the envelope as he turned back to the audience, Del Barbra removed a single sheet, and read,

"From Division Headquarters, Office of Division Commander MajGen William H. Rupertus,

"During the early hours of this morning, three of our 1st Division Marines were murdered, silently and swiftly. PFC Everett Laskosky was stabbed with one blow in the Battalion chapel; PVC Robert Benavidas was stabbed with repeated blows to the chest as he slept recovering from the first stages of malaria in the Pavuvu recovery unit, Wing B, of this building. PFC Laskosky's left carotid artery was severed. Benavidas' heart and left lung were penetrated; death occurring with the third blow. Laskosky died within minutes by choking to death on his blood. Captain Del Barbra will mobilize additional nightly safeguards and defenses, rotating personnel every four hours to patrol all environs of Pavuvu. This nightly patrolling will continue for the duration of the stay by the 1st Division."

"This matter is turned over to the jurisdiction of the military police."

"Signed by Asst. Div. Commander Brig Gen. Leavell C. Shepherd, and Chief of Staff Col. Amor LeRoy Sims."

Neither movement nor sound could be detected among the 40 or more participants. Peter, sitting less than fifteen feet from the captain and podium, was aghast. It meant that as he, William and Ellen were in relaxed conversation on the beach, the multiple-murdering mad Marine was stalking his prey across the channel on Pavuvu.

Within a moment, Peter's horror and dismay was transformed into a fierce rage. The number of Marines dead had jumped to three, overnight, within two days. Someone was running amok, with a fighting knife and no one, neither the military police nor the high staff of the 1st Division, had a single clue who was furiously attacking the defenseless without hinderance or suspicion.

What kind of a personality could be identified? Was there any extreme action that could be taken to prevent further murders? Didn't all of Pavuvu have to be notified that they were in imminent danger? As far as he himself was concerned, didn't he have an obligation to treat the murders with all the intensity his mind could muster? What triggers such homicidal mania? The onslaught of murderous frenzy, assailing recklessly?

"Meanwhile," continued Captain Del Barbra, "There's one more matter. In light of the two additional killings, the Marine Garrison Forces, Pacific, Melbourne, has assigned someone to assist me. After he has spoken his piece, Sgt. Guidi will meet with Battalion Commanders to establish the general patrol grid for us, beginning at 1800, three shifts, four hours each. You'll be dismissed, then return at

1300 with your company and squad leaders' list assignments by names."

Turning towards Peter, the Captain motioned for the Lieutenant to step up to the podium.

"You all should meet and get to know Lt. Peter Albioni Toscanini, who has been assigned to assist me. Because of the lateness of the hour, I must refrain from the usual proper introduction. He's a rising star in the Medical Corps because of his interest in the mind and brain of the murderer, especially the one who kills multiple times. He is being allowed in the medical corps to think differently rather than in the typical homicide mode."

As Toscanini stepped forward, the Captain smiled for the first time that morning,

"What say you, young man?"

"Thank you, Captain."

Pausing a moment, he said quietly, gradually raising his voice as he noticed all eyes were focused expectantly upon him.

"A rifleman understands that in action, he can die," the lieutenant said. "But in battle, in pitched fighting, he feels a certain tranquility, comparable to finding himself in the eye of a storm. So, he fights as trained; competently, bravely. For a handful, the task is to fight heroically, certainly nobly."

"But what causes him to flinch, to cringe, not in fear or terror, but in the utter disbelief a fellow Marine is ambushing other Marines? That is devastating for a warrior."

"Now, five of our good men are lying in the infirmary, with severed, slashed arteries, some punctured to death. The slaughters are not at the hands of the Japanese Empire, but by a unknown native, or one of us."

"This is what we know. He kills randomly among our men. He maneuvers freely. But that freedom is at night, between 2200 and 0200. Those who have seen him running in the shadows, hopping across roads, weaving his way between the tents and utility areas and warehouses, always reaching the edges of Tent City, then plunging into the densely black jungles."

"Because he obviously knows the dense tropical growth so well, I want to assume he's a Pavuvu native now housed with the other hundred or so in the old Japanese colony barracks on the northwest section of Banika. Or, he could be a rare defecting 'fuzzy-wuzzies' brought over from Guadalcanal to assist the Seabees, but refused to return, enjoying Banika and the Russells more. But that's a pure, wild guess, since all 'wuzzies' were accounted for when they re-boarded the transport last week before the Hauser murder."

"But the Pavuvu natives are of interest to us now. The few up-close sightings of the murderer tell us, if we can believe them, the man is dark, he is furtive, stalking, slinking in motion, noiseless. What has us leaning in his direction is how he can adapt to the jungle, boat or swim the channel so easily, so adroitly, from Pavuvu back to his Banika settlement. Throw in that he's supposedly dark, bony-mouthed, fleshy-throated, large lipped. Supposedly, he has fat, thick arms with long, dark hairy mountain bear lumbering hands with thick fingers. He wields a bolo, a large Pacific Island single-edge knife, so highly polished it shines. In short, he's big and dark."

"Now, mind you, these are mere sightings, what shooters giving chase and aiming believe they saw. There could be truth to it and we've taken steps to investigate the village elders, and, if necessary, contain the occupants of their little hamlet, until the multiple - murderer is apprehended or killed. But we aren't sure a Pavuvoan is the perpetrator."

"Nonetheless, native or Marine, five painful letters have to be written and sent to the families of the dead five. And, possibly more letters before all this ends. How difficult to explain that either a jungle monster or a fellow Marine wielded a knife so large with such force, it cut through to the bone of their loved one."

"Now, let me review a few other factors…"

Just then, a hand shot up to ask a question.

"Yes, sir. I should have asked if there were any questions before proceeding. Go ahead, officer."

"How could such a hairy, large native get up close enough in a dense tent area with sufficient lighting to thrust an icepick into the chest and face of an armed sentry?"

"Yes, well, that's the question, isn't it? That fact alone may tell us the Mad Ghoul may not be a murdering native. He would have to be a fellow Marine, one strong enough to thrust a Ka-Bar so strongly, so deeply."

"So," Peter continued, "let's summarize where we are at this precise moment with five fine American men, trusting, loyal boys dead on our hands for reasons having nothing to do with our mission to defeat a deadly foe."

"As hard as it is to admit, there is currently no single accurate clue as to who the murder mad man is. The only method of determining his identity is to be present when he kills again. And, he most certainly will, perhaps as early as this evening, which promises a moonlit night after our normal afternoon showers."

"Although none of us has the experience of a homicide detective, there are certain signs, or points, or indicators we can look for and note.

For example, try to guess at the approximate moment of death, when you find, or are called, to the dead. Ask everyone near the scene when it could have happened. When did they last see the man and when was the corpse discovered. We must try to be as exact as possible to the range of hours, even minutes it happened."

"In addition to determining the approximate minute when death occurred, as the unfortunate Marine praying all alone in the Battalion chapel, pay attention to the position of the body. Was it moved? Did he remain where he fell? Was he still alive when he hit the ground? We need to consider the angle of the instrument as it entered his neck. Was the victim so deep in prayer that he didn't hear the killer, or that he knew him and turned his back on him?"

"As for the factors that may have dissipated with the hours and days, we need not be concerned. The murder occurred at night and the body discovered instantly, or within an hour or so. Same for the rigor mortis, the physical change of muscles. Time of death and discovery was so short, these last two don't count, although note them in your reports."

"And, try not to be opinionated in gathering your clues. And, be careful when dealing with, or working around the corpse."

"Of course, all you come up with are preliminary findings that lead to additional examinations. But the points are the first, what to look for when arriving."

"Now, let me say a few words about possible traits and characteristics of our murder mad."

"Whomever this killer is, and I don't believe it is a native, he is a case study of a man in total agony. All multiple murderers are one minute apathetic and listless, indifferent to all around them, then, the next minute, delirious, turbulent, energized, coiling back to strike.

Look more for the quiet, innocuous, decent fellow in the tents. Although it may seem impossible that someone so strong and violent, capable of plunging a sharp weapon, to the bone, is not the murderer, it may well be true. Prison guards know that the most dangerous men they have to deal with are not the overtly loud, obviously violent ones. The most dangerous are the quiet ones who shrink into corners, or back against the wall in fear. Once corralled or caught, he is apt to strike out with all his force to kill you. He lives in perpetual fear."

"I don't really know if I'm accurate. We've had multiple murderers since the beginning of time, I'm sure. They were never caught except by accident, or they died of old age or natural deaths. But today there's a greater awareness of them. Homicide inspectors are telling the FBI about their failures, their inabilities to catch them in their towns and cities. My dream is to bring the retired inspector into the office to solve such murders."

"What this new awareness is telling us is that the murderer of many is a white male. Well, we've got 16,000 of them right over there. He's smart. He's intelligent. And, he's planned well his killings. He's a kid without a father, from a broken home. He may have been sexually assaulted by that very absent father. And, the kid is depressed and lonely."

"No murder-mads are alike. And, there are several ways they are not alike. One, is the way in which he selects his victims. On Pavuvu, it appears he is choosing his victims only in terms of their remoteness and the nearby access to safety. That means the Marines on the periphery of any settlement, Tent City, or hospital, any area where sleep is inevitable, or allowed, are in danger the most. Those in the core of the sleeping are safe. At the forthcoming meeting at noon, and the planning and assignments of sentries, I'll recommend the majority of our infantrymen and riflemen be assigned out there, rather than in here within Tent City."

"My point is that whomever is going around bumping off our boys in the black night with an instrument designed large enough to kill cows is not just killing for the sake of killing. Here, he has only one type of person to kill; a young white soldier. Out there, he murders 'types' of people he hates or has a grudge on or against. His modus operandi may have been chosen because the victims are all asleep, disposable because they are helpless. Or, the victims could be a certain minority, homosexuals, blondes, etc. The bottom line is that if we look closely at every one of his murders, he is dropping clues as to why he has killed him, and what has made him select who he has selected in those places he can get away easily."

"Our murder-mad Marine may be obsessed with manipulation and domination. Stateside, he uses 'ruses' or 'cons' to get next to his victims. Here, he knows what he is doing and why. 'Is he insane?' you ask. Well, let me put it this way. He will have problems convincing a judge or jury he is criminally insane. This murderer knows what he is doing and he knows the difference between right and wrong."

After a brief pause during which there was a tomb-like silence, Peter concluded,

"Perhaps with luck, today will be the day we either catch him, or kill him. If not, we all have to do what we can in our small way to put an end to it. It will not be easy, because, in a way, we know nothing about who he is, or why he's doing it."

"But remember this as you go about your work. Our minds, or I should say, the mind of the murder mad always has a purpose. He has less control than he thinks. His mind is a labyrinth of complexes, guilt, aggressions, sex, fears, anxieties. People aren't what they seem. All people wear masks. If you don't see beneath the mask, it's entirely possible you may be targeted as the next victim to be slashed to death."

As Peter raised his hand to signal the meeting had concluded, and the audience that had been so rapt and aghast quietly stirred to stand and leave for their respective offices and units, someone asked loudly,

"What about a mental test to administer to everyone?"

Peter looked up with a quick smile and responded,

"Oh, if only it were that easy! A mental test for a special severe type of neuroses that commits murder. I'm afraid we'd find one Marine in every 10 would be suitable for instantaneous admittance to the asylum of the criminally insane. Three out of every 10 would be readied in shackles for the stockade. And, mostly from the officer's corps."

Everyone grinned in agreement.

"Wouldn't it be wonderful if such a device existed? After this war is concluded, it's something for the advance thinkers in criminal psychology to create. I'm afraid most of our combat veterans would not sit still for a mental exam inquiring if they were multiple - murderers. Besides, the organized, intelligent murder-driven killer with a trace of imagination could fake it. How would we know if the test we devised was valid, reliable, and even usable among such large numbers of men?"

"Well, how would you fake it?" someone else asked.

"By telling you what you want to hear."

With everyone pausing, fascinated by this last bit of discussion, Peter, pleased, said,

"We're just in the beginning stages of developing psychometric mental exams that can yield believable scores, shedding light on the mind with evil intent. And, even if I could point to one of you, I would need an eyewitness to corroborate the score, not numbers to substantiate the killer."

As the session terminated, and a hushed rush to return to offices and resume the day's business, Peter, answering a number of brief questions, exited the small patio pavilion into the shimmering white blur of the Pacific sun directly overhead. The cool breeze was welcomed after lecturing at length in the warm air of the hospital structure. Peter's rapid eyes swept the large entrance area and narrow walkways for anyone he knew to have a quick lunch with in the nearby officer's canteen.

Suddenly, from behind him, a familiar feminine voice called out cheerfully,

"Peter! Wait!"

It was Ellen, smiling and walking rapidly toward him. Seeing her enthusiasm in calling out to him pleased Peter. She really was a lovely person and he liked her very much.

"Heard every word you said. What a marvelous lesson!"

"Didn't see you in there with all the others. Where were you sitting?"

"Got there a little late. Had to sit in the back. Did you know another body was found this morning behind the hospital's X-ray unit?", she asked, her voice lowered, somewhat faltering.

Peter paled. He stared silently at Ellen, incredulously. Slowly, he responded,

"No, I didn't hear. No wonder Oscar was so quiet and secretive. Never saw him so deliberative. Who was found and where?"

"One of the nurses in our unit on Banika."

"Banika? That makes a total of six, four in one day! Ellen, I have to get to Oscar's office. I was looking for someone to have a bowl of soup with in the canteen and thank goodness, you showed up."

As she looked up at him, he thought for a moment how much he enjoyed both her company and that of Bill Lundigan's. The very sight of her made him break out into a warm smile, as it did when seeing Bill earlier.

"No lunch today, Ellen. We're not just trying to catch, and if necessary, kill the Mad Ghoul, the whole 1st Division is now at war with the monster. We will kill him on sight. I wish I could cage him to study the mind of the reptile. But I must acknowledge we have to kill him as soon as possible. Now, I must get to Captain Del Barbra's office and learn what time and how the nurse was murdered. Then, I'll examine each of the three bodies to see what I can decipher. I also need to talk to the sentries, and anyone who saw even a glimpse of the murder - mad."

"I understand. Wish I could help you, regardless of how blood-curdling it all is."

"After an early supper, we'll have an hour or so before sundown, you, Bill and me, to catch up on things. Then, I must return to Pavuvu to assist on patrolling all night and being immediately available in case he's killed or caught."

"Yes. I have an intuition you'll come across him tonight."

"So, same place, same time. I'll have more information. Try to get Bill to have something to eat first. He has to chow early, like I will."

Ellen sighed heavily. Looking directly into his eyes, she suddenly was overwhelmed with an irresistible yearning to reach out and touch Peter's cheek. The normal twinkle in his eyes seemed to radiate as an almost imperceptible brighter, luminescent shade of red crossed his face. Ellen smiled, then abruptly turned and walked hurriedly down the road toward the pontoon bridge across the channel to her hospital workstation and nurses' quarters on Banika.

"She's so neat," Peter, thought for a moment as he watched her graceful figure walk away. No nurse's outfit could conceal something so naturally beautiful.

"Fastidious, intelligent, and gentle with an infectious spirit and smile," he mused.

With that, Peter Albioni Toscanini turned and instantly refocused on the matter of multiple murders. His facial expression of delight changed back to a mixture of shock, perplexity, and utter unqualified anger.

CHAPTER TEN

-

Shock, Perplexity, and Insatiable Fury

Friday, August 5

As Peter topped the short rise of the steps to the 1st Division Headquarters, the increasingly strong breeze from the sea suddenly metamorphosed into a typical Russell island afternoon of howling torrential shower.

Pausing a moment to turn and gaze upon the torrential rain now descending in sheets to form little rivulets gushing down the winding crushed coral driveway to the Pacific, he heard the double-glass door swing open and someone call out,

"Hey, you old murderer - hunter, catch him yet?"

Peter smiled, recognizing the voice with a slightly lisping pronunciation. It was that of Rev. Wilfred Pinoe, the 1st Division Chaplain, one of the Lieutenant's favorite officers and a multi-denominational chaplain, a man most of the Marines regardless of religious denomination admired. In addition to being a competent, caring clergyman, attached to the Corps, he was proud of his lisp. Not only did he boast he had it since the age of five, but employed it as a teaching aide for those unfamiliar with the articulation disorder. Pointing to his partially open mouth, he would giggle, "Only comes when I'm unhappy, excited, angry, or plain happy to see you."

Interested as a medical student, Peter would listen intently as Pinoe explained how the tip of his tongue protruded beyond his front teeth, obstructing airflow so that specific sounds couldn't be uttered. He would pronounce "lisp" as "lithp" and, because swallowing was occasionally difficult, his "ch's", "j's", "g's", and "s's", especially words beginning with letters such as "sch", "gho", etc. were slightly stammered due to the incorrect placement of the tongue in the mouth distorting his expulsion of air.

Sturdy, vigorous, and unusually blunt for such an intelligent minister of God, Pinoe pulled Toscanini out of the diminishing deluge into the cover of the headquarter doorway, and said unabashedly,

"I watched all your action with Ellen, you young fox. Everyone knows she belongs to your friend, Bill."

Peter grinned,

"Sorry, friend Pinoe, you're wrong. I'm taken."

"I know," responded Reverend Pinoe, a glitter in his eyes. "Half the 1st Division has heard about a little Nisei named Joan. But, I tell you, old fellow, I mean 'young fellow', that walking down the road half hidden by her umbrella haunts these eyes of mine, clericalist or not. She is so fine she could easily be a famous magazine cover girl, matching Betty Grable, Dorothy Lamour, or Lana Turner, any day."

After a moment, Peter turned and said,

"Let's step out of the wind into the lobby hallway. Glad I ran into you. One of the victims was found in your chapel early this morning?"

"Yes, that's why I'm here. They have a suspect in there with the captain. But I don't think he's the killer. Too frail to repeatedly thrust a Ka-Bar into the praying man's throat, then bludgeoning him with the handle of the Ka-Bar. He then threw it into a dumpster. That guy in there is too skinny to lift anything. No, I didn't hear a thing, not a sound, and I bunk on a cot in the room next to the vestibule."

"I'll catch up with you later. Need to talk to Oscar to let him know I'll be out with the troops tonight, especially near the nurses' quarters on Banika."

"Well, anytime. In fact, why not have a drink before you go on duty tonight. I have a whole bottle of Scotch in my room. In fact, we'll celebrate anything you want. How about Ellen? We'll have the best part of a bottle without water. It'll do you no harm. Scotch might make you think better to catch Charlie the Choker."

Peter laughed,

"Maybe tomorrow, if we catch him tonight. Keep your eyes and years open. You're in a good place and position to see and hear things."

The only residence on Pavuvu, a rambling two-story frame structure painted yellow with a red-painted corrugated roof, served as the 1st Division headquarters. The unsavory looking building was nicknamed "the manor" by the more sarcastic infantrymen. Having belonged to the island's only plantation owners, the Burns Philip Company, a chain of cultivation estates throughout the Solomon area, including both Pavuvu and Banika. It served as the offices for the growing green copra used in a variety of soaps and other health products. Having been perfectly maintained until the Japanese invaded a year or so before, the estate of copra trees had not as yet been overrun by the jungles after the owners and their workers fled the islands.

The exterior of the residence was still in mint condition with high red plants resembling lichen and thick moss-covered walls that surrounded the large house. In the front yard were several lime trees, pepperbushes, and an odd persimmons growth. The low walls surrounding the large house hosted throngs of bougainvillea.

As Peter hastened down the crowded, feverish hallway of tile-appearing blocks toward Captain Del Barbra's office, he noted the old oak-paneled walls, and several hard-breathing grandfather clocks struggling to maintain time. No matter how many times Marine orderlies swept, cleaned, and polished, the interior of the 1st Division

Headquarters seemed soiled. There was an air of desolation about the place that neither cleanliness nor the hustle-bustle of staff could efface.

As Peter reached the door that read in stenciled black paint, "Military Police", it opened suddenly and 1st Medical Battalion commander Everett B. Keck, USN, emerged.

Everett Keck was one of Peter's favorite officers, having been an observer in his introductory "Theories of Personality" courses. Indeed, Peter admitted to friends and fellow students that Keck triggered his interest in the criminal unconscious mind - - "not the preconscious or subconscious, but unconscious", then explaining the differences between the three.

When the 1st Marine Division received its First Medical Battalion, Captain Bruce Logue served as the Division surgeon, and the commander of the First Medical Battalion was Commander Everett Keck. As a 49-year-old Wisconsin native, he saw considerable action on Guadalcanal. "C" Medical Battalion would establish a field hospital shortly after landing as an expanded clearing station. Other medical companies would function as collecting companies for transport of wounded to the clearing station, "C" Medical Company. Upon extinguishing all enemy resistance on Guadalcanal, all the medical units followed to establish and receive evacuated seriously wounded from the Solomon Islands.

By all accounts, not just Peter's, Everett Keck was a good man. His low voice and quaint manner were markedly Midwestern. He was of medium-height, slim, and slightly freckled, suggesting long hours on deck in the sun. He engaged his subjects with dramatic stories, and all who listened found him cheerful, energetic, easy-to-talk-to, and certainly a mentor in the medical field of understanding the criminal mind.

"Well, lieutenant, Captain Del Barbra is expecting you. That was a thought-provoking, intriguing amount of insight you touched upon this morning. You better go on in. There's a lot to inform you about. Time permitting, today, I need you to meet a new arrival in the 1st's Reserve Group's Company, Colonel John T. Selden. We see him assisting your efforts. He's taken a number of advanced psychology courses in Upper Division at the University of Kentucky."

"Eager to meet him, sir."

"Toscanini, who kills with both a Ka-Bar and an ice pick? What kind of man fatally crushes another Marine to death with an ice pick, then after he's dead, use a Ka-Bar to stab the dead man repeatedly. Something is sickeningly wrong here."

"Well, sir," responded the lieutenant. "Some of everything is wrong with the Mad Ghoul, or he wouldn't be killing that way."

"It almost seems two or three murderers are involved in this killing spree. You're the one to figure that out. Then, if he shows up alive; communicate with him."

Someone inside the anteroom of the office yelled out,

"Come on in, Mr. Brains. The door's open."

Peter excused himself, saluted and smiled,

"I'll look him up this afternoon, this Colonel John Selden."

Then, he walked in.

Growing increasingly grim and angry about the systematic murders of three additional fellow Marines, Peter momentarily lost himself in the 1st Division administrative center and its minutiae as he strode into the office of the military police captain. Amid the natural liveliness of high-echelon officers in fresh, newly ironed khaki pants and starched short-sleeve shirts, formal and informal memoranda and other forms of communication were being drawn up, discussed, typed, and routed. All of headquarters seemed engrossed and preoccupied readying everyone for the upcoming campaign, in the Palau Islands, namely, on the island of Peleliu. Reinforcing the 1st Division as part of the III Amphibious Corps was as paramount as catching or killing the Ghoul.

Walking past the sergeant's desk in the anteroom pouring over the deployment map of sentries for the night, Peter nodded at Guidi, who glanced up and grunted. The door to Captain Del Barbra's office was open and Peter strolled in and promptly sat down in the chair beside the desk. Off to his left was a large window from which he could see several companies of sentries patrolling the perimeter of headquarters. With a stern grimace crossing his lips, Peter looked out upon the sunlit drill-ground and the broad sweep of beaches beyond. No soldier posted to guard against the Mad Ghoul or Japanese invader walked alone. Heavily armed, the patrolling was conducted in groups of three.

As he turned back toward his chair, the lieutenant was perplexed. He was toying with various murders and mad Marine scenarios. Although his thick brown hair was carefully trimmed, and his khakis immaculate, covering a slim, healthy figure, every nerve in Peter's body was riddled with tension. He felt the grip on himself was slightly weakening.

Meanwhile, Sgt. Guidi in the anteroom was utterly oblivious to his presence. He had not made more than a casual glance in his direction. Peter, suddenly aware of muffled voices emanating from somewhere, noted that the door to the right of the office beyond Guidi's desk was slightly ajar.

Peter, flashing a grin toward the sergeant, who smiled back, approached the door to listen in. Creeping closer to look through the crack, he saw one of the few Marines he truly admired.

To Peter, Captain Oscar Del Barbra was the iron and steel embodiment of law and justice. So was the immutability of the tone of his voice. He was obviously enraged as he concluded diagraming how the grid schemes for the various acreages of Tent City would intertwine.

"No one can penetrate the encirclement. If so, it'll be damn near impossible to move from one grid to another without being challenged. And, when challenged, the multiple murderer will have to kill two well-armed sentries simultaneously to slink back into Tent City. If he makes it inside there, he'll face small company road and alley patrols all over the place."

After a pause, the captain raised his lead slightly and continued slowly,

"With this plan, the Mad Ghoul's murdering is over. Think about it for a moment. In less than a few days, six murders--five good Marines and a popular, caring Marine nurse. And, all deaths by a fellow Marine. Unbelievable. And further unbelievable, not so much as a glimpse of the Mad Ghoul's face! The man is astonishingly clever. He's certainly no native, or fuzzy-wuzzy. And, he surely can't be a stray, leftover Jap. No, man, he's one of us."

Again, Del Barbra paused, studying his feet.

"What galls me so bitterly is that all of the defenseless Marines enlisted to serve their country, and if necessary, sacrifice their lives. All six saw duty on the Canal, the five riflemen on the island's trails and jungles, the nurse in the mobile care-stations within feet of the line! Here, all six were resting, recuperating, and refitting for the upcoming campaign, except for the young nurse tending our boys in the malaria wards."

"No point in venting my pent-up vengefulness. I've got to get back to work. But, oh God, have your men bring the Ghoul to me personally, for just a few minutes before we send him to the hospital ship's brig. All I need is less than seconds. I will give him back to you in a sticky mass of bloody flesh."

Upon seeing the captain turn away from the blackboard and start walking back toward his office door, Peter glimpsed Oscar's face as he retreated to his chair next to the desk. Never before had he seen such a countenance of emotionally enraged living tissue. The captain was enraged and dispassionate simultaneously. His walk was stiff, yet strong and authoritatively. As he watched the man step toward his desk, Peter decided not to analyze, judge, or understand the captain. Like Del Barbra, he, too, was possessed by an ungodly force. But his facial expression at that moment would remain engraved on Peter's memory well beyond a lifetime.

Slamming his folder on the desk, the captain, without acknowledging Peter, continued toward the broad window. The lieutenant immediately rose and joined him. Neither offered a comment, nor said a word, causing Sergeant Guidi to glance up at the unusual moment. While Del Barbra gazed past the gray bay out to the vast Solomon Sea, Peter studied the half-sunken Japanese barge rusting under the Pacific sun, and, less than 100 yards away, several APD's, fast, light supply transports, and a single LSM, landing ship, medium, unloading cargos of weapons, ammunitions, foods and other supplies onto smaller flatbed craft, including DUKWs, 2 ½-ton amphibious trucks for the docking facilities and nearby warehouses.

Finally, the captain said softly, "Oh, so it's you, lieutenant. Glad you stopped by. I have important news for you. But let me shake off this abysmal gut of feelings I'm afflicted by. And, not being able to shit since the killings began is the least of my problems."

Peter resumed his seat, again turning to face the window. Del Barbra, as well, pivoted his swivel chair, folded his hands, and said nothing. Guidi, head down, continued studying his post assignments for the Tent City grids, listened intently.

"Yup, big news," said Del Barbra angrily. "But first, let's talk. Except for the first, all front-stabbed. How can that be? Are our Marine sentries so weak, especially armed with Thompsons and Reisings, that can't handle some one thrusting Ka-Bars, ice picks, hatchets, or scissors at them? This last murder, the scissors cut so deep into the face, his skull was exposed, then had his head bashed in, his eyes bulging out from under his eyebrows. What matter of man is this Ghoul murderer? You're supposed to be the expert. Tell me."

Peter continued gazing out the window without a word, deep in thought. Then he responded,

"Our murderer is not the Mad Ghoul, captain. And you're right. He's neither a native, nor a Japanese stray. The killer is one of our own officers, an aberration of an American officer."

"Impossible," Del Barbra cried out.

"I don't want to believe it myself."

"How so, then? Explain!" the captain demanded, slamming the face of his hand down on his desk.

"I have only this, captain, and I hope to convince myself that my intuition is as flawed and defective as my intellectual judgment."

For less than a moment, Peter hesitated, then, poignantly, in almost a whisper, he answered,

"There can be only one reason why a presumably trained nurse or sentry, and a heavily-armed one at that, will allow himself to be stabbed to death frontally. Since there is not a shred of evidence there was a struggle, or proof there was a defensive fighting for life, the murdered trusted, had absolutely no suspicion a murderer was approaching him within inches to thrust a sharp instrument into his heart. No! Each of the killed who saw the killer felt subordinate to whomever was walking up to him. The sentinel was submissive, trusting, and friendly. The unfortunate men on duty lowered their weapons, and at that moment, out flashed the ice pick, the scissors, butcher knife, or whatever it was."

The captain, and now Sergeant Guidi, who pulled up a chair, leaned forward as earnestly as each has ever been. Neither of their eyes left Peter's face. Peter, in return, gazing almost unconsciously upon the captain's passionate face-off and tense physiognomy, was certain he caught a sinister gleam in his eyes.

"I never in my career as a Marine met an officer who hated his own men like poison. Japs, certainly. But not his own."

"All I can remind you of is an important truism in the field of psychology: No one, absolutely, no one, is who he or even she, seems to be. Our minds always have a purpose. Each of us, healthy or sick in the mind, has less control than he or she thinks, or believes. The forces in our unconscious are a raging sea of drives, instincts, aggressions, desires, and memories that not only cripple us, but force us to do things, commit assaults we're unable to control. The human mind is a labyrinth of anxieties and complexes not understood. Fortunately, the vast majority of minds don't cause us to commit murder."

For more than a full minute, Del Barbra and Guidi pondered. Then, the captain asked,

"Is it possible the Ghoul, an officer, is a new replacement from the States? We've had over 350 new ones fill in the ranks of those we lost on Guadalcanal due to enemy fire, wounds, and tropical diseases. Hell, man, we had two killed three months ago, in May I think, by falling coconuts! Those replacements fit right in with the veterans, the old timers of the 1st. They all seem to pick up the spirit and enthusiasm. Hard to believe one of those youngsters is murder mad."

"I don't know. The killings started when the 1st Division arrived and will certainly end when the 1st leaves for our island to take. One thing is for sure: He has to be big and strong and powerfully hefty to throw a heavy corpse of a nurse into a dumpster."

Startled, Captain Del Barbra demanded,

"How did you know that?"

Surprised, Peter responded,

"The Chaplain and a nurse. All the nurses watched with horror, I'm certain, as the victim was extricated from it. By now, 16,000 Marines know about it."

"I suppose so. We wanted to keep it secret to possibly entrap the killer in some way. The poor nurse must have been hated awful to be killed and heaved into a garbage bin."

"Yes. But that dead weight is difficult to lift up and throw over 10 or 12 feet."

"Do you think I should recommend we curfew officers from sundown to daylight for a week or so to see what happens?"

"No, I don't think so. For the murder - mad, each killing is like winning a victory, a triumph. His nerves, every fiber in his body, tingles with the thrill of success. It's like he's now addicted. Killing is an emotion he can't describe. It's like an addictive drug, and he likes it. If corralled, he will start killing the sentries assigned to guard him. I wouldn't be surprised if he weren't keeping a written score with name, rank, date, hour, and minute murdered of each of his victims. No, curfew won't stop him."

After a reflective moment, Peter, barely audible and more to himself than Oscar or Leo, whispered,

"Oh God, how I hope I'm wrong. Such thoughts bring on a depression. I've got to stop that oppression--it's creeping all over me. I might even have to have a chat with the chaplain, a friend of mine, about my ambivalence. When I learn the innocent are speared in the chest, my mind... "

"Your mind, what?"

" . . . is interested in the dark forces in man's mind, especially the mind revolving from evilness. It's a minor confusion in me caused by simultaneous conflicting feelings. Like I don't understand me, I don't understand him. But if I have an ounce, even a speck, of courage in me, I'll solve one and fight to the death the other."

"Well, young psychologist who yearns to understand the criminal mind, let's take a moment to look at what you have to deal, with, because it may well be the Ghoul, the Choker, or an immaculate-looking officer, or replacement officer, is a member of your own medical corps."

"Maybe. Regardless, whether an old combat-weary veteran who lost his equipoise, his self-possession, he will go about his duties, his daily work, in a deliberate manner, without ever looking up. There will be no superfluous energy exhibited, not a hint of intensity, all a show of singleness purpose. Not that he's acting to fool us, but because that's who he exactly is."

"Sounds like some of our surgeons," interjected Sergeant Guidi.

"Possibly," reflected Peter.

"Well, we sure have enough of them around here. Just yesterday, I had to sign off on a Cross Reference Memorandum from the Inspector of Medical Department Activities, Pacific Ocean Area, to the

Commandant of the 14th Naval District, with copies to the Command of the South Pacific Force, CinePac and CinePoa. It dealt with our Fleet Hospital 110."

"Well, what the report tells me is that not only are replacements flooding Pavuvu, but also the wounded, the disease-ridden, the mentally ill. I'll bet Mrs. Oscar Del Barbra's panties the murder - mad multiple murderer is among the huge number of recent arrivals."

"Hmmm," Peter sighed. "How many? You may be right. Sneaks out of his hospital bed, murders, then returns to his quarters or tent area. That may be why we haven't seen him disappear into the jungle. But, I'm curious. How many infirmed do we have on the island now?"

"Our new Pavuvu Base Hospital #110 has a normal capacity at 1,000 beds. We can expand to another 400, if we want to. As of this morning, we have 600 occupied. #110 is responsible for everyone on the island, Navy, Army, and Marine, for those on the ships in the harbor. It also has to care for the casualties evacuated from the more forward areas. And, here they seem to stay. Over 100 of our men have been ready for evacuation to the States, but the transportation is meager. Otherwise, we have no problems. Our hospital is considered to be excellently administered and adequately equipped. Our standard profession service has done well for us! We now have attached to us 59 nurses, a number considered excessive. Our #110 is basically Task Force huts with high concrete floors which allow for better ventilation. The operating center and X-ray room are well-dispersed. Arrangement of the huts for the two facilities are considered exceptionally good. Still another distinctive feature of our hospital is the unusually thoroughly precautions taken to safeguard the nurses against prowlers. The nurses' compound is surrounded by a high wire camouflaged fence with the addition of electrified wire. In spite of these precautions however, prowlers have been caught in the premises around the compound. My hunch is that The Mad Ghoul is one of those doctors or surgeons from that hospital area. For some reason, the nurse in the dumpster was murdered on purpose, not at random. It was an easy killing for him."

"And, a civilian nurse at that."

"What?" asked Peter surprised.

"One of our hired civilian nurses, a Hawaiian one," the captain shot back.

"One of Ellen's best friends is from the Hawaiian Islands. Will ask her tonight after supper if she knew the young woman. But, I wondered why so many of our women here look like they are from the Pacific Islands."

"Well, by December of 1942, a little more than a year after Pearl Harbor, we only had 23 American hospitals, several of them the 100-bed mobile unit kind mounted on trucks," Oscar started to explain.

"Yeah, and thanks to my mentor, Brigadier General Earle Maxwell, the Australian manufacturer, began creating prefabricated ones out of plywood and Masonite that could be transported and delivered by cargo craft."

"Well," the captain continued, "also in short supply were medical staffs of all varieties. Since war broke out, we've consistently been 5% below authorized. And, nurses in particular have been in demand. Every hospital is 15% understrength, including ours. So, the need was such our military was forced to go out and hire the closest girls they could find - - those from the Allied Islands, mostly the Hawaiian Islands. And incidentally, the same goes for the 'doctors of the mind', the psychiatrists. But, as we sit here now, the 1st Division psychiatrist is now on duty. Have you met him yet? Dr. Schneidermann arrived a few days ago and is busy providing expert diagnoses."

"I heard a little about him, but that indeed he is at work. I have yet to meet him. I'm anxious to. Was he at the meeting this morning?"

"Yes, in fact he was in the first row."

"But, by your reasoning, a new base hospital, innumerable doctors and surgeons to choose from, and now the murder of a nurse, with more to come . . ."

"Most certainly."

"Well, at least, you may have narrowed down who to look for. After all, surgeons are officers capable of approaching trusting sentries. What's your plan, captain?"

"Well, you'll be included when we sit down to plan a trap, day after tomorrow."

"Day after tomorrow? He'll surely kill tonight or tomorrow night. Why wait?"

"Division Commander Major General Rupertus has been ordered by none other than Secretary of the Navy, John L. Sullivan, to accommodate, accompany, and protect, none other than Bob Hope and his entourage. During a one-day stay, they will entertain our troops on Pavuvu tomorrow afternoon, and Banika tomorrow night."

Peter was utterly speechless. So much so, in fact, the talking, laughter, and chit-chat of hallway and adjacent office activities reverberated throughout Del Barbra's office. As the captain smiled and studied the lieutenant, he could see that he suddenly became grim and lynx-eyed. Now, he was dark, tense, and concerned. Peter was not pleased.

"My God, what better place for a grand finale, a splendorous magnificent setting for homicide by a chameleon. God only knows what the dark matter in his mind will summon up. Use of an ax?"

CHAPTER ELEVEN

-

"Bob Hope? You're Joking!"

For a matter of minutes, neither of the men spoke. Peter was stunned. Del Barbra's keen-sighted eyes under thick eyebrows never left Peter's face.

Finally, the lieutenant who had been gazing out the window in reflection, said soberly,

"A murder - mad Marine on the loose killing his own and you have, of all people, Bob Hope, Jerry Colonna, and several ladies of Hollywood walking around to make us laugh? Are you making a joke?"

"Oh, I hear you, lieutenant…simply put, we catch or kill the Ghoul tonight before Hope and the entourage fly in tomorrow afternoon."

As Peter chuckled warmly, Sergeant Guidi entered the office and, approaching the captain's desk, announced, "Lieutenant Colonel Worthington is coming down the hall."

"Been waiting for him. Glad the lieutenant is here to hear it all. You better pull up a chair, too."

Turning back to Peter, the captain smiled,

"You know, Frank, don't you?"

"I certainly do. One of the best of men. Alongside of Division Commander Rupertus, Assistant Commander Shepherd, and Chief of Staff Sims, you couldn't ask for a better Battalion Headquarters Commander than Worthington. Other than my hero mentor, Brigadier General Earl Maxwell of Medical, there is no Marine more near perfect. Some of us have dark heroes as their life-long teachers, others have mentors with unsavory records and backgrounds, and some have no heroes at all. Both of the men I've selected to serve as my exemplars certainly have their fair share of warts and blemishes. But all I see are two kind, gentle Marines of persistent, resolute, indeed, fierce, defiant, brave, courageous personality traits.Now, a whole lot of Marines around here have those qualities, including you, captain. But what makes them special, and, really, you, too, you old rummy, is your quiet gleam of empathy for the captured, sick, ill Japanese soldier who would just as soon atrociously shoot us in the foreheads."

"What's wrong with being Bacchus? And, I do agree with you about both Marines. No wonder you're the Medical Corps' coxswain in analyzing the criminal mind."

Of course, Captain Del Barbra knew both Maxwell and Worthington well, agreeing with all that Peter had said. Neither officer tolerated fellow officers who liked whisky or enjoyed the concomitant of easy living while serving in combat. Neither was reckless, daring, or frivolous when it came to ordering men into combat. Neither was the least bit intimidated by swarms of "banzai" charging troops, or the continuous pings of bullets spattering all around. Neither officer knew any other occupation other than the corps, each a skilled marksman in the use of all light weapons. Each knew how to read men, regardless of rank, whether their psychological masks were on or off. No wonder, reflected Del Barbra, the young, highly intelligent lieutenant would gravitate to the Lieutenant Colonel and Brigadier General.

With Worthington pausing a few moments to converse with Guidi who returned to the anteroom, Peter continued,

"I'll drink half a small glass of red wine to that, Bacchus. I'm the first to jump up and shout, 'Welcome to colorful, enticing, strangely beautiful Pavuvu, for an excitement of a lifetime. But not this moment,

Mr. Hope. We have a little problem we're struggling to solve--a skillful butcher knife slaughterer of human meat frolicking every which way."

"Didn't realize that on top of being a future psychologist of the murdering - mind, you were also a funmaker. "

"Seriously, military police friend. If for an hour or so, we can protect Bob Hope to bring our bone-weary a few simpers, smiles, smirks, grins, giggles, guffaws, chuckles, titters, cheers, hurrahs, hoorays, shouts, yells and old-fashioned joy, jubilation, and hallelujah, I'm all for it! But suppose the Ghoul being one of us has the same access we have to the entourage, and he puts a blade through Mr. Hope's eye, we'll have a public relations disaster of unparalleled proportions, not just in the States, but throughout the Allied world. No comedian is more adored or revered. I've seen his last five films myself, for goodness sake. Fiasco? The 1st Division will have to answer at the very least to 10 million moviegoers, to say nothing of all the other military personal stateside he's brought a little jubilation to."

"Well, that's Frank's problem. As for me, I'll be with Hope every moment he's here, from the moment the he steps off the plane to the moment he gets back on. The title of his first book or next movie might be, 'I Had A Great Desire to Pee in The Pacific'. Here's Frank now."

"Hello, gentlemen," greeted Lieutenant Colonel Frank R. Worthington, Unit Commander, 1st Division Headquarters Battalion. He was a fine soldierly-looking officer, tall, calm, with a modest appearing face, a slight provoking smile suggesting kindness of heart, yet force of character. He was muscular and obviously strong.

Peter immediately stood up, saluted, and offered his hand.

"Always a pleasure to be in your presence, sir," smiled the lieutenant.

Shaking it firmly, the Lieutenant Colonel returned the smile, asking,

"Catch the killer, yet?"

"No, sir," chuckled Toscanini, "but we will. So help me God, we will."

"I know, Peter. That's why we look to you to unofficially lead the task force to get him. Any clues whatsoever?"

"Only that he must be an officer to approach and close in on the sentries murdered, despite their being heavily armed. He is either an officer in khaki or posing as an officer."

"Well, keep me informed, preferably every few hours. The Marine Corps, or any branch of the service, for that matter, has never been faced with such an internal horror. And, now, with a VIP and his team arriving tomorrow?"

"Makes me very, very nervous, sir," interjected the lieutenant.

"Me, too. But let's take a look at this thing, so you can share the information with those who should know."

"Our recreation officer was informed by a summons from Commander Rupertus to report to his office by 0600 this morning. Since Shepherd and I were already in our respective offices, we were called in. None of us knew what it was about. Bill said he had just sat down at his desk when he received a teletype of the highest priority that Bob Hope agreed only hours earlier to perform on Pavuvu this afternoon before his performance tonight on Banika. We were both surprised and pleased. 'Wow!' was our first reaction, then remembered we're in the middle of a murder spree. By midnight, our time, Secretaries of the Navy, past and present, Frank Knox and John L. Sullivan, had notified the President they were going to sign off approving the request promising Roosevelt the highest security would be in place. Hope said he'd like to meet the multiple - murderer because he might be related to Bing Crosby. Furthermore, he wanted the killer to know he didn't mind being a victim as long as his handsome face was left intact."

Del Barbra and Guidi laughed softly, as Peter smiled.

"So, this has gone all the way to the President's office?"

"Yes. Roosevelt said he had no problem with Crosby heading for Pavuvu, since he was a solid Democrat. But, as for Hope? A Republican? The Japs might be so infuriated Tojo would personally lead a landing assault."

Everyone laughed loudly.

"Apparently, when told the Relax and Refit men on Pavuvu had nothing compared to the luxuries of Banika, he insisted on performing. He said something to the effect, '50,000 Marines to watch us perform? When Crosby's ventriloqials will generally mobilize, maybe 5, lemme-at-em!'"

Again, loud laughter from Del Barbra and Guidi, and a smile from the lieutenant.

With that, Peter added, "Unless needed, I'm off to the hospital morgue. I need to examine the murdered. Was he killed by someone right-handed or left-handed? How tall was he to form the thrusts of the wounds, etc."

"No, lieutenant, do what you have to do. We're going to review our safety and security preparations on Pavuvu for the performance. I'll be roaming Tent City tonight. We'll catch up then."

"I'll be among the hospital wards, but will seek you out, unless you want to tour our arrangements there."

"I'll see. Be prepared to attend the 0700 meeting tomorrow morning for the final summary."

"See you then!"

With that, Peter hurried off, past Guidi with a nod and smile, and down the hall through the half-hysterical activity of headquarters, and out onto the front concrete porch. There, a mid-afternoon bright blur of shimmering light greeted him. Below, his rapid eyes swept the spread of Pavuvu, its bay and dock, crops of coconut palm trees, warehouses, utility facilities, armored vehicle lots, and the vast Tent City of the 1st Division. Farther out was nothing more than oceanic solitude. He had to hurry, since he would cross to Banika after examining the dead; then, after chow, a brief respite with Bill and Ellen, followed by a double back to assist in patrolling for the Ghoul.

Descending the steps, Peter walked toward the new Base Hospital #110, past the fresh landscaped plantings and their rustic fences. Off to his left was the medical supply depot, the dispensary, and the four-celled stockade for neuropsychiatric cases.

Within the base hospital, amid the steady luminous light heat, Peter walked down the hall filled with numerous hospital personnel past the wards of patients with malaria, dengue, various skin disorders, hernias, infected wounds, appendectomies, etc. Since the Solomon and Russell Islands suffered heavy flooding from inordinate summer rainfalls, various sections of hospital #10 were inaccessible. Entering the staff workroom and lounge, Peter immediately noticed the large refrigerator box morgue next to the embalmer's chamber. It appeared unaffected by water damage. The five cadavers, four Marines and a civilian nurse, lay naked awaiting dissection should the Division assign a coroner to determine the need for autopsies. Low, incandescent lighting lit the interior of what the medical staff referred to as the "ice box", projecting eerie shadow images amid the dead.

Since not a single murder weapons had been located, Peter quietly observed the sharp force bloodstain patters on each of the bodies for unusual significance. Atypical stab wounds, attacker handedness and frontal positioning, direction, penetration, order of wounds, etc. yielded a helpful overview of injury variables and death interpretations from sharp-edged weapons and their effects on the body. from a recent lecture Peter attended, he recalled two salient facts in stabbing murders: (1) The minimum safe distance from an unknown assailant wielding an edged weapon is 21 feet; from a known assailant, less than six. (2) Most homicidal slashings occur from behind, and, (3) screwdrivers are usually the murder weapon of choice, with two deep stabs accomplishing a death.

For a moment, Peter reflected on the beginning of pathology science as a subspecialty of medicine in murder investigations in the late 1880s. In 1890, a city ordinance in Baltimore authorized the Board of Health to appoint two physicians as "Medical Examiners" to conduct all autopsies upon the suspected murdered. Twenty-five years later, New York City eliminated the coroner's office and created a medical examiner system to investigate all deaths resulting from criminal violence. Systematic efforts at managing death investigations by a medical examiner was less than 30 years old.

In the ample visibility, Peter studied each of the dead, recording notes and necessary surface anatomy, anterior and posterior blade thrusts for the external post-mortem findings submitted to the Judge Advocate, or legal officer, in Honolulu. The early afternoon hours flew apace. Noting the penetrations, punctures, wounds, and their depths and widths soon sickened Peter. Breathing heavily, he was laboring under powerful emotions. His weary face was a pallid gray, analogous to those of the victims.

Stepping back from the cadavers, Peter seemed transformed for the first time in his life. His hair and clothes were disheveled. His body seemed to writhe in agony, his tear-filled eyes wanting to cry out, reflecting a heartfelt sadness.

Pulling the white bed sheets over each of the dead, from toes over their heads, he thought to himself,

"Men die in combat die all day long. When the soldier is calm as he accepts death, he is at his glorious. Knowing his end is near, never to breathe again, to never see or feel the presence of joy, and happiness of his loved ones; mother and father, wife and children especially, and yet fight to the last second, bloody with back to the edge, weapon, out of ammunition, useless, he is among the Warrior Gods of America's Heritage, beyond further elevation, with the exalted and aggrandized. Admitting, conceding esteem and wonder and veneration by one's deadliest adversary is the goal, the highest victory of every fighting man."

"But to know these unfortunate five died at the hands of inexplicable murder is beyond definition."

Peter, nonetheless, remained composed and resolute. He had a job to do and he would complete it to the very best of his ability. Furthermore, he was gaining a reputation among the Marines and officers of the 1st Division for being dispassionate. That one adjective was well-earned and under no circumstance did he want to jeopardize such a fine accolade.

Suddenly, the metal door of the refrigeration unit swung open and two officers strode into the semidarkness. Uncannily, the daylight from the staff lounge-workroom silhouetted Peter in sharp relief.

"Oh, how ghastly," the shorter, more muscular, of the two officers exclaimed, good-naturedly.

"Well, Reverend Pinoe. A nice surprise. What brings you here?"

"Have come to offer the deceased a sock full of prayers to assist them on their journeys. At least one needs help being ushered where he's going. Plus, to familiarize myself with the offensive reek of death I must learn to get used to. I must be here," he responded, his lisp as pronounced as ever.

Peter glanced at Pinoe and couldn't help but smile. The chaplain always appeared like he slept in his clothes--he was so desultory, disarranged, and dissonant. There was a certain restlessness about him, even a hint of roguishness. Nonetheless, he was wildly popular because he was always available, regardless of hour, especially for Marines who received "Dear John" letters. Because of his innate geniality and happiness, he was all-animation with a constant contented smile.

Quizzically, Peter glanced at the lean, lanky officer behind the clergymen who was now standing before the sheeted cadavers.

"And, you, captain? A division replacement?"

"Yes, having arrived over two weeks ago. I'm to serve as the 1st Division psychiatrist. I'm Dr. Stuart Schneidermann."

Peter drew a deep breathe, a glint of excitement lit his wide eyes with an unabashed excitement.

"Welcome, sir," Peter said quietly, as he offered his hand. "There's a great deal of work awaiting us, either individually or as a team. We'll talk later, especially if you're on duty tonight."

The man smiled lightly, and sat somewhat gloomily. Peter's first impression was that the lean, lanky captain was the silent type, grim, cold, and taciturn. In fact, in shaking his hand, he felt a certain foreboding. His voice was all military, snapping yet lifeless. Behind close-cropped hair, and rigidly set facial muscles, were disquieting eyes and an obvious penetrating, razor-sharp mind.

"Oh, nice," thought Peter, the blood pounding through his heart so strongly that a slow, angry chill began to creep over him.

Reverend Pinoe, after lifting the white sheets of each of the five to observe the wounds of the corpses, turned to Peter with a slight shine in his eyes and whispered huskily,

"The great Renaissance artist-sculptor, Michelangelo, more than any other sculptor, was able to capture the soft, flaccid silky muscles right after death better than any other sculptor. That's why my favorite work of art is his taking Jesus Christ down from the cross and placing him in Mary's lap. I forgot its name, but I saw it in the Vatican before the war in Europe."

After a thoughtful pause in which Peter and the psychiatrist looked on, Pinoe continued,

"Notice," as he lifted the sheet of the female victim, "her muscles in death now--solid rigor mortis, rigid without shortening. All the muscles are affected at a similar rate, but rigor is more evident in the short, smaller muscles earlier than in the longer, larger muscle masses."

For an unsettling moment, Peter, very surprised, said nothing. Then, he asked,

"How do you know so much about all this?"

"Oh, I read it somewhere. After all, I deal with a lot of suicides, and especially those who die in combat before their burials."

After a slight pause, he added,

"To me, muscles are muscles, but they are the most aesthetic right after death."

"You sound like you're the Mad Ghoul," Peter said jokingly, yet studying Pinoe's reaction.

"Oh, not me. If I were, I would use poison or simple strangulation. I wouldn't go around plunging huge sharp instruments into hearts, chests, and stomachs. Too much damage to the muscles."

Eager to change the sickening subject, Peter glanced at Dr. Schneidermann and asked,

"Any thoughts?"

"Plenty. Multiple - murder is a subject with few known facts. And, we know less about who a multiple - murderer is than we do about what and how he does it."

With that, the psychiatrist walked over and yanked the white sheet off the man who lay in rigor mortis next to the nurse, stabbed through the heart, the blade's second thrust pierced the Marine's lung.

"This man, and the others lined up here, were victims of planned, systematic acts of violence. Neither he nor these others expected death. Now, their eyes turned up and young faces little more than yellow pallor, we have to consider the motivations behind their murders. Let's look at the known facts."

"Multiple - murders, as opposed to mass murders," he continued, are the murders of separate victims with time breaks, from two days to weeks or months, between victims. You might say that the time breaks between the killings are 'cooling off' periods."

"In psychiatric terminology, a multiple - murderer is either psychotic or psychopathic depending on the information examined as well as the facts of the crime. From what we can gather, multiple - murderers are rarely psychotic. They are usually psychopaths, often sexual psychopaths, who have profound personality disorders, but are very conscious of their own criminality. There is no question they are in touch with reality."

"With the psychotic killer, he kills because his psychosis drives him to kill. In the case of the psychopathic killer, especially the multiple - murderer, from what little we have learned about his mind, kills because he likes to kill. He is usually intelligent, charismatic, street-wise, charming, and usually handsome. He is mobile, traveling around in search of the 'right victim'. He prefers a certain type of victim, someone who is vulnerable and easy to control. Often the victims will resemble each other."

"The multiple - murderer is extremely manipulative, leading the victim into a certain 'comfort zone' in order to better control for the murder. Some have a fascination for detective and police work and procedures. A few have been police officers. We might even look at our own MP's on Pavuvu. Some have even interjected themselves into the investigations, even returning to the scene of the murder to assess the investigation, or to tease the police with additional clues."

"Remember that these are basically assumptions based upon observations by a variety of people. Trying to delve into their personalities is new to those of us so rooted in old, standard investigative procedures and explanations to account the reasoning of the multiple - murderer."

Peter interjected,

"This is very helpful. How did you accumulate such traits and characteristics?"

"By reading old case files, by listening to old psychologists, by applying personality theories to behaviors and the like."

"Well, go on. I've never heard it said so well. This is a learning lesson for me. I surmised in the recent years some of what you say, but I . . . Anyway, please go on. What else can you tell us about the multiple - murderer?"

Dr. Stuart Schneidermann displayed a slight smile for the first time.

"Well, despite their outward appearances, they are very weak and insecure. They have no power or strength until they have a victim under control. Then they feel a sense of security, a temporary superiority. We think they enjoy the publicity of their murders and follow the news chase closely, loving every minute of it, satisfied they are defeating the authorities."

"We psychiatrists consider multiple murders as the ultimate extension of violence. The killer sees he has the power of life and death over someone else and is thrilled by the cruelty of his act and will indulge in torturing his victims to death. The sounds of the victim's screams and pain are music to his ears, enhancing his dreams and fantasies. Unfortunate victims are considered 'play things'. Mutilating them also shocks the police, which pleases the killer. He has no capacity to love, or relate, so his only self-gratification is in the feelings that come with murder."

"Naturally, their earliest years, whatever they were, influenced their evilness years later. Child abuse certainly is one factor. Alcohol or marijuana or other drugs don't make multiple - murderers. No, it goes much deeper than drink or drugs. Child abuse has everything to do with his hatred, his drive to kill, perhaps a drive for revenge against his parents."

"It's interesting to note that the multiple - murderer's murders tend only to increase. It appears that they have to kill more often in order to enjoy the 'high' they get from the act. Most multiple -murderers have been caught by accident as they become bolder in their murders and disregard the risks for the 'high'."

"Some old timers, retired homicide inspectors, estimate there may be as many as 30 stateside multiple - murderers at work now. They will continue until caught, killed by the authorities, imprisoned and to die there or die of natural causes. Outlining who the multiple-murderer is, is the art and science of the future. That is, you gather every known fact and detail of the crime, sit down with other experienced investigators, throw in an authority on the violent criminal mind, and you will probably have a map, a diagram, a chart as to who he is, making finding him an easy task."

After a long pause, Peter smiled and said,

"Dr. Schneidermann, I am so pleased you are among us. You will be an invaluable source of assistance. For me, personally, I will bind myself to you to absorb all that you know."

Peter lingered for a moment as the three officers silently stood before the dead. Then, abruptly, he turned and hastened out the door. Pinoe and Scheidermann remained behind gazing upon the corpses.

CHAPTER TWELVE

-

Eve of Hope

Friday, Aug. 5

It was late in the afternoon when Peter walked past the surgical unit and various ward tents, then out the door of the hospital and into what would soon be a gathering dusk. Without stopping to talk to the officers and enlisted men he recognized or knew, he hurried down the main road and turned off, toward the rutted roadway leading down to the channel and pontoon bridge separating Pavuvu from Banika. His plan was to return to his Banika quarters for a quick shower, then chow down on the hot food from the officers' galley. His only concern was he would fall asleep in his serving tray while enjoying his early evening dinner. He so yearned to meet Bill and Ellen on the beach prior to assisting patrolling Pavuvu that he even considered doing without a healthy meal. An hour and a half with his best friends would be enough to offset both dinner and that night's sleep in a warm, dry bed.

Although there would be no moon that night, the starlight would be sufficient to distinguish objects in the roads, clearings, and in-between the narrow lanes and alleys that separated the pyramidal tents.

"It's not all knives and murder," Peter pondered as he rapidly crossed the bridge and continued hurrying the mile toward the base headquarters and officers' quarters.

Meeting Dr. Schneidermann was special, certainly fortuitous, when Reverend Pinoe, providing the replacement officer with a tour of

Pavuvu, the 1st Division's first psychiatrist, brought him into the morgue earlier in the afternoon. In his lengthy lesson, Peter understood him to say that as far as the Mad Ghoul was concerned, all humans are a trifle mad, but the more perceptive understand that. 'We may not be multiple murderers, but we, as humans, all indulge, from time to time, in minor vagaries and instabilities of madness. The multiple - murdered on Pavuvu left a galore of clues; if only any of us had the imagination to see laterally, on all things, rather than vertically, or in a straight view without glancing from side to side for help.'

Peter smiled, 'My thoughts, precisely. Only point I can't agree on is that reason helps more than intuition. And, that you can never search hard enough. I believe intuition is more important than reason and that generally we try so hard to find clues that we miss the ones right in front of us. In other words, don't make finding the Mad Ghoul difficult. Look, watch, think, and feel, that is, allow your instinct, your seeing, to locate the murderer. Remember, the Ghoul is not a lunatic, a genuine cockeyed loony from a nearby asylum.'

After trotting into the two-story Medical Corps officers' barracks without stopping to address the callers, and scurrying up the stairwell to the second floor's sleeping quarters of more than 50, Peter stripped in as few motions as possible, showered in the stalls at the end of the dormitory near the cots and bunks, and, in a flash, dressed in clean underwear and fresh khakis and a dark brown sweater. After rubbing a damp towel over his recently polished shoes, the lieutenant looked as fresh as he did twelve hours before when he breakfasted.

With that, he leaped downstairs and across the short walk into the 1st Division General Headquarters, again avoiding medical staff and colleagues who hailed him, in order to see if Commander Everett Keck (MC) USN, 1st Medical Battalion, of the 1st Division, was available for a quick update on his assessment of the cadaver wounds. He was not.Keck was in a meeting with Division Commander Major General William H. Rupertus, Assistant Division Commander Brigadier General Leonard Shepherd, Chief of Staff LeRoy Sims, and division and unit commanders.

The lieutenant manning the office desk said,

"I know he wants to talk with you. Best you catch him on patrol tonight. He'll be back and forth between Pavuvu and Banika. We're expecting another killing or two tonight. And, the Hope people flying here at around 1000 in the morning. They will be coming in from Cape Gloucester where he performed the night before. He'll lunch, along with all his entertainers, with our entire command at noon in the mess hall. At 1400, he'll jump into a piper and fly over to the strip across the channel. The others will be driven over in two of our armored vehicles, just in case.They'll be all yours from 1500 until midnight tomorrow night. We're all keeping our fingers crossed The Ghoul will be in the audience laughing his head off rather than trying to murder him or some hapless Marine."

Peter, nodding gravely, said nothing, then turned and headed for the day's final hot meal.

At the entrance of the officers' mess hall, Peter was greeted by the mess sergeant who asked,

"Shoot the bastard yet? You tell me who he is, I'll kill him myself, barehanded. If you do, I'll tell you the surprise we have for supper."

Peter chuckled, glanced at the mess sergeant, and whispered,

"I'm sure we'll know tonight who he is. I'll have someone fetch you, then we'll lock you both in the morgue so you can enjoy a few minutes asking him what his problem is."

"Wait until fellas hear this!" he laughed aloud. "Ok, for that I'll tell you. Guess what five YP tugboats fitted with 'reefers' brought this afternoon from Guadalcanal?"

"Reefers? You mean the drug tobacco wrapped in thin paper for smoking?"

"God, no lieutenant. Smoke that garbage around the Japs and they are sure to shoot your ass off. No, our reefers are refrigerators. And, the brass over there decided to share a special meat with us, not a new kind of spam, but porterhouse steaks; not just for the officers, but one for every Marine on both islands!"

"Unbelievable!"

"But the steaks have to be eaten tonight. The YPs had to get back by sundown for serving. In the morning, they head out with more porterhouses for our men in the outer Russells."

"Well, sergeant, let me do my part in this war. I'll enjoy mine now."

Since it was well past 1700, a line began to form behind Peter as he picked up his tray and utensils, then headed for the next counter where the porterhouses were piled high in a glass cylindrical container. Other foods and provisions were available cafeteria-style. The smell of coffee permeated the hall as Peter sat alone, a plate filled with mashed potatoes, steamed Brussels sprouts, fresh baked bread, ice cream with chocolate topping, and newly flown-in apples and oranges. He was in no mood for idle chatter, gossip, backbiting, rumors, or to share letters from home. He ate quickly to erase the faces of the dead Marines and their wounds.

As Peter exited the mess hall and walked at a measured pace toward his favorite secluded covert on the beach to rest and reflect, a cool breeze swept in from the Solomon Sea Slot. Glancing skyward, he noticed that although the sun hadn't yet sunk below the waves of the Western Pacific, the hint of cold stars appeared.

Scurrying along the raised path of crushed coral, remaining aloof from all troop contacts along the way, Peter wound his way down the main lane to the edge of the swamp then over the ground ivy to the abandoned Japanese-constructed shore defenses to the debris-laden, rubbish-strewn beaches. All along the way, he pondered why it was he who usually was capable of reading the minds of men by the signs they left behind and around them. But for the life of him, he was baffled, completely and angrily perplexed, by the Mad Ghoul and his motives.

Approaching his retreat before the arrivals of Bill and Ellen, Peter was accosted by one of the hundreds of beach sentries,

"Lieutenant Toscanini, is that you? For your usual hour?"

"Yes, sir, it is, too soon to be joined by cameraman PFC Bill Lundigan and Nurse Ellen. You know them."

"Yes, I do and they'll pass through to you. But with the black of night approaching, I suggest you three retire to the amphitheater for the movie."

"Oh, what's being shown tonight, despite 'The Ghoul on the Loose'?"

"Believe it or not, sir, 'Call Out the Marines', a 70-minute comedy-musical starring Victor McLaglen, Edmund Lowe and Binnie Barnes."

"'Call Out the Marines'? Are you kidding me? We don't need to call them out. We got over 16,000 1st Division here already. Then, add another 35,000 miscellaneous Navy and Army and you have all you need to catch one mad Marine who enjoys murdering fellow Marines!"

"Have you already seen it? It was in the theaters two years ago, two months after Pearl Harbor."

"Oh, I saw it advertised, but wasn't interested. I had no idea then that I would be in the Navy-Marines then or showing any signs of being interested in the Marine mind that goes around killing his own."

"Well, if it'll make you laugh, why not go see it?"

"I'll send Bill and Ellen. I'll be on duty patrolling Pavuvu. I think the Ghoul will strike again tonight. Stay alert, young man. He's killing youngsters like yourself," the lieutenant concluded as he turned and walked the few feet to his favorite niche of repose.

Peter's "private beach" was no more than 10 yards of pure white sand, debris-free because he personally cleaned it for himself. For some reason, the sand on the north west side of Banika facing the Solomon Sea Slot was deeper and more pure than anywhere else in the Russell Islands. From his restful position sitting on the white sand, with his back leaning on an ancient shore ridge that had receded, he not only valued the solitude for an hour or so of thought, but also enjoyed observing the beautiful rare cream-colored cockatoos skimming over MacQuitti Bay waters for food. Adding to the early evening color of the overall setting were the green, blue and red parakeets and the sounds of their rhythmic flow of chirping sounds. As the sun slowly descended, then disappeared over the horizon, the birds buzzed, cowed, then with diminishing chatter, they flew into the coconut palms where they would be safe during the night hours.

As he waited expectantly for Bill and Ellen, Peter studied the dock activities now that the harbor lights were on. Preparations were well under way for the following week's invasion by the 1st, 2nd, 5th Marine Divisions; of the Palau Islands, in particular, one called "Peleliu", less than a mile wide. Tinian had been declared secure on August 1, and, in a matter of hours, all resistance on Guam in the

Mariana Islands would be over. Weeks earlier, Saipan had been taken and fully occupied.

The island hopping and long leaping were accelerating. Rumor had it that if all went well, the 1st, 2nd, 5th Divisions would be occupying Tokyo by Christmas.

In Europe, the prognosis for surrounding Berlin was just as promising. The week before the allies had broken out of Normandy and within the week invaded the south of France. Rome had been liberated and the siege of Leningrad lifted.

All was going well in both theaters of World War II. Little Pavuvu was living proof of it. Never before had seventeen freight-laded merchant ships anchored in the Bay, waiting to be unloaded, two at a time at the only dock in the entire Russell Island group. For more than 36 hours straight, Liberty and Victory freighters had been disgorging and discharging their tons of crated cargoes, supplies, and vehicles. For Peter, watching the activity and listening to their muffled sounds at his distance away from the one dock carried a special significance.

His middle-aged uncle on his father's side worked at the Richmond, California shipyards, one of more than a hundred in America, helping to turn out a Liberty or Victory freighters and transports every week. Gus worked as a welder next to " . . . hundreds of lovely 'Rosies the Riveters', enjoying them more than his specialty, joint and butt welding," as he explained.

Now, in the moonlight, gleaming in their shades of gray and black, Peter could distinguish by their silhouetted profiles the liberator EC2 (emergency cargo medium size) and Victory VC2 (Victory type cargo medium size). Sailors, Marines, and merchant mariners themselves teasingly referred to them as "ugly ducklings". Of course, it was with utmost fondness since each carrier was the source of survival with its five cargo holds of 12 deadweight tons of life and death loads of food, medicines, and munitions. And, no military man was more respected than the merchant mariner because his class of serviceman suffered the greatest percentage of deaths while delivering supplies.

Meanwhile, Peter's attention was diverted to the troop transports arriving with replacements and combat veterans returning for retraining at stateside bases. To his left, within the channel itself, Marines were enjoying the final swim of the day, plunging and immersing, soaking and splashing in the calm, luminescent seawaters of early evening.

MacQuitti Bay and its channel was especially active, and beautiful, that night, the eve of one of the greatest entertaining events in the history of the USMC.

And, with a murder mad Marine on a killing spree.

Suddenly, quick, soft footsteps on the moon-blanched bluff could be heard behind him. Forgetting for a moment that he was expecting his friends, apprehension gleamed in his eye as he automatically reached for his .45 holstered to his belt.

The radiant moonlight threw her slender figure and graceful stride into strong relief, her face and hair as blonde, lively, and lovely.

It was Ellen, and Peter, despite his longstanding love for Joan, had to admit she was special.

"Where's Bill?" Peter asked smiling.

"Here's a towel we can sit on. I'm tired of getting sand in my panties when I sit here with you and Bill."

"He would rather go to a stupid prewar Marine movie than engage in a quiet, thoughtful conversation with us?"

"Yes. When he heard the title, he laughed. He was on the set next door while they were making whatever the movie is called, 'Wake up Marines' or 'Here come the Marines', whatever."

"Yes," chuckled Peter. "He told me he was making an RKO film in February, 1942, called 'International Squadron'. The guy wanted to be a lawyer, and here he was by the age of 30 having more fun being a co-star of over 40 movies. He says the year before he was in two of his favorites, 'Sailors On Leave' and 'The Case of the Black Parrot', making maybe $300-$500 a week. Around the same time, he was narrating Looney Tunes cartoons for Warner Brothers because the executives there said his voice had a 'smile to it'! Did you hear any of this?"

"Oh, a little. I know he was making a movie, 'Salute to the Marines' after finishing 'International Squadron', and he walked out of the studio to join up."

"Yes," continued Peter, "After 'International Squadron', in the middle of 'Salute', he said, 'Who am I to play a hero when so many of our boys are now fighting for me to 'act' a hero. I can't be a hero when so many heroes have already lost their lives.' So he walked off the set and drove over to a Beverly Hills Marine Recruiting Office and enlisted!"

Ellen added softly,

"He was draft-exempt, wasn't he?"

"Yes, due to a physical back injury. The guy joined up out of patriotism. He was under a newly signed contract with MGM. His boss was Louis B. Mayer. The head of MGM was furious with him for enlisting! He shouted, 'You signed up to be a Marine just as we were about to promote you to be a big star. Do you realize what you've done? Well, you're fired!"

"No, he never told me that part of it. This afternoon, he came to my ward and said he heard a tugboat convoy from Guadalcanal just arrived with steaks for the whole island, 1st and 5th Divisions, for every person on the island. Well, one boat brought a copy of 'Call Out the Marines'. He tried to find you. By the way, where were you?"

"In the morgue, believe it or not."

"He knows Binnie Barnes, who is the waitress in the café the two Marines flirt with. Because Binnie and Bill are good friend, he was over there at the time. She introduced him to the two actors, Victor McLaglen and Edmund Lowe, who he says were perfect gentlemen and very nice to him."

For the longest moment, the two were wordless and each reflected upon their friend, William Lundigan, the moonlight shimmering off the eroded white sand crystals of the beach before them.

"Did you see any of his movies before you, too, enlisted?" Ellen asked quietly.

"A few. But when I saw Bill in boot camp standing in line for chow like the rest of us, I knew I had seen him before. At first I couldn't remember, but there's only one smile like his and by the end of chow, I knew it was some motion picture I had seen him in."

Again, there was a long silence as Ellen slipped her soft hand inside Peter's arm. Surprised, a pleasant shiver perplexed him. Not that he was embarrassed with the sudden thrill of a woman, Ellen, who he knew clutching his arm, but he was confused, and therefore troubled by his ambivalence. A shadow crossed his face.

'Her eyes are magnificent, her body so lithe, and I've never seen anything like her hair', he thought. 'Fortunately, this having conflicting feelings won't last. But I am puffing and panting without her noticing it.'

Not for a moment had he forgotten or dismissed Joan, although at this moment the Mad Ghoul was of little concern.

"Is something disturbing you?" whispered Ellen, poignantly.

Smiling, Peter said affectionately,

"More than you can possibly know. I'm slightly uneasy because I think I've gone 'Asiatic', as so many of my fellow Marines, friends and colleague say."

"What's that mean?" queried Ellen, seriously.

"Oh, it's what every Marine out in the middle of the Pacific does if he's been here too long: strange, eccentric, silly, idiocy, goofy. It's a term peculiar to a region, a geography, a class of people. When a Marine begins to break apart, as I'm doing now, Marines diagnose the collapse as 'Asiatic', having been in the Far East, or anywhere else, for that matter, far too long. Pavuvu isn't in the Far East, but close enough."

"So," she asked with a twinkle in her eyes, "You believe you have the 'Asiatic'?"

"Sure do."

"But why?"

"Look, Ellen. Right now, bright moonbeams are enhancing the soft radiance of your amazing golden hair. You have a slimness accentuated by your poise, even while sitting here next to me. The beautiful tenderness of your face makes you more exquisite than ever. How do you think all that affects me, lonely in a war zone, and the murdering - mad going to kill again, even as I shudder saying all this?"

Peter drew a deep breath to slow and quiet the pounding of his heart. Ellen, here, at this moment, was as stunning as his Nisei, Joan, yet it just couldn't be. They couldn't be one and the same.

As the two gazed up at the stars, a cold foreboding seemed to drag Peter down. All his thoughts and emotions were now of Joan. To further break Ellen's grip on him, his growing embarrassment, and his growing affection for her, he asked,

"Think the Ghoul will strike tonight, Ellen, the eve of a most deserved day for the Corps in the South Pacific?"

"He may have, already. Oh, my God, I hope not. If he's waiting for me, he has to go through you, and later, Bill. But Peter, he doesn't frighten me, even without you two. I know how to aim and fire this .45 at my side.

After a smile and a pause, she asked,

"What movies of Bill did you see? I saw some, too, but can't recall their names. Like you, I remember his warm smile, his animal warmth."

"The movies with Bill in them that I saw were 'Santa Fe Trail', 'Sea Hawk', 'Dodge City', 'The Fighting 69', among a few others. He was helping to make two or three features a year, because he was so popular. And, what stood out in every film, no matter what role he played, was his natural charm, his kindness, his goodness."

"Yes, when I was introduced to him a number of weeks ago, I had heard I was meeting a movie star, but couldn't picture him. When he walked up, I had to laugh because that 'natural charm' is exactly what I remember the most long after I saw his pictures."

"So, Ellen, it all leads to this. I will be perfectly honest with you because I will always consider you two as my lifelong best friends."

Peter paused, then continued gazing straight ahead across the channel into the darkened coconut groves of Pavuvu.

"You and Bill make a handsome couple. You've heard him refer time and again to Rena Morgan who he met on his last night of leave while in New York when he was in transit to boot camp. He writes to her every single day, even about you. But I honestly believe he loves you. He'll often say when you're not present that he misses your gentle voice as much as your whole being. And, I agree. With you, as with my Joan, it's the feeling of wholeness, of peace, of a kind of completeness when you're within feet, of actually seeing, hearing, even smelling you. Is there a better definition of love? Maybe. But that emotion of having you within reach comes close."

"Well," responded Ellen, "That's how I feel about you two. Complete relaxation, an unwinding, being yourself, total peace."

"Joan and I have that. As you belong together, Joan and I are one."

Ellen had tears in her eyes that Peter did not notice. She remained quiet for a moment, then asked with a forced cheerfulness,

"Tell me about her, Peter. You're always talking about her, little things, your obvious feelings. But who is she, really?"

"Well, Ellen, I'm not certain when Joan entered my life in south Stockton. It turned out we lived only six blocks from each other, but she went to a different grammar school. But in the ninth grade, the first year of high school, the kids of Hazelton and Jackson grammar schools, about 15 blocks away from each other, merged into ninth-graders at Edison High School. Since we both were on academic tracts, we were in the only Latin 1 class. She sat in the first row near the teacher's desk, and I sat in the second row near the windows. Three or four desks separated us, but for some reason, we kept exchanging glances. Joan insists our love for each other began right there. But I don't think so."

Ellen, clutching his arm more forcefully, eyes cast upon the sand before them, implored softly,

"Why?"

"Well, Joan must have been 13 or 14 years old before the war working at a small soda fountain and snack bar next to the El Dorado Street Lincoln Theatre, making milkshakes, ice cream sodas, frosty cones, and preparing hot dogs. OF course, she could only work on weekends for 75 cents an hour. I'd go into that soda fountain on weekends because I was an altar boy at old St. Mary's Church and had to serve Mass at noontime. She was younger than I, but I used to think she was the loveliest of all the girls who worked for nice old Mr. Hagio, the owner, who took the tickets and kept the lobby neat and clean. Everybody loved Mr. Hagio, including my dad, who was the projectionist for Emily Perino at the Star Theater on Sonora Street around the corner. My father always said the Issei Japanese-Americans were the gentlest, hardest-working, respectful, kindest people on earth, even more so than the high-mountain Italians of Northern Italy from where my family came. To dad; Mr. Hagio, and the owner of the three movie theaters within a block of each other; the Lincoln, across El Dorado street, the Imperial, which showed only Spanish-language movies, Mr. Hayashimo, were even nicer than all the others! Joan's father respected the man so much he insisted he be her 'baishakunin', the 'go between', when the time came after her internment to marry me. It is a custom I wholly agree with. Mr. Hayashimo and my Italian-American father approving a mixed marriage! Unheard of in Stockton, California! So, both dad and I saw Joan at work on weekends when we both walked up and down the stairs at the end of the fountain up into the projection room. Remember, dad had two or three jobs, one was driving a Union Oil Company truck delivering gas and oil to gas stations during the day, working the projection booths at night at the Star, Imperial, and Lincoln theaters, and working relief at Austin Brothers' hardware warehouse, selling to Stockton. So, in short, I paid no attention and yet I paid attention to a skinny, no-breasted teenager black long - haired, Nisei before I noticed her sitting in the front row of Mrs. Hofmeister's Latin 1 on the first day of school. I think I loved her before she noticed me that morning before class began."

"That's a nice story, Peter. I never knew nor heard of Japanese or Chinese or Koreans marrying anyone outside their races. It's sad what our country did to her family, her people. I'm so ashamed what our country did to them, rounding up the nicest people on earth, throwing them into cold, dusty barracks, for nothing. They are Americans, aren't they?"

"Of course; virtually all of them are. And, their so-called 'apartments' within the barracks are maybe 30 feet of space separated by blankets stretched across a rope! Some of the elderly were so depressed, so confused, so humiliated, they began to commit suicide! What kind of America has America become? I'm sorry, Ellen, that I become enraged just talking about this. Most of my best friends are Nisei. Oh, Ellen, how I want you and Bill to meet Joan, to be at our wedding, when this war is over."

"But, Peter, is it really love that you feel for Joan, or pity, or sympathy, or simple anger at injustice. You still haven't told me about her. Who is she?"

"First and foremost, Ellen, she is brave. That's not the number one reason I worship her. But her courage in every aspect of her family's life is something to behold. Like her brothers' courage. There are three Ikeda boys, the family still refers to them as 'boys', and each of them personifies it in length and depth. For example, the brothers were the second to sign up for a newly formed combat unit to fight in the war. Mike Masaoka, from Fresno, whose father knows my grandfather in Galt because they both have almond and walnut orchards, is the National Secretary and field executive of the JACL, the Japanese-American Citizen League. He was able to convince President Roosevelt to authorize Nisei volunteers form the camps to join the armed forces. Mike was first to join up. Then, Lloyd, Dan and Cyrus signed. These good men, and hundreds and hundreds of others, from all the two-dozen other internments, enrolled to prove they were

Americans, that the United States was their country, too. They wanted to risk their lives just like the other boys they went to Edison High with; Hispanic, White, Chinese, Black, every nationality that lived in south Stockton. I think that unit is now called the 442 Regimental Combat Team. General Joseph Stillwell, our commander in Burma, said at a meeting in San Francisco two months or so ago when I read in the June issue of 'Yank Magazine' that the fighting men of the 442nd were buying an awful big hunk of America with their blood. I'll never forget those words because they are so true."

After a minute or so of reflective silence during which Ellen studied Peter's lowered facial expressions, every muscle flexing in incensed passion at the government's evacuation of more than 115,000 or so good, decent, proud people to cold, lonely barracks of deprivation and despair. He was thinking of the photo of an elderly Issei, perhaps 80 or 90 years old, in her black overcoat and black hat standing in an empty Tanforan, California, racetrack horse stall with only straw on the floor, straw soiled with horse urine and manure. The look on her sad face was of bewilderment and anguish, as if to ask, 'What have I done to deserve this?'"

Then, after a moment longer, Ellen watched Peter's quiet rage engender a grin. He smiled,

"If a 442nd Regimental Combat Team for Nisei women is formed, Joan will be the first to volunteer, and lead it."

Again, a short pause.

"So," continued Peter, "her bravery is one of the first reasons why I came to love her so much. But, obviously, Ellen, my feelings, my emotions, go much deeper than her bravery. And, it's even more than that she loves me so much that makes me love her even more. To me, Spanish Philosopher Ortega Y Gasset expresses it best why men often fall in love. I was always looking for written words to say what was in my heart. Reading his "On Love--Aspects of a Single Theme," which Gosset wrote in 1927, I found the closest words yet. He described beautifully Lord Nelson's love for Lady Hamilton. It's how I felt for Joan. Then, he introduces Orlando, a highly intelligent man, but not an intellectual. Regarding intelligence, writes Gasset about Orlando, his mind reacts to happenings with a certain sharpness and precision, Orlando tells Gasset since that he's always involved in sharpness and precision, he is apt to fascinate over the 'hidden deer in a woman'. That is, the more of a man one is, the more he is filled to the brim with rationality. Everything he does and achieves, he does and achieves for a practical reason. A woman's love, that divine surrender of her ultra-inner being which the impassioned woman makes, is perhaps the only thing, which is not achieved by reasoning. The core of the feminine mind, no matter how intelligent the woman may be, is occupied by an irrational power. If the male is the rational being, the female is the irrational being. And that is the supreme delight, which we find in her! Do you get it, Ellen?"

"No."

"I'm going to have to go in another minute, but will walk you back to your room. You know, don't you, I will be on duty tonight to catch the Ghoul. But, before we go, let me say that it's Joan herself, her very core, her intrinsic femininity, her truly deep mystery, her often-silly irrationality, her wondrous womanhood, her eternal maidenly, her unconscious wish to be matronly, her natural effeminate side that drives me into her arms."

"Can't any woman give you all that?"

"Freud and other psychoanalysts say any of, maybe, half a million."

"Could I be one of those 500,000?"

"If Bill and Joan weren't in the equation, you bet your life you would. But, enough now, Ellen, I must walk you back. I have work to do."

With that, they both stood up, brushed off the sand, and, after Ellen folded the blanket, walked back to the hospital barracks where Ellen's quarters were located.

"Aren't the stars wonderful?" asked Ellen, gleefully, but softly.

"Yes," responded Peter, glancing up into the sky, but obviously preoccupied. "Are you going to meet Bill? The movie has probably just started. It's only 70 or 80 minutes long."

"No, not tonight. I'll rest for tomorrow's big day. I just hope the noiseless ghost leaves us alone tonight and tomorrow."

Peter, walking alongside, didn't respond.

Armed Marines of various grades, alone and in small parties, hurried by, on their way to Pavuvu by way of the pontoon bridge.

"How many long hours do you expect to work tonight? You have to rest up for tomorrow, too," Ellen implored.

"Oh I know," responded Peter glumly. "Sleep is the least of my thoughts. This night might have no end, if a dead Marine turns up."

Bonfires of gas-soaked litter had been started, illuminating the 1st Division Headquarters and the general hospital next door.

"Golly, I hope I don't have to substitute for someone on the night shift," Ellen breathed more to herself than to Peter.

"Yes, I hope so, too. A huge day coming up tomorrow."

"I so want to be fresh for whatever assignments I receive. It'll be in and around the open space of the amphitheater, I'm sure. Wish it would be close to the stage. Our captain is trying to arrange the nurses' schedules so that all of us are on duty to watch the performance."

"Well, I'll look for you since I'm sure I'll be with Del Barbra and Guidi circling throughout. Don't you enjoy the peace and quiet when everyone is asleep in the ward?"

"Oh, I hate night duty. It's more disconcerting than any of my duties. It was quiet and peaceful before the Ghoul showed up. Now it's eerily quiet, thinking the Ghoul is behind everything, ready to pounce on anyone in the wards. Then, when you look into the neighboring jungle, all you're able to see, if you have an imagination, are evil things."

"Yes, all because of the Ghoul."

"And, if he wasn't on the loose, I'd be right back down there to your 'private beach'. You and Bill don't know this, but I have had a little dory, a flat-bottomed fishing boat with high sides, hidden yonder through the grove on the bluff above the beach not far from the old copra warehouses and docks of the plantation. My first boyfriend here in the Russells and I used to dive off the end of the coral blocks of the long jetty which extended from the first of the six warehouses."

Listening intently, Peter asked, "But aren't there crocodile nests near the berths where the coasters and copra boats used to dock?"

"Yes, but it didn't bother us since no one ever went there because of the crocs. We actually repaired an old half-sunken dory. He patched it up with oakum and tar he found the Japanese left behind in one of the warehouses. He and I would row out in the channel with a bottle of wine he got from the Navy medical corps over your way. With the stars overhead, we'd swim, drink wine, and swim until curfew. Often, we would just watch the sun go down in the west. The crocs never bothered us and we never bothered them. Their main nests were among the patches of the mangroves. Occasionally, we would enjoy the bitter-tasting milk from the green coconuts he would cut down."

"Sounded like fun. Who was . . . ?"

For all her nonchalance and bravado, Ellen's chin began to quiver, slightly from fear, mostly from a general, uncontrollable anxiety. But she neither flinched nor lowered her head. She reached over and up, placed her arms around his neck, and allowed herself a single, soft whimper.

Nearing the general hospital's covered ramp during the day that functioned as a verandah, Peter was pleased the sentries for both headquarters and the medical facilities had been tripled. All were heavily armed, as were those circling the adjacent military installations and low buildings and barracks. Within the surroundings, all was quiet, and the atmosphere heavy. Everyone they encountered was gloomy. Few words, if any, were exchanged. Wounded or ill Marines were strolling singularly or in two or three party groups, their heads bowed.

With silver-white stars sparkling overhead, and a cluster of motionless coconut palms forming a canopy, Ellen abruptly pulled Peter off the walkway under it. Looking up into his face, Ellen said quietly,

"I'm leaving you tonight for tomorrow. You and Bill should know that after tonight, I will no longer be able to live without you two easy-going, handsome guys, both of whom have little bone and absolutely no muscle, yet high intelligence, infinite kindness, courage, and old-fashioned, decent respect. And, on top of all that, both of you are nice."

CHAPTER THIRTEEN

-

"Any Murders Tonight?"

With Ellen well on her way to either rare white sheets on a cozy cot, or to learn which hospital ward she would substitute in, and Bill enjoying the remainder of "Call Out the Marines", Peter, flashlight in hand, hurried back down the road leading to pontoon bridge. Lanterns and drum bonfires helped illuminate the way. Although fuel was not necessarily in shortage, it wasn't wasted on Banika. If the Mad Ghoul was to kill that night, he would not strike in the dark.

With a backward glance and a hand wave at Ellen as she smiled and waved back entering the hospital, Peter was surprised to see a jeep slowly rumbling down the road toward him from the general hospital parking area. Seeing it was Lieutenant Toscanini, the driver pulled up alongside.

It was the multi-denominational chaplain, Reverend Wilfred Pinoe, with a large grin on his face.

"Well," chuckled Peter, "Looks who's just come to rescue me from a long walk to Pavuvu, no less than a Minister of God, the clergyman of all clergyman with the ever - so -slight lisp!"

Pinoe had to laugh,

"Aw, get in. I walked over here to visit the sick in the various wards. Now, that I've borrowed the jeep from the motor pool, I'll drive you wherever you need to go."

As Peter climbed into the front seat of the Jeep, Pinoe stretched his leg out to the floorboard in order to retrieve the Zippo lighter in his khaki pocket, then fumbling with it to light a cigarette. A big black Lincoln sedan leftover from the plantation owners and hidden from the Japanese occupation force in early 1943, passed by with 1st Division commander Major General Rupertus in the back seat with an unidentified officer.

Turning back toward Pinoe framed in the brief blaze of the Zippo lighter, Peter saw that the chaplain was pale, worn and somehow older.

"I'm so exhausted," Pinoe confessed. "Working, counseling and praying with more than two dozen recovering riflemen leaves you a bit short of breath."

Peter, to stimulate the clergyman, was friendly, conversational, and commenting on the activities along the way to the bridge. Natives, under bright portable lights, were still being supervised by officers in clearing away underbrush where the Ghoul might hide near the road, as well as cutting down tall coconut palm trees for new warehouse material.

Driving along the embankment near the bridge, Peter was surprised how well lit the permanent warehouses were, again to eliminate as much darkness as possible. There were permanent structures, well maintained, and guarded by highly disciplined sentries. Dozens of hastily built sheds, and larger 'wattle and daub', flimsy, badly paint-splashed, plywood frameworks harboring piles of crushed coral, extended beyond on unpaved roads.

"Where can I drop you off?" Pinoe queried.

"Don't exactly know. Better drop me off at the Captain Del Barbra's second office in the Pavuvu administration unit. Tonight, I'm roaming all over the island on my own, probably with Sergeant Guidi. So is the captain. We may not catch or kill the Ghoul tonight. Meanwhile, there are two with whom I want to spend some time, my mentor, Brigadier General Earle Maxwell, and Dr. Stuart Schneidermann, the new psychiatrist for the 1st Division."

"And, you, Wilfred? Grueling, I bet. Marines think chaplains have the easiest, lightest gig-work. But, you fellas, are really unsung heroes."

"God Bless you, lieutenant. You are one of the few who sees it, except for the men we serve. Right now, we have some 6,000 chaplains in the combat theaters, with another 3,000 on their way to sustain and promote wartime chaplaincy. The Office of the Army Chief of Chaplains is doing all it possibly can to ensure every military man, American or not, has access to someone of God to talk with. Makes no different if the soldier or sailor is Catholic, Jewish, Lutheran, Baptist, Protestant, Northern Methodist, Mormon, Christian Scientist, Greek Orthodox, Buddhist or whatever he is, that trooper will have an open door to a man of religious teachings to comfort or assist him."

"I think that's wonderful," Peter said softly. "But what denomination, or particular religious body do you belong to and preach about?"

"Lieutenant, we are all men of faith, religious freedom, religious liberty. For example, evangelicals and Mass-attending Catholics have the freedom to practice their faith while in combat. But I am available, night or day, any hour, to listen and help. That's our clear message, and that's why I answered over here on Banika this afternoon."

"War, and all the tragedies it brings... " Peter breathed quietly.

"Such a dastardly thing," echoed the Reverend.

As the jeep slowly drove down the slope to the pontoon crossing, Peter glanced at Pinoe who was lost in thought as he firmly clutched the steering wheel. Two terms crossed his mind--selflessness and unity. Selflessness, because this man of God was a helper, a genuine caring helper. Unity, because his kindness was natural to his personality.

Simply put, he was a loving man. And, as a loving man, his entire being was devoted to fixing broken hearts, broken minds, broken bodies.

At the pontoon crossing, a captain was in the process of unravelling a traffic jam of several dozen dump trucks hauling crushed coral from one of the Pavuvu beach hollows to the dock warehouses. He motioned for the jeep to cross against the oncoming traffic. Peter, who knew the captain, suggested they wait until he waved all the trucks across so that they could learn the latest deployment information for the night, as well as any rumors about the Ghoul that surfaced during the afternoon. But noting Pinoe's weariness, Peter merely stood up in the slowly moving jeep and waved, the captain waving back in acknowledgment.

Reaching the edge of Tent City, Pinoe pulled up, paused, and Peter jumped out.

"I'll catch up with all my people in and around here. You going back to the chapel?"

"Yes, until daylight, then back to the hospital on Banika. But I'll cross back for Bob Hope. Wouldn't miss that for anything."

"We can call you later tonight, if we need you."

With that, Pinoe drove off to the car pool to return the jeep, while Peter began to search for any officer he could find. A sentry greeted him, asking for identification. Then he explained that the Ghoul was still on the loose, and that the Russell Islands were temporarily considered a combat zone. Consequently, all officers were on duty and the Officers Club was off-limits. A voice on the Tent City PA system loudly announced that the curfew would begin in 30 minutes and all Marines except those pulling the night's first assignment had to return to their quarters. Under no circumstance was anyone to appear on the grid's roads, alleys, or public places.

As he slowly roamed the periphery of Tent City, Peter was impressed with the discipline exhibited by all aspects of the 1st Division. No one, including naval and Army personnel in the medical units assigned to the wards, displayed a relaxed attitude, or routine-as-usual mentality. In addition to being heavily-armed, everyone was in combat fatigues, helmets or caps in place, insignias clearly in view according to regulations, troops saluting snappily, and words spoken only when necessary.

"These men," Peter thought to himself, "loathe the Ghoul more than they do the Japanese."

Although Peter encountered just about everyone he knew, he was in no mood to discuss anything. That included with Dr. Stuart Schneidermann, the new 1st Division psychiatrist, and Brigadier General Earle Maxwell, the officer he respected and trusted the most. Strangely, his thoughts that long night fluctuated between his beloved fiancée, Joan, and the eyes of the murdered in the base morgue, and their young faces, of yellow pallor.

As Peter walked past extra troops hurrying to position themselves around both ends of the pontoon bridge, he was jarred into the realization that he would soon collapse from exhaustion. The Ghoul, Joan, and Ellen were taking their emotional toll on the young lieutenant.

By 1:00AM, and not a hint of murder from any quarter in the entire Russell Island group, and with an enormous day about to begin in less than five hours, Peter decided to trek his way across Tent City to the second office of Captain Del Barbra in search of a cot and a blanket. He would gladly sleep in his clothes if he could close his eyes for a few hours.

Every step of the way to Captain Del Barbra's office, Peter's thoughts were of Joan. How he yearned to hear her voice and giggle again, her melting gaze of pure emotion. Now, at this hour, he knew he could very easily love Ellen. But it was Joan he would marry. She would bear his children and live her life with him. Ellen, hopefully with Bill, would be their lifelong friends.

Irrespective of the emotional thoughts bringing him almost to his knees, Peter was being gnawed by undefined, unexplainable doubts-- would the Mad Ghoul ever be identified? Could the multiple - murderer be a USMC officer? Were the clues so apparent everyone was oblivious to them?

As Peter reached the crest of the slope and the triple-guarded annex of Division Headquarters, he turned right toward the well-lit general hospital which by its extension overlooked all Pavuvu. He virtually bumped into an advanced guard of four submachine gun-carrying Marines accompanying the 1st Division commander.

Following the guard which quickly placed itself in strategic protective firing positions were Major General William H. Rupertus; his Assistant Division Commander, Brigadier General Lemuel C. Shepherd; and Chief-of-Staff, Colonel LeRoy Sims. Three additional Reising - wielding Marines followed the party of seven.

"Well, hello there, young lieutenant!" the major general exclaimed affectionally. "You on track to catch the monster tonight?"

Peter smiled, acknowledging the 1st Division Commander's sincere feeling toward him.

"Sir, more than anyone can possibly know, how I wish that was the case, especially after spending the afternoon at the morgue with the five victims," Peter said gravely.

With steady, unwavering eyes, then a fierce expression of anger, Rupertus said,

"Soon, our bewilderment will be over. We'll catch the son _ _ _. Then, very quietly, I'll shoot him in the head myself," he smiled softly.

Where some of the major general's staff felt he was often indecisive, even flawed in strategic combat planning, Peter like the man he unconsciously regarded more as a father - figure for not only himself, but also the other Marines of the 1st Division. Bronzed, lean, clear-eyed, individual, and unafraid, William Henry Rupertus was all of 54 years of age.

Peter, as well as every Marine in 'Rupert's Old Breed outfit', knew the major general's biography. Amid the man's remarkable military achievements, there was enormous personal tragedy as well.

After participating in jungle warfare in Haiti, following World War I, he was assigned to command the 4th Marine Brigade in Peking, China, in 1929. There, within a year, a terrible scarlet fever epidemic broke out, resulting in the deaths of an appalling number of Chinese civilians, including Marines of the 4th. Especially anguishing was that William Henry's wife and two sons perished.

Soon, thereafter, Rupertus became the CO of the Marine Barracks in San Diego, There, in his off-duty administrative work, he became an expert marksman and wrote, "The Marine Corps Rifleman's Creed" to encourage recruits in all branches of the Armed Forces to always place trust in their weapons.

After Pearl Harbor, Rupertus was assigned to the 4th Marine Regiment of the 1st Division as commander. When General Vandegrift left the 1st Division in July of 1943, William Henry assumed temporary command until six months later, in December of 1943, he was promoted to Major General and led his 1st Division to victory over the Japanese at the Battle of Cape Gloucester.

Now, during the heat of a murder - mad Marine multi-murdering fellow Marines, he was planning, and preparing, for the invasion of the Palau Island group, specifically Peleliu.

"Well, young man," the major general smiled, "catch him tonight before the Bob Hope Show arrives and I'll see to it, personally, that you're named commander of the Pacific Fleet, and Admiral Chester Nimitz reduced in rank to Assistant Commander."

"Well, sir, you'll have him by daybreak, and I'll be happy to borrow and use your .45. But, may I nap for just an hour or two, that is, if I can find a cot somewhere in here. It would take too much time to return to my quarters at Banika."

"Well," Rupertus responded, "We are just on our way to tour the Ghoul defense arrangements on Banika, but you sleep until sunup, breakfast here, get fresh underwear from Colonel Sims, who will let you in my office where there's a cot and blankets in the back room.Amor, see to it, now. We'll wait. And, as we do, tell me your thoughts. Will he kill tonight?"

As Colonel Sims hurried to his office bunk for fresh underclothing and the key to the major general's office, Peter, William Henry, and Lemuel Shepherd huddled.

"I suspect he will strike again tonight, too much notoriety to pass up. I so pray I'm wrong. But the prestige of murdering another Marine on the eve of an important entertainment event will make him famous throughout the Pacific. Then, if he can kill Bob Hope himself, he will enter the Assassin Hall of Fame, joining the evil likes of John Wilkes Booth and others. The Ghoul lives in an organized world of madness that is fed by publicity, acknowledgement, repute and renown."

"You think he'll kill on Banika tonight, then?"

"Yes, sir. I thought for sure it would be an assault on Pavuvu since the Ghoul undoubtedly lives in Tent City. But after spending a few hours browsing the roads and alleys and observing all the preparation for safety and security, I believe he wouldn't risk murdering among such activities and measures. Best to engage in killing where few preparations have been made."

As Rupertus and Shepherd pondered Peter's thinking, the lieutenant added,

"And, one more reason, sir, why I feel he'll strike on Banika. His latest murder occurred in a medical facility. He apparently knew how to get around in, and make his escape from. My intuition tells me that he'll go back, simply because it's easy picking for an unsuspecting, probably wounded, Marine."

"Well, he hasn't struck yet. And, the hospital area is triple-picketed. He can't worm his way through that string of sentries," Rupertus said calmly, glancing over his shoulder as Colonel Sim hastened back.

"Besides, Lieutenant," echoed Brigadier General Shepherd, "We have a kerosene lamp every 10 feet. The whole medical unit, including the general headquarters is lit up like a carnival, except with only one color, white."

"Yes," grinned Peter.

"Lieutenant, there's a small cooler where the cot is. Orange juice, Coca-Colas, cold-cuts, and the like. Help yourself. In the toilet room, you'll find an extra toothbrush and shaving kit. Make sure you don't oversleep. No brass bugle to awaken the drowsy. Meeting starts at 0700 in the conference room down the hall from my office. You must be there. The only item on the agenda is Bob Hope."

Everyone laughed, including the escorts.

"I won't embarrass you, sir. I'll be the first to take a seat."

With that, Peter turned and headed for a much-needed hour or two of slumber. He would be up by 0500, breakfast, shower in the major general's back room bathroom, and seat himself before all the other participants arrived.

Alone in the back room of the 1st Division Commander's office, with the door slightly ajar, Peter, as exhausted as he was, again felt that dull, strange sensation that's bothered him since earlier that day. Mechanically, and virtually asleep standing up, he began removing his clothing and placing them atop a nearby chair. He noted the cooler next to small sink adjacent to a box cupboard in the first of three rooms. Each had a single window, its shade pulled down, facing the Solomon Sea. Although all three had well-polished floors, the rooms were bare, with the exception of rude tables, a few chairs. One wall of each room held a medium-sized gun rack with M-1s, Thompsons, Reisings, and other light weapons.

After helping himself to a Coca-Cola, Peter laid back on the well-blanketed cot and tried to make himself comfortable. Despite all the splendor of quiet and peace, the few hours remaining in his night promised to be bitter, perhaps the bitterest of his life.

"I'm so played out, that even the air seems difficult to breathe," Peter thought to himself.

Something, a thought or thoughts, words either imagined or actually heard, body languid on the part of someone, something triggered pounding in his heart, mocking and challenging his intelligence, battering and beating him, left him sleepless. For the next hour and a half, Peter lay awake. Half a dozen times, he went into the bathroom to pee. Unable to, he returned to his blankets. Finally, with his inner struggle beginning to subside, and with one hand clenched until the nails bit into the flesh, he began to slip into sleep, weighted with the restlessness of a brain trying to decipher what was a strange intuition about the murder - mad marine who was multiple murdering his own. Deep, sound, sleep, he knew, would come quickly, as it normally does for the extremely weary. And, not long after, hopefully, pleasant dreams of his Joan Ikeda. As he drifted into oblivion, he smiled, realizing that here, in the back room of the major general's office, there was an absence of rots, land grabs, mosquitoes and mosquito nets, and, above all, the putrid smell of rotting coconuts and their milk.

Within a moment, it seemed, Peter was abruptly startled back into consciousness. A large, human-like figure breathing heavily was in the dense darkness of the room, Peter sensed, lumbering straight toward him. The odorous two-legged monster appeared to be raising a large, sharp instrument over his head as if to plunge into his face. With his .45 in its holster attached to his belt draped over the chair where his clothing was, Peter panicked. Death was inches away, his only protection a navy blanket. As the large knife-like weapon thrust toward his eyes, the scene instantly changed.

A face suddenly appeared on the smelly, wild man-like beast within an army pyramidal-issued tent as he repeatedly struck a hapless Marine in the stomach as he slept. It was the face of Major General William Henry Rupertus, the Commander of the Old Breed 1st Division. Then, just as suddenly, as Peter, slightly aside, watched motionlessly as Military Police Captain Oscar Del Barbra, with a tray of scalpels and other razor-sharp knives used in surgery was slicing in long, deep cuts the legs of the murdered nurse in the morgue. Just as abruptly, the scene changed for the fourth time, and Peter found himself at dusk buried up to his shoulders in the sand at his favorite hideaway beach near the observation post facing the Coral Sea. A faceless man was poised behind him holding a small hatchet over his head as the trapped lieutenant awaited his decapitation in paralyzed terror. He could not see who his executioner would be, although he sensed the khaki-dressed man was an officer and a friend. No one was on the beach and the world's sounds and activities seemed to have vanished. Then, unusually stark sneering and snickering utterances were heard as the Marine, with hatchet still in hand, walked around to face him. Although he remained faceless, the man's stature was familiar. Then, his face slowly faded into that of his best friend, Bill Lundigan, who, without a word, swung the hatchet down upon his head.

A gentle tap on his partially-opened door awakened Peter from his nightmare, although the violent pounding of his heart continued. Sweat had coagulated every vein and vessel in his body. He wanted to remain motionless, but the tapping grew louder. A voice, cold, loud and hard, demanded,

"Peter Toscanini. Are you all right? Urgent news. I'm entering."

With that, an officer with a flashlight entered, searched for the light-switch and turned the lights on. Peter, up on one elbow, bewildered, asked,

"What's up? Who is it?"

"You're needed right now, lieutenant, at the Base Hospital. The Commander personally sent me over to get you out of the back room. Two more murders tonight, a nurse, around 2300 was discovered after the sentry's body was found around 2150. General Rupertus is waiting. Let's go. And, by the way, if you don't recognize my voice, I'm your Number One mentor, Brigadier General Earl Maxwell."

Peter was stunned beyond movement or words - - two more murders; a nurse involved, possibly Ellen; summoned by the major general, personally; and Earl Maxwell, his favorite teacher himself standing next to his cot.

"I'll dress, sir," he said, stumbling out of bed. "Do you know who the nurse is? Was she on duty in one of the wards? I have a friend there, a nurse."

 Maxwell said gravely,

"Helen, Lou Ellen, Anne, some name like that. They're doing a lot of soul-searching over there, because apparently, she was very vulnerable, being left alone on the ward. Stabbed frontally, but not fatally. She screamed, was struck with probably a butcher knife or bayonet or a "Ka-Bar". She died on the spot. The nurse who rushed over from the next ward was sliced on the upper arm near the shoulder. She's being treated there."

Sitting on the bed, slipping on his socks, Peter asked quietly, "Could the murdered victim have been named 'Ellen'?"

Putting a hand to his chin, Maxwell whispered hoarsely,

"Yeah, that's it."

Peter felt his heart sink.

CHAPTER FOURTEEN

-

"Ellen, You Live?"

Both Lieutenant Peter Albinoni Toscanini and Brigadier General Earl Maxwell of the Medical Corps were exhausted by 5:00am Monday, August 7th, 1944, and the day hadn't even seen sunup yet. Maxwell hadn't slept since the night before, and Peter less than two hours since midnight.

Now, while being driven by jeep back to the hospital annex on Pavuvu, each was lost in thought, Maxwell on the security measures for Bob Hope and his entourage that afternoon and evening, Peter about Ellen's death and his resistance to falling in love with the young nurse. Underlying their silent meditations was a premonition of trouble that day.

"Is the meeting still scheduled for 0700?" Peter inquired without glancing at his mentor.

"No. With this development, it's postponed for two hours. It'll still be in the new conference room of the annex. Try to get a little breakfast before it begins at 0900. You may not eat again until Hope and his crew leave, or are put to bed tonight."

"A cup of hot coffee would be welcomed, but as for food or breakfast, I can skip a morning. The way I feel this morning, I'd rather single-handedly extract two dozen Japs from a deep cave than continue the day with the madness tearing my mind apart - - the certainty of my friend Ellen's murder; the series of horrific scenes in a two-hour long nightmare in which different Ghouls stab me, if I'm to believe Sigmund

Freud who says we are everyone in our dreams; and, my intuition screaming that the world's funniest and most popular laugh-maker is going to be assassinated on my watch."

"Oh, my God," responded Maxwell, continuing to drive without taking his eyes off the road, "but I have the same dream, the sense there will be some kind of an attack, not by a fired weapon, but in a way the others were murdered, close, up front, the plunge of a razor-like blade into Mr. Hope's abdomen. It means an officer is the only one allowed to get that close, and it means the Ghoul will have to get Hope alone so that after he kills him he can slink away."

"Like I say, it's madness, sheer unmitigated madness--to have to go through what we're going through," Peter said, brokenly. "And, after having studied the stab wounds of five unfortunates in the morgue yesterday afternoon, I now have two more of the victims to study. How I hate this part of my work."

Not another word was spoken between the two for the rest of the drive. Maxwell was drained, emotionally and physically. Yet, he tried to seem relaxed, but could only do so mechanically, stiffly, without any physical movements.

Peter was struggling, too, under some kind of spell or shock or despair, which was consuming him. Something was laboring, indeed, masticating, in his entire cardiovascular system that he simply couldn't interpret. Someone did something, behaved in a certain manner, or said something that at the time seemed so innocuous, so harmless that it "was like water off a duck's back". But, what was it? Whatever it was, it must have somehow resonated in his subconscious, or he wouldn't have dismissed it. But, why, then, is he so forlorn and vexed? Something didn't make sense, and no amount of rest, no number of hours of sleep could change the dark outlook of the day that was just beginning. A few minutes later, slightly before 6:00am, with the jeep parked on the far side of the joint general headquarters-hospital annex parking lot near the small coconut grove that fringed the hillside, Peter, with Maxwell at his side, walked up the green slope toward the hospital entrance. Both officers were amazed by the number of armed Marines stationed around the perimeters of the two virtually connected units.

Dawn was breaking over a cloudless sky, and already a suffocating heat with near 90% humidity promised an oppressive, body-drenching day.

"Hopefully," said the brigadier general, "the discomfort will be relieved by humor and entertainment."

At the hospital entrance, two empty ambulances with flashing red lights had backed up to receive the deceased. Over by the entrance was a neatly painted sign, in capital letters boldly black and evenly bordered, that read,

"IF YOU SIT, YOU RUST!"

Every time Peter walked under it into the hospital, he smiled, as any knowledgeable doctor or nurse would. No one knew who painted it or put it up. But no one took it down.

"Truth was never truer," commented Peter. "To live a long life, move, and keep moving. And, to help you move some more, eat anything green, the darker the better. And every vegetable there is, in every color nature has given us. And, when not moving, sit quietly and read or create something, or anything. Even when stationed in places like miserable Pavuvu."

"You learned the secret to longevity, did you now?"

"Yes, sir, partly from your teachings."

Watching the two officers maneuver through the sentries and arriving medical personnel and staff officers investigating the murder victims and scenes, a lieutenant verifying identifications for entrance, walked up and said,

"Brigadier General Maxwell, the major general is where the nurse was struck down, next to the malaria ward, D, outside the first exit in the small garden patio."

Hurrying through the hospital lobby and down the main corridor past the wards to the patio of death, Peter and Maxwell heard faint strains of "Have I Told You Lately That I Love You?" sung by Bing Crosby and the three Andrew Sisters.

"So early in the morning to hear love songs in the wards? The men haven't even had breakfast yet."

Maxwell chuckled,

"It's therapy. You know that. We keep it soft and play only the like early in the morning. Sort of a 'to-wake-you-up music'. Later, during the routine of day, we play 'big band'. After dinner, from 0600 to 0800, we allow, even encourage, the recovering men and off-duty nurses to dance together. That kind of activity is good for the heart and mind. No mildewed atmosphere here. Depression is almost nonexistent. When the wounded, sick, afflicted dance and sing, only good things happen; the most important being they heal faster."

Peter nodded,

"I know."

Standing with a group of military police officers in the corridor alcove nearest the nurse's murder patio were Captain Del Barbra and Sergeant Guidi. Walking past them, Peter's gaze met Oscar's, as he glanced toward the two passing officers. Peter had never before seen such graveness on the face of an officer of the armed forces. Grimly, and downcast, Captain Del Barbra simply shook his head negatively.

Continuing their hurried pace down the indoor canvas-tent corridor to the murder scene of the nurse, Peter and Maxwell paused a moment to gaze into Ward B, the 160-bed malaria unit.

"Sad," commented Maxwell slowly, deliberately. "Out of 1,000 beds here, we have over 160 men down with that disgusting infectious disease. The number is considered excessive compared to other combat zone hospitals in the Pacific. But, fortunately, our station or base hospital is considered excellently staffed, programmed, and administered. So said the Inspector of Medical Department Activities, Pacific Ocean Area. We're proud. But, spoiling our pride and recognition is a lunatic Mad Ghoul."

"Yes, 'Charlie the Choker'. Very humorous," Peter responded despondently. "Furthermore, I detest this part of my work. I hate walking past the wards along here, seeing so many of our healthy men feeble, shivering, perspiring profusely, and all with horrendous, splitting headaches."

Lingering another moment, Maxwell concluded,

"Well, they serve as a lesson why you must take your Atabrine pill, as well as wear all-body-covering clothing, regardless of the heat and humidity, that covers every aspect of flesh, especially the neck to protect you from the anopheles mosquitos."

Past Ward C, they skirted, housing another 100 or more men down with equally debilitating illnesses, such as typhus and amoebic dysentery, then Ward D, with less than 75, bedding the Marines in shock, exhaustion, malnutrition, and the perennial, unidentified "jungle fever".

"Luckily, no battle-wounded on these premises. After Guadalcanal and Gloucester, they were all shipped stateside by hospital ship. Even those two or three who have since been shot accidentally," commented Maxwell, casting quick glances down each ward.

Then, amid an assembling group of ambulatory patients out of bed peering through the line of windows between Wards D and C, Maxwell commented softly,

"They're peering at the nurse's corpse on the patio leading to the alley. She's still there at the murder scene, under blankets. So, so sad. She couldn't have been more than 30, and now all we see of the poor thing is her blood slowly oozing out from under the blankets. Right now, I could kill the Ghoul with my bare hands, personally, all alone."

"I know…" Peter said softly, in tears.

For him, the moment of truth arrived. Beyond the windows in the patio stood Major General Rupertus in a circle of six or seven members of his staff. At their feet was the blanketed body of his very heartfelt friend, Ellen. Now, having to survey her stab wounds as factors of medicolegal importance was going to require mustering courage he was certain he didn't possess. How could he possibly not flinch, or succumb to grief, while following the wound track, number of wounds, width of the knife, depth of penetration, and murder instrument(s) used. He would have to answer whether a serrated knife was used, and how were angulated wounds achieved, by two or more separate thrusts, whether by the assailant twisting the knife, or whether the nurse twisted herself after the instrument entered the body.

Of all the data he had to collect, the most difficult would be defining the cause of Ellen's death: (1) hemorrhaging by massive perforated penetration, such as arteries of the neck, heart, lungs, and aorta severed; (2) air embolisms; (3) pneumothorax; (4) infection; (5) asphyxia due to blood aspiration. And, to determine the answers to these issues, he would have to multiple measure every wound to increase the death wound accuracy.

Gazing through the windows at the Rupertus group in quiet discussion, then the two blanketed deceased victims, Peter was in no position, psychologically or physically, to conduct two such surface autopsies, especially the stabbing on Ellen. He faced the most unsettling situation of his life.

As he turned away from the window and the gruesome scene, Peter cast about where to redirect or disperse the increasing ambulatory crowd. As he did so, sweeping the corridors and open adjacent rooms, he noticed in sheer relief whom he thought was his buddy, Bill Lundigan, seated at a table down the hall with a nurse heavily bandaged around the right shoulder. They sat leaning forward toward each other in what appeared to be a serious conversation, as medical staff, visiting military personal, and the usual amble patients in pajamas leisurely roaming the corridors without purpose.

In the only two wicker chairs leftover by the Japanese occupation months earlier, Bill and the bandaged nurse sat comfortably only a few feet from the entrance to the large nurses' station where all medications, drugs, and assorted remedies were maintained and dispensed. In addition to supply records being maintained in the inner office, fresh bed sheets were issued when either new arrivals were assigned their wards, or routinely once a week.

With an agonized pained smile, Peter motioned to Bill, commenting to Maxwell,

"Other than you, that's the most important man in the world to me. I'll be back in a moment. I need to say 'hello' to him."

"Take your time. If Rupertus or Sims needs you right now, I'll come and get you. Meanwhile, you may want to talk to the nurse who actually fought with the Ghoul. She can identify him. How is it he allowed her to live?" After a slight pause, he continued,

"She screamed so loudly that half of the Corps came running down the corridors from all over, inside and outside, the hospital. He ran like a frightened rattler."

"At last a witness!" exclaimed Peter, then called out,

"Bill!"

As Bill and the nurse turned to see who was approaching their table, Peter continued, extending his hand,

"Always have time to say hello to an actor friend! Didn't expect this! How'd they let you in here this morning? Thought you'd be sleeping off 'Bring on the Marines', or whatever that movie was named you saw last night."

Bill, now standing bolt upright, laughed,

"Well, lookie here! No less than Sherlock Holmes! I searched for you after the movie. Was told you were strolling around Tent City, looking or someone appearing sinister."

Peter stood for a moment, puzzling over Bill's jovial tone. How was it possible he hadn't heard about Ellen's cruel death?

Just then, the usual August corpulent tropical thunderhead burst open with a solid soaking of rain momentarily flooding all the Russell Islands. The pounding on the rooftops of the wards and their hospital was deafening.

"Better the downpour now than when Hope arrives with his entertainers. I was so tired trampling around Tent City with no sighting than rather than return to Banika, I simply walked up to the captain's back office where he has an open cot. Later, I'll have to tell you about a woozy of a nightmare I had. You'd have a good laugh, if it wasn't all so tragic. Ellen…oh…Ellen," his voice trailed off, a tear on his cheek.

Turning to be introduced to the seated, obviously frail, bandaged nurse sitting comfortably and relaxed, facing him with an ear-to-ear grin, Peter found his vision partially blurred from tears. Coupled with her face flushed with redness from a peculiar sort of guilt or embarrassment, and the orange-yellow pall cast by broken morning sunlight from perforated clouds passing overhead, seeing through the light dimness made the nurse appear much older than she was. Wearing an old-fashioned grey roughened fabric of linen, cotton wrap-around dress and dark blue sweater with a white blouse commonly worn by night duty ward nurses added to her stigma of aging. In fact, there was such aura about this silent, smiling, mysterious figure she almost appeared to emerge from some imaginary ether. Stunned beyond belief, Peter felt his knees buckle. His entire vision was focused upon the sedated nurse, all the flesh and blood of her, in a wicker chair directly facing him as he stood before her. A shimmering light had replaced the haze and dimness in the corridor, accentuating her splendid features and golden hair.

Although smiling, as were her clear eyes, the face was a puzzling mosaic of emotion. She stared at him, with a frozen smile. And, Peter, in sheer disbelief, as if he were seeing a ghost, stared back hard. With so much blood pounding through his heart and mind, Peter's trance, his power of seeing at that moment, his cognition, intelligence, feelings of empathy were in hopeless bewilderment.

Although he was momentarily paralyzed, he saw all this in a single flash. And, now, as the eyes of Peter and the nurse met and locked, his widened in a mixture of incredulity and utter joy as he recognized Ellen.

"Ellen!! ELLEN!! I was told . . . I thought . . . I THOUGHT . . . I was told that the nurse out there . . . I . . . can't believe this! . . . You LIVE! . . . BILL! SHE'S ALIVE!,... "

Ellen, with her heavily bandaged shoulder, struggled to stand, her other arm reaching up to him. The sunlight again lit her features as she whispered softly,

"Hello, Peter."

"Tell me, Ellen…How? I was told…darn that Brigadier General Maxwell that, that... "

"No, Peter. It was my friend Pauline who was murdered. Apparently, she ran out from the corridor, probably this very nurse's station, when she heard the sentry patrolling the back area scream after being knifed in the stomach. Pauline was on night duty like myself, she in wards D and E, and me with Rachel in A, B, and C. The Ghoul, about to leave after the murder of the Marine guard, saw that Pauline had bravely run into the patio. The dead sentry was at the end of the alley. He saw her and came back. I was approaching, hearing all the commotion, and as I entered the patio with poor Pauline already dead, and the Ghoul running halfway down the alley, he turned and saw me, ran back and took one swing, slashing my right shoulder. I fell, stumbled back, fell to my knees, and he raised what appeared to be a butcher knife or Ka-Bar. When he saw Rachael watching and screaming from the window inside the corridor and wounded patients coming up to the window as well, all in their issued pajamas and seeing the faces, he dashed off down the alley."

Peter, standing next to Bill, who had resumed sitting, listened intently. Bill was wordless as he watched Ellen.

Peter, a cold anger sweeping over him, asked haltingly, "Did you see what he looks like?"

"Oh!" she exclaimed, recalling the horror of the encounter, and swaying slightly lightheaded.

"His entire head under his cap was wrapped in a flesh-colored towel, as a mask. Its front had slits for his eyes, nose, and mouth. He wore khakis, like the other reports said, and his pants and shirt seemed perfectly starched and pressed, like an officer's. From a distance, he looked normal, until you got up close and saw the face was only a wrap of sorts."

Ellen's eyes fixed narrowly on the door leading to the patio, as she continued,

"I'd say he was Bill's size, not massive as some have insisted, medium build."

Ellen paused, shifting her gaze to the increasing number of MPs and other military personnel crowing the corridor. Numerous officials, tense and conflicted, entered and exited the patio area.

Ellen continued, her voice growing softer and more steady,

"But what surprised me was despite his power and energy to plunge his dagger into the heart of victims, he seemed worn and tired. His striking me, my shoulder, his action of swinging at me with his slicing motion seemed pale. Rachael told Captain Del Barbra and General Rupertus that he was heavy-set, and that his officer's hat had fallen off and was lying next to poor Pauline, in her pool of blood. I didn't see it quite her way. She said his tan towel didn't hide his sleek dark-brown hair, which glimmered in the broken moonlight. I agree with her that he moved quickly, smoothly, almost like an animal."

Peter, heard Maxwell call out from the door of the patio-alley crime scene, "Lieutenant, General Rupertus is calling for you."

As he turned that moment, he saw Chaplain Pinoe maneuvering down the corridor through the crowd toward Bill, Ellen, and him, as

Dr. Schneidermann, about three yards behind him, waved at Peter but turned toward the patio murder scene.

"Ellen and Bill, I'll see you at the Hope Show. The psychiatrist has just come up and I have my work to do. Ellen, you're shaken and dizzy. Go and nap for a few hours. Come with Rachael to the performance. I'm so relieved there was a mix-up. I still can't believe it. Two more dead, one a nurse. I'm so sorry. See you two this afternoon. Get there early for good seats to see better. The first row, if not reserved for the brass," the reverend lisped, obviously distressed.

"Do you think the Ghoul will strike at Hope himself?", asked Pinoe, as an afterthought.

"Yes, I do. If he succeeds, the whole world will know who he is. The USO provided murder - mad with a perfect opportunity. Now, I have to go."

Reaching the patio door as it opened, Dr. Schneidermann greeted and opened it for Peter who turned for a quick glance at his three friends. Bill, with his head down, a grin on his face, stood by as Pinoe embraced Ellen despite her arm in a sling, whispering energetically in her ear as she nodded and smiled.

During the 90 minutes that followed, Peter hurried through his tasks. Standing before Nurse Pauline's punctured corpse sprawled in a pool of her own blood, he met for a few moments with Division Commander Rupertus, Assistant Commander Shepherd, Chief of Staff Sims, and Nurse Rachael who fought the Ghoul.

"You have your duty to do, lieutenant," the Major General said glumly as he gazed upon the murdered woman. You have less than 90 minutes. By 095, I want you to join us in the ride over to the Pavuvu hospital for our 1000 meeting. Although we'll be going through all the last-minute safety and security issues of the USO people arriving, I'll want you to say a few words about what happened here last night. My entire staff and all unit commanders will be present. Of course, you'll address the question on everyone's mind: Will that damn Ghoul, or the so-called Charlie, the Coker, or Choker, or whatever the hell name he has, go after Hope, or me and Shepherd, or anyone of my high officers this afternoon during the performance? After the meeting, you are to lunch with Shepherd and Sims, then meet and greet the arriving entourage and escort them to the amphitheater stage area where I'll be waiting with the rest of my people."

"Yes, sir, I'll be through within 90 minutes. I've already gotten Nurse Ellen's description of the Ghoul. I'll talk to Nurse Rachael in a moment."

"Yes, and the Graves Registration lieutenant who is with the body of the sentry at the end of the walkway. I'm off now to my office next door. No matter where you are in your notes, stop at 0930, and leave. The three of us will be in my staff car waiting for you. At least, we'll be back to heat and sweat. Thank God, Hope will be here. He'll lift the sullen atmosphere around our boys. To have a 5 cent monster break down our morale is impossible to believe."

As the commandant began to walk toward the patio door, he turned, and asked,

"Your impressions of Nurse Ellen, lieutenant? Is she doing well?"

"Yes, sir. She suffered a terrible laceration to her shoulder, the blade penetrating a depth near her rotary cuff. She was sutured, and has her left arm in a sling. It was Nurse Rachael here, who screamed for help, then staunched the flow of blood, saving her life, all by herself. Nurse Ellen lives thanks to Nurse Rachael."

The 90 minutes that followed were a little less than a whirlwind. He interviewed Nurse Rachael; met with the Graves Registration lieutenant; perused the sentry's personal belongings, emptied from his pockets; collected and identified scraps of paper and other unimportant items that may have spewed from the Ghoul's pockets as he fought off Ellen and Rachael, then fled down the walkway; removed and secured the sentry's cbg tags; met with Reverend Pinoe after he consoled Ellen and Nurse Rachael; called for the full names of the victims in order to write their next to kin; when questioned, sat with Captain Del Barbra, Sergeant Guidi, and Dr. Schneidermann and shared his thoughts about the misconceptions of multiple murderers, outlining who he believed were the four basic types, and the common psychological thread that connected them all, then, quickly found his way to the hospital mess for a late breakfast and a cup of coffee.

Then, within a few minutes of his scheduled appointment time with the major general, Peter returned to the crime scenes to sketch in his pocket notebook the positions of the dead and their wounds. As he did so, Pinoe produced a shiny Leica camera and took a number of photos of the victims, including closeups of their death agonies.

Exiting the hospital, Peter saw the Commander's staff car, motor running, less than 20 yards to his right, in front of the 1st Division's Headquarters. As he hurried toward it, he could tell it was occupied by a driver and three officers, undoubtedly Rupertus, Shepherd and Sims. For the first time that windless morning, he felt the heavy moist heat of early August, which literally dripped from the body. The shadeless crushed yellowish red coral of the path connecting the hospital to the island headquarters was too hot to touch.

"Well, at least," thought Peter, "the entourage won't face tropical showers as they perform."

A final glance around him before stepping into the backseat of the staff car told him that everywhere around the headquarters annex must have been at least 100 heavily armed Marines.

As Peter stepped into the vehicle, and took his seat in between Rupertus and Shepherd, there was nothing but a solemn silence. No one said a word. Peter could decipher anger in Sim's face as he stared straight ahead on the passenger front seat. Shepherd sat frozen, looking out at the troops milling about, and Rupertus apparently preoccupied.

As the staff car pulled away and drove toward the pontoon bridge, neither word nor emotion was expressed. Finally, nearing the crossing, Rupertus said slowly,

"After Chaplain Pinoe left his chapel, one of our men kneeling in prayer was stabbed to death."

CHAPTER FIFTEEN

-

Bob Hope Arrives

Restlessness was prevalent throughout the open dining mess patio area where more than 40 Division headquarters staff and unit commanders were assembled. Wordlessly, they awaited Commander Rupertus, Assistant Division Commander Shepherd, and Chief of Staff Sims. With the teeming shower earlier that morning over, heat-clouds so normal in the Solomon Sea climbed on the backs of other clouds, producing a withering heat, heavy and wet.

No one seemed to notice.

Everyone was absorbed with the horrendous reality of it all. Never before in the history of the American military, had the dead piled up by the murder madness of one of its own. The arrival of Bob Hope and his entourage was imminent, and the officers were angry and frustrated. The count of the deceased was growing, three within the night and early-morning hours alone and no one had an idea who the individual was that was multiple - murdering and why. What was supposed to be a festive few hours of entertainment was clouded by a Ghoul.

With the arrival of Rupertus, Shepherd, and Sims, with Peter trailing behind, the gathering perked up, leaned forward, and prepared for the afternoon's task.

Immediately, indeed, precisely at 10:01am, the major general called the meeting to order. In his hand was a single sheet of typed assignments for both the duration and departure of the Hope entourage.

"At ease, gentlemen. After a few statements and announcements, a final roll call of our participating personnel will be taken with a review of his specific safety and security assignment."

As he paused, he scanned the audience, as if in search of someone. Then he asked,

"Is 1st Medical Battalion Commander Everett Keck of the Navy's Medical Corps here? I don't see him. He may have some new information about the Ghoul." After glancing around, he continued,

"If he arrives, call it to my attention. Meanwhile, as you have undoubtedly heard, the Ghoul struck three times last night, two at the Base Hospital on Banika and the other early this morning where he killed previously, the Pavuvu chapel. That makes seven killings in less than a week. Some firebrand, this Mad Ghoul, or Charlie the Croaker, or Choker. We have conflicted information as to what he looks like. I'll let Lieutenant Toscanini bring you up to date on that."

"But what we have to discuss now is whether the murderer will strike during the performance. At me and my staff? At Hope and his people? While more than 16,000 combat veterans look on? At the beginning or end of the entertainment? We need answers, men, and we need them now. Lieutenant, step forward, please."

Peter walked forward from where he had taken a seat between Shepherd and Sims. As he approached Rupertus, with one hand holding out the small microphone, he noticed out of the corner of his eye, Bill and Ellen, followed by Pinoe, entering the pack of the patio seating area from a side entrance.

"Gentlemen, the mad-murdering Ghoul is one of us, an officer, sitting among you. Remember, and never, ever forget, the first lesson in the study of the mind, whether it's healthy or sick: No one, absolutely no one, is who he or she seems to be. Our minds always have a purpose.

All of us have less control over it than we think. If it turns out that Major General Rupertus is the Ghoul, or Assistant Division Commander Shepherd, or Chief of Staff Sims, or, for that matter, me, you will be shocked, but not surprised, because you see, don't you, that there is potentially a Ghoul in all of us."

"I say he's one of us because other than the first murder through a cut hole in the victim's canvas tent, all the murders have been the same, up front and less than 18" from the victim's heart. Only one familiar person would be allowed that close to the armed sentry without being challenged. An officer the victim respected."

Peter paused.

"And, not just an officer. He would have to have been an officer of high rank, of unequivocal acquiescence and obedience, once his bars and stripes and badges and emblems were noted as he approached the victim."

He continued,

"We have varying descriptions of the Ghoul by those who chased and shot at him. But, the nurse sitting back there with her arm in a sling because she fought him and was slashed almost to the bone saw him best. As the mad murderer dashed into oblivion after each of his evil deeds, it was... "

Just then, Commander Rupertus stood up and announced,

"Excuse me, Lieutenant, but Commander Keck has arrived. After we hear what he has learned, we'll continue where you left off."

As Peter immediately stepped aside and observed the second-most admired man in his life walk forth, he cast a quick glance at Brigadier General Earl Maxwell of the Medical Corps sitting in the third row of the semicircle. What more could Peter ask of the tragic situation? The special bond and fondness Keck and Maxwell had for each other elevated his admiration and respect for each. Both officers were exceptionally brilliant. Not only were their commands administered with nonpareil competence, but then also conducted their staff in kindness and patience. No one questioned the intrinsic bravery and courage of each man.

"Rarely have such men of quality looked upon each other with such reverence," Peter reflected. As he glanced at Maxwell, the brigadier general smiled and winked at Peter. Then, a quick look at Bill and Ellen showed the two beaming at him.

"Hello, lieutenant," nodded Keck, "and officers of the 1st Division and its Medical Corps. The news I bring you this morning amid our difficult, no, wrong word, our tragedy, is directly from the Federal Bureau of Investigation in our nation's capital and its Chief, J. Edgar Hoover. I was looking to communicate with an assistant director of the Murder Department. While I waited for a connection, Mr. Hoover wired,

"How are your boys doing against the Japs out there?"

Everyone in the audience laughed loudly.

"In any case, men, he gave all of us a good pat on the back, said the nation was watching our fighting, island to island, certain of our final defeat of the little bastards of the Rising Sun. He also said he was sorry for our crushing blow - - a Marine killing a Marine. Then, he said I was to communicate with one of the leading homicide detectives in the country, Howard Teten, a highly respected expert on multiple-murderers. Mr. Hoover concluded that with the large number of men congregated together here, he's surprised there's only one Mad Ghoul. Stateside, there are undoubtedly several dozen scattered throughout. They are impossible to identify because most kill at random and over varying periods of time. Rare does one murder as rapidly as the one among us. The FBI has no answers. It's trying to recruit Teten to join its staff. All his bureau can do now, until a Teten-type steps forward, is to gather information, case studies, keep records, search for patterns of unsolved murders."

"Well, naturally, I was eager to wire and communicate with Mr. Teten, of the Homicide Division in the Hayward, California, Police Department.

He was very eager to help us, although he admitted he was just as much at a loss as we are at a loss to whom the Mad Ghoul could be unless we provide more details on his manner and fashion, his modus operandi, of his killings."

"So, in short, we're on our own out here in the middle of the Pacific Ocean, trying to figure out who this Ghoul is. But, to help guide us, Mr. Teten offered four, maybe five, types of multiple-murderers. Listen carefully and see if any of these types trigger a personality we can look at among our troops."

"The demented, deranged killer. He claims he sees with clarity things we can't. He hears voices, we can't. He'll say things like the darkness and impenetrable demand he murder. He is an outright lunatic. There is nothing rational, sane, or real about him."

"The Ghoul isn't crazy, insanely, delirious, nuts. He plans. He's smart. And, he's organized."

"The second is the emissary type. He feels he's on a special duty, or task, to murder a special group of people, like call girls, priests, and major generals."

With that, everyone in the audience laughed uproariously, causing General Rupertus to wince, yet with a slight smile crossing his face.

"In other words, this type of murderer displays nothing abnormal. He just wants to do his part of murdering off the evil Marines.

"Well, again, that's the Ghoul."

"Third, there's the type of killer who kills for the sport of it, the amusement. It's the tingle, the sensation, the kick that comes from murdering. He's cruel, almost fiendish, because it provides him with a certain intoxication. Know any Marines like this? The Mad Ghoul is more like this kind of murderer. If he's caught, rather than shot to death, he'll boast about it. Search your minds. He'll probably give himself away in some manner, by words or actions short of murder."

"Then, there's the sex-driven killer. Teten says that for such men the amount of their pleasure is in direct correlation with how much torture can be inflicted, how loud the screams are from the victims. The more atrocious, brutal, torturing he can be, the better, the more stirred up, the more excited he becomes. Teten says he's carnal in his behavior, and, again, you would know him by his behavior and words. Again, the Ghoul is closer to this type rather than the first two."

"So, gentlemen, we're looking for someone within the last two types. Teten says the FBI is establishing a list of possible 'multiple-murderers' from across America who had been reported to have behaviors such as these, and we'll see if any of our 1st Division men are on that list. We have a crew of officers working on this as I speak to you this moment."

"Now, let me turn this meeting back to the lieutenant. And, as I do, let me tell you about Peter Toscanini. He's my lone rover, my wanderer, and roamer in search of the Ghoul. In brief, he's the 1st Division's own psychotherapist, although he's not that just yet. You might say that he's in training to be a future psychologist, or psychotherapist. Peter is on his own, taking him wherever he feels he needs to go. His sole responsibility, his goal, is to find, arrest, and if necessary, kill the Ghoul. He reports to me directly. Peter, step forward."

As he did so, Peter glanced around the open, saw that Bill and Ellen were still among the officers, accepted the small microphone from Keck and said,

"Gentlemen, I'm no certified psychologist, psychoanalyst, or anything other than a proud lieutenant from the Medical Corps assigned to special duty. I've been interested in human nature for a long time, and at the University of California was taking courses in psychology, personality theory, with a special interest in the criminal mind. While there, a visiting professor by the name of Dr. Salvador Minuchin further triggered my interest. My fieldwork consisted of helping him pioneer work with teenagers as he began to shift his focus from individual symptoms to their relationships with their families. No little boy or girl at the age of three or four says, 'Oh, I can hardly wait to grow up to kill people', unless he hates everyone so much he wants to strike back later in life. That amount of hatred can only come during the first years of life. The Ghoul may have just started killing while on this island, but the core, or, the basis, the foundation, was laid as a child not being loved, not being wanted, not being valued, not being held and acknowledged or appreciated. The Ghoul is empty of any human emotion and fills it, homicide detective Teten believes, with the thrill and excitement that comes from murdering."

"My courses taken under the guidance of that good man, Salvador Minuchin, helped me define who the future therapist should be. He began disputing the traditional methods of the fathers of modern psychology, Sigmund Freud, Carl Jung, Alfred Adler, and so, so many others who searched and search the subconscious, then the much deeper unconscious, for illness to look at the broader perspective of family role and social environments to shape a person's behavior. Minuchin rejected the therapist's traditional role as a passive listener to become an inquisitive, traditional interventionist who challenged the patient's preconceptions and preoccupations with evil thoughts. He would ridicule, plea, praise, pull away, demand, insult, fight, then say he was sorry to the patient. But the point was the patient began to think, which, in turn, led to feelings, new feelings of hope, a certain liveliness, empathy, and ultimately, love."

"If only he were here today to study what's right in front of us, the clues that we can't see staring us right in the face. If only, Mr. Teten were here to help us."

Peter paused for a moment, glancing at Dr. Maxwell who was listing intently, and Dr. Schneidermann who just entered and took a seat in the back.

"I will leave you with this thought before returning the meeting over to Commander Rupertus. Howard Teten spoke once in Dr. Minuchin's 'Advance Personality Theory' class. The men were good friends. The detective said simply, and please mark down these words, 'Don't be afraid to listen to your intuition. Use it as a lamp, a guide, follow it, because it may lead you directly to the obvious. And, when you come to the obvious, don't be afraid of it. Don't turn away from the obvious, don't fight or disregard the obvious. You may think that the obvious is too easy and therefore can't be the answer. But, damn it, the obvious is most often the right conclusion and answer. More than likely the obvious will allow you to crack the case wide open."

With that, Peter turned to Major General Rupertus who rose instantly, walked forth, nodded to Peter, and turned to the audience,

"Gentlemen, we will now turn to the issue of Mr. Hope's safety. When we conclude, we'll have a brief sandwich lunch, then, go about our tasks. He will be arriving with his performers in less than three hours."

"First, let me give you a brief background of today's gala affair. As our division started to prepare for the next campaign last week, the recreation officer learned that Bob Hope and his troupe were to pay a surprise call on our men next door at the Banika airfield. Staff Sergeant Harold Broome immediately asked permission to wire Hope if he would also perform on Pavuvu. I understand that within minutes, the famous vaudeville actor and popular radio comedian and movie star, a legend who's already won the hearts of servicemen in North Africa, Italy and France, agreed to hop a Piper and fly over here, 20 minutes away, with all his crew of six. Since the Cub is an observation plane, a two-seater, six of them will be required. They'll be arriving around 1400 this afternoon, performing immediately in our makeshift amphitheater. In between, the entourage will be escorted by a team made up of Lieutenant Toscanini and Commander Everett Keck of the Navy's Medical Corp, Lt. Col. Earl Maxwell, the Chief Surgeon of USAFISPA, Captain Oscar Del Barbra, and my entire staff, Shepherd, Sims and the D-1, D-2, D-3, D-4 chiefs. They will tour Pavuvu Island and its facilities, defenses, and see the ocean views, then spend an hour or so at the hospital where Toscanini and Maxwell will assume the roles of guides. They will then be taken to our Pavuvu headquarters for an early supper in our officers' mess and finally over to our Banika theater for the performance. By 1800, they'll be back on the Piper Cubs for the short return flight to Banika. There, Mr. Hope insists they immediately perform for the Banika boys until 2200. They'll stay overnight in the Base Hospital, and, after an early breakfast, tour the hospital in the morning. By 1000, they'll be on their way back to Guadalcanal."

"Who's coming?" an officer of the 1st Division, 1st Battalion asked with a smile.

"I'm glad you asked, Lieutenant Colonel Walker Reavers," responded Rupertus.

"Well, only six. Bob himself, fellow humorist singers Frances Longford and Patti Thomas, guitarist Tony Romano, and some other comics and musicians whose names I've forgotten."

"We've heard he likes being with the troops, the fighting men," said another.

The major general smiled.

"Well, I understand a few months ago, Jack Benny and Larry Adler, with his harmonica, were all over the Middle East. Then, awhile back, Martha Raye went into the foxholes of Tunisia, as Al Jolson, with his harmonium, headed for Egypt. Only Judith Anderson and Ray Bolger were out this way, Anderson with the troops and Navy in Hawaii, and Bolger in Guadalcanal."

"Now we get to the prize of them all, the best the USO, the United Services Organization, has straight from the Aleutians, where our men in tiny posts up there get nothing, no leave, no entertainers, nothing but cold, sleet and rain."

"Every officer I've spoken to has said the same thing about Mr. Hope. He's a tornado in himself. No one has seen anyone from the ranks of Show Business travel as far, work harder, make as many masses of troops laugh more, and risk his life almost daily. For us out here in the Russells, he'll do two shows, back to back. One from this afternoon on Pavuvu, and, on Banika tonight, then up at 0700 to tour and spend time with our men who are hospitalized. An amazing man!"

As Rupertus paused, Reverend Pinoe walked into the open patio area, searching for a chair among those in the audience of the semicircle.

"Reverend, I'm glad you walked in. Are you available this afternoon to join our welcoming party to meet Mr. Hope and the troupe at the landing trip and remain with him until he and his troupe fly back to Banika at 1800?"

"I'd be honored, sir," Pinoe responded, with a broad grin.

"Then, take the seat up here next to Lieutenant Toscanini since you'll join him and my staff in welcoming the troupe. Meanwhile, let me finish telling you what I've heard about Bob Hope. Sure, I, too, have gone to the cinema at home, always with my wife, Beth. We have seen every one of the films he's made. I remember 'Road to Singapore', 'Road to Morocco', 'The Ghost Breakers', 'My Favorite Blonde'. We even saw one of his earliest, 'The Cat and the Canary'. But my favorite, one that dealt with Nazi spies in New York, was called 'They Got Me Covered.'"

After glancing around the assembled group, and seeing their intense interest, Major General Rupertus continued,

"When it comes to mingling with our brother servicemen, it is said Hope is extraordinarily friendly. It's known among our troops, here in the South Pacific, and across the Atlantic in Western Europe, that Mr. Hope will only eat with the fighting men, drink what they drink, use the same personal facilities, read the same monotonous drool and drivel we all read, and listen to the same as our boys listen to. He sincerely feels he's one of them, is with them, and wouldn't mind be given an M-1 so he can join the front line."

Rupertus again remained silent, searching for words to express his innermost thoughts. After a pause lasting a full minute or so, the commander said quietly,

"I'll let you go in a moment. Those with specific custodial duties will meet back here with Assistant Commander Shepherd and Chief of Staff Sims. Now, go get a sandwich and a cup of coffee or glass of milk. The rest of you will go about your assignments."

"If there is an incident, anecdote, or vignette that tells you exactly who Hope is, what his character is all about, what the core of his heart is all about, it is this one:

"Recently, there was one camp in the Aleutians, he couldn't get to for one reason or another. So, in order to watch his performance, some 600 troops marched more than 10 miles across rain-swept countryside to see and hear him. But by the time they arrived, exhausted but eager, the show was over and Bob and his entourage were gone, already at his sleeping quarters preparing for a sound sleep. But suddenly an officer knocked on his door, and, after Hope responded in his pajamas, was told the 600 riflemen were walking back to their camp. Hearing this, Hope instantly called his troupe together, threw them into jeeps, and after six or seven miles, overtook the troops, cold, wet, and discouraged, and started performing on the spot, in a drenching downpour, including the sleet, winds, and heavy rain. That one incident where Bob, Jerry, Frances, Terri and the other two in which everyone clowned around in heavy sleet, strong winds and in the rain for 90 minutes, endeared him to our troops more than any other story."

"Well, men, that's all I have to say. Mr. Hope is coming to give us an enormous lift with his wonderful sense of humor, and I have seven decaying Marines on slabs in the hospital refrigerator," said Commander Rupertus softly, as tears began to well up in his eyes. Peter and Pinoe, the two closest to him, were amazed. Neither had ever observed such a high-ranking military officer allow himself to break down under any emotion.

Finally, the major general, controlling himself not to wipe the tears away from his eye, concluded,

" . . . and so, men, amid the ribbing humor, the adlibbing, hollering, the often-risqué dialogue, remember that lurking in the shadow somewhere is a murdering Marine who undoubtedly will strike today or tonight to make a name for himself. Don't let the Ghoul do it."

As the major general turned to walk out to the jeep for a ride back to his Banika office, Reverend Pinoe suddenly stood up and approached Rupertus, saying,

"Neither your wrath do I fear, nor any disciplinary action I may have coming, but I must say this. Never did I expect to see a tear in the eye of the Commander of the 1st Division, Marine. Red eyes are rare among men who order men into certain death day after day. Yet, to observe you of the high rank to allow your officers to acknowledge your humanity is the privilege of my lifetime. God bless you, Commander. I wish every warrior of all our services could know such empathetic decency."

With that, Peter stood up and said,

"He'll come this afternoon or tonight, men. Alert everyone, especially all on Banika. The Ghoul craves darkness for his deeds. And, all of the dead learned this the hard way. My hunch, intuition, and my unconscious, say the same thing: He strikes tonight on Banika during that performance. He'll come up close and personal, this officer of ours. Then, he'll plunge a Ka-Bar into your chest and stomach. No one from his troupe, especially Hope himself must be left alone for even a moment. If he needs to nap, you nap beside him; if he needs to pee, you pee right alongside of him; when he eats, we'll all eat alongside of him."

"This $7,500-a-week Hollywood legend, this inexhaustible man who comes to make us grin and laugh, didn't have to come to the Russells. Now, he faces murder. Your only job, men, is to keep the Ghoul at bay until we finally catch or kill him. Keep our visitors safe and secure."

With that, the meeting was over and the participants headed for the sandwich counter with soft drinks and coffee, then their assignment posts, or an additional where they were now.

Peter, with Pinoe in tow, walked over to where Bill and Ellen sat. Keck and Maxwell huddled for a moment, Keck shouting over to Peter that several jeeps would be ready for departure to the landing strip at 1300. Hope was expected within the next two hours to arrive.

"Well, you two, fancy meeting you here! Ready for roars of laughter?" Peter asked, grinning.

"Yup," responded Bill, standing up with an ear-to-ear smile. "It'll be just like being home when mom and dad sat in their cushioned chairs and sis, big brother, and I laid on our backs on the living room floor. Then, at exactly 5:00pm on late Sunday afternoon, the Pepsodent Hour came in on our small radio and for 60 minutes, we heard nothing but wisecracks and funny stories."

Pinoe nodded, then added,

"It's well known in our military circles that Hope's an indefatigable man, running himself wild. All of us chaplains received brief biographies and summaries of his USO work in case he suddenly dropped in, like he's doing today in our theater of operations. The bulletin mentioned he didn't care if he did six or eight shows a day, since he not only loves our boys, but also wants to do his part for the war effort. He says he wants to disprove the photo that says when he's shown with countless of our fighting boys shaking his hand, it's not because he's too old for the draft. No, sir. I agree with Bill, Bob Hope is a direct and straight link into our living rooms back home."

Turning to Ellen, Peter exclaimed, "Ellen, what are you doing here? I was hoping you'd be asleep until showtime. You just went through hell, young lady! Are you in pain?"

"For a little scratch? Of course not. Just couldn't sleep with all the excitement. Bill and I discussed the situation after you left us on Banika and decided to simply walk over here. I'll go back with the other nurses after the afternoon performance to relieve one or two of our nurses in the Base Hospital so they can attend tonight's performance on Banika."

"I'm delighted, Ellen. Let's head over for a sandwich or two; it'll be a long afternoon before we have another meal."

As they walked across the open-air patio in the hospital, Peter noticed for the first time how subdued everyone was who was eating, or about to eat, sitting at tables or standing in the queue. The usual aura of assurance that accompanied officers in starched, freshly ironed khaki uniforms was replaced by a gloomy apprehension. Silent officers in neglected, wrinkled uniforms stood in line, waiting to help themselves to cheese and tuna sandwiches stacked high on silver trays. Ample raw vegetables, freshly baked bread and Australian butter were also available on the single table. Coffee, pastries, and fresh ice cream were also present. Green-leafies, soft drinks, and Pacific Island fruits were made handy on a third table. Amid the absence of the usual chatter and chuckling, a prerecorded baritone soloist was singing "The Road to Mandalay."

Peter nodded to Bill,

"I'd swear half these officers think they're going to a firing squad rather than lunch."

"Sullenness commingling with feeling of expectancy, not only for Mr. Ghoul, but also Mr. Hope," Bill responded, equally sullen.

"I heard," interjected Pinoe, standing side-by-side with Ellen, "that six Piper Cubs will land on the dirt road down from Tent City, and that our 12-member band will be playing 'God Bless America' as the group assembles after landing. One of the nurses is supposed to sing it. Will make a wonderful impression on Mr. Hope."

Suddenly, Ellen, unable to contain herself, began to weep uncontrollably, unashamedly.

"Why, Ellen, what brings this on?" asked Peter, knowing the answer all too well, as Bill stepped toward her, and Pinoe placed an arm around her, whispering a quiet reassurance in her ear.

Stepping away from the queue, and its inquisitive onlookers, Peter asked quietly, "Need to return to the nurses' barracks? What is it, Ellen?"

In between soft sobs, Ellen said throatily,

"The vocalist chosen to sing 'God Bless America' was Pauline, my friend, who was murdered last night. She had been told about it last night before her night shift, and was proudly telling me and Rachael; she immediately wrote her mother and father, and was flying so, so high, then stabbed so brutally, laying in a pool of her own blood, so young, such a dedicated nurse, engaged to a boy who was part of the Normandy invasion, she... " Ellen was shaking so emotionally the three men sat her down at the nearest table.

Pinoe, seeing the utter anguish on Ellen's face, said in a lowered voice to Peter and Bill, "Get something for all of us to eat and drink. Ask if you can crowd in at the head of the line - - you have one of our nurses in pain. I'll stay and counsel with her until you get back. Then, I'll leave for the hospital where I have men waiting. I'll be back for the 1330 departure to pick up the Hope gang."

Peter turned to Ellen, struggling to control her weeping, "Ellen, we'll bring back whatever's on the table. We'll all share. After some fresh food and coffee in your stomach, you can decide what you want to do."

With that, Peter, accompanied by Lundigan, walked hurriedly to the front of the queue. Turning back for a quick glance, Peter saw that Pinoe was embracing Ellen, whispering into her ear. She was smiling and waved, indicating Ellen was well again.

Then, with trays in hand loaded with sandwiches and beverages, and dishes and utensils placed on the table, the men snacked. No one said a word for a few moments. Peter finally said,

"Ellen, help yourself. You really should eat if you're going to be up all day."

Pouring a cup of coffee from a small pot Bill borrowed from the main table, Ellen said quietly,

"Pauline told me confidentially she hoped that if she had to die in this war, it would be peacefully. Preferably, as she slept in her bunk in one of our wards. Her call to service, she said, came on the Sunder afternoon of December 7, 1941, knowing that our boys were hurting and in pain across the Pacific and she should be with them. The next morning, Monday, December 8, she enlisted in the Army. The Army grabbed her because she had a Bachelor's Degree of Nursing from St. Mary's College in Moraga, California. Without any Army training, she was commissioned as a lieutenant to develop a fast-paced plan to recruit and train young women for the program. Then, for three years, she tended our boys in the Pacific because the 1st Division was in an urgent, desperate need. The Army loaned her to the Corps. Pauline was on leave from the Army to help the Corps, then was murdered by a Marine!"

With that, Ellen began to shake and sob uncontrollably again. Peter and Pinoe placed their arms around her shoulders without words and soon Ellen regained her composure. She continued,

"For us, the veteran nurses and the new ones, she's been a legend, a model of what nursing service is. She always worked 80 hours a week, without comment or complaint. And, she was a fighter, too. All the Medical Corps dealt with her because she was a tireless advocate for quality of patient care, and a spokesman for patient rights. No one messed with her because she was as unafraid as she was merciless in her beliefs, and tireless in seeing to it they were achieved."

"And to see her cut down by perhaps a man she helped," interjected Pinoe.

"That's very right," stammered Ellen. "While under her care, all patients were treated equally. Each man was treated with kindness, gentleness, and dignity. She even offered a whole new concept, one that encouraged the wounded or ill to be actively, not passively, in their own care. She went out of her way to praise those nurses who worked just as hard, cared just as much, and felt as much as she did that private or general, kitchen cook or invasion strategist, was a brother, and she was going to love him, exemplified by her basic care. She didn't care about herself, but she was determined that those such noticed would not go unnoticed. But in her case, she did receive notice, proven by the awards she received. The rest of us chucked when she merely packaged them up and sent them home to mom."

Again, there was pause as the sobs and tears began to flow again. Ellen concluded,

"What endeared me as well to her was her care for domestic animals. The Japs left two dogs behind. God only knows what breed they were and who they once belonged to. Skin and bones, they were near death. But, so typical, she simply made them her own. They are up under her bed waiting for her to come off-duty to take them for a walk, then feed them. She honestly believed, not just in words, but in her warm heart, that all living creatures were sacred and deserved life as long as it lasted, naturally."

"I loved Pauline, and now she's gone, having died at the hands of a murderer she would have given her life to care for and protect."

With that, Pinoe raised himself, stood up, patted her on the shoulder and walked away.

Meanwhile, Peter and Bill remained silent, heads lowered, offering nothing except their soft breathing.

Ellen understood. Then, very slowly, with both her hands, she stretched across the table, each hand reaching for Peter's and Bill's. Clasping them, she said softly, "Will one of you, I don't care who, or which of you, but will one of you be intimate with me later tonight? I really need for one of you to hold me, to caress me. Please?"

CHAPTER SIXTEEN

-

"Is that him?"

Neither Peter nor Bill said a word. For a full minute, neither of the two friends moved a muscle other than their facial features, which somehow produced the emergence of grins.

Blushing, Ellen cast her eyes down.

"Doesn't matter who, just so long as it's one of you," she continued in a mumble. "Not interested in anyone else in the whole of the Allied armed forces in the South Pacific . . . I so want someone to touch and hold me... "

Her eyes remaining drooped, more embarrassed than guiltily, she insisted, a hint of mirth creeping into the tone, "It's not romantic or sexual pleasure I seek, only you, Peter or William, to hold me, to hold me dearly, with strength. Nothing more... "

Regaining his composure from a stance of reflective silence, Peter said hesitantly in a barely audible voice,

"Well, if Bill who's not pledged to anyone won't, I will, with your understanding, Ellen, that my Joan is the only woman on this earth that I can embrace... "

"But I have my Rena Morgan in New York who still doesn't know that... "

"Oh, for goodness sake, I wasn't asking either of you to get a ladder and climb up and grab the moon for me, I simply wanted one of you to allow me to rest my head on your shoulder. I'm over it now. And frankly, your reluctance helped me return to reality."

"Ellen, I fully understand and am ready to engage in that with one of the few women on this earth I want as a lifelong friend. Freud once said, 'Women don't become prostitutes because they yearn for money or sex. They become 'women of the night' because they simply want to be held.'"

"Yes, that's it. With Pauline gone in less than a few hours ago, she and I relieving girls too exhausted to work last night, and tonight to give up her own enjoyment so others would have theirs . . ."

"Oh, Ellen, I understand, I understand... "

"I tried to save her, I tried... ", and she burst into tears again.

"Bill, I must go now, and fetch Mr. Hope. Why me, I have no idea, but I must report to the Commander's car. Stay with her, and when I see you at afternoon's performance either here or tonight, over there, I'll tell you all about Hope the gossip and insights of all who are with him."

As Bill smiled, and nodded at Peter, as he placed his arm around Ellen, Peter nodded approvingly, and without further word, turned and walked through the open patio area toward the hospital entrance where he was to meet Major General Rupertus.

What immediately struck Peter as he exited the open structure of the hospital was the force of all the early noontime wind sweeping across Pavuvu from the Solomon Sea "Slot". Wind-swirling sand off the high dunes near the channel beaches attempted to penetrate his eyes, throat, lungs, all adding to the pain of his cracked lips. Although not a full-blown sandstorm, it was nonetheless barely bearable.

"How sad," he thought, "if the performance was hampered or halted because of tornado force winds,

Swallowing dryly, Peter looked all around him. Rupertus, Shepherd, and Sims would be along in a few minutes, followed by other officers of the 1st Division. Five staff cars were lined up, their PFC drivers standing outside by the drivers' seats with the back seat doors open, and the car motors idling.

Behind the staff cars, were 10 large platform trucks capable of conversion into troop carriers, their motors idling as well. Helmeted Marines carrying an assortment of weapons, mostly machine guns and rifles, were lounging, relaxing, smoking, talking quietly across the street from General Headquarters on and around the benches in the tiny memorial garden the center of which was the post fluttering the American flag. Of the ten trucks, four carried moveable searchlights and anti-aircraft guns, the weapons poking their long, covered muzzles skywards.

"Wow!" thought Peter, "are we going through these melodramatics for 'show' to impress the USO, or is there a real threat on the lives of our visitors?"

Glancing at his wristwatch, Peter saw that it was two minutes after 1330. Suddenly, the front door to General Headquarters swung open and Major General William H. Rupertus, Division Commander, stood there in a Marine wrap. Exiting behind him were Brigadier General Lemuel C. Shepherd, and Chief of Staff Amor LeRoy Sims, equally resplendent in their respective uniforms garnished in earned medals. All casually and calmly walked down the steps, exuding confidence. Bringing up the rear were a dozen well-armed, heavy-jacketed, binoculated, goggled, scarfed motorcyclists who would lead the parade to greet the Hope troupe after landing.

Rupertus appeared friendly and cordial, even cheerful, despite the wanton murders of his troops. As Peter waited patiently by the lead staff car, the Commander, with his assistant commander and chief-of-staff in tow, walked across the road in order to mix and talk with his soldiers, patting some on the back, laughing heartily with others. For an afternoon and evening, all was well in the commander's mind, and he was grinning for the first time in a week.

With Rupertus and Shepherd in the back seat at the windows, and Peter in-between them, with Sims on the passenger side of the front seat, the lead car pulled away on the road of crushed coral and slowly headed down the straight road to the landing stip. Six Marine motorcyclists with machine guns perched on their backs assume position on each side of the staff cars. All six drivers impressed Peter with their handling of their respective bikes, as their speed increased, and a good deal of ground was covered. As they assumed the point positions, they began to skid and bounce as Peter searched the roadside for anyone who could pose a threat to the guest and his entourage.

As the welcoming convoy proceeded slowly along the slender, and high-backed roughhewn, prickly roadway, several jeeps conveying six Marines, each bearing Browning Automatic Rifles, intercepted and replaced the motorcycle escort, which immediately fell behind the retinue. Although squeezed and smashed, the crushed coral from the tropical sea showed the wear and tear of small tank treads and the wheel marks of countless heavy army trucks, gun carriages, and jeeps.

Along the way, all side traffic was halted, congesting much of the normal vehicular movements on Pavuvu, all the way back to the pontoon bridge. They drove past several ration dumps, collapsible water tanks, and Marines manning heavy-duty machine guns that had been set up that morning all along the route. Marines either waved or saluted the Commander's staff car.

Rupertus asked, a twinkle in his eye, "Remember how all our roads used to bog down in the mud and the common name for Pavavu was 'mud hole'? All the men of the 1st blamed me for it."

"Heck," interjected Shepherd, "They blamed you for all the bad things about this stink hole. Now, after only a few months, the men are eulogizing you for all the improvements you've made, regularly rationed beer rations being one, along with a solid recreation program with ample bats and balls, boxing gloves, volleyballs, basketballs, horseshoes, badminton, among all the card games."

"The lighted screened mess halls you had installed when we got here in February and March meant an enormous amount. Now, they serve the men for letter-writing and playing cards."

"Well," responded Rupertus, "much of that came from Melbourne, Honolulu, and San Diego, including having the USO and other stateside organizations collect current magazines from families that were through with them for distribution, not only on Guadalcanal and the Russells, but all over the Pacific. Headquarters has seen to it that every area has a shower and a laundry. Thank God, a Division order finally came down authorizing quartermasters to cut off khaki trousers above the knees for daytime shorts the men have been clamoring for. They were right: the Japs were better at issuing tropical clothing than we were."

"Not to change the subject, General, but what can you tell us about Bob Hope?" asked the Chief of Staff.

"Well, let's first of all hope they all come in safe and sound, and not crash into the post at the end of the runway," responded the Major General.

"Well, the part of the strip we're having them land on," added Shepherd, "is where we evacuate our seriously wounded by plane. It's also the smoothest part of the road-runway our observation planes land and take off from. So, the Piper Cubs have the best area to land in the Russells. It's no longer a little, ole lonesome strip uncared for."

Commander Rupertus added,

"Supposedly, Ernie Pyle may be with the Hope entertainers. After the invasion of Normandy in June, his people reassigned him from Europe to out here. So, gentlemen, on our watch, for a little more than 10 hours, we have one of the most popular comedians in the world on our hands, and certainly one of the most important war reporters in America. Suppose for a moment we lost them both on Pavuvu to the Ghoul, while we were in charge of their lives... "

After a long minute of silence, while everyone was in deep personal thought, and within sight of their airstrip parking lot destination, Peter asked,

"Isn't the new Seabee-built Red Cross building beautiful? It's the best looking structure in the whole Pacific world."

"Yes, it is," answered Rupertus. "But some of us feel it's more of a tribute to our Red Cross girls, to our 1st Division Command, and to our troops themselves."

Shepherd chimed in,

"You see, Peter, there was never a problem with the girls on Pavuvu as there were on Banika. Here, at the old plantation house, the Red Cross girls lived. There were only six of them, with 16,000 Marines who hadn't seen a woman for a year since the Division left Melbourne. There was not a single, tension, disrespect, or sexual insult exhibited. Of course, our M.P.'s still patrolled the plantation facility right up until the girls moved into the new nurses' facility a month ago. On Banika, the M.P.'s had to employ war dogs and high barbed-wire fences which were inundated by high pole floodlights."

Sims added,

"Our boys haven't shunned that new Red Cross building, or blackballed or ostracized it. However the men feel that going there shows a certain weakness in them. To show their open prejudice, they mock the regular visitors by calling them 'Red Cross Commanders'. The six Red Cross woman themselves remind us that Marines are brought up the hard way, not to expect any favors such as 'Red Cross'."

"Well," Commander Rupertus smiled and said, "I love those two nice buildings although my boys are not 'taking' to them. But the troops are in high combat morale, ready for the next campaign coming in a few weeks. Along with a lot of spit-and-polish, and healthy, fulfilling activities rather than gathering up rotted coconut . . . Oh we're turning into the airstrip's parking lot. Soon, the first Piper Cub should be landing. Let's get out and stretch our legs. Once the landings have taken place, we'll walk over and welcome them all. I hope Ernie Pyle is with them."

Of course, Peter had been on the landing strip innumerable times, rarely acknowledging the area. Now, he looked around in earnest. There were no taxi ways, no buildings, only an open control tower with a thatched roof adjacent a coral strip 7,000 feet long running east to west on a narrow tongue of land. Almost from water's edge to water's edge, there were no squadrons of heavy Corsairs, no refueling facilities, no huts of mess halls and sleeping quarters, only a long white landing strip from a roadway. The only movements that were discernible were three men, an assistant operations officer, a control functionary, and an observer leaning over the tower railings talking to the medical emergency rescue force of physicians, nurses, and corpsmen waiting around three ambulances and two fire trucks. Half a dozen yards on a strip of shade along the perimeter of tall palms was a flatbed truck with a dozen or more Marine musicians tuning up or playing their musical instruments. Known as the USMC Pavuvu "Hashbangers", the potpourri of trumpeters, violinists, banjo players, and varying other brass, string, and drum players were rehearsing "God Bless America."

"Tropical heat running into solid fronts with clouds this time of year tends to ground all planes extending from 3,000 feet to 10,000 feet," said Sims. "Even Piper Cubs. Hope nothing goes awry."

"It could," interjected Shepherd. "Small observation planes like the Pipers always have a greater chance of hydraulic problems and their thin fragile tails and wheels falling off."

"That's a very prejudicial comment about an Army-designed airplane," grinned Shepherd.

After a pause, Rupertus, still cheerful, added,

"Well, at least our beautiful coral air field isn't muddy . . . Praise God for that!"

Then, at precisely 1400, two P-38 Lightnings roared overhead so fast no one saw them until a second later as they twisted in broad turns. Two VMO-251 Corsairs followed within a moment, tipping their wings to the welcoming committee below waiting in the parking lot.

As Peter looked skyward for the "Lightnings," Rupertus chucked,

"Wish the Corps gave me such escorts as that."

Then, the faint, muffled sounds of light-engine aircraft could be heard approaching and suddenly, six tiny dots could be seen approaching from the southeast, the P38s and Corsairs continually circling the evenly spaced Piper Cubs.

"Wow!" exclaimed Peter, bringing smiles from the three command officers.

Now, every eye of everyone on the parking lot and in the observation tower were on the sky not only on the six light planes in a row, but also throughout the sky's panorama. It was always possible that Japanese aircraft could be lurking at low levels from the other seas.

"They are here, safe and sound. Now, let's hope, no pun intended, that they land without any mishaps. The winds have calmed, nothing is in their way to cause an accident, yet... " Rupertus worried quietly.

After maintaining their cruise speed and significantly reducing airspeed, thereby coping with the high turbulence in the light aircraft over Northwestern Pavuvu, the first Piper Club slowly and smoothly approached the long touchdown.

"I'm so thankful the Seabees added the Martson steel matting atop the crushed coral last month. The lessons of constant crackups, flip-flops and turnovers at Henderson Field on Guadalcanal last year and this taught us matting saves pilot and passenger lives."

"Plus, we know", added slightly anxious assistant commander Shepherd, "From our months of using this little strip which is nothing more than an elongated taxiway requires more than just guts and hope to putting that tinker-toy Cub into this pea-patch. It takes an imperturbable art of flying."

"Well," added Sims, "Henderson became an important air base for the region. The original fighter strip was improved and expanded into a larger bomber strip with hard stands and taxiways. We have plans in the works to turn our little observation plane strip into a much-needed fighter runway."

As Peter and the Command staff observed touchdown after touchdown of all six of the light aircraft, the lead Piper Cub taxied to the far end of the runway and turned abruptly into the end of the parking lot. The passenger sitting next to the pilot clasped his hands and waved them over his head. Then, he started clapping.

Taxing to the leveled and surfaced area in the corner of one of Pavuvu's coconut plantations that had been cut down earlier in 1944 to serve as a storage lot for 100 LVT-1 (Landing Vehicle Tracked) amtracs of the 1st and 2nd Amphibian Tractor Battalions, the area was guarded 24 hours a day as the popularly known "Alligators" were being serviced and prepared for the Peleliu assault. Thick jungles virtually surrounding the lot helped camouflage and conceal the precious water-land vehicles.

"Yes, sir," smiled Rupertus, "very tidy landings, very doctrinaire flying, very text bookish. Those cute little Cubbies are something to behold in action."

"Yup. The pilots, the best the Corps has in this part of the Pacific, flew the Cubs from Henderson to Banika this morning, then around 1330, picked up the six member entourage and flew them here, one passenger per Piper. Those pilots know how to handle them, how to track and fly them in current wind, true ground speed and time to this very point from dead reckoning to true, experienced, veteran pilotage. Not once did they stray or have their engines stall."

After climbing back into their respective staff cars, trucks and motorcycles, the reception party drove over to the first Piper Cub to land that was quietly parked waiting for the other five to taxi over and line up next to it.

"Here, the planes are the most vulnerable. We have security around the lot, but is it enough? Supposed a group of superior Jap officers and troops waded ashore and hid out in the jungle for reconnaissance to verify where our lines are in preparation for an attack, a concentrated attack, on Mr. Hope and his people. Or, a strafing and bombing mission just about now by 'Zeros', the AGM2 Kokutais, single-engine fighters, flying out of the main field on Rebual, or the one at Buin on Bougainville. Just two or three of those Zeros could turn this field, and Pavuvu, into a wild melee. And, trust me, the Japs would love to diffuse, better yet, quash the Hope phenomenon."

Within moments, headquarters staff cars, army truck flatbeds laded with heavy antiaircraft guns and machine-gun carrying Marines, and jeeps converged on the lead Piper Cub. As the commander's car sped the several hundred yards toward the first plane that had lined up to be the first in a row for later departure. The single engine still idling, the pilot had quickly emerged from the Cub to place a four-step stool at the passenger side of the plane to assist the passenger in stepping down.

Pulling up within half a dozen yards of the passenger side of the Piper Cub, the driver hadn't turned off the car's engine before Rupertus opened the car door to his back seat and literally bounded forth to greet the arriving guest.

"Well, would you look at him?" an astonished Shepherd asked softly. "The old man can still scamper pretty well."

"And, for a few hours, not preoccupied about the seven dead in the Pavuvu refrigerator morgue, and then son-of-a-______ who'll probably kill a few more of our boys before we catch up to him," said Sims somberly.

At that point, actor Bob Hope climbed out of the cockpit, giggling standing atop the ramp with arms spread wide apart, he began singing loudly, "Oh, happy days are here again."

"Yup," responded Sims, "it's Hope all right, shorter than I remember him in all the movies I've watched him in. The skid nose sure stands out. It actually complements the slope of his chin."

Peter, who said nothing other than chuckle at the comments of the highest officers in the 1st Division command, was riveted by what he observed. Watching Rupertus rush the plane, and hearing his commander ask enthusiastically, his eyes wide and bright,

"Mr. Bob Hope?"

The passenger, pulling his travel bag out of the cockpit, turned, smiled at the general, and answered,

"No, I'm Bing Crosby. Hope is back in Hollywood rehearsing his acceptance speech before a mirror for the Oscar he's certain to get next spring."

Everyone within hearing laughed uproariously.

"Mr. Crosby," responded Rupertus, "we're happy to have either one of you, you or Mr. Hope, out here in nowhere sea and sky. Welcome, on behalf of all 16,000 Marines of my 1st Division troops. Every single one of us grew up loving both of you."

"Well," responded Hope, "in case we're too tired to return to Banika, tell me you have clean and fresh bed sheets on the cots. No more bed sheets sewn out of discarded tent canvas. Promise me, unlike that island next door, that you don't have lizards, scorpions, and rats copulating with the land crabs. And, more important than sleeping in dazzling white linen, and watching oversexed creepy-crawlies, dance toward each other, tell me you don't have any Jap snipers hanging around in your treetops."

Just then, the flatbed Army truck transporting the 1st Division's makeshift band of volunteer musicians pulled up. More than a dozen musicians leaped off carrying their horns and stringed instruments in hand and quickly assembled a few yards from Rupertus and Hope. A crude, primitive PA system was set up, and as the general and comedian turned to observe the group, the band began performing the "Star Spangled Banner", immediately followed by "God Bless America."

With everyone standing at attention, Hope held his right hand over his heart. With Rupertus, and his two assistant commanders, including Peter, following suit, hands over their hearts, everyone spontaneously began singing "God Bless America." Even before the refrains were concluded, Peter swore later, confirmed by Shepherd and Sims, Hope was observed wiping a tear from his eye while Rupertus, eyes to the ground, wept unashamedly. Patrols and sentries throughout that third of Pavuvu Island reported the sounds of the band and singing of those participating.

When it was over, one of the Marines in the band handed his stringed instrument, a violin, to the fellow musician and lifted a short, portable flagstaff on a tripod from the flatbed and raised the "Stars and Stripes" to thump and flap over the scene.

Then, after a moment of silence, everyone turned back to the comedian and his five performers, and the six pilots who successfully flew them in.

For Peter, the moment was so overwhelming, filled with emotion he wanted to cry. All of it, of course, was due to patriotism. But it was more than that. It was the sight of each of his murdered Marines he had to examine. How could a Marine kill a fellow Marine? The moment was so poignant, he could feel his face flush red.

As the P-38, "Lightenings, and Corsairs flew back across the parking lot for the final time that morning, the pilots, in unison, waggled their wings. Hope, his hand now on Rupertus' shoulder smiled and shouted,

"Go lick the Japs, boy, so we can go home, damn it! Otherwise, we'll be fighting them in Seattle, San Francisco, and L.A."

So many thoughts, so much excitement, so varied the images, and all at once, commingling with musings over Joan incarcerated in an internment camp, and brooding about the Ghoul, anger, nay, a fierce hatred for not only the multiple murderer, but also that the Pacific War might last another year, possibly two, Peter knew he had considerable thinking to do sort it all out.

With that, Rupertus turned to Hope who said, in all smiles,

"General, and all you nice officers, musicians, rifleman, and pilots who risked your lives flying us in, I want you to meet, face-to-face, the Hope Gypsies, whose eyes, like yours and the others of the 1st, are turned defiantly toward Japan."

Somewhat awed, everyone turned to look upon the five "Gypsies" who had lined up before them.

"First," continued Hope, "meet 'Mother' Frances Lanford, our dancer. She's the oldest of the Gypsies at 31 and, also a darn good singer."

As she stepped forward, smiled, and waved, Hope continued, "You all know that FDR, in 1941, created the USO, the United Services Organizations, to raise your morale, and to keep your morale, among another thing, high. Well, I could make a naughty funny that the girls there, 'Mother' and Patty, are delighted to do so, but I won't."

This triggered an amount of titillating giggles, causing Rupertus to blush red and Hope and Jerry Colonna to grin from ear-to-ear.

"Boys, Frances already serenaded tens of thousands of our troops with ballads like 'You're My Lucky Star' and 'Hurray for Hollywood'. She's more a singer than dancer and actress, and her legs are more beautiful than her voice. 'Mother' Langford, as you'll see, knows just how much sex to pour and still be dignified. I can tell you fellas that the girls back home are encouraging her to represent them as the 'All American Girl Waiting At home'. And, I can tell you on the sly that neither Frances Langford nor Patty Thomas have any problem raising your 'morale' and keeping it hard, I mean high, not hard but high," Hope said somberly, fighting back a sheepish grin.

"Which brings us to the second beauty of my Gypsy Six, Patty Thomas. Why do I keep saying, 'hard'?"

As the modest number of servicemen began to hoot and applaud, General Rupertus flinched, and turned, eyes flashing, so much so, there was instant soberness.

Hope chuckled,

"I get it, men . . . Well, as you can see, fellas, Patty, who is only 22 years old, is what you're fighting for. When she's on stage, and in her flimsy outfit, you won't be able to take your eyes off her legs. This dedicated, sincere young woman is more a dancer than singer and comedian, proven by her dedication. She dances on hoods of jeeps in the rain, she dances on boards over mud, and especially looks forward to being near the front lines and emergency wards of hospitals. Like Frances, she is made of the real stuff. She doesn't show off her legs, she flaunts them in order to get your guys for a few moments to not only forget what you've seen and experienced, but also what you're about to see and know . . . Patty's a real sweetheart, men. She lives to entertain you."

"And now, for the professor, 40-year-old Gerardo Luigi Colonna of Boston..." as Hope continued his introductions, as Peter, with natural curiosity, mused for a moment over Frances and Patty,

"The younger woman is giggling openly to herself because some of our younger fellas are starting to behave ridiculously. Sure, they haven't seen the uncovered legs of women in more than a year, but they don't have to act like teenage boys. Patty is at least 10 years younger than Frances. Hope is right. She is calm and womanly. Patty is almost a teenager herself. I wouldn't say that the two are beautiful, but they certainly come down on the side of being good-looking rather than plain appearing. Each is beaming, suggesting self-reliance and quiet confidence. It's obvious both want to be among us. They care. They weren't assigned to visit troops. And, look at how they adore their boss, Bob Hope."

Hope continued,

"Jerry Colonna is one of my three original Gypsies; Frances and Tony Romano, our guitarist, standing there, hands in his pockets, being the other two. You may have seen my pal, Professor Jerry Colonna, in 'Naughty But Nice,' made in 1939, and 'Sis Hopkins,' the year later. His trademarks are wide, rolling, bulgy eyes, those plus his walrus mustache and bellowing opera-lampooning voice. If we perform before the Navy, he dresses as a sailor. If we appear before the Army, he dresses as a soldier; then the Air Force, he's a pilot. That's how loyal he is. He's one with all the armed forces. He's a great entertainer, a better comic actor than I am. He was so bulgy-eyed in my movie 'Road To Singapore,' made in 1940, and Crosby's 'Star Spangled Rhythm,' that Bing asked if he buy could those eyes. Everyone loves them! Wait until you see them at work this afternoon!"

"Tony is special. He's been with me the longest. He arranges all the music, and accompanies our singers when you boys request various songs. He knows them all. He's only 29 and, as a guitarist, he can play jazz as well as classical, new or ancient. Tony is our musical sideman, a more loyal man you could never find. Because he loves me so much he works cheap, and I take advantage of it."

"Jack Culpepper, the homely one over there, is the oldest of the lot. He's 41, and performed as a dancer, singer, radio comedian. He teamed with Ginger Rodgers as a dancer, then had the gall to marry her. Their team was known as 'Ginger and Pepper'. Like 'The Professor', he was in our 'Road to Singapore' and with Bing in 'Rhythm on the River' and Crosby asked him if he could have Ginger. Cul popped him on the nose. You think you can ski down mine? Try his new slope!"

"Barney Dean, standing next to me, is 'my man Friday'. He's 40 and a gag writer. Some of his stuff is good. He was writing for Crosby, got bored with his crooning, and joined me. He broke into show biz as a dancer in minstrels, vaudevilles, and was in my 1941 movie, 'Louisiana Purchase' where he embarrassed everyone because he couldn't take his eyes off Vera Zorina, my co-star. He can't get her out of his system. Walked around in tears. His other problem is that he hates flying in PBY's Catalina Flying Boats. Throws up all the time."

With that, the troupe waved and the men and officers of the 1st Division welcoming committee howled and spontaneously applauded. Then, with everyone mingling about and talking to the Hope performers, General Rupertus asked "Stash" Colonna,

"How was your flight coming in on the Piper?"

The "Professor" answered,

"The Cubs we came in on apparently are used by the Army for spotting Jap artillery. This was fine with us as long as the enemy knew we were just visitors. After riding in that bouncy PBY, the Cub seemed so slow it would just hang up in the sky and rock in the slipstream made by the seagulls whizzing by. It gives you the feeling that you're riding a kite with no strings attached."

"Mother" Langford, with her bright, endearing smile, added,

"Waiting for us on the beach waving were at least 18,000 Marines, all veterans of Guadalcanal, I was told in my plane, veterans also from the fighting on Munda and Bougainville."

"Yeah," added Colonna, "my pilot told me that the Marines below us on the beach had gathered on landing crafts which had been drawn up from Banika, and other islands. The riggings and every vantage point on the ships were filled with hundreds of men."

Patty Thomas chimed in, to the delight of the circle of Marines around Colonna and Langford, "In my Cub, we circled low, including our Corsair and P.38 escorts, and buzzed them a couple of times before being set down on that rocky road over there near the baseball field and stage area near the beach."

Colonna interjected," . . . and the pilot I was riding with yelled, 'Okay, pile out!' I answered, 'Out?' I've been out since the first bump back at Henderson Field.'"

Patty chimed back in again, "It was a rough landing. Bob shouted to me a moment after landing,

'Fancy meeting you here! You'd think Pavuvu airport could afford a better waiting room than a parking lot with no buildings.' "

"As for me," smiled Colonna, "I hope no one starts throwing rotten coconuts, if he doesn't like our routine."

"Well, Gypsies, let's go see Pavuvu, with the emphasis on 'P U' warned the boys back at Guadalcanal when we told them we were coming here today."

Rupertus said, "Throwing coconuts will get a Marine a month in the brig. It's serious business around here. This past spring, two of our boys assigned to cleaning them out of the swampy area were killed when they were hit on the head by natural falling coconuts."

Hope responded,

"We're used to troops throwing things at us; believe me, general. Even their shoes and boots."

"Have your audiences always thrown things at you while performing?" asked Assistant Commander Shepherd, a twinkle in his eye.

"Yes, sir, and Thank God they did, especially in my early years. I wouldn't have had anything to eat if it wasn't for the stuff the audience threw at me."

With the young Marines from the military police security detachment, drivers' pool, and Piper Cut pilot unit lining up before Bob Hope, Jerry Colonna and Frances Langford for autographs, virtually everyone talking at once, ignoring Patty Thomas, Tony Romano, Barney Dean and Jack Culpepper, the day suddenly turned dark gray and within moments as the Pavuvu installations, facilities and palm groves began looking unusually bleak and ill-tented, it started to sprinkle.

"The shower's nothing, certainly drenching, but fast-moving. What I fear for your show is the inferno that is certain to arrive in the next half hour," said Chief of Staff Sims.

"Inferno? What inferno?" asked Colonna. "Japs are not invited. If so, I'm going home."

"The increasing tropical heat, the blowing tropical sand and the biggest pain in the a-double-s there is--the tropical torridity, the hot moisture, or humidity," responded Sims.

While Hope, Colonna, and Langford chitchatted, gossiped, and talked idly with the men, they scrawled away their autographs. Meanwhile, the six Cub pilots, and six drivers of the staff cars prepared their engines for departure. As the drivers pulled the cars around, the Piper Cubs began taxiing toward the narrow road for departure to the Banika Airfield for a late evening flight back to Henderson Field on Guadalcanal. Major General Rupertus had ordered them to do so since Peter, with an armed vehicular escort, was to drive the Hope entourage over to the Banika amphitheater for the evening performance.

Soon, all staff officers and entertainers were climbing into the cars and making themselves comfortable. The tropical shower ended and the early afternoon sun burst through the cloud cover. Inside their respective staff cars, everyone fastened their seat belt. One after the other, the cars were driven down the road of the airstrip to a side road that led directly to the baseball field which would serve as the Pavuvu amphitheater. Marines here were already pouring onto the field, finding for themselves whatever seating pleased them. In certain stretches, the drivers slowed down to less than 15 mph, peering through the thick Jeep windshield. Peter, marveling at the banter, was in a perfect position to observe Hope sitting in the front seat next to the driver. He sat in the back seat next to the window with Rupertus between him and Shepherd next to the far window.

"Well, Mr. Hope," smiled General Rupertus, "if you and your troupe choose to remain overnight on the island of Banika rather than return to Henderson Field on Guadalcanal, you'll be given V.I.P. rooms at my general headquarters, rooms for each of you with fresh sheets, new blankets on actual beds instead of used cots. Plus, as V.I.P.s, each of you can take a 'real bath', not having to use helmets as your washbasins. Now, I'll be on the same second floor as you, and available at any time of the night or morning. If you want to talk with someone here on Pavuvu, the hook-up is done manually by telephonists sitting in front of switchboards 24 hours a day in the three 8 hour shifts. Only one line is available on this island, down the hall from my office."

"Well, we'll see, general. The standby pilots can find lodging on Pavuvu?"

"Why, of course!"

"I'll let you know halfway through the performance."

During the 20 minute journey to the Pavuvu baseball field, no faster than 15 to 20 miles per hour, the conversation was primarily between Bob Hope and Major General Rupertus, with Peter, the driver, and Assistant General Commander Shepherd absorbing every word. The comedian was somber as he showed an amazing acumen regarding both theaters of war.

"We're already agreed, the seven of us. If we all go down together, we're certain we're going to Heaven together to perform before all the religions of the universe. That's why we've done benefits for all religions, starting five years ago. We decided that by doing all religions, we wouldn't blow the Hereafter on a technicality, having missed, or ignored, a religion. And, no matter where I am entertaining the troops, and I'm killed there, somebody or other will ask me,

'Where do you want to be buried?'"

"I answer, 'Surprise me.'"

"We will! We will!" laughed Rupertus. "Did you hear that all organized resistance on Guadalcanal is ceased as of this morning?"

"No! That's good news. I also heard on Guadalcanal this morning that Tinian was declared secure last week. By the July 4th last month, I heard our troop strength in the Pacific reached 475,000, which included 33,000 officers and 443,000 enlisted men and women. How are we going to lose this war with manpower like that?"

As the comedian and the commander bantered back and forth with Marine Corps campaign chronologies since February 1st, 1942, Peter enjoyed sizing Hope up.

"And for all four of you here with me now, please get the word out how much the Marines on Pavuvu meant to me less than an hour ago. You see, these two shows we're doing today, one here now, and the other back on Banika tonight, aren't on the schedule. Our little band of

Gypsies flew over here in those model toy airplanes; the cute Piper Cubs, because the recreation coach over there asked if we wouldn't mind the extra show. You provide an audience of our fighting boys, even if we have to go to Purgatory, then Hell, we'll go."

"Well, we were told your 1st Marine Division men were preparing for the invasion of the Palau Islands. That's all we needed to hear. We were coming over here, even if it meant the show was scheduled at 3:00am. On our short flight to your landing strip road, we buzzed the baseball field next to the beach, rapidly filling up with young fellas from all over the island. Imagine, six Piper Cubs, all in a row, circling the baseball field, tripping our wings to say 'Hello, you lucky fellas! We're here, and we're going to make you giggle and laugh."

"Well, buzzing that stadium with 16,000 guys looking up, cheering, and waving at each plane then flying toward the landing strip road is by far the most exciting thing that has happened so far on my USO tour, in Europe and North Africa, and the Pacific - - probably even the whole war. My pilot said as many as 40% of the men waving and cheering will never be seen again. I'm sure the other 60% I'll see again in the recovery hospitals stateside, such as the new, modern one in Oakland, California. On Banika this morning, just before we flew over here, we visited the guys in its hospital. The wall behind one fella's bed, a recovering veteran from Guadalcanal, had so many pinups of Betty Grable, and now Patty Thomas and Frances Langford, on the wall the land crabs and mosquitos were drooling. Another guy had only pinups of Betty Grable. Many were duplicates. You know the one I mean, her back to you, as she turns her head with a wicked smile and gleam in her eye. Every American fighting man, no matter where he is in the world, has the same photo on the wall or in his helmet. Who can resist an a-double-s like that? I said to him, 'Don't you know Betty

Grable is married to Harry James, the band leader and famous trumpeter?' The wounded Marine answered, 'Who cares? After the war, we're going to kill all the buglers anyway. Especially, the early morning ones!"

As Peter listened and watched, he rapidly came to the conclusion that Bob was a genuinely an affable man, approachable and sincere. Because of his fame and wealth, the comedian was not a "stuck-up". His legend was justified. While treating throngs of troops to laughter, he was gracious, kind and generous with his time. In 1941, even before World War II broke out, he received an Oscar "for humanity". It was no accident or whim that he was the first entertainer to perform for the armed forces.

And, he was as fearless as he was tireless. The fact that two USO performers, including the popular Tamara, were killed in a Lisbon Clipper airline accident en route to perform at a Mediterranean base, was non-deterring. Everyone enjoyed his gags, the endless ad-libbing, his timing, and coordination of vaudeville pantomime. Peter believed the comedian when he said, "When I get home one of these days, my kids will think I'm been booked there on a personal appearance tour", and "When this war ends, it'll be an awful letdown for me personally."

"No," thought Peter, "it's impossible to dislike him, on the radio, the screen, the stage. He's himself, real, a kindly man with a soft heart, which makes him all the more endearing. He's one of America's great treasures, and he's here in this car, with me assigned to guard his life from the Mad Ghoul."

Suddenly, from far in the rear at the intersection where the dirt landing strip road met the long roundabout side dirt road leading to the baseball stadium temporarily converted into the day's amphitheater, a heavy roar could be heard rapidly approaching. Emitted from an armored three-seat reconnaissance vehicle with an open top racing after them, the roll and rumble of the accelerating noise was accentuated by a horn blasting violently.

As everyone in the general's lead staff car, including Hope himself, turned their heads to see who was chasing them, the cyclist waved for the driver to slow down, then pull up.

"Urgent dispatch, urgent from general headquarters at Banika. Dispatch! Stop!!"

As Rupertus' car abruptly skidded to a halt, the brakes screeching loudly, the cyclist of the scout car pulled ahead by 10 or 15 yards, then kicked the foot brake, parking the vehicle in the middle of the narrow pounded earth and coral road, blocking further movement in both directions.

"Did you see that? How the driver handled the three-seater?" asked Shepherd, amazed. "He was ripping it, wasn't he? Zipping past us, skidding on the crushed dirt-coral, bouncing into the air, while in total control passing us, then cockily planting the scout car in front of us so we can't move forward or backward. Who is that guy?"

"Crosby evading one of his Internal Revenue Service tax collectors," quipped Hope.

Removing his goggles, the driver stepped from his driver's seat and stood silently next to his vehicle for a long moment, peeing long and hard at the squad car's front window.

"My God," Hope exclaimed as everyone in the staff car sat in stunned silence. "Is that a .45 sagging at his right hip, or could it be his…"

Even Rupertus had to smile, as the others in the car, including the driver, chuckled knowingly.

"I think it's 'Old Clodhopper', Del Barbra's favorite MP now assigned to the second shift guarding headquarters on Banika," smiled Shepherd.

"Yup," responded Rupertus. "Clodhopper is the biggest, most massive, almost jauntily conceited MP in the whole South Pacific. Right now, the way he's approaching us, I'd say he's aggressively self-confident."

Peter, unusually quiet being the lowest ranking officer in the staff car that afternoon, spoke up.

"I know him. A good MP, in fact, one of the toughest we have here. But he's usually stone-cold calm. Now his eyes are bristling with anger, even disgust. Something is up, General."

Old Clodhopper, handsome in a heavy fashion, a bearing of mannerisms that boasted he appreciated himself very much, reflected by his carefully groomed coal-black hair, close-cropped and wavy, slowly walked up to the driver's window and motioned for the driver to roll it down.

"Commander Rupertus, I have an urgent confidential communiqué form General Headquarters, Banika. For your eyes only, although permission is granted to share it with proper staff."

With that, he stretched through the car window and handed the major general an envelope. Rupertus reached across Peter and accepted it. With that, cyclist Clodhopper saluted. Turning, he trotted back to his scout car, swung himself into the driver's seat, kicked the handbrake off, and started the ignition, triggering the engine to throb jumpily. After a sputter or two, the fast, armored reconnaissance open-topped vehicle turned around, and roared back the way it came.

Meanwhile, Rubertus ripped the confidential envelope open and read the single sheet of buff-colored paper. As Hope chatted with

Assistant Commander Shepherd, Peter studied Rupertus' facial expression as he read the contents. His face was ashen and contorted, his eye softening into narrow slits. With his mouth slightly open and ajar, his lips appeared crusted. He attempted to clear his throat, which resulted in an unintelligible hoarse whisper.

Eyes now wide, sitting upright, staring out his side window, the Commander of the 1st Division tried again, speaking to no one in particular.

"In a linen closet, far back of the Banika hospital in the hall behind Operation Room 2, Nurse Marguerite Chapman, who, disappeared near the end of her third shift. Everyone believed she returned to her room and bed ill. They just found her in a corner of that obscure room behind boxes stabbed to death, frontally, drenching in her own blood."

CHAPTER SEVENTEEN

-

The Happiest (and Hottest) Potty in the Pacific

After a stunned silence, Rupertus ordered the driver to proceed on to the stadium amphitheater. Then, he leaned forward and asked,

"Bob, you've heard of our trouble?"

"All Banika is talking about us."

"And, yet you stay with it?"

"Of course. There won't be any gags, wisecracks, jokes, witticism, or quips, if I can get my hands on his throat," Hope answered solemnly, staring straight ahead, teeth clenching.

Again, a brief silence. Then, the commander of the 1st Division said softly,

"Few men have earned my admiration for kindness, ability, and courage. You are one of the three I've encountered in my lifetime. God Bless you, Bob Hope."

Rupertus glanced across from him at Peter and Shepherd, then added, "A copy of the note the Ghoul pinned to Miss Chapman's breast was included in the dispatch envelope. Read it out loud, Peter."

The young Lieutenant accepted the envelope and retrieved the note. It read,

"Hail Commander General Rupertus - - grieving over you and the droll jester begins before midnight, twilight to the very dark; courtesy of an anomalous Mad Ghoul Marine. What a piece man is who relishes murder. A very odd creation. Neither animal, who knows not how to murder, nor the earth's outer reach inhabitant who has no word for it, I am human, one of the supposed civilized of the civilized, and therefore capable of unimaginable horror. What a wonderful mystery I am, enjoying the pain in your eyes as my shiny blade plunges to your bone this night."

Without comment, Peter and Shepherd perused the murder note. Peter noticed the grim expression on Hope's face as he handed the Ghoul's murder message back to the major general who, continuing to look straight ahead, was still sitting bolt upright.

As the small caravan of six staff cars and security guard motorcycles following from behind entered a clearing that had once been a coconut grove behind left field of the Pavuvu baseball stadium now serving as the temporary site for the afternoon's performance, Rupertus, calmly, commented,

"Three months ago, this island began an amazing transformation overnight, from unworked plantations of rotting coconuts to a thriving military seaport. Under Seabee guidance, the Pioneer Battalion of our 1st Division did virtually all the construction. The field we're coming up to was leveled in less than two days. Now, it's covered with a thick grassy turf where our boys play baseball on a diamond; football; rugby; on a real field; and even soccer. As we drive to the parking area behind the small grandstand, and the facility to change in, you'll see how we built a boxing ring, handball court, volleyball area, bowling alley, and basketball court adjacent to it. We're so sports-minded it pays off both in combat and rehabilitation, we of the 1st are renowned for our athletics program. We engage in regiment-sized competitions against Army, Navy, and Seabee Teams. And, I might add, we always win."

Hope, with his eyes wide, could hardly believe that suddenly he was in the middle of a mass of Marine humanity. With perhaps more than 20,000 assorted troops at leisure waiting for the performance to begin, the amphitheater was a noisy, restless, thriving center of agitated combustible activity.

Level as a plate of glass window or a wooden tabletop, the huge field stretched to the edges of a short rise, which then, in a carpet of green-grey-brown vegetation, slumped down to the cold channel water separating the two islands.

At the far end where the hastily constructed makeshift stage had been built, the view of the channel, beaches, and beyond the Pacific was partially blocked at the neck of the wide basin by small tents, tent houses, and minor metal huts. One was conspicuous because it was so pretentious, having been painted blood red and trimmed in white. Gingerbread architectural moldings and projections serving as showy and tawdry decorations painted in light pink adored the doors and windows.

The building, a new officers' latrine painted in the bizarre colors with the grotesque ornaments, was designed by a Seabee sergeant as a practical joke. His explanation,

"Low level USMC officers are known to have difficulty finding privies, thereby winding up messing themselves. My color combination will guide them to the proper pee hole."

As Hope listened to the explanation, he laughed aloud,

"Exactly the kind of explanation I would offer . . . if I didn't like the Marines."

Everyone laughed, General Rupertus the loudest.He added, "We've come to love that little 'pee hole'. Truth of it was that he was being facetious. Those colors were the only paint colors the Seabees had in the Solomons. We also liked the wooden structure because it had two back doors leading to a small channel beach that's private and quiet."

After a long silence during which the staff cars wound their way through the multitude rushing to the caravan and surrounding it, applauding and cheering, Peter addressed the comedian who was thoroughly, deeply engrossed enjoying the spectacle,

"Mr. Hope, as General Rupertus mentioned earlier, I've been assigned to linger and over you throughout your stay on this island. I am not to leave your side regardless. You are free to perform, eat, nap, and relieve yourself, but only with me at your side. Not for an instant are you to be out of my actual eyesight. And this at the risk of court-martialed. While you are on stage, I'm to be no less than 25 feet from you."

And, Peter, at the risk of insulting Mr. Hope, thereby incurring the wrath of the Commander of the 1st Division, couldn't help himself,

" . . . and should you wish to engage in intimacy with one of... "

"All right, lieutenant," laughed Rupertus, Shepherd and Hope.

"Sorry, sir, couldn't help myself."

"Hey, no issue with any of that, including the 'intimacy' part. What you'll really enjoy," exclaimed Hope with a wide grin, "is being present when I relieve myself. Even mom objected to that. She complained she always had to wear a gas mask when she changed my diapers. The first words I heard while being born were, 'Just look at the sizes of his yuck-a-do's. God, what did you bless me with? And their smell! We could have won World War I in the first days, if we had a smell like that bottled and released at the front. Churchill told me he heard about the smell when Parliament began debate for its use in the House of Commons after that fateful May 29, 1903, day in Eltham, London."

Everyone giggled.

"But in all seriousness, lieutenant, I'd love to meet and then be left along with that son - - - for a minute or two. Don't forget I was born with timing and coordination. That's what makes me a great, great comedian. But I was born with no looks, except a ski-slide nose, with no personality, no courage or bravery, no ability to write, no special speaking gift, no art for pantomime, and no character."

"But the timing and coordination helped me in the prize fighting ring. I learned how to fight in a house of six brothers with only one bathroom. We didn't stand in line. We fought it out. The winner went first. But I will say that having one toilet and six brothers, plus mom needing to use it, taught me how to dance."

"Were you much of a prizefighter?" asked Shepherd.

"Not bad. I'll prove it, if you turn the son - - - over to me. I learned the skill of punching and art of the knockout at Charlie Marotta's Athletics Club on 79th Street in New York. I wanted to enter the featherweight division of the Ohio State Amateur Boxing Matches with my best friend, Whitey Jennings, under the name of Packy East. I was certain my fists fit the ring. I won my first official fight with a lucky punch, when the other guy turned to ask the other corner for advice. Then, in my second fight, I faced a more seasoned fighter. He made a quick end of my career in the first round. It was also an abrupt end of my two fists. But, I'll take them out of cold storage for Mr. Mad Ghoul."

"Then you went into showbiz?" asked Rupertus.

"Oh, something like that. I always had a touch of hankering for the burlesque music hall, vaudeville. When I was born, the doctor said to my mother, 'Congratulations, you have an eight pound ham'. And, when mom felt the sizes and smells of my 'yuck-a-do's' she said, "he's proven by this he's slated for showbiz and stardom.

"And I'll say one last thing on the subject. Jack Benny is always bugging me for a turd lump to place around his money under his bed.

'Why pay a bank to guard my cash when no one will get near your smell?'"

Outright laughter rocked the staff car as it entered the edge of the outskirts of the open field. Meanwhile, hundreds of Marines dressed in the A-1 class khaki shirts and pants and caps, all starched, pressed, and neatly folded, with shoes just polished, hurried for bench seats cut from trunks of palm trees, or the long rows of sandbags to sit upon. Fortunately, the earlier showers hadn't affected the baseball field-amphitheater, other than leaving behind puddles and mud. Hope smiled broadly at a glimpse of the huge mass of men already seated, the wounded who could walk and amble from the Pavuvu hospital commingling with staff officers on comfortable cushioned chairs.

Then, skirting the edge of left field, the commander's car in the lead of the small caravan proceeded cautiously through arriving Marines toward the back to the temporary stage that had been constructed atop home plate. Among the hundreds of grinning soldiers seeking places to sit, Peter recognized innumerable men he knew, as they in turn saluted Commander Rupertus and acknowledged Bob Hope with thumbs up, cheering, and otherwise hooting it up.

Parking in an area behind the makeshift stage, no more than a roofless platform now roofed with a stretched waterproof double-canvased tarpaulin, Peter, upon climbing out of the staff car alongside of Hope, saw a hodge-podge of 16 square foot tents, small Quonset huts, and other recently constructed structures, all connected by wooden plank walkways because of Pavuvu's eternal seepage and mud.

Although several latrines accommodating large numbers of Marines were positioned around the open field, only one medium-sized privy with three urinals and twelve stalls was available for the officer staff. It was a red-painted framework with two small windows at each end. As elsewhere around the field and stage, red, white and blue bunting decorated the facility. Above the entrance was a permanent large sign that read, "All USMC Officers Wash Their Hands After Handling Danger." A second sign, leaning against the outside wall next to the entrance, recently painted with perfect lettering, black on grey, read, "Make Us Laugh, Bob, Make Us Laugh."

The area was familiar to Peter. Recently, he had joined the 1st Division 'Mudhens' softball team. With a sidelong glance, he noticed Chaplain Pinoe, laughing alongside Jerry Colonna, as the others of the troupe exited their staff cars. Remaining by Hope's side, Peter waved, and motioned Pinoe over. As Hope engaged in conversation with a number of officers while Commander Rupertus looked on, Pinoe led Colonna through the mingling crowd to Peter's side.

"I just asked 'the Professor', or 'the Mustache' ", said Pinoe with his excited lisp, "if that was him when his Piper Cub circled the field, and the pilot switched off his engine for a few moments. Someone put his head out the window of the plane and screamed a famous cry,

'Yee-oww-oww-oww-oww!'

"You weren't here, but our men already here went crazy with laughter, cheers, applause, hollering and... "

At that point, Colonna, tweaking, pinching and twisting his mustache, said,

"What's wrong with that? I say hello to everyone that way."

Just then, Captain Del Barbra and Sergeant Guidi shoved their way through the crowd and approached Toscanini and the others.

"All is well, I presume," he said laughingly. "I'm very pleased you were selected, lieutenant, to watch over our honored guest."

"Thanks, Captain. I truly appreciate that compliment. Meet Bob Hope and Jerry Colonna. That's Barney Dean over there, Bob's gag-writer. The other fellow is Tony Romano, Bob's guitarist."

"And, both my best chums out here... " smiled the comedian.

"Well, Mr. Hope, welcome! We certainly hope the 113-degree heat and humidity don't bother you. Our men are so appreciative, as much, if not more so, than our officers. Men started arriving here by late morning as the rumor of you coming over here spread like wildfire. You saw them on the channel beach by the thousands waiting for the Pipers to fly over. They knew the direction from which you would come, your flyover route. And, they started assembling on the beach over there at 1100. We estimate that at least 80% of all the Marines on Banika and Pavuvu are out there waiting for you."

Serious for a moment, Hope placed his hand on Captain Del Barbra's shoulder, and glancing at Rupertus and Shepherd, said quietly,

"I'm sure it will be one of the most pleasant memories I'll have in this war . . . now, let me on that stage!"

Rupertus waved for two Marines each carrying a 5' by 6' signboard to walk over and positioned themselves before Hope and himself. One board posted read, "First in the hearts of all servicemen," the other, "The Bob Hope Show."

Smiling, Rupertus glanced at the comedian, who he saw was beaming from broadly, and said,

"These two fellas with their signs will go first. The Marine band, our own 1st Division boys, is seated and awaiting the signal to play your theme song, 'Thanks For the Memory'. When they start playing that, we'll follow the sign-carriers and we'll stop under the huge marquee hanging from the roof over the stage that reads, 'Hiya, Bob!' You'll step forward with me and I'll say a few words of introduction and when the huge acclamation that's sure to come simmers down, I'll hand you the microphone. By the way, I'm sure that sooner or later, you'll have to pee. Remember, and I'm very strict and will hold you to it, you are not to do so unless Lieutenant Toscanini is at your side, watching every dribble. Are we in agreement, absolute, total agreement?"

Hope, realizing the sincere solemnity of the commander's tone, nodded appreciatively.

"O.K. Shepherd, signal the band and we'll go, twos following twos, me and Bob, first, Peter, and Shepherd, second; then two women next, Patty and Frances following, etc."

As Shepherd started toward the steps leading to the bandstand, Chief of Staff Sims broke into the surrounding observing crowd, raised his hand, and asked,

"Commander, can we hold off for a few minutes? The final contingent of our headquarters personnel and hospital nurses not on duty are headed this way in a dozen trucks as we speak. They've just been waved across the pontoon bridge. Less than 15 minutes, I'd say. It'd be nice if they could see the performance from the beginning... "

Rupertus glanced at Hope, eyebrows up. Hope nodded, "It'll allow us a few moments to become acquainted with your cute little red outhouse."

The major general smiled, then asked Shepherd if he would take the stage and "Tell the boys we're waiting for the Banika crowd to arrive. Less than 10 minutes, that's all."

Then, the commander turned to Peter, "Lieutenant, take me, Hope in tow, and the Miss Langford and Miss Thomas, as well as the others, and introduce them to our price and job, yonder. Since there are no facilities for women, they should use it first, followed by their leader.

Quickly. We begin in 15 minutes, whether the staff is here or not. Make certain our sentries assigned there are up to the task. No one is to enter when anyone of this team is in there. When the nurses get here from Banika, I'll assign one or two to stay with the ladies."

Sims added,

"I had a cleaning crew in there this morning scrubbing the dinginess and dampness out of the crappy officers' toilets."

Amid the ongoing whirlwind of activity and emotion going on behind the stage, including chanting, hooting, and hollering of the impatient thousands in the waiting audience, to say nothing of the arriving Banika trucks, and their disembarkation of administrative personnel and hospital nurses, Peter led the way. He turned toward Hope, with the rest of the procession following, and said,

"It might be painted an embarrassing red, but the officer's latrine is better than anything I've used in the South Pacific. No mildew, I'm told, between the tile cracks. Rupertus says that while he's in charge, there will be no 'potty hells' for any of his men, officers or not."

While the Hope group quickly rotated turns in and out of the facility, the comic, first one in and first one out, stood outside the wooden frame structure with Peter. Meanwhile, several musicians exited the last trucks to arrive, and, with their stringed instruments, started to hasten toward the bandstand. Hope, seeing them, cupped his hands over his head and waved, shouting,

"Thanks, fellas! You all make us feel real welcome. After this damnable war is over, and you are back home, we'll form a band and call it 'The Boys from Pavuvu - - A Band of Exotics In A Sea of Rolling Coconut Trees'! Yes, sir, men! We'll recruit the Big 'C', Crosby, as our featured coconut."

Everyone cheered, causing the waiting audience to chant,

"Bob Hope! Bob Hope! Bob Hope!"

"Well, general, we better hop on stage. My crew is ready, and I've been ready since I was born and where and when I was present."

As the troupe trooped up the steps of the bandstand, the lieutenant honoring his assignment's every step, Peter heard his name being called out,

"Peter! Peter Toscanini! Lieutenant Toscanini!"

It was Ellen! And, with her, was William Lundigan! And behind them was Dr. Schneidermann, the 1st Division psychiatrist.

"Wow! You three! Wonderful sight. So happy you came. Take the first three chairs in the first row by the steps there. I have to remain close to Hope. I've been assigned to be his 'bodyguard'. Stay nearby, so I can catch you up on what's going on. I want you to meet Hope, but I can't take my eyes of him, fearing the Ghoul will strike, if he is given the chance."

As the commander and the comedian led the short two-by-two procession up the steps of the bandstand and onto the stage, the phonograph records' recordings of Glen Miller, Harry James, the Andrew Sisters, among others, diminished in volume.

Suddenly, with Rupertus stepping away as the Marine band leader handed Hope the microphone, "Thanks For the Memory", the comic's signature theme song from the 1938 musical comedy, "The Big Broadway of 1938" which won the Academy Award for best movie song of that year, was played by the band.

Over 20,000 Marines and supporting staff who had been waiting patiently in the pure, white light of Pavuvu's shimmering August heat and humidity, broke into unmitigated applause, cheers, shouting, and other assorted hoopla. Peter, relishing the loud moment, thought to himself,

"Here's a world-famous man dressed in ordinary baggy trousers with a thin open-neck collared shirt, wearing argyle diamond-patterned knitted socks, a punster with an illimitable intrinsic sensibility of the humorous performing in torridity's sweat, risking his life before so many, including the Mad Ghoul, who is surely observing out there to prepare to murder him in the blackness of nightfall. Bob is a model of youthful spirit, with good-nature in his eyes that squint joy and eagerness, as he sees all our men! He is truly a delight, on the stage as he was in our sedan, in the staff car as he is now. Himself, true to the bone. Nothing false or fancy. Just real wherever he is."

Then, as the final phrases and verses of "Thanks for the Memory" drew to a close, a rapid succession of light, playful pitter-patter and teasing began.

"Hiya, boys. You know me, the vaudevillian wanderlust, Bob 'Mosquito Net' Hope, hopping from island to island with you, until we all land on Tokyo together, the huge sign hanging from the ceiling over my head that reads, 'Hiya Bob' should read 'Hiya boys! Thank you for making the Japs take it on the lam....' This afternoon's performance is part of the 'Somewhere in the South Pacific show of the Art of Living Series aired over the NBC Affiliates. Everything from this point on will be impromptu."

"Boys, before I properly introduce you to my Gypsies, first the girls with legs and other alluring appendages and accouterments that you're fighting so fiercely for, then the altar boys, Big Beautiful Moustache Colonna, and the other brave knights who watch over them, including the homely kid on the block, Tony Romano, guitarist, I'd like to take a few minutes to tell you how it is we all happen to be here waiting to be murdered by a murdering-mad lunatic Marine."

"And, by the way, if you're out there, in all seriousness, give yourself up. You don't want to hurt any of your buddies anymore. Why? You're just temporarily off-track, plodding away to kill good American boys. We all wander from the course. We don't go around killing our brothers, our friends, our own. You do, and, because of that, you need help. Just walk up to the nearest MP or high-ranking officer and say, 'It's me. Stop me from hurting another fellow Marine.'"

"Okay, that said, let me go on for a few moments about how we got here this afternoon. When this war started, me and my Gypsies, sometimes five or six or seven, if you count me, under the auspices of the USO got involved as often and as much and as best we could. And since then we've been bombed, strafed, shot at by snipers, and generally cussed out on the battlefield, from North Africa, across Sicily and Italy, and now the South Pacific. We've been cold in Alaska, foggy in England, hot in Egypt. But none of us would trade a second of those happy times. And besides, we love the applause. But wherever you are, the Hope Vaudeville Circus will be ready to make you laugh. Out here, it'll be known as the 'Pineapple Circuit'. Same laughs, but more women, more legs, more . . . well, you know what I mean. Occasionally, in between, we'll make a musical feature film comedy or two, and say funny words on the radio. Now, you guys here in the Pacific are our focus."

"Along the way from island to island, we heard of you boys training for the past six months, on this tiny island for the invasion of some island you never heard of. We heard that you were all but forgotten, that you hadn't seen a movie star for over a year when Gary Cooper came by to say 'Hello'."

"It seemed to us the islands were getting smaller and smaller, the Marine crowds larger and larger, the Japs closer and closer. Then we hit the island next door, Bonika, or Banika. As we prepared to perform, the 1st Division recreation sergeant asked me if I'd take the Gypsies to Pa-poop-poop-u, or whatever the hell the name of this wanna-be . . . piece of sh - - is, this dot of crab crap, that's not even on the map. He started to beg, 'there are almost 17,000 guys over there and they need to laugh. They're forgotten. They don't know how to laugh anymore. They've had no entertainment. Please go see them!'."

"Can they wait another 10 minutes?" I asked. "I'll round up my people. You get the plane or cars ready and we'll go now!"

He laughed and said, 'The island has no airstrip, meaning we'll have to land on a road of crushed sea rocks. It's not that dangerous, yet it is a bit dangerous. Do you still want to go?'

'Is Crosby there?' I asked.

'No, of course not. Pavuvu is nothing but a swamp, a cesspool, a hellhole of rotting coconuts.' He said you would fit right in since you always smell something decomposing."

'Is it a good place to hide from my draft board?'

'Mr. Hope, even the snakes can't find it. The Japs had it and said they'd rather lose the war than live on it.'

'Then we'll go. We'll give those forgotten boys the best show we have yet given on our tour.'"

"Well, as it turned out, we'd had to wait until today to come over. All six Piper Cubs had to be flown from Henderson on Guadalcanal to Bonica or Banika, whatever that damned island is named. All I can tell you, men, before we start, is that seeing you by the thousands cheering on the beach over there as we flew in, seeing you on this baseball field, cheering as we buzzed over twice, low enough so that we could see you looking up with your smiles, made us want to be here even more. My God, what we wouldn't do for you guys!"

For Peter, the introduction was one of the most exhilarating presentations and remarkable sights of his life. Smiling, Bill Lundigan, sitting next to him, elbowed his friend. Dog-legged from his mesmeric trance, the lieutenant glanced past his best friend and noted Ellen next to him, followed by Dr. Schneidermann, Captain Del Barbra, Sergeant Guidi, Assistant Commander Shepherd, Major General Rupertus, and Chaplain Pinoe. All his friends, all chuckling, giggling, tittering, and outright laughing until tears filled their eyes, were there in the first row adjacent the stairs on the side of the bandstand.

Then, as Bob Hope began the show's impromptu patter, the one-liners, the introductions of all his Gypsies, the gags, jokes and songs, a hint of discord seemed to creep into and disturb Peter's mental equanimity. Usually, Peter showed himself as capable, self-reliant and confident. Now, as he watched and listened to the performance, some vague imminence seized him. His marvelous self-control was weakening and a troubling anxiety seized his mind. Despite the mass of men in the audience behind him, and his colleagues and associates, all armed with .45 caliber automatics holstered at their sides, Peter slowly descended into a mild depression, a return to an earlier unidentified apprehension, a foreboding of danger, toward himself and those around him he loved. But of what? Certainly, he felt a presentiment of impending peril as he grinned saturningly at what Hope was saying on stage.

Sitting silently, preoccupied with Hope's every movement, his lip stiff, face rigid, and sullen, eyes coldly piercing, Peter only heard the final words of a long one-liner, " . . . want to put me into mass production." As everyone roared with laughter, clapping, hooting, and hollering, Peter steely agreed, the mass production of a kind, generous man, the absolute antithesis of a murder - mad Ghoul spinning death over everyone. And, amid the few moments of fun and joy, what better place than to spoil it all, in the open and in the daylight, than with a famous murder or two? Why wait until midnight to kill, in the blackness of night, unseen?

Riddled with such questions, Peter could only brace himself for the rest of the day's events. But, somehow, it wasn't the thought that the afternoon performance would be the perfect scene for the murder that made him uneasy. He was unnerved because of something he noticed, or what someone said in the last few days. But what? And, by whom?And, why? The Ghoul was certainly an officer, a recognizable with bars and stripes that allowed the Ka-Bar to rise within inches and plunge into his heart and chest. Who? And what was said?

Meanwhile, Frances Langford was on stage a few feet in front of Hope beginning to sing, "I'm In The Mood For Love."

"I'm in the mood for love
Simply because you're near me
Funny, but when you're near me
I'm in the mood for love... "
"Heaven is in your eyes
Bright as the stars we're under
Oh! Is it any wonder
I'm in the mood for love?"
"Why stop to think of whether
This little dream might fade
We've put our hearts together
Now, we are one, I'm not afraid"
"If there's a cloud above
If it should rain we'll let it

But for tonight, forget it!
I'm in the mood for love!"

Just then, a young Marine in the second row jumped up, his cap clutched in his hand, ran into the main aisle, and up to the stage before Frances, and with arms held wide open, shouted.

"You've come to the right place, honey!"

The thunderous clamor that followed lasted a full minute, Hope, Colonna, Langford, Thomas, and the others on stage, including the members of the Marine band, buckled over in uncontrollable laughing convulsions. Peter, too, had difficulty maintaining his composure, laughing so hard.

Hope's show that afternoon promised to be no more, and no less, no better or no worse, than any of the hundreds he had performed since 1942 in England, North Africa, Sicily, and Italy. It would be held impromptu, and with no preparation, not that it would suggest a casualness, or offhandedness. Each rendition of it would be based upon the success of the preceding one, not in a studied manner, but a reflective one.Months earlier, Hope wrote in the Preface of his newly published book, "I Never Left Home" (1944), which in its first four months sold more than 1.5 million copies,

"I saw how they worked, played, fought, and lived. I saw some of them die. I saw more courage, more good humor in the face of discomfort, more love in an era of hate, and more devotion to duty than could exist under any tyranny. I saw American minds, American skills, and American strength breaking the backbone of evil... "

Bob's opening monologue was always a variation on the theme of the ordinary soldier's daily experiences. His skill at improvisation coupled with an intuitive sense of satire, gentle ridicule, and silly sarcasm made "the boys laugh, saving the day". He learned almost from the beginning that "the boys" laughed the hardest when the one-liners and jokes dealt with the men themselves, the man who fought from the foxhole, who struggled to endure to stay alive.

Thus, when Hope and Colonna used the infantryman lingo, joking about their lister bags, Atabrine tablets, armor artificers, the soldiers in the audience laughed the loudest. "They were speaking our language, which made their gags even funnier," wrote Lieutenant John D. Saint, Jr. to his parents, Mr. and Mrs. John A. Saint of South Claibone Ave. in New Orleans.

Later, Hope recalled facetiously,

"Whenever I came on stage and delivered my opening monologues, the crowded, overflowing audience was so 'excited' by my words that not a sound came out of them. Often we'd be in gullies, on hillsides, or on the flat ground, often drenched by rain, or even snow, or the blazing sun overhead, their rifles and machine guns cocked and ready to fire."

"Then, when I would introduce Tony Romano, Jack Pepper, and the other Gypsy boys, those thousands upon thousands of wonderful fellas cheered like mad. But when I brought out and introduced Frances Langford and Patty Thomas, they stood up en masse, as a whole, as one, and cheered and whistled so loudly, so forcefully, its wind blew me right off the platform. When my two girls came forward to the edge of the stage, MPs positioned themselves all over wearing rubber gloves ready to push the eyes back in the sockets of men who hadn't seen women's legs in more than a year."

And, so it went for more than an hour, Frances singing and Patty dancing their hearts out. In between their solos, Tony Romano, "Who could get more out of a guitar than anyone, including the world's great classical guitarist," played with such feeling that even the men with the hardest combat-experienced hearts suddenly felt tears flooding their eyes.

With the completion of singing two songs each, with the minimum accompaniment from the band so as not to interfere with her beautiful voice, Patty handed the microphone back to Bob. Having spotted during the interlude several hundred Seabees in the middle of the audience, he spontaneously, as was always his want, to pay tribute to members of the Armed forces rarely recognized for their brilliant achievements.

"I see out there members of the 48th Naval Construction Battalion . . . Seabees, they call you. You are the guys who transformed coconut plantations knee-deep in rotting oval edible fruit with white meat oozing sweet milky fluid into airstrips, runways, and parking lots for aircraft. You build anything, and everything buildable, wharves, docks, road, chapels, hospitals, country clubs, houses of prosti…, no, I'm kidding. Who needs those? You're not afraid of swamps, open sand, or hip-high mud. Unhampered by flooding rains, typhoon winds, and endless Jap snipe fire, you put up 16-foot tents, Quonset huts, mess halls, and beautiful luxurious silver privies with golden toilets for officers while digging one-foot deep trenches for the run-of-the-mill trooper. You are the guys who can't care less about freezing cold, searing heat, bugs and land crabs, scorpions, and officer reprimands and insults. What you can't stand, however, is boredom and abstinence. Your only relief from the reality of the Jap eyeing you over there is falling in love with the hula dancer tattooed on your buddy's arm. You're the one who'll dreamily ask if she has a sister."

"All you guys are special, every member of the armed forces. Everyone here. But, the Seabees? A unique edge, I would say. What you guys build is almost as important as what the others around you capture. The Seabees allow supplies to be brought up through the jungle, and airfield to be constructed in places so remote even Club Med hasn't found them. And, MacArthur adores the Seabees. When he left Corregidor, he waded through the ocean to a submarine. It's not true he left his footprints on the water. When he said he would return to the Philippines, he added the 1st Division would lead the way with the 48th Naval Construction Battalion building the bridges connecting all the islands."

"No sir. The Seabee has a bit of a shine to his edge. These sailors with hammers in their wide pants read blueprints part of the time instead of Esquire Magazine all the time. They're really rugged, and although the Seabees are only two years old, they have a great reputation as a corps. When you hear the 1st Division landed some place the chances are the Seabees built what they landed on."

"Well, enough of heaping praise. But as my Frances and Patty come on next, and my Gypsy boys play in between and, when appropriate, fondle, I mean 'feel along', I'll check out the officers' toilette, powder room, chamber pot, or whatever else you want to call where you peepee, or do your yuck-a-do.I think I saw it out there behind the grandstand, a reddish color thingamajig with decorative trim."

So, as the audience hooted and hollered, clapped and cackled, Bob concluded, "Where's my bodyguard? Oh, there he is, the youngster sitting there in the first row. He looks young enough for me to be his bodyguard. The kid could be Crosby's new baby boy."

Glancing behind him and seeing "his two girls" poised to perform, laughing and waving at the audience, Bob, pretending to look nervous and worried, said,

"I don't know if I should give up my microphone to these two Gypsies in order to go tinkle. Look at the sillies, ready and roaring to take my place as I innocently and lovingly answer a 30-second call of nature, maybe more, since it involves number two, the yuck-a-do. What kind of friends are these? Put them in their place, boys, by answering, my question, WILL YOU MISS ME IN THE NEXT 10 MINUTES?"

In virtual unison, more than 16,000 troopers stood up in unison and roared, "HELL NO!"

Pretending to stagger backward, Bob shouted indignantly,

"OK, OK, I can take a hint! I can take a hint! They'll sing as a duet, even songs meant to be sung solo, 'Boogie Woogie Bugle Boy', 'I'll Be Seeing You', "I'll Never Smile Again', 'Sing, Sing, Sing', 'Fools Rush In', 'I'll Walk Alone', 'Over the Rainbow', and 'Hooray   for Hollywood'

As Hope moved off to the side, and Frances and Patty heartedly and lively stepped forward, the massive audience, still standing, raised a din that was so loud that Hope shouted, "Be careful, you just woke Tojo and Hirohito up."

Meanwhile, in the jarring cacophony of approval, the two women stepped forward. Both were stunningly dressed, although skimpily and simply. Hope smiled broadly, thinking how wonderful it was for "the boys" to revel for a few moments in good, clean girls who spoke their language, thought as they thought, believed as they believed.

Then, as the two began to sing, accompanied by various band members and their instruments from the band, Hope quickly descended the side steps of the grandstand, nodding to Peter to follow.

The officer's bright red and showy privy was some 35 yards behind the grandstand. Earlier, Chief of Staff Sims had assigned two officers armed with machine guns to guard it, one at the entrance, and the other at the back door, which led to the trail which wound its way down to the nearby channel beach.

As Peter and Hope walked side by side toward the recently-constructed privy, the comedian commented with a twinkle in his eye, "You know, I've peed in some of the best, and some of the worst piss-pots in the world. I couldn't believe it when I saw that red outhouse as the sedans pulled up behind the grandstand. As I looked upon it through the staff car window, I thought to myself, 'That has to be the happiest, and hottest, peepee hole in the Pacific'."

"Yes, sir," responded Peter. "With everyone watching the show, you'll have it all to yourself."

"Oh, I don't mind someone watching. I always pass on to whoever is standing, or sitting, next to me what an old, old professor told me as we urinated side by side in a university urinal. 'Pee now that you can, my boy, because soon enough you won't be able to. Enjoy, enjoy!"

CHAPTER EIGHTEEN

-

Yuck-a-do

Surprisingly to Peter, neither of the two sentries were evident in front or in back of the officer's lavatories, especially since the Commander of the 1st Division personally assigned the men and their weapons to their exact positions.

"Both will catch hell, if they left their posts to watch the show," Peter said, an angry edge in his voice.

"Well, if you like, lieutenant, I can hold my yellow river and yuck-a-do until we're back on Guadalcanal tomorrow."

Peter chuckled.

"No, not necessary, even though I don't holster up until we get back to Banika and your performance there at 7:00pm tonight. Besides, we have patrols all around us in the nearby jungles, and treetops, coconut groves, and on the perimeters of the baseball field. Up on the ridge we have three 155mm guns manned by fully armed artillerymen. Four light machine gun nests, partially hidden, are within shouting distance once I blow my whistle. In fact, if I do, that whole mass of manpower will come running because I'm certain everyone knows what we're expecting to happen."

"Besides," added Hope, the Ghoul told us himself he would strike by midnight on Banika. By then, me and my Gypsies will be in the air back to Henderson Field."

Peter said nothing.

Then, outside the latrine, Peter said quietly,

"I'll go in first, Mr. Hope. You follow me, about 10 to 15 feet from behind. I'm certain the facility is vacant, but once I check out the interior, I'll also take a moment to glance around in the back area. The officer sentry assigned there has probably joined his buddy guarding the entrance and the two now arguing who's going to take my empty seat to view the legs of the girls better."

"Oh, for crying out loud, lieutenant. I told you officers I know how to fight, and win. Remember, I've made five pictures with the 'Big C,' fighting him on everything."

"Yes, but we can't be cautious enough. If you have to be murdered, Mr. Hope, please arrange to have it done on someone else's watch. Who would take your place with the 'Big C' in the 'Road' series?" Peter chuckled.

"Hey, kid, no problem. My choice is the obvious one: Gregory Peck. If worse comes to worse, then the other 'Big C', Colonna. His moustache alone would smother the little dwarf with no voice."

Entering the darkened foyer of the latrine, Peter, with Hope a dozen feet behind him, silent and serious, flipped on the door's battery operated light. The lobby was vacant, and not a sound could be heard other than muffled applause, singing, hollering and laughter from the audience on the field. A string of ceiling light fixtures running the length of the foyer was switched on by Peter, providing a subdued glow which reinforced the dim light overhead. Under the golden glow were several long tables, countertops with simple faucets, mirrors, and more than a dozen chairs. Coat racks were strategically placed all around the anteroom.

The overall impression of the entryway was aesthetically pleasing.

"It's the easy accessibility that appeals so much," Hope commented.

Peter responded,

"You know, of course, that diseases cause more casualties than bullets. Hygiene is stressed over and over and over. Even during combat shell trenches are always dug when practical; if not, each Marine has to dig his own hole and then cover it.

When Peter shoved open the double-doors leading to the lavatories, Hope exclaimed,

"Wow! Would you just look at the big potty room! It's a wonderful resting, lounging place, really for presidents. What an imposing impression it makes, and all constructed without stonework and modern steel. Just old-fashioned plywood, common nails, and inexpensive, ordinary hardware store-bought enamel paint. This fancy hall of toilets doesn't advertise glitter, but a relaxing ambiance. It's the best one I've been in during my travels."

"Yes, especially when we've been so used to filthy bamboo water closets built on crushed coral you could see through, wooden toilets without seats. Look there in the stalls, each toilet is new, with fly-proof seats, and falling lids on each pail!"

For a long moment, each man stood in marvel appreciation as he gazed upon the best restroom facility of the entire Pacific War. The officers' Little Red Painted House was comfortable, safe, and private, with clean, attractive stalls, all as hygienic as any found stateside.

"It's so clean it could be part mess hall, part potty," Hope offered. "Just look around you, nothing broken, everything in near-perfect sanitation, no bad smells, no dirty wash counters, no empty or jammed toilet paper dispensers, no trash on the floors, no empty soap or paper towel dispensers, no wet floors, and I bet no need to stand or wait in line. What I like the most is, I bet, no hideously stained seats, or Out of

Order signs, The only thing missing are female attendants to help your unzip your pants."

"Everyone knows we're doing all we can to inhibit the spread of germs and bacteria. Upkeep is important for building morale. Poor restrooms set a negative tone. Privacy, safety, cleanliness, and hygienic add to health. And, we had it built without a budget, from bits and pieces, leftover materials. We're very proud we have eliminated the horrendous!"

"Well, it sure strikes me as an intelligent toilet house, one I'm certainly happy to put to use!"

After verifying that the dozen or so swinging-door stalls were empty, Peter glanced into the small storage closet with several ceiling-high windows. Located behind the mirrored urinal wall, the storeroom had sufficient space to locate the facilities' cleaning materials and assorted stage equipment, including marquees and wall posters.

The room was so crowded with theater furniture. Items and scenery, lights, and low scaffolds that in a quick, furtive peek, Peter realized it would be next to impossible for the Ghoul to lay in wait within such a limited confinement.

With that, Peter hurried to the back door of the facility in order to exit and locate the second Marine officer assigned to guard the back of the officers' privy.

Thrusting it open, he was partly blinded by the mid-afternoon sunlight. For a moment, Peter considered what was in front of him. First, he saw a path leading down to two trails, one, rather obscure, proceeding, directly toward an empty channel beach, the other past a raw, unsophisticated verdant with hundreds of different types of fern.

Peter was fascinated. It was an area of the island he was unfamiliar with. Beyond the verdant was an old corrugated heavy, leaky tin-roofed warehouse no longer in use. Until the Japanese had occupied the island a year or so before, it had stored Polynesian war canoes, and before that, served as a meetinghouse. Until the new iron shelters for munitions and light machine guns and other small weapons had been completed five months before, the 1st Division had to store and canvas the items in the ancient structure. Some 50 yards away, Marines interested in ornamental horticulture volunteered to maintain formal flowerbeds, gardens, and lawns. All were irrigated by Pavuvu's only volcanic spring, the island's main source for pure water. Across a small palm grove was the huge coral quarry, the only sourced of coral rocks to be crushed and used in all building.

As Peter turned to his right to gaze down the straight wall line toward the baseball field where barely audible strains of Frances Langford's "I'll Be Seeing You" could be heard, he noticed a green canvas tarpaulin covering a large lumpy mass of what appeared to be gravel or small irregular debris. Unable to continue his scan of the panorama from the edge of the structure to the distant palm groves and jungle to his left, he momentarily studied the lumps and humps under the waterproof tarpaulin. It was then that he noticed what resembled half a boot protruding from under the wide canvas cover.

Suddenly, fearing the worst, Peter jammed the back door with a nearby rock to keep it from shutting, and ran over to it, knowing what was there before lifting the canvas.

Despite being forewarned by his intuition, he was jolted by the sickening sight of two dead Marines heaped haphazardly, one on top of the other. Both were still bleeding from huge protrusions to their stomachs. Their machine guns and holsters .45s gone were missing.

Horrified, Peter noted the facial expressions on each of the young dead officers' faces. Their eyes were wide open, so frozen in stupefied astonishment as to who was killing them that each was utterly defenseless at the murder weapon plunged repeatedly into their abdomens or hearts. Peter had studied each of the Ghoul's murdered victims, the cadavers with the same surprised questioning looks. These two unfortunate Marines had looked into the eyes of pure evil and before they could raise their weapons in defense, they were already dead. The sight was the grimmest and most grisly the lieutenant had yet seen.

In a flash, Peter veered and literally hurled himself back toward the rear door of the facility, which to his relief was still slightly ajar as he left it. Now, completely lynx-eyed, in the dim golden light of the interior, he first noticed that the door of the storeroom behind the wall of the urinals was also slightly open. Obviously, someone had been hiding in the ordered chaos of the room when Peter had first glanced in.

Turning his greatest fear toward where he left Bob Hope, he saw that the comedian was talking to someone, his voice asking,

" . . . well, before you murder me, will you kindly tell me if Crosby sent you?"

The nonchalance tone of the question, the measured movement of his words, and rhythmic flow of their sounds, was so bizarre and unexpected that the shining Ka-Bar fighting-knife poised to plunge into the face of Bob Hope quivered for less than a second, allowing Peter to scream frantically, "No!"

Between the astonishing question and the sudden reality that he had been discovered by an adversary, the murder-mad Ghoul was momentarily disoriented.

Peter, with a barely audible profanity, then clenched teeth, sprang toward the would-be slayer, stretching out his right hand for the

Ghoul's wrist holding the long, thick battle knife. Reeling from his own diving force and simultaneous striking blows to his head, Peter's bitter fists found the murderer's face, nose, and jaw. The assassin, staggering and sagging, nonetheless remained on his feet. Clearly, Peter now recognized the assailant. For a moment, he froze in utter shock and agonized disbelief.

"PINOE, YOU! NOT YOU? Oh, my God!", he thundered, "HOW COULD YOU! OF ALL PEOPLE??" YOU? ALL ALONG? NO! NO!"

Then, as the Ghoul clenched his teeth, he attempted to spring forward. In his mind, he knew MPs were undoubtedly on their way. If he didn't kill Peter now, he was finished, either by a USMC firing squad, or if unlucky, by the military's hangman's noose.

Believing he could make fast work of the lieutenant who he perceived as "puny", he figured he could dash down the back trail of the facility to the channel beach where his private Micronesian dory could be retrieved from its hiding place amid the flora. Within minutes he would paddle across the channel to the Banika hospital where he could claim he was administering to the ill. Without a gun, he would have to kill Toscanini with the Ka-Bar he still held, or if lost in the struggle, strangle him to death with his hands.

Although the grim, sneering Chaplain was some 20 feet away, ambling toward him, the fighting knife firmly grasped in his right hand, Peter remained perfectly calm. Without further shouting, he studied every muscle, every moment in Pinoe's body. The lieutenant's life was on the line, within seconds of obliteration, and, without his usual holstered .45 automatic at his waist, he was defenseless, other than his brilliant mind and the surefootedness and nimbleness that emanated from years of playing singles in tennis.

In the minute or so that transpired, the Ghoul had not uttered so much as a word, grunt, snarl or scoff. Then, he spoke, lisping more than usual, the sounds of which Peter understood so clearly just hours before,

"You're sure making a lot of fuss over a few worthless Marine deaths. But you and Mr. Hilarious there will be joining them on the slabs soon enough."

"Mr. Hilarious, that would be me, you son-of-a-bitch. That is, unless you're referring to my sidekick, Mr. Colonna," Bob Hope commended somberly as he stepped closer to the two. "Remember, lieutenant, I know how to fight. Let me take him down."

"No, no!" shouted Peter. "Run for help. Run! Run!"

"The audience can wait. I want to help you nail this bastard."

"Go get help! That's a direct order. Get help . . . Go! Go! Damn it, GO!"

As Hope finally whirled and darted toward the lavatory outer entrance doors, Pinoe, although more than a dozen feet away, panicking in fear the few minutes he allocated for murder were evaporating now that the comedian was exiting the facility for assistance, leaped forward the best way he could with a limp, waving the Ka-Bar in repeated slicing motions. Peter, sidestepping the swinging arm, then dodging and evading the Ghoul as he pressed forward, a hateful, sickening smirk on his face. Ka-Bar or no Ka-Bar, the pudgy chaplain was no match for the young lieutenant, strong-framed, athletically svelte, in near-perfect condition with ideal weight, height, and strength, and obviously a man of far higher intelligence.

By a narrow margin, and a certain amount of acrobatic skill, Peter eluded and averted the Ka-Bar, parrying and warding off the knife blows and left-handed fist. Peter, with the cleverness of faint attacks was able to hold off the Ghoul's arm holding the large knife. His right fist managed to thrust upward and into the Ghoul's midsection. Despite blow after blow, the burly murder-mad Marine, smirking maliciously, managed to break away from the tight embrace a few feet and in savage rage lunge back again.

Breathing heavily, Peter, aroused by passionate hatred to near violently explosive action, remarked implacable with his hard-hitting punches.

"So you're the vile, bestial creature that all brave men despise, nothing more than a thug assassin who strikes in the black of night. I would never have guessed the venomous snake was you."

Stepping back, Peter observed the Ghoul, slightly stooped from the repeated blows to his belly, cursed gutturally through his clenched teeth.

Pinoe, his cold, merciless deep-set eyes glittering with rage, snarled in his imperfect, falteringly pronunciation,

"If I die, I'll come back and destroy you and the whole 1st Division."

Angrily, Peter retorted, hoping to stall for time,

"The hell you will. If you don't drop that Ka-Bar and submit to the court-martial, I'm bound by duty to kill you here and now, which I will surely do."

Meanwhile, with a "Damn it, GO!" still ringing in his ears, Hope, surprisingly agile for his age, was racing well down the walkway toward the grandstand MPs assembled in small groups watching the performance. When he ran past a nurse hurrying in the opposite direction toward the officer's restroom facility, he shouted.

"No! No! Don't go over there! The Ghoul is fighting with Lieutenant Toscanini! Help me find armed MPs!"

"Yes, yes," she responded, continuing on.

With animal ferocity, Peter and the Ghoul again embraced each other in a life and death struggle, the lieutenant as yet having unsuccessfully yanked or grasped the fighting knife away from the murder-mad marine. Peter, with one hand now on the Ghoul's throat, strained with all his might to get his other hand on it. Meanwhile, Pinoe fought with such ferociousness that he was able to thrust a thumb on the lieutenant's face in order to gouge an eye out, while simultaneously endeavoring to get the large knife high enough to thrust down into Peter's face.

Then, both managed to break away from one another. With several deft movements, Peter, being far more fleet of foot, again dodged the swings of the sharp weapon. Peter was a few inches shorter than Pinoe, although the two were more or less the same weight and strength. All in all, it was a fair fight for each. The Ghoul had fighting lessons as a youth in a Boston boxing club, while Peter was learning the basic strokes of tennis; i.e. forehand, backhand, lob, volley, serve and drop shots. Each shot required a different footing.

Although Peter's movements were surprising to the Ghoul, the murderer managed to inflictfour additional minor slashes on the lieutenant's right shoulder, abdomen and left hand and arm. Each was bleeding, one, the shoulder, profusely.

Weakened by the loss of a moderate amount of blood from all the cuts thus far endured, Peter, realizing he would probably be cut open in less than a moment, and that he could no longer skirt and dance around the Ka-Bar, remained calm and at peace with himself. Seeing the lieutenant's condition, Pinoe, with a set, tightly drawn smile, inched forward toward Peter who was bent backward. Seeing the Ghoul's arm lift with his hand firmly griping the long, wide knife, he knew one swooping slash would either cleave his head in two, or sever it from his throat.

Without a sound, and with every fluid ounce of might idling in his veins, Peter swung his right fist in an uppercut thrust that sent the murder-mad, still clutching his large knife, wheeling and stumbling so that Pinoe momentarily lost his balance and as his hand holding the Ka-Bar hit the shut door of a toilet stall, last in a line of a dozen, and, it miraculously slipped from his grasp.

Realizing he now had the advantage, Peter pulled himself up and walked slowly toward where the Ghoul lay in a stark heap. With his turn to stand over the enemy, Peter could not help but smile cynically. Leaning over the Ghoul, the lieutenant's fist went to work on Pinoe's head and face, so much so that the murder-mad no longer had the strength to shield himself. Head wobbling, body nothing more than a limp, unmoving mass of uniformed flesh, the Ghoul was in excruciating pain where he could no longer utter a word.

All Peter could do now was to wait for the arrival of help, and, in doing so, ensure the Pinoe would not get away. Underlying the increasingly savage grin of satisfaction on Peter's face was a genuine hatred for the murderer of fellow Marines, a wish to kill him with the Ka-Bar weapon laying less than a few yards away. "Best," Peter thought to himself, "If the MPs arrive quickly, before I lose self-control and kill him myself."

Then, Pinoe, prostate before him, groaned, and slowly lifted himself sufficiently from lying downward, to an inclined sitting position, all accompanied with low, mournful sounds of both physical pain and sorrow for himself, having been being discovered and caught. Staring at the floor, he kept mumbling in a thick, grating lisp, 'give me a gun', 'watch the fun', 'big-son-of-a-gun', 'water, jam, gun', 'watchman's gun', 'washerson gun', 'son-of-a-gun', 'laughing gun', 'shrill gun', etc.

Rubbing his eyes to see more clearly, Pinoe looked up at Peter now clutching the Ka-Bar and, with a vindictive light in his eye, he grinned evilly, then almost triumphantly. He uttered, "I'm only one of three Ghouls. The 'silly gun' will kill you for me."

Peter, drained and almost depleted of all his strength and energy, allowed himself to slip into a complacing quiescence. Only a moment before, he had been a bitter, raging avenger resolving to kill the Ghoul, totally missing the obvious, sudden glint of exultation in the eyes of the muttering murderer. And, as he mediated on the harmlessness of the barely conscious Mad Ghoul struggling to stand, the grim lines on the lieutenant's face also relaxed slowly from their ruthlessness.

"Pinoe, why you?" Peter challenged softly. "You, the Man of the Cloth, the clergy, that every Marine admires, and respects, and trusts. That's why our men were killed up close and frontally, without resistance, because they never dreamed you, of all people, could murder so cruelly, you cowardly son-of-a-bitch!"

Again Peter growled within, allowing an inner anger, an uncontrollable rage, to consume him. As he waited a second or two for a response, Peter sensed Pinoe had not heard a word. Even worse, the Ghoul wasn't even looking at him. He was snickering in what appeared to be in jubilation at something behind him.

Suddenly hearing short, soft steps running toward him, Peter whirled to see Ellen, pallid in face, shaking of body, a Ka-Bar of her own raised and poised to plunge. Peter, mustering his remaining strength to defend himself against certain slaughter, swayed backward in a delirium of disbelief. Although he still firmly gripped the Ghoul's fighting knife, he had no intention of using it to defend himself. After all, Ellen was a friend. No, he loved Ellen.

"ELLEN! It's me, Peter! What are you doing?" Peter screamed as he lurched backward. The nurse, meanwhile, repeatedly plunged and swung the Ka-Bar, missing as Toscanini darted and danced slowly backward until he was stopped by the lavatory wall, his knees sagging to the point that he went down. For a moment, all he could see was a blurred figure holding a long, wide object approaching with quick firm steps.

Eyeing her calmly, he gazed into Ellen's hard, expressionless face.

"Hello, Peter . . . Why did you have to get involved with all of this? Killing Hope, and with luck, Rupertus, and a few of his staff today was going to be the last of the spree. You were supposed to keep out of it. Now, I'm obliged to put you to sleep, too."

Ellen's death sentence didn't faze or frighten Peter. Even the painful bruises and cuts, one still bleeding profusely, didn't matter, he thought. She was the Ghoul, too, and an unexpected accomplice. If he could manage to keep her talking a few more moments, it was possible the military would come bursting through the facility doors.

"But why the killing of our own?" Peter asked softly, "Why them?"

"Oh," she responded angrily, "I asked the chaplain to help me murder that asshole Johnny Houser, who betrayed me for the nurse we killed last night. He said he's murdered before, stateside, members of his congregation. He lusts for the terror in his victim's eyes. But, since we were all confined to these islands, we first began killing the ones we wanted dead. Then, to hide the fact, we began eliminating a host of others like we're crazy, and no one will ever guess that Hauser was the only real victim."

As Pinoe, struggling to crawl toward them shouting hoarsely, his lisp more than ever. "Get him, you fool! Shut up and kill him! They'll be here in a flash! Can't you see he's gotten a stupid trusting female to yakity-yak while Hope has run for help! Kill him!"

Peter remained deathly still, allowing the seconds to pass as he pretended to listen. In reality, his depleted energy was replenishing itself for one final hefty trust at Ellen. If help hadn't arrived by then, he was finished anyway.

"After the hours we spent together these past two days," Peter said slowly, knowing they would impact her dramatically. "I was beginning to love you, Ellen."

"And, me too!" she yelled in a muffled voice. "How ironic I wanted you more than that cheap B actor! All you had to do was tell that Jap woman in the internment camp back home you were through with her. Now I'm going to send you to Heaven. Sorry, Peter, but I have to."

At the very instant Ellen stepped forward, her hand with the Ka-Bar raised to strike him, Peter wheeled to his left, flinging his smashed and deeply sliced shoulder up and toward the plunging knife. As large as it was, the heavy knife ripped through the loose collar of his shirt. To his amazement, his right arm, which had hung uselessly at his side for the past several minutes, blocked the thrust aimed at his face. As he painfully lay with his back to the facility wall, he used his right leg to continually kick and block any additional Ka-Bar swipes. Peter knew he was already dying and there was no longer any hope the MPs would arrive in time to save him. Ellen, seeing the spurting blood from the long, deep shoulder slash, marveled that her Peter had not screamed in pain from the gash, which appeared more as a gouge than a long slit. Resting on his side, back against the wall, Peter smiled grimly as he looked up at her.

"Go ahead, you f…ing slut."

As Pinoe, waving his arm, was shouting, "Yes! Yes! Yes!", Ellen raised her arm a second time, not to slash or slice, but to plunge. With it, held as high as she could possibly get it, an indistinguishable gleam surfaced in her eyes, and, looking down at Peter, ready and still defiantly prepared to absorb the plunge into his head, a bullet from Bill Lundigan's .45 entered the back of her skull, and exited through her left eye.

CHAPTER NINETEEN

-

Sealed Orders

"Wow! What a sickening sight you look! To say nothing of the messy mass of broken bones, cut flesh, and painful wounds you must feel. You could be the start of a horror movie! Yes, sir!" Bill Lundigan chuckled uncomfortably as he stood over Peter huddling against the back wall near the exit door. Less than two yards away lay Ellen, deceased, right eye wide open, blood oozing from her left eye after Lundigan's .45 bullet entered the back of her skull and exited a few inches above her nose dangling the eye from its socket.

"And look at him," Lundigan continued, casting his chin toward Pinoe, the Mad Ghoul, or Charlie the Choker, more than a dozen yards away, attempting to crawl in their direction. "Limp and bleeding, pale and ashen, unable to get up, or stand, realizing he's caught, facing certain death, a firing squad or noose and struggling to reach us so he can strangle you. Are you up to all this drama and comedy?"

A faint smile lingered around Peter's lips.

"Oh, I'm not damaged much, Bill," Peter whispered weakly, staring at the Ghoul. "I wish he could reach me, the loathsome aberration."

Lundigan, with one eye on Pinoe, knelt by the side of his wounded friend and said softly,

"Medics are right behind me. When Hope called for help, I was out of my seat and flying over here. Ellen had left my side a few moments before. Hope passed her. I somehow knew then that she was part of the killing spree. The medics called after me if you were still 'a-going it', and I laughed. 'Are you kidding me', I thought to myself, 'You can't easily kill a nice kid like that'. Now, let me take a quick tally of your wounds and bruises. I hear the medics bouncing in now. And, look at me, still holding my .45 in the air! Damn, look at the huge monkeyshine on your rotary cuff, sure to affect the first serve of your tennis game."

"It'll heal," Peter said nonchalantly. Glancing again at Pinoe, he said, "I should have known. When he and Schneidermann, the psychiatrist, visited the morgue while I was studying the corpses, he hinted how much he enjoyed looking upon and touching dead flesh."

"Well, you got the Mad Ghoul, all right," Bill smiled, shaking his head admiringly. "And my Lord, what a roaring cookout party you made of it!"

Holstering his .45, Bill, with no further comment, gazed past Pinoe, as several medics, military police, and other officers swarmed into the lavatory. For such a relatively compressed restroom, debris of various materials was now scattered about. Anything that wasn't bolted down was smashed--small wooden tables, potted plants, Ka-Bar slashes on the walls, broken mirror glass on the floor, etc.

Skillfully, two medical officers began administering first aid to Peter's wounds and preparing to place him on a stretcher for immediate departure to the Banika hospital. As one cut open Peter's bloody shirt, the lieutenant seethed,

"Oh, for goodness sake, I'm fine. Look after that pitiful creature who soon enough will be dead and thought of no more. He's shattered and has grown weaker and more quiet. He's given up attempting to crawl toward me with an evil intent. We should try to at least save him from embarrassment and discomfort from all the pageant and parade sure to come in the hours that follow."

"Soldier, be soldierly. He can wait. We're not through with you yet," one of the medical officers said. With three medics working in synchronization, each of Peter's wounds was carefully bathed, the bleeding staunched, and then dressed.

More than a dozen rugged, burly experience-appearing MPs filed silently through the lavatory doors, their .45s readied, all with grim faces, savage gleams in their eyes, thinking of vengeance for the murdered Marines. Dividing into groups of two, the MPs checked the storeroom and each of the closed door, toilet stalls, finding all of them empty.

Once the MPs declared the facility cleared, the 1st Division command staff, including that of the Military Police, were allowed to enter. With more than half a dozen heavily armed officers surrounding the Ghoul seated double-chained and handcuffed, everyone wanted to see him, the Chaplain the 1st Division Marines adored.

Rupertus remarked to Peter, who was now being placed upon a stretcher for delivery to the Banika Hospital,

"Well, my boy, the mystery is at last cleared up."

"And, how!" echoed Bill Lundigan.

"And, double, how!" Captain Del Barbra echoed laughingly. "After more than a week of murder after murder, the ordinary killer stateside must seem like a Messiah. There wasn't much any of us could do. But apparently, you fought heroically, saving Bob Hope's life, from what Hope said. Of course, I'll write up the whole story for the Brass in Washington. You're certain to make promotion. And, naturally, we'll arrange to have you fly in for the execution."

"I'll be there. Soon as I leave the hospital, I'll want to interview him, especially if he's murdered before, why and how he joined Ellen. The real question, which he can't answer, is, 'How does someone like you become so fiercely cruel in one hour and so compassionate and understanding in the next."

Pinoe, barely able to walk when so heavily cuffed and double-chained, was now on his feet and being prepared to be led to the Banika brig. Overhearing the exchange between Rupertus, Toscanini, Lundigan and Del Barbra, he began laughing in a low tone, with a glint in his eyes, he said,

"How can such a travesty as myself happen in America, or the great U.S. Marine Corps? My head is spinning at such a stupid question? Cry out with your questions! Cry out for my execution! With Ellen gone, you will learn nothing of her motivations, and all I'll give you are warts on your asses. You won't . . . you can't prevent a reoccurrence by another monster like me. The brutal, heinous murders were orchestrated by me, so you try figuring out all the 'whys'."

A feeling of revulsion swept over Peter.

"Yeah," responded Peter, "you're right. You're too sick to even know the reasons why. You'll soon find yourself in the lowest depths of Hades justly meeting your hellish rewards."

As Pinoe was led through the back door of the facility, limping and smirking simultaneously, officers in the back of the crowd by the front door cried out,

"Make way. Make way! VIP coming through. VIP, VIP coming. Man of God headed for Hell!"

The circle surrounding Peter on the stretcher parted and Bob Hope entered, glancing all around. Walking up to Peter and the medics, with a blanket stretched over Ellen a few feet away, he glanced around and commented loudly with a grin,

"I see so many lively men in khaki holding big guns, I feel I'm back on the Paramount Lot in Hollywood marking the 1942 war comedy

‘Caught in the Draft’ with Eddie Bracken and Dorothy Lamour. I’ve got to complement you MPs indulging our hero: You all look like Madeleine Carroll with muscles.”

Although there were the usual chuckles, smiles, titters, grins, and outright laugher, very few were amused. Noticing the absence of the usual mirth, Hope paused, and apologized,

“Fellas, I’m sorry for my feeble attempt at humor when death is bleeding there in front of us. She was an American nurse who during the day cared for, administered to, and watched after you soldiers. At night, off duty, for who knows why, she killed you. There’s no humor today, really, in here, or out there. Sure, you caught up with them, the Mad Ghoul, and, who would have guessed, his beautiful accomplice I passed as she ran in to stab him to death. And, a USMC-assigned nurse, at that, they watched their brothers, the victims, writhe in pain, squirm, wriggle, and struggle against the battle-knife plunged into them, crying out one word, ‘Why?’ But that lieutenant there, being carried out to the hospital on Banika, showed implacable iron in his veins, and a fierce resolution, saved my life and cornered him singlehandedly.”

After a short pause with everyone riveted to listening to what appeared to be a different, a deadly serious Bob Hope,

“No, men, there’s no humor here. And, it’s only fair people Stateside know that the Mad Ghoul was not just a Marine problem, but a mental illness issue. All of you officers joined the Corps to fight the Japs, but you never dreamed they enemy on Pavuvu would be one of your own.”

During the days that followed, Peter was confined to a Banika hospital bed, while waiting the slow healing of the heavy bruises and the larger wounds Pinoe had inflicted. Deeper than first believed the

Ka-Bar gouges had penetrated deeper than originally believed, forcing Peter's admittance into the officers' bedridden ward.

On the third morning that Peter was confined to bed, under the strict order if he violated this provision for convalescence, he would not only be handcuffed to his bed, but also strapped under the blankets. Captain Del Barbra, with Sergeant Guidi trailing behind him with his clipboard in hand, entered the ward shouting in his usual jovial, ebullient manner,

"Guess what, Toscanini. They just honored you by lifting the beer rations for the whole 1st Division!"

Barely awake, Peter frowned.

"Very funny. And, I thought all the comedians had flown back to Guadalcanal."

"And, Rupertus named the order after you, 'Honoree'!"

Peter, struggling to sit up by himself, smiled.

Del Barbra couldn't stop talking loudly.

"What a wacky farce it's been! Amid the sad multiple deaths, it's been sheer buffoonery. A broad comedy by the world's greatest comedian, a burlesque without the hoopla and hum-dog music led by the top mimic!"

"It was fun, wasn't it?" Peter smiled.

"And, Hope said to tell you and Bill Lundigan that the two of you will always have roles with Paramount Pictures, if you want them. A long letter will be forthcoming to you personally in appreciation for you saving his life. For now, he wants you to heal, and heal quickly. He says to tell you all gags aside, you are his hero, and that you saved his life. And, above all, he says to you personally, 'Thanks for the memories.'"

"Well," responded Peter, "I now know, having seen it for myself, why the men love him so much. Of course, there are several reasons.

But, underneath them all, there is a genuine man who's good, who's kind, who cares. We could both go on about his generosity, spirit, and love for us all. He gave us all something we'll never, ever forget."

After a moment of reflection, Peter added,

"Bob Hope gave us soldiers a laugh and a grin as our lives are changing forever. Even for those of us who are fortunate enough to live through this war to tell the tale, our lives, for the rest of our lives, will be changed, vastly changed. For a mere fraction of a moment in time, Bob Hope, and all his gags, monologues, and soliloquies, made us smile and forget how awful war is."

During the several long days that followed in mid-August 1944, Peter, 'feeling stuck' in the officers' wing of the Banika hospital, surrendered to formal interviews, USMC reports, and teasing ridicule, especially by his closest friends, Bill Lundigan, Dr. Larry Schneidermann, and Oscar Del Barbra, and a host of others.

Ellen's warranted death wrought havoc on the hearts of both Peter and Bill. Each "loved her" in his way, akin to the platonic, the inevitable intimacy between two fine, healthy men and a kind, gentle, beautiful American nurse. It was still impossible for Peter and Bill to believe Ellen was intent on killing the lieutenant to save Pinoe. For Peter, it was difficult to believe that he fought a desperate life and death battle in which, for all intents and purposes, he lost. He was within two or three seconds of certain death from the plunging arm's raised Ka-Bar until a single bullet from Bill's .45 entered the back of Ellen's head.

In attempting to explain how and why Ellen joined Chaplain Pinoe in multiple murdering fellow Marines, Peter could only repeat what little was known about the profile of the woman criminal. The lieutenant said,

"We know so little about her. And, even less, actually nothing, about the female multiple-murderer. We know that since 1900, during the past 44 years, the patterns of female crimes have been growing more violent. The popular myths about the women of crime don't apply in Ellen's case. Today, about 10% of all women criminals are convicted of murder. Before 1900, it was less than 1%. Because of the women's movement? No. Money crimes count for at least 40% today. Usually, it was cocktail waitresses with kids, who became prostitutes and drug-dealers. Forgery, larceny, and embezzlement are doubling. Those women don't need to be punished, they need to be rehabilitated. Women accomplices in petty, even major crimes, are pictured as the 'dumb broads'. And, the woman who murders by herself, without an accomplice, male or female, rarely commits it for money. She doesn't murder for stolen goods, check forgery, and embezzlement. She doesn't even murder as a head of a household to help support her children without the aid of husband or parents. Economic crimes have little importance. She, and include Ellen with her, for some deep monumental reason deeply buried in her psyche, a damage that occurred so long ago in her life that she has more or less forgotten, murdered for an unconscious hatred even she doesn't understand. Early in her life an occurrence occurred that wounded her so that she sought revenge. In Ellen's case, PFC Houser abandoned her. And that abandonment echoed her abandonment as a child. She asked Pinoe to commit the act for her. And, thus the spree of killing was so relieving, and thus enjoyable, why not kill the same man over and over again?"

On the fifth day of Peter's "confinement", during which his wounds were healing nicely, Major General William Rupertus arrived for a visit, in addition to handing him orders for a new assignment. He was accompanied by virtually the entire 1st Division Headquarters

Command Organization, including Brigadier General Lemuel Shepherd, the Assistant Commander, his soon-to-be replacement for the "Stalemate II" Operation in the Palaus Islands; and, Chief of Staff, Colonel Amor LeRoy Sims, along with the four Division colonels. Also, in tow were a few of Peter's favorite officers, Commander Everett Keck, USN, of the 1st Medical Battalion; Colonel John Selden of the 5th Marine Battalion, and five or six nurses.

Peter, in the tradition of Bob Hope and Jerry Colonna, quipped,

"Is the war over, or did Sharon from back in 12th grade of high school finally turn me in for having roving hands when I parked dad's car on the levee?"

After the nurses abruptly halted, roaring with laughter, and the officers, including Commander Rupertus, ceasing their soft chuckling, guilty grins, and shy smiles, the major general said, as he handed Peter an official 1st Division Headquarters envelope,

"Son, your new orders were drafted in Honolulu for special assignment Stateside. You are not to open the envelope until your fifth day at sea then destroy it by fire or disintegration by the ocean itself. The letter is to be presented to the captain of the USS Morgan, who will maintain it in the ship's vault in his Captain's Quarters. The letter is sealed and ribboned. No one else is to read it. Neither are you to discuss its contents, by written word or verbal, of the letter's content. Are you clear on all this, Lieutenant?"

"Yes, sir," Peter smiled broadly.

"Quite frankly, Lieutenant Toscanini, I don't know what your new assignment is. Neither does Commander Keck."

"In addition," Rupertus continued, "the request for air transportation to San Francisco, California, is being typed as I stand before you now. At midnight, a Piper Cub will arrive from Guadalcanal to fly you to Henderson. There, you'll board a transport returning to Melbourne. Upon arrival, you'll taken to a stripped-down B-29 to fly you and a dozen or so others also assigned for special duties to the McClellan Airfield near San Francisco, California. There, after a series of meetings and in-service sessions, you'll begin a long furlough, a leave of absence for 18 days. Upon your return to the Frisco Presidio, you'll begin a series of simultaneous recovery reassignments, and retraining sessions. General Shepherd has a number of administrative issues paperwork to go over with you following our little celebration in a few moments. He is to remain behind with Commander Keck. Together, they will draft a request from me that you be nominated for no less than the Navy Cross. As you know, it's the highest decoration, other than the Congressional Medal of Honor, for extraordinary heroism in operations against an armed enemy. They will write the first draft, I will edit it, adding and deleting here and there, then send it up the USMC chain of command to the Commandant for recommendation that he send it onto Frank Knox, the Secretary of Navy. I will add a personal note saying that only around 60 have ever been issued, but you deserve to receive one for your investigative work and final confrontation with the multiple-murderer. If he is not in agreement, and only Heaven would know why because you're a Navy Lieutenant, not a Marine Lieutenant, then would he consider recommending you for the Distinguished Service Medal, of which only three have been granted. If not that, then certainly the coveted Navy and Marine Corps Medal of which there are only 15. I will argue for the Navy Cross most vehemently. Now, with all this said, young man, and prior to preparing for your departure this evening, we have concocted a celebration, an old-fashioned toast for who you are and what you've done."

With that, the doors of the officers' recovery ward swung open, and leading a parade of officers, hospital patients, and medical personnel four abreast, filed in. Bill Lundigan and Nurse Heather Gordon led the way, Bill carrying a huge punch bowl fashioned from the Plexiglas bubble of a B-17, undoubtedly filled with a drink, a combination of various fruit juices and odd alcoholic beverages.

Heather Gordon, the R.N. who was most responsible for Peter's recovery, sitting with him next to his bed on a daily and nightly basis, carried several tin platters with recently baked cookies. Behind Bill and Heather, Captain of the Military Police Del Barbra and Sergeant Guidi followed, the captain playing a violin and the Sergeant strumming a guitar, with others behind them at work on a variety of small musical instruments, all struggling to perform in unison, "Thanks for the Memory", Hope's signature tune. By mid-afternoon, many, other than Commander Rupertus' staff, found themselves inebriated beyond delirious. As Heather carefully packed his duffle and satchel bags for departure to Anderson by Piper Cub on the Pavuvu road air strip, Peter huddled with Bill, Oscar, Leo and others finalize the life and death encounter with the Ghoul and to say a temporary aloha to each.

Smothering humid heat and the Pacific's seasonal summer winds floating equatorial clouds northward led to teeming rains early that afternoon, so soaking that Pavuvu was virtually flooded. Just as the arrival time of the Piper Cub was about to be postponed, the ocean sun, as usual, broke through, ensuring a dry crushed coral road-runway. The inescapable heat and humidity would return within minutes.

Climbing aboard the Piper Cub and gently settling himself comfortably in its single passenger seat with a movable back, Peter waved farewell to Bill Lundigan, Oscar Del Barbra, and Leo Guidi who accompanied him from the officers' sickbay on Banika to the main airfield departure area. As the small observation aircraft lifted off, and the friendly drone of the motor kicked in, the lieutenant, encouraged into drowsiness, fell asleep for the entire hour flight to Guadalcanal's Henderson Airfield.

Awakening from his nap just as the Piper Cub began its descent to Henderson, Peter reflected for a moment on how the 3,600-foot airstrip had been the primary objective for the Japanese invasion of the island on August 7th, 1942. Below him now were the clearly defined defensive positions consisting of trenches and antiaircraft emplacements, well-built and equipped, several hangars, numerous auxiliary machine shop buildings, circular revetments, taxiways to the main runway, and the original pagoda-type control power that was set up by the enemy to control their airfield operations.

The short flight arrived long before sunset, allowing Peter several hours of liberty before reporting to Lunga Point for embarkation aboard the USS Morgan transport at 10:00pm that night. Refusing the opportunity to rest and relax at either the barracks near the airfield, or the docking facilities, Peter requested a guide and jeep to tour the major battle sites, Mount Austen, Alligator Creek, the jungles and terrain of Matanikau, the beaches at Tenaru where the Japanese made their desperate suicide changes, and, most important of all to him, the infamous turning point in the Guadalcanal Campaign, the Battle of Bloody Ridge.

Just after dusk, Peter was driven to the Officer's Club near Guadalcanal's General Headquarters less than a mile from the wharf. The best the Seabees could offer in the way of a structure was a large split-bamboo building hastily constructed with a thatched roof.

Nonetheless, Peter enjoyed an unusually fine dinner, and the continuous singing of the Andrews Sisters from one of the few

American jukeboxes to be found in the South Pacific. His favorite song, "Have I Told You Lately That I Love You," sung by the three sisters, and accompanied by Bing Crosby, was repeatedly played since it brought him all the closer to his beloved, Joan Ikeda.

Arriving by jeep a few minutes before 10:00PM that night at the long pier, Guadalcanal's main passenger landing-docking wharf, embarkation of passengers had apparently begun after the arrival of a three-freighter convoy two hours before. A light drizzle which had begun around twilight for the second time that day turned into a 20 minute torrential downpour of horizontal sheets.

Escorted by his captain-ranked driver to the waiting launch at Guadalcanal's primary pier's ramp, Peter had to maneuver between the native "fuzzy-wuzzy" waterfront workers piling and unpiling, stacking and unstacking boxes and crates, empty and filled, with every imaginable resource needed by men at war preparing for invasion. Lined up on stretchers under rain-protecting tarpaulins were more than 100 severely wounded Marines readied for relocation at Army-Navy hospitals in Melbourne. Corpsmen were milling about. Some were actually dressing wounds that had opened while transported from both the main hospitals of Banika and Guadalcanal. Peter overheard a Navy doctor sadly pronounce that one man with severe abdominal mortar wounds had passed away en route.

It was at that point that Peter learned he would not be boarding the transport USS Morgan but the USS Pinkey, an evacuation transport, a combination troop transport and hospital ship with an augmented medical staff and wardrooms for casualties.

It so happened that Peter, to expedite his journey Stateside was ordered to board the USS Pinkey, one of the smaller ships among the four transport groups of Task Force 71 assembled at Lunga Point's long pier. The USS Pinkey was assigned to join Transdiv. 12, the destroyer transport group, Five of Task Force 71 destroyers were ordered to the U.S. Naval installations in Melbourne for refitting of the newest, most advance radar system equipment, and retraining of each destroyer's personnel in its use.

After being escorted to his private single-berth quarters with a bolted-down waiting table, Peter was delighted. It was a far-superior stateroom, in space, cleanliness, and minor conveniences, than any he had occupied in his Pacific War travels thus far. Placing his duffle bag on the tautly stretched Navy blanket of his bunk, Peter, deeply curious about the unusual medical tender he was sailing upon, wandered the vessel at will. Invariably, an officer, corpsman, or gob in blue shirt and dungarees asked Peter jokingly,

"Are you one of those raggedy-ass Canal boys?"

Grey-hulled, the USS Pinkey was neither painted white nor displayed a Red Cross. It was not a "non-combatant" since it carried various small cannons and heavy machine guns. Its complement was 12 officers and over 60 corpsmen. The Pinkey's role was mainly to transport Marine regiments from Australia, unload their weapons and munitions, then return with serious casualties. It was staffed by five surgeons, an otolaryngologist and urologist, with assorted American and Australian nurses. Since it had numerous operating rooms, emergency operations were conducted on board.

Fortunately, the entire 6½ day journey occurred without mishap or misfortune. Indeed, the convoy of Task Force 71's four transport groups, more than two-dozen ships escorted by seven destroyers, one of the largest convoys to set sail to Australia from an advance battle zone in the summer of 1944, sailed under a protective overcast and not once were challenged by Japanese naval, air force, or submarine forces.

At precisely 0100 on the morning of August 21, the convoy was well on its way, and during the week that followed, Peter again experienced the tedium of ocean travel in the vast South Pacific. The dark, cloudy, gloomy weather encouraged remaining below deck, usually playing cribbage, blackjack, or poker, the medical personnel's favorite card games. On deck, the infinite sky above was a monotonous blue, the ocean waters intensifying the tiresomeness of it all. Even an occasional glorious sunset couldn't alleviate the "Long Sail", as the wounded 1st Marines on their way to Australian and Stateside hospitals facetiously referred to the journey.

Meanwhile, a budding camaraderie quickly developed between Peter and the officers of the medical staff. They discussed all military issues pertaining to their involvements, politics and sports at home, as well as plans after the war. There was plenty of good food to eat and snack upon, Peter feeling the strength returning to his muscles. On the third day out, the USS Pinkey made a sweeping turn to the southeast, skirting New Caledonia then passing the Loyalty Islands. Soon, the Task Force would be leaving the southern Coral Sea and gliding parallel to the northern Great Barrier Reef.

On that fifth day, just after supper, while at the railing toward the stern of the Pinkey observing a brilliantly colorful sunset, Peter carefully opened the sealed letter and read the official stark, blunt, two sentence typewritten order:

"Lt. Peter A. Toscanini, USN (MC) temporarily assigned to the 1st Medical BN, 1st Marine Division (REINFORCED), Cape Gloucester ("Backhander") Operation to Palaus ("Stalemate II") Operation, is formally detached for pending assignment. He is to report no later than 20 days from this date forward to Comdr. Emil E. Napp (MC) USN at the Oakland-Alameda Naval Air Station, San Francisco for

Redesignation Communique 174 RM13SXT1446, with 18-day furlough granted."

Of course, Peter had no idea what the Redesignation Communique would contain, and he would have to await arrival in the San Francisco Bay Area to find out, but he was delighted about the number of leave days ordered, sufficient time to travel by train to the Rohwer Interment Camp in Arkansas, four days to and four days back from the air station.

Meanwhile, the monotony of five additional days and nights aboard the Pinkey would have to be endured. And, adding annoyance to the wearisomeness, lifejackets were mandatory, even within sight of Eastern Australia's Great Dividing Range. Few were bothered that deck space was virtually nonexistent. Off-duty sailors, relaxing corpsmen and other medical staff, as well as anxious "hitchhikers", such as Lieutenant Peter Toscanini, simply sprawled themselves everywhere, and anywhere playing cards, sunbathing in the ocean air by the Pacific sun. Occasional training classes i.e. "Know Your Enemy - How to Recognize a Jap" and the two hot cafeteria-style meals a day were the certainties of the routine, although every other night offered a movie or special performance or two. But even these were difficult to endure due to the overcrowded conditions.

Although Lieutenant Toscanini was a deeply emotional man, he was writhing psychologically, unconsciously under the grip of an intuitive feeling he couldn't define, classify, or understand. And, the qualm was intensified during the journey's lazy days of rest, white sunshine breaking through the low, gray overcasts, stretched out on blankets on deck "shooting the breeze" and "scuttle-butting". While the deep wounds on his body and the bruises that marred his face inflicted by Pinoe slowly healed, Peter's thoughts of the Mad Ghoul and his accomplice intensified, assailing his consciousness. His confidence in the tragedy's conclusion decreasing, Peter's vague doubts and disquiet turned into terror. In the final throes of the hand-to-hand struggle, Pinoe had muttered something gutturally and profanely that bitterly poisoned his positive emotions about the outcome.

What was it?

Why couldn't he remember what was said? Was it too painful to recall?

As the USS Pickney sliced its way through the lapping Australian waves, and he was as relaxed as if he were at home on his front porch, he simply couldn't recollect the lisped words. No amount of deck skylarking could convince his memory to bring back the utterances. Repeatedly, he recalled and relived the scene in the lavatory, its silence, gloomy dimness, the atmosphere of solemnity stiffened his determination to get to the bottom of it.

Ellen's attempt to murder him left him in a strange cold calm, less wary, more implacably irresolute. For her, he felt more pity than condemnation in his heart than he did for Pinoe. Yet, the chaplain deserved a bare touch of compassion. Yes, he multiple-murdered young Marines. But, Pinoe insisted he be in the first wave ashore during the invasion of Guadalcanal when he could have waited for the third and fourth waves when there was no longer the threat of being killed while wading ashore. Later, when asked about his determination, he said simply, "It's always in the first wave ashore when the boys need me."

Although Ellen would have plunged the Ka-Bar into the deepest part of his face, reflecting about her brought a sympathetic, almost kindly, glow in his eyes. Because he liked her the moment he met her months before, he would have easily fallen in love with her had it not been for Joan Ikeda. Even now, he was still haunted by the fury in her wide blazing eyes as she lifted the Marine knife over her head. How could he erase the image, her hair disheveled, her frozen face chalk white, every fiber in her young body intent on killing him. Even now, the tornado of the life and death struggle with Pinoe was less important than what she meant to him, even now.

Past Cairns, Townsville, MacKay, Rockhampton, the Curtis Islands, Fraser Island, Brisbane, Southport, Sydney, the Task Force sailed until midmorning of the sixth day when shouts were heard throughout the USS Pickney, "Melbourne! Melbourne!"

Appearing to rise out of the sea were the modern high-rises of a beautiful Australian city. Its harbor was crowded with warships from all the allied Pacific nations since by August of 1944, a number of island invasions were pending. Later, after the USS Pickney dropped anchor, Peter awaited a launch, or landing craft, to transport him ashore, heard his name announced over the ship's intercom system to report to the bridge cabin where Captain Henry Fallon was expecting him.

Hurrying up the steps to the bridge in a drenching shower, he was greeted with a smile and handshake,

"Lieutenant, a radio signal arrived moments ago. Air transportation to the McClellan Air Base is available within the hour. A launch is on the way, and the Military Police is already at the pier waiting your disembarkation. There, you'll be met by G-4 Lieutenant Colonel Harold Deakins, 2nd Provisional Military Police Battalion, 1st Marine Division, who will read your new assignment to you. He will take no questions. Your flight will last 22 hours, arriving at the McClellan Air Base by 0300 day after tomorrow, stateside date and time. Your duffle bag has been packed and awaits you at the boarding ramp. The launch, I see, is arriving just about now. Good bye, lieutenant, and good luck whatever your new assignment is."

Within minutes, Peter was in the launch and less than a half hour later, in the backseat of a military police staff car alongside of Lt. Col. Deakins.

"No one knows your full assignment, lieutenant, or to whom, how, and when you'll report your results. My orders are to ensure you arrive at the airfield and that the departure is on schedule and routine."

With that, Peter smiled, turned away, and enjoyed a final glimpse of the city of Melbourne, his thick duffle bag in between his legs.

CHAPTER TWENTY

-

Headed Stateside

To Peter, Melbourne at the end of August 1944, the end of winter below the equator since the Northern and Southern Hemispheres were reversed, was a wonderful sight to behold. A stopover for a few days would have been a pleasant "tag" to his 18-day furlough. A city of more than a million, the Aussies were known throughout the Allied forces for their generosity and hospitality. A fighting American like himself was not regarded as a foreign troop, soldier, or sailor, but a "hero" like every member of the Australian military. But, for Peter, there was no time for such a relaxing pause.

For his two-stop, 33-hour journey aboard a stripped-down B-29 "super fortress" to the only airfield in Northern California capable of accommodating such a large bomber, the McClellan Field closer to Sacramento than San Francisco, Peter was driven to the Point Cook Base of the Royal Australian Air Force for a back seat. More than 60 other military passengers would be returning stateside with Peter; Army, Navy, Marine, and Air Force officers, along with representatives of various Intelligence Services, Technical Divisions, the American Red Cross, etc. Two air groups occupied the aviation parking lots next to the "Superfortresses", 30 in all. They were the newly arrived 374th Troup Carrier Group and 60th Air Depot Group. Since the summer of 1942, the American Airforce (USAAF) and the Australian Airforce (RAAF) had shared the base. On the fringes of the base were parked

US A-20 Havocs, A-24 Dauntlesses, and worn-out, virtually obsolete, B-17 Flying Fortresses.

Peter, now standing on the edge of the runway, marveled at the sight. On the opposite side of the field were over 100 C-47s of the 54 Troop Carrier Wing and some 80 CG-4A gilders in preparations for whatever island invasions were being planned. Behind all these planes were parked troop carriers and huge storage dumps of gasoline, ammunition, and other supplies. Suddenly a roar overhead forced Peter to look skyward, and there, flying low, four P-51s flew past, perhaps on a mission since their route was upward. What part of the field they emanated from, he had no idea.

Then, a welcome sight was gazed upon: four Australian-affiliated Red Cross women dressed in clean, starched uniforms walked forward from the nearby terminal kitchen with trays of pastries, doughnuts, and warm enthusiasm. Peter hadn't eaten since the night before on the USS Pickney. The large coffee container a young lieutenant wheeled up behind them was welcomed even more.

As Peter munched upon a small tasty Australian pastry, a cup of hot black 'Joe' in the other hand, as one of the Red Cross teenage girls referred to American coffee, two of the Seventh AAF Command staff cars pulled up and parked on a rise of reserved ground area some 20 yards from the tarmac. Peter, standing adjacent to his duffle bag, conversing with an officer also waiting instructions to board, knew the several officers emerging from the vehicle were coming to direct his departure.

A tall, slender captain with a thin toothbrush mustache below a perplexed, quizzical expression, asked,

"Where can I find Naval Lieutenant Toscanini?"

"Here, sir. Would salute if I didn't have my hands full," Peter responded with a smile.

"Sorry for not being present upon your arrival at the pier. We were informed earlier this morning you were to be handed a memorandum, sealed and confidential, from Headquarters, 3rd Marine Division, Fleet Marine Force, revising your previous stated orders unopened until read a few days ago aboard ship. Per instructions on the face of this dispatch's envelope, you are not to open or read until your arrival at the McClellan Field in California. If I may suggest, lest you lose it during your 5,000 miles of flight, stopovers, and possible change of planes, you tape the envelope to your leg," the captain said somberly.

Peter nodded without comment.

"You are to be seated," continued the captain, "among four officers of the Pacific Aviation Engineer Battalion. They design and construct our airstrips, island to island. They are not Seabees, but the instructors of those who instruct the Seabees. I believe I see them to your left, approaching from the little-used emergency landing grassy field. Come, I'll introduce you to them now."

Just then, however, a minor pandemonium broke out among the scattered assembled six or seven groups totaling more than 60 as the B-29 "Superfortress" taxied toward them from one of the dozen hangers at that end of the runway. En masse, some 60 officers carrying their various bags and briefcases surged toward the embarkation stand and ramp. A staff sergeant holding a pen and clipboard quietly asked the first arrivals to begin lining up. He immediately started checking their names off.

Amidst the continuous din of the four-engine propeller revolving hubs, the thinly mustached officer who saw no point in even introducing himself promptly yelled,

"Sorry, Lieutenant, the airman aboard will show you the cabin area assigned to the Pacific Aviation Engineers. You'll have to introduce yourself. They're on their way to McClellan Field, too. Stay close to them. They know their way around the in and outs of the journey. Although I'm not positive, and even if I were, names and personnel change at the whims of whoever happens to be writing or typing the orders. But as far as I know, you'll be greeted and whisked away from McClellan to the Oakland-Alameda Naval Air Station, an hour's drive away, by Colonel Logan Gaulding himself, of the MPs, Force Special Troops (FFACF), Marine Garrison Force Pacific. Apparently, you're V.I.P. stuff, to have him not only pick you up, but personally drive you 80 miles to the Alameda Naval Station. In our office, the speculation is that he will be your mentor on a special assignment for the 18th Service Battalion of the 1st - 3rd Base headquarters III AC-VAC. You are holding the envelope, witnessed by six of my officers. My responsibility was to see you board, which you are about to do. And, now, lieutenant, you are on your own. Good luck to you, sir."

With hand waves and their abrupt departures, Peter turned to stand in line to board. He was in a near-perfect position to study the Boeing B-29, "Superfortress", or "Flying Fortress", or "Superfort", the familiar names of the American public for the spectacular aircraft.

"My God," he thought, "for all its massive potential for death and destruction, it's the most beautiful machine for war ever created: A shiny, flush-riveted, non-camouflaged silver aluminum monster. And, damn, look at those four Turbosuperchargers, probably more than 2,000 horsepower each with four-bladed propellers capable, I've heard, of flying well over 4,000 miles without bombs. And guns! Look at 'em! At least a dozen .50-caliber machine guns and, look-at-it-there, in the tail, a 20-mm cannon! Supposedly, the airship has remote-control turrets. Supposedly, one of these returning from a bombing mission a month ago fought off more than half a hundred Jap fighters, Zeroes, Bettys, black, shiny Zekes, Vals, Tonys, etc., every one of them with large red rounders on its sides. All the way to California, more than 7,800 miles away, there will be no need to anxiously search the skies for fast single-engine Jap fighters. They'll be afraid to attack!"

With that, Peter stepped up and into the aircraft. There, an airman issued him, and everyone else who boarded, a parachute and a long-billed flight cap. He was told the Pacific Aviation Engineers were to sit near the stern gun tub. Although the 60 or more officers quickly climbed aboard, putting out their cigarettes, they continued to talk loudly, some even excitedly. Behind them followed various ground crew inspectors checking, double-checking, and triple checking all the exterior props, gun emplacements, etc. Crew members checked the interior for overloading, power failure possibilities, safety of fuel tanks, the props that prevent against burnt-out engines, the central fire-control system, adequacy of the newly-installed radar equipment, and all other intricate, complex instruments, devices, machines, and systems pertaining to the safety of flight control. The final inspection was conducted by the ground crew who surrounded the Fortress, listening nervously for any sound suggesting a troubled engine.

As command staff cars, jeep, aircraft prime movers, supply trucks, and gasoline tanks began dispersing from on and around the main runway, final preparations were made for liftoff.

Having introduced himself to his four traveling engineering-officer companions, Peter leaned back, gazing out the small window. He thought to himself, "The Central and South Pacific they would be flying over was the largest water theater in the world, 16 million square miles, five times the size of the United States. They would be flying at more than 20,000 feet over thousands of miles of emptiness. At times, there would be nothing but ocean for over a thousand miles. The feeling of being left alone would be overwhelming for the new aviation passengers.

It was with a wonderful feeling of suspense combined with exhilaration that Peter, sitting back, felt the B-29 "Superfortress", with a mild lurching, take off. Now airborne, he wondered how the 38-ton bomber would handle the soft, moist air of the Southern Seas. He wondered, then smiled remembering someone back in line say that its pilots were recipients of the Distinguished Flying Cross Awards for previous B-29 missions over southern Japan. Furthermore, they were employing the newest navigational technology. No, traveling at 360 miles per hour with several stopovers for most refueling was of little concern.

The entire furlough, despite the promise of being marred by constant nagging by the memory of the multiple murders of The Ghoul, was a welcomed rest and opportunity for relaxed visits with Joan in Kansas and his parents, as well as extended family later in California.

So it was that during the long hours that followed, with the exception of a brief stopover in Wellington, New Zealand, to pick up officers awaiting passage to San Francisco, that the droning sound of the four Wright R-3350-23 Turbosuperchargers put Peter to sleep. When he awakened hours later, islands were before him, broken rings of coral built on the peaks of submerged volcanoes. Virtually all were bare, white, and treeless. They belonged to the southernmost group of the Tuamotu Archipelago. By morning, the B-29 would be well past the Christmas Islands, a large number of them, less than an additional seven hours to the Hawaiian Islands.

Wide awake, and with nothing to read, Peter became acquainted with his four new friends.

"So, you are the guys who build the bases for these big things," he said, pretending sarcasm.

"Yes, sir," a young USAF captain smiled. "At least five dozen on the drawing boards throughout the greater Pacific, plus a dozen for Formosa alone. Brand new B-29s, that's what going to win the war for us. They'll be staged, along with long-range single-engine aircraft, on new runways, in such a way that no part of the Rising Sun will escape being bombed to Hell. We'll be able to have these Superforts on bases between New Caledonia to the Marianas, all the way to that little spec of volcanic ash called Iwo Jima, the one with the reputation of being the most unpredictable target in the Pacific. All stepping stones to downtown Tokyo. All 30 VHB groups under the auspices of the Seventh Air Force."

"Nice," nodded Peter, an ear-to-ear grin crossing his face.

The captain continued,

"Lieutenant Wayland, here, answers directly to CINCPOA. Sergeant Jackson is adjutant to Vice Admiral J.H. Hoover, Commander, Forward Area. I can't share with you what I do, or who I report to."

"Certainly. I understand. I only know the geography of the Western Islands, the Solomons, Canal, and the Russells. Our Henderson Field is the longest runway in that part of the ocean. But it's less than 3,000 feet, only for single fighters. On my Pavuvu Island, the only runway we have there is a rarely-used dirt road with crushed coral."

"Well, we're all headed to San Francisco, and, upon landing, off to our separate assignments in different directions, to meet and confer with civilian engineers and manufacturers regarding a number of technical and logistical issues. For example, I fly down to Downey, California, near Los Angeles for a meeting with the big-shot executives and engineers of the Consolidated Aircraft Company that made the popular Liberator and is now making at that huge plant the B-29s. And, by the way, Hoover, my boss reports directly to Admiral Chester Nimitz."

"Listen, Lieutenant Toscanini, make the Marines aware that our guys work 24 hours a day supervising the Seabees, overseeing the Seabees while they construct the airstrips and runways, hard stands connecting the taxiways, service aprons, various roads, low-project warehouses, storage sheds, underground facilities for bombs delivered to be used by heavy bombardment units, housing for personnel, mess halls, latrines, washrooms, etc. etc. Very few in the Armed Forces know the extent of what we do to help win this war in the Pacific," interrupted Sergeant Jackson the adjutant to Vice Admiral Hoover.

"Peter", added Lieutenant Wayland, who answered only to CINCPOA, "We're so pleased that the first 12 groups, 30 B-29s per group, are in the air, on their way to our advanced bases to replace, relieve, and add to what obsolete bombers we already have attacking every day. In fact, we'll wave at them as they fly past in the opposite direction in our flight path tomorrow around noon. We'll leave Hickory Field in Honolulu on our long final leg to Frisco."

The relaxing camaraderie between Peter and his new-found buddies would last until the five clasped hands to bid au revoir on the McClellan tarmac until they met again somewhere in the Far Pacific. It wouldn't be easy. For seemingly endless hours, they had explored and conversed about a kaleidoscope of subjects, issues, military victories and defeats, including personal joys and tragedies. And, while they spoke quietly and dispassionately under the great rumbling noise of synchronous propellers, they drank can after can of tomato juice. Since smoking wasn't allowed, they sucked different colored candy "Lifesavers", as they gossiped and shared rumors, about mechanics and crew chiefs to the members of the Joint Chiefs of Staff. Meanwhile, vibrations and reverberations seemed to accentuate what was beneath them--the eternal, empty, covetous sea, and above them, ice-cold overcasts.

Across the wide Pacific they flew, hour after hour, napping, lost in thought, each to his own, reflecting, ribbing, and surprisingly for grown men, debating the pros and cons of World War II's comic book heroes such as Captain Marvel, Joe Palooka, Terry and the Pirates, Boy Commandoes, Superman, Boy Submariner, Dick Tracy, etc. etc., as each hero fought Tojo, Mussolini and Hilter. Unless asked directly about the rumors already circulating throughout the Pacific bases about the attempt on Bob Hope's life, Peter would not utter a word about the Mad Ghoul and his involvement in capturing the murder-mad Marine.

In the final 90 minutes of the flight, the closer the Flying Fortress approached the West Coast of the United States, California and its principal city of San Francisco, with McClellan Field only 25 minutes of descent flight time away from touchdown, the more impatient and excited the passengers became. Surprisingly, a significant number were subdued, even sullen. Peter, a psychologist, understood the dynamics of anxiety of suddenly being Stateside, a rush of home life and activities overwhelming the man in direct proportion to the length of his absence. And, entering one's hometown or city, the familiar sights, food, noises, horizons and skylines, and the welcomed sights of streets, trees, parks, schools, hospitals, theaters, churches, traffic corners, businesses often suddenly restrained, even stultified, rather than release pent-up emotions or fulfill longing. For some, coming home, even for only a short visit, could be cruel or joyous.

But not for Peter, and his new friends. Although no one would admit it, all five were a bit giddy.

Just then, wind-driven elephant-size clouds, accompanied by thunder and lightning, burst open, unleashing a deluge of thick, heavy raindrops that pummeled the B-29, slightly swaying the massive steel and aluminum bomber.

"Oh, hell!" someone sneered. "Looks like we gotta land in this. No fun. Not a proper welcome for five courageous fighting like us."

"I agree," someone else added, "hate massive downpours and even hate more the lingering showers. Doesn't help morale."

"Won't last," interjected Peter, "I already see sunlight streaking through the broken clouds there to my right."

Then, almost as quickly as the thundershower unleashed itself, the storm was over, the clouds dissipating, or simply evaporating. The late-afternoon sun seemed to engulf all the northern world of California with magnificent bright yellow-orange colors some 10,000 feet below.

"Land ahoy!" shouted a pilot from the Superfortress's cockpit over the intercom system.

And, sure enough, far, far ahead of the aircraft was the historic, six-year-old, Golden Gate Bridge, one of the world's most remarkable engineering marvels. Basking in the late afternoon sun, the new span not only represented America's genius of engineering and construction, but also superb planning at the financial level to pay the high cost of the achievement. As applauding erupted accompanied with shouts and yelps of joy, hand-shaking all around, and laughter, much of it nervous, followed by a shed tear or two, the feelings of well-being saturated everyone.

Wheeling slowly, less than 200 miles per hour, like a massive winged pterosaurs reptile, the popular plane gradually settled on a course straight to McClellan Field, less than 100 miles away in the northern San Joaquin Valley. Already, the pilot was calmly requesting landing instructions, which he assumed would include a downwind approach. Although Peter was born and raised in nearby Stockton, less than 60 miles away, and knew the San Francisco Bay Area well, he had never seen the area from that height and perspective.

He was captivated by the unlimited cloudless visibility. To his right, as the "Flying Fortress" soared over Alcatraz and Angel Islands, were the cities of San Francisco and, across the Bay Bridge, San Pablo Bay, Richmond, Berkeley, the Oakland Army Base, Alameda Naval Air Station, Hayward to Newark and San Jose.

Then, almost immediately, Peter felt a slight vibration and he realized descent had commenced, and once over Mount Diablo, within minutes, the McClellan runways could be seen. Within a moment the B-29 "Superfortress" was entering the 3,000 acres, 3.3 million square feet of the USAFF Training Airfield, a major Command responsible for training pilots and aircrews of swift fighters and heavy bombers.

As the "Superfortress" continued its long descent, reaching the B-29's minimum decent altitude, and maintaining the aircraft in level flight, it was less than three minutes from the runway. Peter, gazing out his small window, and enjoying the slow, smooth approach, saw more than a hundred maintenance buildings, several dozen steel hangers, and innumerable machine shops in various clusters throughout the huge base. Little-used emergency landing fields dotted the areas in between. And alongside of them were flimsy, temporary warehouses.

Within seconds of touchdown well beyond the midpoint of the 4,000 feet long strip, four engines began to soften their heavy burbling, the dull sound of a bump and its accompanying shimmying signaled a successful landing. When the taxiing was complete, and the four supercharger engines switched off near the main airport, the flight was over. Everyone aboard again broke out in spontaneous clapping and cheers, Peter joining in. But to him, it meant even more. There was an exhilarating sense of deliverance, first to feel the gradual decent, then hear the landing gear released, followed by the sound of the impact of the drop.

Peter's only disappointment upon being back home occurred as he stepped down from the Superfortress: the suffocating, broiling dry heat of the western San Joaquin Valley in late August.

For some of the officers returning Stateside, being home wasn't the remedy for the emotional turmoil of recent combat.

Although Peter's parents, grandparents, and extended family, as well as the proud city of Stockton, California were just beyond the horizon to the southeast, he was consumed by an inexplicable sadness.

Why was he occasionally preoccupied with the final utterance of the Mad Murderer? Did he miss a fact or clue, as to the identities of the Mad Ghoul? Was a third murderer involved? Whatever was operating at his unconscious level, he was irritable, anxious, depressed, and agitated.

Now, however, he was faced with the immediate reality of "What happens now?"

Among the first to emerge from the B-29's fully pressurized main cabin and disembark down the wheeled up stepped ramp, Peter felt the full force of the searing dry 115-degree heat. From near-perfect comfort to miserable, debilitating heat, he was near wilting until he heard, then saw, a large number of greeters, friends and relatives, well-wishers in a large mob, crushed and confused, beyond the tarmac within a fenced area near the baggage claim area. A dozen yards from the cabin ramp, a group of high level officers, all grey haired or balding officers with bronze furrowed faces, most holding files or satchels, waiting patiently. Each had a job to do, and the sooner the better. Sprinkled among them were a few Army Nurses (ANC) and Women's Army Corps (WAC) officers, and several Red Cross young women with trays of fresh doughnuts, pots of steaming coffee, and decanters of cold orange juice.

Then, the depositing of the B-29's cargo of officers began. Every one of the travelers was exhausted. With packed gear, shoeboxes tied with string, small cartons and assorted bags, canvas and otherwise in hand, each officer descended the aluminum steps and quietly lined up in a queue. There was sorting out to be done by the McClellan Field administrative staff prior to release and transportation assignment to respective assignments. As those queued up waited patiently to be processed and released to the crowded fenced-off outer yard, the five pilots of the Superfortress walked past clutching their baggage of personal belongings. Not a word was spoken as spontaneous clapping began, an applause lasting a full minute as the embarrassed pilots simply raised their thumbs in pleased acknowledgement.

Despite the pervasive heat, Peter, as exhausted as everyone else, was pumped up, especially when a small Army Air Force band among the greeters behind the fence began playing Glen Miller's, "In the Mood"; the song made famous by the Andrew Sisters, "Don't Fence Me In"; and "Boogie Woogie Bugle Boy", sung by a young Red Cross teenager atop a large wooden crate. Such big band music usually appreciated in the barracks was certainly welcomed as the officers were processed. But when the band, minus a number of key instrumental players, began playing Irving Berlin's 1918 composed "God Bless America", beautifully sung by another teenager, undoubtedly still in high school, did the usual inviolable, Peter feel a tear or two run down his cheek.

With scarcely a backward glance at their friend, the famous Flying Fortress of World War II, everyone scattered in varying directions with those awaiting their arrivals, many headed to base offices, others to the nearby parking lots.

Peter, standing on the street curb outside the small terminal, had no idea, not the faintest inkling, what to expect next. His plan was to quietly open the confidential envelope with what felt to be a single sheet of official military stationery in the presence of the Military Police Captain or Lieutenant he expected to meet. If he had questions, they could be answered by whoever welcomed him. But no one was there to greet him! Neither an envelope, written message, telegram, nor a simple phone call. He decided to reenter the terminal and request a lift to Base Headquarters.

With a slight touch of anger, Peter, with his duffle bags in hand, turned and stepped toward the terminal entrance, when, suddenly, he heard a the honking horn from a Command staff car, with a second Buick following.

As Peter abruptly turned, and the initial car pulled up to the curb where he had been standing, waiting, an officer, colonel in rank, jumped out and asked, almost frantically,

"Lieutenant Peter Toscanini?"

"Yes, sir!" Peter answered, turning around with an appreciative grin.

"Whew! Hoped we hadn't missed you!"

"I'm relieved you arrived, whomever you are, colonel. I was on my way back into the…"

"Well, we were delayed. We had an urgent order to await the latest word from your key contact in the assignment you are to undertake."

As he shook Peter's hand, he introduced himself.

"I'm Colonel Stuart Paige from the Marine Garrison Forces, Pacific. Mine is currently the 6th Company, Force Special Troops. Our sole duty is to guard Japanese prisoners of war captured by all services at the Iroquois Point Stockade at Pearl. We were formed just this past March. At the end of next month, September 30, I'm reassigned to return here at McClellan Field from the Canal to command all Stateside Provisional Military Police companies, detachments, and platoons formed on various American bases. We'll headquarter here at McClellan in this inferno of the San Joaquin."

Just then, a hefty, medium-sized, middle-aged officer with a kindly face and gentle gestures and movements approached with his trailing adjutant clutching a clipboard.

Colonel Paige said, "This is Captain Harry Wallace of the Atchison, Topeka and Santa Fe Railway who reports to the Officer in Charge of the Passenger Section of the U.S. Army Transportation Division. Following him is Lieutenant Edward Irby of the Southern Pacific Company of the Military Railway Service."

As Peter awaited the punch line, his new assignment, he noted the unmistakable tone of urgency. Everyone was in a hurry due to a sense of major importance.

"We must leave immediately, Lt. Toscanini. You are to catch the SP all military train out of Sacramento to Los Angeles. Since we had no time to cut your orders and travel papers, Captain Wallace will accompany you to a point south. I will leave you at the Southern Pacific Station in Sacramento. I'll read your orders to you in the staff car on the way. You are not to have a copy; it's that confidential."

"Wow. Can you at least tell me where I'm going?" Peter asked slowly, quietly.

"Why to the Rohwer Relocation Center in McGehee, Arkansas, of course!"

CHAPTER TWENTY-ONE

-

On to McGehee, Arkansas

Stunned, amazed, enormously pleased, Peter gasped, "Huh?"

"With all due respect, lieutenant, get in the damn car. We've got to move, if we're to catch that all troop streamliner."

Somewhat in a shock of awe, Peter shoved his bags into the passenger side of the front command car next to the driver's seat and climbed into the backseat with Colonel Page. Captain Wallace and the two adjutants entered the second command car.

Within a moment, the two Buicks were driving at the maximum speed limits of the McClellan Airfield toward the Base's easternmost exit that led to Highway 580 and, beyond, some dozen city blocks, to the Southern Pacific Railway Station.

For Peter, the experience of seeing the massive base, one of only three in California capable of accommodating B-29's required 4,000-foot runways, was a joy in itself. Although he was born and raised less than 50 miles away in Stockton, he had never once stepped on the McClellan grounds, let alone toured the facility. He knew of its remarkable reputation as not only an instructing airfield born out of the need for to train skilled single-engine fighter pilots in the last year of World War I, but also as a staging area for transportation of as many as 30,000 troops at one time.

Past row upon row of two-story olive drab colored barracks, they sped, leaving Peter in a trance-like state. McClellan was as monotonous as the Pacific. As the funnel through which fighter and bomber pilots poured into to recently captured Pacific bases, the site wasn't chosen for its beauty. Only a few miles from San Francisco Bay, it was selected because it was large enough for the advance aircrafts of the future.

"Well," chuckled Colonel Paige, "Aren't you going to ask any questions?"

After a moment of reflection, Peter, still observing the layout of the base, said weakly,

"I'm a bit embarrassed because I believe I just peed all over my seat. Rohwer is the one place I want to go on this earth, just about now. How on earth did you fellas know?"

"What an uproar of logistical managing and planning by a number of high officers in diverse important offices to get you to some placid, dull, podunk Arkansas small town. And, having to read every communiqué, starting with 'For Your Eyes Only. Destroy Upon Reading'. You certainly are V.I.P. to get there without delay."

"I'm on a 18-day furlough, most of which is to be spent with my finance at the Rohwer Relocation Camp in the Vicksburg Engineering District guarded by the U.S. Army Corps of Engineers."

"Yes, I heard she is a Nisei."

"What? You people know all this? How so? Why?"

"O.K. I can tell you all I know. When you return from visiting 'Joan'. You're going to be on a streamliner just moments from now all the way to McGehee, Arkansas. After visiting with Joan, three days, you'll board another train for the nine-day return trip, but to Stockton where you will spend three days at home with your parents. At that point, your 18 day furlough will end and, on the morning of the 19 day, we will pick you up at your parents' home to report to me at either my McClellan or my Oakland Army office for final instructions and deployment."

"Where?"

"The Camp Elliott brig outside San Diego. You'll be going into it as a prisoner in an undercover operation. It seems that in that stockade, an inordinate, an excessive number of killings of Marine inmates, some of our boys simply disappearing. Your job will be to find out what's going on without you being murdered yourself. You'll be all by yourself, you and the killer, or killers, who are reportedly the guards and officers themselves. Somehow, you are to learn if there is an unmarked burial ground of Marines, supposedly cremated remains in the brig's ovens. Not one officer, will know, absolutely no one will know who you are and you'll therefore not have anyone to lean on, to call for help, aid, or assistance."

"What proof do you have such murders are going on?" Peter asked quietly, wide-eyed.

"None, or we would have made arrests and closed it. But, rumors have persisted for almost a year now due to a significant number of unexplained dead, dying, and unaccounted for, and deaths from so-called, supposed, 'inmate fights'. Almost 24 deaths within one year! By going undercover, you'll see for yourself. When you report to my office upon your return from Arkansas, you'll be permitted to read all the reports, observations and analyses. We're in the process of creating for you a file of information on who you are, your crimes, sentences, and where you served time. It will follow you into the stockade and brig. You'll arrive at Elliott aboard a prison bus with inmates from numerous other western states, but you'll be the one from Oakland. The only help you'll have will be a phone number that you'll be able to access, of course, 24 hours a day. These are only a few of the aspects we'll go over when you return and are ready to assume your assignment. Upon the success of this project, there are several other assignments awaiting your expertise."

"I'll be ready, Colonel Paige, and will work with you accordingly upon my return. I understand why I cannot be provided paperwork to peruse and study. So, I must remain patient until I return. But can you tell me who, and what agencies and officers were, logistically involved in the nightmare my furlough caused?"

"That information is undoubtedly restricted, although no one has indicated it is not. I will tell you, Peter, if you and I have an agreement that the information I share will not be provided to anyone else lest the superb coordination allows insight about the special methods we use in joint - participation operations among agencies."

"Yes, you have my word."

"Well, in each area headquarters, like mine for Northern California back at McClellan, blackboards keep commanders like me informed on carefully monitored Lieutenant Peter Toscanini's movements. Apparently, your assignment changed twice during your journey here, including the one I received less than an hour ago. The Army Transportation Office in San Francisco has ultimate jurisdiction over your safety, security, and success of arrival. I don't know who those officers are or who's overall is responsible for you between Pavuvu, Rohwer, and McClellan. Upon touchdown, I received a radiogram you had safely arrived. I immediately informed the Transportation Command Centers in Honolulu and San Francisco, adjunct offices of the Army Transportation Office. Both offices carry the authority equivalent of the highest authority, other than the Chief of Transportation Troop Movement, Division of Special Services in Washington, D.C. The detail desk there is who I'm in regular contact with, and, believe me, Major John Dunne and Lt. Colonel George

Barney, like the tub of fat, Captain Wallace, in the car behind us, are old, hard-boiled, ignorant gruffers, puny to say the least, who make it all the more tedious and difficult."

After a pause, Peter grinned,

"Believe me, I know the type."

"Now, let me have your sealed confidential letter. I will destroy it for you. I will read your new order. You will listen to your new order and, once again, not receive a copy. In this instance, as well, the order will be destroyed. All you have in hand for your new assignment will be a pass document Captain Wallace will give to you for train travel to and from Arkansas, and my phone number."

Peter remained silent as he handed over the old confidential envelope.

Colonel Paige tore open the newly arrived radiogram; showed it to Peter for a moment, then read him the contents:

U.S. Navy Department
Washington, D.C.
August 21, 1944
In Reply Refer
To Number
M/O 12/1164
From:The Director
The Officer-In-Charge, Security

Reference:

1)You are temporarily ordered for the duration of the spoken word assignment as an undercover agent, special and unencumbered, to the

1st Provisional Military Police Battalion FMFPAC. All modes of travel will be Class A (Special)

2)Colonel Stuart Paige, temporarily commanding the 2nd Provisional MP Battalion, will be your exclusive monitor.

Major General Homer Isetti

As the two Command vehicles screeched to a halt in front of the Southern Pacific - Union Pacific Station terminal in west Sacramento, the busiest in the San Joaquin Valley, and the third busiest in the state of California, Peter was dismayed that the colonel had ordered the driver to drive past the long line of local autos dropping off or picking up passengers. An M.P. traffic officer waving his baton and calling out there was no parking in the area, Paige jumped from the auto and confronted the M.P. with a document. The MP immediately waved Peter, Paige, and Wallace through, then pointing to where the drivers were allowed to park.

Entering the station-terminal on the western outskirts of Sacramento, Peter was amazed how the station had grown and developed in less than four years. For decades, it had been the main starting point for long-distance central California travelers to all points east, especially New York and Washington, D.C. Lined up on the sidewalk outside the terminal's entrance were more than 200 troops with M-1 rifles, backpacks, and carry-on gear waiting to board Southern Pacific's 3767 for transportation to the Oakland-Berkley Ferry for passage across the Bay to San Francisco's Fort Mason, the west coast's main point embarkation for the islands of the Pacific.

"Let's go, Peter," Colonel Paige said somberly. "Captain Wallace will accompany you. I'll explain in a moment."

Into the terminal Paige led Peter, with Captain Wallace following. Long noisy lines of civilian passengers standing before ticket booths greeted them. Cutting straight through, Peter overheard such comments as, "Lady, stop shoving me! You ain't going nowhere," "Oh, dear! I've got to meet my sailor husband in San Diego tomorrow and he's only got a one-day pass," "All I've done since I got here is stand in line to get a back seat", "I hear the ticket agent hasn't slept for six months' "I should have had my reservation before I gave up my hotel room", etc.

Paige, noticing Peter's curiosity, chuckled, "Lieutenant, this is precisely why we have millions of posters throughout stateside reading, 'IS YOUR TRIP ESSENTIAL?'"

As Peter nodded, soberly, the colonel said, "Hopefully, we're going to miss the 'Big Rush'. I see through the far windows a troop train is just pulling up. All the boys on that train will be running in here to the two canteens. Happens every few hours. The train pulls in for less than half an hour and everyone on board dashes for the station canteens, one where you pay, the other free of charge. Never fails, a few don't allow enough time to buy their 'goodies', and the train pulls out leaving them behind or running down the track after it. It's really quite hilarious. They walk back, some of them almost in tears, because they know they are in huge trouble."

As the three continued toward the departure-arrival platform, Paige pointed to his left at a "waiting canteen" that had been setup. He said with a smile,

"The ladies and women, mostly housewives of Sacramento, all volunteers, now wait for every troop train going through the Capitol of California that stop to drop off and pick up troops. They put up that big sign, 'Come and enjoy our way of saying thanks for protecting our shores'. God bless them. They always have ready for the soldiers hot coffee, cold drinks, doughnuts, homemade cookies, and sandwiches.

With Captain Wallace bringing up the rear, Paige led the three-man group through the lobby of the main station to the military passenger boarding platform. Wallace had not uttered a single word since being introduced.

"I'd say, by my watch, she'll pull in about seven minutes from now," commented the colonel.

"You're that exact?" Peter asked, "Marvelous! But look around this place. That yard over there: Unloading vehicles, crates, weapons; tanks, half-traks being loaded on flat cars. And, look at those coaches with troops leaning out the windows talking to ground personnel. On the other side there, more military trains awaiting departure from staging area landing platforms. And, there," he pointed, "Pullman Company Streamliner sleeping cars with a detachment of WAAC's, 46th Company, I think, waiting to board."

"You bet. Lots of action at this key railway center, especially on the Union Pacific and Southern Pacific yards. So much needed equipment pouring out to fellas spread offensively across the Pacific. And, the newly-designed troop carriers, or trains, with army kitchen cars at the head-ends," Paige enthused excitedly. "And all headed to either Fort Mason by ferry, or by freight car or flatbed to the Oakland Naval Supply Center, near the San Francisco-Oakland Bay Bridge. And, Peter, I don't know if you know this, but see all those 'old timers' around here and on the yards over there. Every one of those old guys is between 40 and 85 years of age. They've taken over the jobs of the younger men assigned to the Military Railway Battalions. They are the conductors, brakemen, flagmen, porters, cooks, etc. who wear gold insignias showing their lengths of service. For example, a gold star depicts 25 years of service while a gold bar indicates five years of service."

"No. When there's time, I want to research and read about the activities of the Military Railway Battalions formed directly from the Railway Companies themselves. A great concept!"

"Peter, here comes your Southern Pacific train now. It's the Southern Pacific's 4313 Troop Train No. 9, the 'Fast Mile'. It won't be the most comfortable of troop trains because it's made up of mail and express cars with a few passenger cars at the rear end. It's a very fast train that carries the California bulk mail. Someday, after the war, the airlines will carry all that mail."

"For me, the faster the train to get me to the Rohwer Internment Camp in McGehee, Arkansas, the better. If necessary, I'll stand all the way. Believe me, colonel, she'll do."

"Peter, we have less than a few minutes. Let me explain. When Major General Commandant Rupertus informed us the top-secret aspect of your next assignment, and the fact that you had an almost three-week furlough coming, and that you had shared with a friend or two your desire to travel to the Rohwer Camp, several officers in different transportation departments, as I've outlined, planned everything for you. They chose the fastest, quickest method to get you there and back in the shortest amount of time. The Union Pacific route would take 2 ¾ days, the Southern Pacific, less than two days. There is no single route between Sacramento and Rohwer, or McGehee, the town. Either way, either railroad company, means endless stops, but less so by the Southern Pacific across the deserts of Arizona, New Mexico and Texas. For example, the route to Arkansas using all Union Pacific trains take you through Nevada, Northern Utah, Southern Wyoming, then change to UP trains to travel through northeast Colorado, Northern Kansas to St. Louis, then another change to the Dixie Line, I think, to Little Rock and a bus to Rohwer. Along that route, you'd be service by mostly the 'old timers' since the company has more than 7,000 employees."

"Well, we put you on the Southern Pacific which is coming up. It's not the 'San Joaquin Daylight', 'Sunbeam', or 'Lark' streamliners, which are far more comfortable, but, as you say, 'It'll do'. Mail train, No. 9, the 'Fast Mile', will take you to Los Angeles, over to Phoenix and Tucson, over the Continental Divide to El Paso, San Antonio, Houston, and up into Arkansas and McGehee on or near the Mississippi. You'll cross pleasant valleys, mountain ranges, deserts, and both beautiful and ugly territories. You'll be in the thick of America at war railroading, which, in a way, is quite thrilling. So, sit back window-side and enjoy the scenery."

After a pause, Colonel Paige glanced at Captain Wallace, and with a slight wave of hand, added, "Lieutenant Toscanini, you are now at the full mercy of this officer. He'll see to it that all your travel documents to and from McGehee are in order. He'll also see to it your seating, sleeping berths, and dining needs are met. All in all, we've done the best we could on such short notice. I will be monitoring the best way I can all your movements. You'll report to me immediately upon reentering California. Goodbye, for now, lieutenant. After meeting you, I'm certain you're the right man for the job to come. It'll be a pleasure working with you."

With that, a sharp strident shrill of a locomotive whistle pierced the terminal, and as lieutenant Peter waved a final "Then, until... ", Paige quickly departed, Captain Wallace stepped forward. In a low, dull voice, he uttered sullenly, "Follow me."

And, within moments, Peter found himself relaxing in the window seat of the last of six passenger cars attached to the heavily laden mail train. As Captain Wallace wiped the seat clean opposite the lieutenant, and shuffled the papers in his carry-on, searching for a memorandum, Peter noted Southern Pacific yard workers attaching a string of flatcars loaded with heavy antiaircraft guns and M3 tanks to his car.

"Strange to see all this so close to my home in Stockton, down the road," he said more to himself than Captain Wallace.

"Happens every half hour," responded Wallace, without looking up.

Peter, with his duffle bag on the seat next to him, nodded silently.

Leaning back on the cushioned padding of the leather seat, Peter studied Wallace for the first time since being introduced to him less than an hour and a half before. He certainly was heavy, large, and powerful. Although a high-ranking officer in the U.S. Army Transportation and Movement Division, he offered not a word of explanation, advice, or guidance. If anything, he walked in a manner suggesting sententious petulance. He was ugly, and his behavior didn't offset that apparent façade. It wasn't that Peter felt unsure of him. He simply didn't like this man who appeared to be a deaf mute.

Then, after two shrill whistles from the locomotive cabin, the Train #10 began to pull away from the military passenger terminal for the 400-mile journey to Los Angeles and the Southern Pacific yards there. Opposite Peter, Captain Wallace looked up and said with a touch of anger,

"Now that the little shit is gone, I have things to tell you. First, the Mad Ghoul hung himself early this morning. He was assigned a single cell in the Guadalcanal stockade and had virtually the entire hospital staff on Canal at his service. He left you a long letter and the commandant is studying it now."

Shaken to his core by the news, Peter was instantly, alert, wide-eyed, and speechless. After a long silence, he asked weakly, almost inaudibly,

"Say it again, please, and how? Besides, how would you know?"

"He used one bed sheet, and a dozen boot laces. He somehow managed to hang himself from the upper bunk of his bed since he was in his cell alone. And, he was supposedly being watched 24/7. Today, he would have been placed aboard the hospital ship in a super secure cell and taken to Honolulu, presumably for trial and execution."

"Do you know who I am?"

"Why, of course. Everyone is talking about you and how you saved Bob Hope's life. I know little of what the Ghoul did. No one really does, because the USMC wants to rid itself of the incident forever. Can't have that in the Corps, a Marine murdering Marines. So, the news people will never hear of it, and, if it gets out, the Corps will deny it. So, no details about him and his nurse partner. But the officers know, and won't tell, or will deny, deny, and deny. But everyone knows about Lieutenant Peter Toscanini."

Peter turned to gaze out the window as the train, well on its way south, was approaching the northern limits of Galt, California.

"Lieutenant, allow me to give you a clue…"

"Damn, I needed to talk to him. He kept muttering, 'Give me a gun' or, 'wonder man, will you lend me a gun?' something or other about a 'wonder man', as he grappled for mine! But I couldn't quite make out what he said as he was cursing me at the same time in his thick overworked lisp. I've been bothered since his identification and capture about something; I just can't figure out what. Were there additional murderers operating together? If so, whom? And why? Why our own men? And, now he's cheated us out of answers unless he put it all in his letter to me. How do you hang yourself with shoelaces? How do I make out his words?"

"I have no answers for you, lieutenant. Our offices were all informed so as to get you where you wished to go. But I do have information on what follows after your next assignment, should you survive it."

"Go ahead," Peter asked, intently, leaning forward forgetting the upper San Joaquin Valley scenery that glided by. The air, hot and a bit stale, in the coach couldn't be ignored, however.

"Nothing about as violent as you've just gone through, and are about to go through at Camp Elliott," the stocky, taciturn captain began, "but certainly an interesting story."

After a pause, Captain Wallace continued,

"It seems that the USMC has a Jap turncoat on its hands. Not an ordinary 'Banzai' screaming foot soldier, but a highly intelligent, English-speaking lieutenant who was born somewhere in California in the 1920s, taken by his parents to live and go to school in Japan in the 1930s, then became an officer in the early 40s, served on Guadalcanal fighting our boys of the 1st Division, then suddenly one night, made it through his and our lines by crawling among the millions of land crabs, and finally walked up to a sentry outside one of the camps, introduced himself and said he really was an American and not a Jap enemy. He needed to speak to an officer, then be turned over to our Intelligence Division. The sentry was about to shoot him when another sentry intervened. Since then, he's been helping our people plan strikes against the Imperial Army's various Divisions, especially the 100th. He's continuing to help, and everyone who deals with him likes him. I forgot his name, but he's a Kibei, a person of Japanese descent born here, but returns to Japan. Your woman is a Nisei, born here by parents who were born here, but whose grandparents emigrated to California from Japan, I think. It's something like that."

"Well, the upshot is this: The guy is helping us a lot. But is he leading us, our intelligence people, down a primrose path to the ultimate battle that will win the war for Japan by betraying our Allied Forces? He's been grilled for months, trying to discern whether the Jap is nuts, or an elaborate subterfuge to lead our militaries into a huge trap. Your job will be to get next to him, befriend him, with your Nisei woman, and get to the truth. In fact, you're not to know any of this. You are not to even tell your woman about any of this. You may even have a change of assignment as you arrive back and meet with the little traitor. I'm telling you all this because it's only fair, and my way to sticking it up the ass of that little shit, Colonel Paige. I hope you'll never tell, or bring up, what I forewarned you about. With this, you won't be caught off-guard."

Occasionally, the train's whistle blew, and, approaching Woodbridge, Lodi, and North Stockton, slowed down to less than 40 miles per hour. For several minutes, Peter said nothing, as he gazed out the window at the beautiful flatlands of varying agricultural crops growing in the late summer heat. Finally, he looked over at Captain Wallace and said, pensively,

"Captain, thank you. I truly appreciate your well-meaning forewarning. It will help me and may even save my life in the assignments to come. I'm indebted and won't forget. Thank you, sir."

A bare grin played upon the captain's clenched lips, as he nodded. Both men then fell into a long silence as each gazed through the window. Without stopping, the troop train slowly passed through the northern southern Pacific Station. Peter, changing seats, could look down familiar streets to his grandmother's home on East Sonora Street 25 blocks away. He knew she would be busy in the kitchen.

For the following three hours, Peter sat or stretched out on the upholstered seat watching pedestrians, or the scenery, small towns, and large cities roll by. He saw for himself at virtually every stop of the train #10 how the war's great demands for fighting men, munitions, and equipment were making on transportation's normal freight and passenger priorities.

And, for the first time, he saw for himself how patriotic everyone was, per railroad managers, ticket sellers and ticket takers, railway military police, shippers, government agency personnel, and yard workers, handling every type of movement locomotives wielded, including livestock, vehicles, baggage of every imaginable shape and size.

As Captain Wallace put it when he shook Peter's hand, bidding him farewell until they met again, standing together for a final moment on the military passenger platform of the Southern Pacific's Union Station in Los Angeles,

"Well, lieutenant, you'll only see a fraction of the 41,000 locomotives of America's fighting railroads, of the 2,000,000 freight cars deep speeding over 230,000 miles of rail lines. You'll see an incredible amount of handling and tendering. The whole nation is at war against the Krauts and Nips, and you'll be thick in the machinery that will bring about victory."

And, Peter indeed saw it all, including what all civilian and officer passengers did when cold, wrapping themselves in blankets; when hungry, waiting for a seat in the diner; when in need to relieve themselves, taking turns in the passenger restrooms; when again hungry, enduring the taste of usually hamburgers and pop; when crowded, sitting among veterans on furloughs or quick visits home, or sitting with fully-equipped recruits who had no idea where they were going once they reached their port destinations; and, in the Pullmans, sleeping wherever assigned, frequently in Upper Berth 4, usually reserved for kid raw recruits.

He watched and waited as train #10 deposited and picked up mail. He watched and waited at hundreds of railroad sidings as troops disembarked or climbed aboard. He watched and waited as flatbeds and passenger coaches were interchanged, added or suspended, etc. etc.

It was always the same, Southern California, Southern Arizona, and the Rio Grande Valley, his mail train rolled east while troop trains sped west. If he saw the sign once, he saw it posted a thousand times in urban areas throughout the entire route to McGehee, Arkansas:

"Victory Rides on Wheels."

CHAPTER TWENTY-TWO

-

Rohwer

As an avid reader of western historical fiction, Peter enjoyed the relatively smooth, rolling ride across the American Southwest. Gazing out the window of Train #10, his creative imagination recalled many a story by Zane Grey, Charles Alden Seltzer, and Steward Edward White who often wrote stirring stories about pioneers, Apaches, bandits, feuds, and, above all, romances in remote corners of where such classic authors claimed motorized tires never tread.

While many passengers in the coaches drew their shades, reclined in their seats, rested one leg upon the other and dozed, Peter reveled in the beauty and grandeur of vast sage seas, round barren hills, jagged mountaintops, flat glaring deserts, deep colorful canyons, and wild, and unpopulated mesas. Gliding along over worn, slick tracks, Peter was comfortable and slept easily in his lower berth. Of course, the 2,650-mile rail journey was hot, dusty, wearing, and toilsome. But, for a soldier, it wasn't hard, especially when he reflected upon honorable men and women, courageous and brave pioneers who defied wild men in wild times in the wilderness. Someday, he vowed, as he gazed upon the incredible desert landscapes and mountain Rangers of southern Arizona, southern New Mexico, and central Texas, that he would return with his beloved Joan to kneel before the graves of the noble. He would consummate his unbounded love for her under the stars of a Southwest spring and its illimitable wild flower, especially as they began to bloom.

Yet, his spirited daydreaming didn't dull his consciousness. No matter the resplendent natural setting, or the speed at which the train sped by, the same chill that engulfed him during the Ghoul murders returned to corrode his instinctive intellect and intuition. Vistas and views were no match for unresolved unconscious struggles.

"What in damnable hell did the murder-mad Chaplain mean when in that bitter life and death struggle he repeated in his slight lisping, 'kill-me-with-your-gun, wonder-man'; 'will-me-with-your-gun', shadow-man'; 'still-me-with-your-gun, hiding-man'; or, some such figure of stuttered speech. Intermittently, the undefined sense of calamity that was less than a few weeks old returned, triggering a brooding in Peter that lasted for hours.

"What really happened," he wondered "prior to, during, and after those murky nights of murder? Was it only the Ghoul's idea to launch a spree of killing his own trusting Marines? He probably murdered prior to enlistment, but where? And why wasn't he caught? How did Ellen become involved with such a man? And, more importantly, why? Although motivation was near impossible to determine during a spree, clues as to who the killer was were rampant, if one knew how to find then decipher them. Above all, what could Pinoe have meant, despite the difficulty of his aroused, agitated lisp, when he seemed to be pleading, 'Kill me with your gun', or 'Will you give me your gun, sighing man?'"

"Thank God, it's over," he grimaced in disgust. "The Man of God, appointed by the Men of God to assist in salvaging the weak, the ill, the emaciated of spirit and hope from sin was evil-personified."

Such was Peter's quandary within hours from being in the arms of the love of his life, yet burdened by questions he wasn't even certain were apropos.

It was near midnight when the Southern Pacific pulled into the small McGehee Railroad Station. As untiring as Peter was, he was nonetheless very tired. He knew his days of travel from the Russell Islands and long hours of reflection were over, and that if he was ever intimate with the wild, endless Southwest again, it would be with Joan. Less than three miles away, in the Rohwer Relocation Center, Unit, she was asleep by now, unaware she was in for one of the grandest surprises of her life.

That night, he hadn't retired to his berth after a late supper, because he learned from the conductor he would be the only passenger to disembark in McGehee. Peter remained in his comfortable padded seat, dozing until awakened by a porter.

Now, peering into the dim light of the railroad station as he stepped off the mail train, he could tell by the size of the nearby water tower after that the two-minute stopover McGehee was a larger community than he was led to believe by the conductor. Peter had never been this far, East and knew very little about the histories of its states. Neither had he heard of McGehee, Arkansas, nor how the small American city received its Irish name.

Now, at midnight, in late August of 1944, all that greeted the single-passenger holding two duffle bags was silence in near darkness. Focusing his vision, he noticed the vague shape of a large depot behind the station. Obviously, it was an Army warehouse storing military supplies. A large five-word sign had been painted in red on the windowless side of the wooden structure, "More teeth, less flat feet," a phrase from the Bud Abbott and Lou Costello feature film, "Buck Privates," produced in 1941 by Universal Studious.

Then, as the air-brakes of the mail train hissed, and Peter watched the locomotive pull its passenger and flatbed cars away, he heard footsteps approaching him across the wooden planks of the arrival-departure platform.

"Lieutenant Toscanini, please follow me. We received a telegram from Honolulu in the Hawaiian Islands in the North Pacific, no less, that you'd be arriving tonight on the 11:57pm stopover. You, sir, are now in my care until you leave the station premise after sunup for Rohwer. Follow me, please."

Peter, grabbing his bags, anxiously heeded the command. The small, dingy frame station was painted a chocolate-brown color and appeared as an ancient-appearing oddity, adjacent two parallel shiny, reflecting ribbons, that somehow distinguished the community and its surroundings. A small American flag was in every single window of an ordinary American town.

Entering the arched doorway of the flat-roofed one-story wooden building, the night station master introduced himself as "Timmy" Timms.

"Been looking at rails and beckoning locomotives for nigh a half a century. Almost live here. Enjoy watching people and families come and go, assisting them when I can. Lot better than sitting with the dawg in the backyard, or yacking in saloons and betting parlors."

Peter, appreciating he was being taken in tow, considered "Timmy" the epitome of a railroad station supervisor. A tall, thin, lanky fellow of more than 60 years, a balding man wearing day and night an aged sun visor, forest-green with projecting orange brim, fading black suspenders holding up well-worn trousers that only extended to the top of equally well-worn socks, Peter was instantly drawn to this man who, although oozing gentleness and kindness, was not a fan of brevity.

"Our three hotels close at 10:00pm. If you show up at 10:01, you wind up sleeping on the park bench. Besides, the hotels change the bed sheets once a decade. So, that being said, you have two choices: sit up in the waiting room the rest of the night or lay down on my office cot. The blankets are fresh and the sheets are clean. In the morning, whenever you're ready, I'll drive you to the Japanese camp down the road thataway. I don't know if anyone among the Rohwer Relocation Administrative staff knows you're coming. Anyway, if he's in his office, I'll turn you over to Ray Johnston, the Project Director of the Rohwer Red Cross Unit. They'll call me when to come and get you because you can't sleep there at night. Now, you get settled in my office. The washroom, and, believe it or not, a real life-size shower next to it, are waiting to meet you, I'm sure. While you're showering, I'll cook you up bacon and eggs sunny-side up, plus a pot of coffee. Are you hungry?"

" . . . and so sleepy. But right now, I'd rather eat than lay down."

"Give me your rumpled khakis to wash and iron - -I'll have them ready and fresh for your visit in the morning. Get along now; it's well past midnight. By the time you've finished, your late dinner will be waiting on the table. Throw your clothes, including underwear, in the basket outside the shower stall."

Half an hour later, the strong fragrance of fried bacon and sizzling eggs floated throughout the entire small empty station. For Peter, who had showered and was sitting on the edge of the cot, searching his duffle bag for a pair of clean underwear, the odor served as a lighting-like aphrodisiac. He was already soundly asleep before his back hit the blankets. "Timmy" Timms, with a plate of bacon and eggs held in one hand, pulled a blanket over Peter with the other. Gazing down on the young Lieutenant who appeared in a dreamlike state, "Timmy" smiled, thinking to himself he was "taking a liking" to the young officer. After consuming the hot meal, he began the tedious task of hand washing, drying, and ironing his new friend's disheveled clothing. Ethics, a deep sense for loyalty, respect and the ability to engage in careful thinking were personality and character traits important to the station master, and Timmy intuited Peter had them in abundance. Toscanini would be his friend.

Even before dawn, and with less than five hours of sleep, Peter rolled out from under his blankets and was delighted to find his uniform carefully washed, pressed, and hanging from the back of a chair a few feet from the cot. Putting on his shoes, which somehow had been polished, he began the day with a zest.

"No time for breakfast, Timmy. Much too excited. Since I'm certain the camp's main gate won't be open for several hours, let's drive around on a short tour, and have a quick cup of coffee at one of numerous diners along the highway. Then, we can approach the gate and wait for it to open."

"We'll have to wait for my relief manager to arrive at 7:00am before we can leave the station. But, meanwhile let's scramble some eggs. Coffee is all ready.

An hour later, with Timmy driving, and Peter seated on the passenger side, the train station's small flatbed truck, more a dilapidated jalopy, jerkily thrust forward on a "tour" of eight square blocks of McGehee, Arkansas. For more than an hour, Peter remained anxiously silent, nodding only as Timmy related the history and culture of the Mississippi community. The cool, efflorescent river mist had long since dissipated and, by 8:00am, the rising sun was at work broiling eastern Arkansas.

Meanwhile, he enjoyed watching the mostly male citizens leaving their homes for work, and their children with dogs at their sides heading for school. Wives and mothers with soiled aprons covering their worn housedresses watched from their front porches, waving white handkerchiefs and towels. It was an image of every small town in the western hemisphere, if not the world.

Timmy waved a hand at McGehee, "My people, our town, last century, this century, next century. Let the Japs and Germans try to take it away from us. Our only sadness, as a unified people in a fighting town, is whether we've done enough, and continue to do, to help our boys, fellow Americans, who are as gentle, kind, and loving, and, I might add, brave and courageous, as all those in our proud history have been."

Peter grinned, glanced at Timmy who appeared to have a tear in his eye, then back at the downtown area of McGehee. He said softly,

"Looks almost exactly like my own hometown, Stockton, California, for other than the surrounding woods and fields. Business fronts and houses are exact replicas. And, every face that glances at us, smiles, including the local police there at the corner. Like Stockton, every business is opening up early. No business is closed or boarded up. Yes, I see a few tent houses mixed between some noble-designed homes with flanking small garages. Then, there are empty lots, none of which are strewn with any garbage. The streets and the few parks are spic and span. And, now that we're emerging form the town, I look back and I see no building over four stories high. I see faded billboards, strong telephone and utility poles, here and there gas stations some either closed because of gas rationing, or outright abandoned. Way over there is an old roundhouse for locomotives which apparently hasn't been in operation for a half a century, other than it's heavy repair shops, My God, if this part of town isn't south Stockton where I grew up, Center Street and Charter Way, the industrial section and poor house surrounding it."

For a long moment, there was silence. Then, Timmy Timms said, softly,

"You're a good man, lieutenant, a very good man."

Again, a silence at the end of which he continued,

"We're now on our way to the camp. It's at the end of these pine trees, carpets of cotton greens, level as a table. All agriculture sections, then, four miles away, camp, and who you want to see. Here, I've written the station phone number down. I'll be there at all times of day. When you're ready, call me. I'll fetch you back here to catch your Southern Pacific 'Daylight' back to California."

Handing Peter a slip of paper with the station number on it, which he pulled from his pocket with one hand while the other was on the steering wheel. After a pause, he added,

"Let me give you a brief background on what you're to visit. We're not happy of having the infamous incarceration camp down the road, but would be proud to have all 9,000 of the Japanese Americans living among us as neighbors."

Although there was a ton of gladness in Peter's heart that at last he had put almost 10,000 miles from Pavuvu behind him, perspiration began to appear on his forehead. For no reason at all, he was suddenly apprehensive. Although it was unlike the "Ghoul business" that vaguely disquieted him from time to time, an unsettling emotion seemed to flow in his veins. It troubled him, making him conscious of a reality other than his dreamy thoughts of Joan.

"Nervous?" asked Timmy Timms.

"I don't think so. I'm really tranquil and happy. Soon, I believe, my Joan will be in my arms. No, something else is at play in my mind and I don't know what it is. But I so want to see her."

"Well, you can barely see the water tower in the morning haze. There are 10 relocation project sites in the U.S., two of them in Arkansas, the other in Jerome, same everything, also 10,000 residents on 10,000 acres. We're on Mississippi River Delta country and cotton is mainly what we grow. We're also known for our woods and swamps. Work started in July of '42 and cost the government almost $5,000,000. They have good water, all they need, sewage disposal, electric power and lighting, telephone facilities, and, from what we hear, pretty decent military police watching over them. It's the evacuee housing that's not right, that's not fair, that we McGeheeans resent. Those are Americans behind barbed wire who did nothing, nothing and that housing isn't fair, I say."

"Joan, in all her letters never once, not once, complained about how they lived."

"Well, hear this then. I'm sure they won't allow you to roam with her at will throughout the camp. No visitor has so far been allowed to do so."

"What's their living like? I'm sure they'll allow us to be together in a visiting area. And, there is so much to talk over about our marriage that I won't ask her about the living and sleeping quarters."

"Well, lieutenant, as you can already see from this position on the road, barbed wire encloses 51 blocks of barracks. There's a patrol road all around the camp and eight guard towers. Twelve barracks are in each block, and each block includes a women latrine, a men's latrine, mess hall, laundry room, heater room, and recreation hall. And, remember, there are 51 blocks per camp. In the 10,000-resident camp, there are designated areas for military police, hospital, administration, future schools and community activities, and two large play areas, combining children with adults."

"How many people per barracks?"

"It depends. Out in the McGehee community, we guess a typical barracks is about 20' x 100' divided into five 20' by 20' rooms or apartments. Each camp administrator can change the sizes of the apartments to accommodate family sizes. One family per one room, or 'apartment'. Know how changes in 'apartment' sizes are engineered?"

"Not a clue."

"With a blanket over a thin rope which can be easily hooked to the interior walls of the barracks."

"So, beds are crammed into small spaces called 'apartments', each 'apartment' separated from the other by a blanket hung over a piece of rope, about 6 to 8 feet high!"

"And, toilet and bathing facilities? How's that done?"

"One barracks devoted to them in the middle of the 51 blocks."

"What?"

"Yup! That's how it is. You can see it all as we approach the main entrance. Look to your right. The unique feature of the Rohwer camp is its cemetery over there. And, notice how it faces the internment camp. It holds internee burial spots marked by headstones with two large monuments, one dedicated to those who died in the camp, and the other to the Nisei men of the 100 Battalion, and 442nd Regimental Combat Team. For the civilian internees of the Rohwer dead, the monument off to the right there reads something to the effect, 'May the people of Arkansas keep in beauty and reverence the dead who died on this soil . . . Let us never forget them who lay asleep in our earth', something like that. This is where I turn into the camp off Arkansas State Highway 1. The large sign to my left announces, 'Rohwer Relocation Center, Vicksburg Engineer District, Corps of Engineer,

U.S. Army speed limit, 20 M.P.H., Report to Military Police, 1st Building at Camp Entrance.'"

"What's that monument?"

"I'll pull over so you can read the inscription. It's dedicated to the camp boys who have died in North Africa, Sicily, Italy and France. From Rohwer, a dozen or so have given their lives to America."

Pulling into the entrance of the camp, and across from the Rohwer Military Police Office, Timmy turned the motor off of the flatbed jalopy truck in the parking lot in front of the monument so Peter could study the inscription of the two-story obelisk. The tall, four-sided stone pillar tapering to a flat top which supported a large metal wing-spread eagle atop a sphere of the world. At the bottom, engraved in Japanese and English on the foundation block was the inscribed dedication,

"To him who sleeps eternally here a descendant of glorious Yamato who came in his prime with hopes and ambitions heroic to battle, the fortunes of life, peace and bliss be yours."

After a somber, reflective moment reading and rereading the chiseled inscription on stone, Peter nodded quietly,

"I understand from my Brass-powers-that-be that we have as many as 15,000 Japanese-Americans from the camps fighting alongside our Army forces in southern Europe and now in France. In the Pacific, there's a group of Niseis who are serving as interpreters with our Marine, Navy and Air Force. They are also interpreting for the Army units that joined the Marines units. Some 18 to 20 Medals of Honor have been earned by those brave guys. Maybe another 10 or 15 before the end of the way. By next July of '45, there may be as many as 20,000 to 23,000 Nisei men. Almost every teenage boy in camp wants to sign up like his older brothers. I was told by Major General Rupertus that the 442 Regiment Combat Team is well on its way to being the most decorated unit for its size and length of service in the U.S. armed forces."

"Yeah," responded Timms, "we heard that, too. Can you imagine what kind of spirit they have? Before the outbreak of war, they and their families faced terrible discrimination in certain parts of our country."

"All parts, California included. I saw it often in Stockton."

"And, yet, of all peoples in America, they are, always have been, the nicest, gentlest, generous, honest, cleanest, forgiving, caring and loving."

"Because of where I grew up, the neighborhood, and because of Joan, I've known hundreds, mostly my age, and I've never known one, not one, to badmouth another human being, or cheat in a game, or curse a swear word."

"Maybe after the war, even our McGehee citizens learning how many were killed in action serving our country, will feel differently about them."

"Joan and I don't want our children to have to go through the prejudice, bias, and outright discrimination she and her parents and family had to go through."

Glancing at the monument again, Peter reflected for a moment, then said,

"And, in terms of their courage and fighting spirit? Let me say this. Joan wrote to me that when her brothers volunteered to join the 442nd, her parents told them the same thing all Japanese-American parents told their sons: always follow the Bushido Samurai; Code of Death. She said her father put his hands on their shoulders and said, 'Departing sons, try hard to live. But if you must die, and there is no longer the possibility of remaining alive, fight to the end with honor. Never bring shame on your family or country.'"

Timmy also looked long and hard at the monument, then added,

"How fortunate you are to have a Nisei girl. Even at my age, single and alone, I would gladly share the rest of my life, and her life, together. O.K. Enough of all this. I can go no further and have no reason to accompany you into the Military Police offices. I'll turn around and leave you. With your order in hand, explain that after all is said and done, you request that Ray D. Johnston, the Project Director of the Rohwer Red Cross Unit of the Relocation Center, take you under his arm to arrange for your visit with your wife-to-be. Upon your completion of your first visit, you will telephone me, as I explained. You will stay with me for the second, even third night, should you remain extra days. Regardless, the entire Southern Pacific Railroad Company is ready to assist and will remain at your disposal for the duration of your visit to Rohwer."

With that, Timmy Timms shook Peter's hand as the lieutenant exited the flatbed. The station manager watched Peter walk across the street, saluting various officers and personnel in and about the entrance, walk up the porch stairs, and, with a final wave, disappear into the building.

Inside, Peter drew a deep breath to steady his excitement. Despite consumed by the fidgets, a vibrating, head and a pounding heart, he remained calm and composed as he crossed a small walled-in lobby-waiting room toward the obvious receptionist seated behind a large desk, typing at professional speed. Glancing up and seeing a smiling lieutenant approaching her, she rose to greet him with an equally endearing smile.

"Sir, we've been expecting you. Even though I'm a civilian, I was tasked with tracing your movements on the rails from McClellan. I've spoken to more station managers, conductors, porters in three days that'll be enough for a dozen lifetimes of train travel. In addition, I've been in contact by radiogram two or three times a day with Captain Oscar Del Barbra on Pavuvu Island in the Russell Group. I take it you know him?"

"Boy, do I!" explained Toscanini.

"Well, sir, less than an hour ago, two radiograms arrived within minutes of each other. They were marked 'extremely urgent' and 'classified-confidential'. Without reading them, Red Cross Project Director Ray D. Johnston had them sealed. He'll hand them to you in person in his office."

"I'm certain they are congratulatory in nature, that I arrived safely." Peter smiled. "We got to know each other pretty well over this past month."

"One is from your Commander, General Rupertus."

"Oh, really? He and I got to know each other especially well."

"I'm to bring you to Mr. Johnston's office immediately, he's right down the hall, there" she pointed "The camp's civilian administrators are away in Washington. All camp administrators are in a weeklong conference. I'm sure our people would have enjoyed hearing first-hand, what our boys are doing out there on those cold-water islands. And, by the way, you're the first serviceman to visit one of our residents since camp began two years ago."

Led down a hall of half-empty offices in an administrative unit surprisingly quiet, Peter inquired,

"Yours is the only typewriter that works around here?"

The receptionist chuckled, "No work to be done. All 9,685 internees are honest. Never had a problem with anyone. The older boys can't wait to join up with the 442nd, the younger ones are policed by their own internal security policy authority, the same way their 12-member fire department crew handles all fires. We don't even need the gun towers. Our staff could be cut by two-thirds. Five of us could handle the little work and investigations 20 M.P.'s do. Our only problems revolve around the occasional suicides. We don't carry guns, and there are no guns in the towers. Same for all camps, except for the Tule Lake camp. But the suicides hurt us staff very, very much. Usually older, lonely men, and young women kill themselves. So, so sad. Men hang themselves, women will hang themselves, too, but a month ago, one young woman threw herself under the locomotive that supplies our materials off a SP branch line."

Entering an obviously large double office area, Peter's first sight was a young woman with blonde hair sitting behind a desk at work on a stack of papers, pen in hand. Morning light from the window near her desk cast a soft glow on her, producing a gentle, glowing result. Her eyes, measuring every step he made into the room were wide, pure, and vivid. She was beautiful, and, suddenly, he flashed on Ellen and the first time he saw her. As a tense sadness momentarily overwhelmed him, he continued following the receptionist into the office of the Red Cross Project Director. Peter turned and flashed a smile at the young woman behind the desk who was still staring at him, an ever-so-slight smile crossing her lips.

"Hello there, Lieutenant Toscanini. We've been waiting for you. You're quite the sensation, I understand. These two radiograms marked urgent and confidential are for you. No one here has read them. Came in about the time you were being driven over here."

As he handed the two radiograms, to Peter who stuffed them into his pocket, he smiled,

"My people back on Pavuvu congratulating me for getting here safely, I'm sure, sir."

"Well, I'm Ray D. Johnston. Let me say we've been made privy not only that you were on your way to see fiancée Joan Ikeda, the shining star of our internment camp, but also your remarkable achievement of saving Mr. Hope's life while defeating the so-called murder mad Mr. Ghoul."

"Only one question, sir, does Joan know I'm here?"

"No. Only the Rohwer Camp administrative staff does. But since all this broke within a week, there's been little time for rumors to filter down to her level. I can't be 100% certain she doesn't know. I even had a phone call from a reporter at the San Francisco Chronicle about you."

"How soon can I see her?"

"Right now. I've cleared my desk to get you two together this morning! We'll go through the back door there. I know where she is and what she's doing."

"Is there any way I can observe her for a few moments without her seeing me…and then surprise her by just walking out? I so want to surprise her... "

"I don't see why not. I'll be with you, observing, telling you the do's and don'ts. Let me show you on the camp map behind me where she lives."

Peter liked Ray Johnston instantly. He was obviously a gentleman with a warm gleam in his eyes. Like Timmy Timms, he was a kind, gentle man who made friends easily. A slender, sinewy, thin waist body held up broad shoulders, while a thin mouth and small nose seemed to be topped by short balding hair.

Sitting behind the usual sparse governmental wooden desk, scattered with papers, contracts, documents, etc, the Project Director sensed Peter's inquisitive stare sizing him up. Especially interesting to the lieutenant was the large map with various colored pins, colored rectangular designations of the maps entire 10,161 acre capable of accommodating 10,000 internees. In addition, it indicated the perimeters of Desha County, and directions eight south to Watson and 25 miles northwest to Arkansas City. To the east, the shores of the Mississippi River were noted.

"Interesting, is it, Lieutenant?" Johnston asked, standing up and facing the map.

"I have all 51 barracks numbered with the block and barracks' managers listed underneath. For example, Joan Ikeda is there, Block 25, Barracks 3. Mr. Hayashi, a wonderful man, is in charge of her block. The barbed-wire 12-foot fence runs alongside of her barrack, which is adjacent in the middle of the outside length, which means the guard tower is virtually overlooking her barracks. There are three towers on each side of the camp quarters occupying less than 1,000 acres of the camp's 10,000."

"I see," said Peter, slowly, perusing the map. "I see how the colors identify all aspects of normal life, the various churches in each of the blocks, the libraries, recreation areas, elementary schools and nurseries. Even the pine trees within each block are identified. My goodness, I'm impressed."

"You understand, my office is separate from the U.S. Farm Administration's responsibility. The American Red Cross, for our supplies and activities, including the salaries for me and my staff, are donated. The US Army, in general, and the Military Police in particular, handle the costs for interning the residents. I operate on less than

$10,000 a year. The cost for each relocation and internment camp in America is well into the hundreds of thousands of dollars."

"Thank you for the time explaining much of it to me. Very little, if anything, at all, is ever reported about life in the camps in the national newspapers and magazines, especially the locally- oriented newspaper in my hometown, Stockton, California. In the various military offices I've been in, especially the waiting rooms, there are puff pieces celebrating how wonderful life is behind barbed wire."

"I know. I know."

After a pause in which both men continued gazing upon the map, the Project Director said,

"I know how to get you as close as possible without her being aware of your presence. Then, when you're ready, watching you step out in front of her, and seeing her expression will indeed be something to behold. Never has it happened before. I'll bet you a thick, juicy doughnut, she'll start crying."

"I know."

"Well, as it so happens, today is special, the noon hours being the most important. Sponsored by the Rohwer Red Cross Chapter's executive board, 12 members, all Japanese-American; the more than 100 block and barracks managers, and Home Service Office staff, and 70-member Community Council, are celebrating the Annual Tomonokai Day. In preparation for the ceremony and luncheon, Joan, and a host of at least 200 teenage girls and their mothers, are busy setting up the chairs and tables. I thought you'd have at least a half hour just watching her before surprising and joining her."

"Won't the people resent me showing up and just stepping in?"

"On the contrary, they would be proud. After all, their sons, their brothers and uncles are being led in Italy and France, even the Pacific, by officers like yourself."

"Well…"

"When we get to the supply closet window, I'm thinking of where you can observe her at work, and the small patio where you can step forward to surprise her. As we make our way over there, I'll tell you what the ceremony of Tomodachi is all about. Tomodachi means 'friends'. Tomonokai, which comes from 'Tomodachi', refers to 'the gathering of friends'. But more of this later."

"Yes, I've often heard Joan speak of that ceremony because it's one of her favorites."

"Let's go!" Johnston's voice snapped vibrantly, as a feeling of excitement swept over Peter.

A quarter of an hour later, Johnston, with Toscanini at his side, walked hurriedly down the green slope leading from the main administration building, and the administration and personnel apartments, toward the small picnic area adjacent to the main hospital. From the Military Police building they had crossed the street before the parking lot, the warehouses, the motor pool, and main post office. Meanwhile, Johnston greeted everyone who crossed their path, while Peter saluted all officers and smiled at every internee. More than all else, he wanted to be alone with Joan, to hold her, to make sure she was still his fiancée, to convince himself beyond all fears she was still his and worth to go on living and fighting for. Somehow he sensed her nearness that she truly was less than 100 yards away and that standing before her in an unexpected surprise would be the major drama of his life thus far. This is the hour, Peter thought, and the scene is ready, the veil within minutes to be raised, and the last act performed. How excited he was!

A third of the way down the sloping path, the Red Cross Project Director slowed and pointed,

"Look beyond the roof of the hospital. There's the picnic area and your Joan Ikeda is among those women setting up folding chairs, hauling portable tables, spreading tablecloths. Soon, the guests will walk over from their barracks. I'm taking you to a linen closet where there's a window to watch. Just outside of it is a partially ivy-covered patio. When you're ready, you can merely step out into it and walk over to get her. Are you certain she won't have a heart attack? There are several two-seat benches there where you can talk. I'll always be within hailing distance because as a visitor, even as a high-priority officer, you can't be allowed to be alone on grounds, with her, or any internee for that matter."

"Let's hurry, please, Mr. Johnston."

The Project Director glanced back at Peter with somewhat of a sarcastic smile. He said nothing as he entered the Rohwer Relocation Center Unit hospital with the lieutenant trailing close behind. They hurried down a hall off offices for doctors, dentists, and nurses, the Office of the Rohwer Board of health, reception room, nurses' aides' area, dental clinic, x-ray room, operations center, obstetric ward, several classrooms for first-aid instruction, before reaching the unlocked linen closet Johnston had in mind.

Entering the room, Peter saw the window he was to peer through beyond the shelving of bed sheets, towels, various linens and other supplies. Several startled aides who were busy unpacking boxes of linens for empty shelves looked up as the two men entered.

"Don't mind us, nurses. Go on with your work. We're going to use the back window as an observation post."

As the aides smiled at Ray Johnston, they continued unpacking and recording the contents on clipboards. Peter was the first to reach the window. Quickly, he rearranged several unopened boxes so that he could sit and watch. The morning sun was reflecting in such a manner that the shadows cast prevented anyone from the patio area attempting to see within. Peter was allowed to look out, but no one in the picnic area would think of attempting to look within.

"Perfect, isn't it, Lieutenant?"

Peter didn't hear him since he was so intent on scanning the large number of female faces busy setting up for the ceremony.

Then, suddenly, there she was, in green pedal pushers and a white short-sleeve cotton collared shirt carefully placing embroidered tablecloths, with her two sisters, Kimi and Sayu, on tables. He allowed a tear to run down his cheek as he watched her work authoritatively and competently with the young teenage girls.

Observing Peter's marvel and wonder as he watched Joan arrange the Tomonokai party tableware for the Rohwer senior citizen group. Johnston smiled and said softly, slowly,

"No question about Joan being popular in to our community. I hear everyone, men and women, young and old, even the elderly address her as Ne-san, 'big sister'. Now, she's arranging the Bingo materials for each table This Tomonokai is a big deal around here. It's supposed to take place once a year, but here in camp we do it once every two months. The McGehee bakeries help out because they deliver boxes and boxes of free pastries by noon."

"My understanding," said Peter, is that each community, say, Stockton, California, has a slight deviation of the name. There, my

Stockton high school friends called it 'Tanoshimi Kai'. 'Tanoshimi' means 'something to look forward to.'"

"'Tomonokai' comes from the Japanese word 'Tumo' which means 'friend'. So, 'Tomono Kai', according to what Joan taught me back in Stockton, refers to a social gathering of friends, especially senior friends, for fellowship. To the delight of the elderly, hot lunches are always served."

"Wish we could afford them here," Johnston added. "Just tea and pastries. Several of our internees owned restaurants and they work together when our extra supplies permit them to create unimaginable good tastes. The tiny cakes are always intricately detailed."

"In Stockton, Joan loved attending the December Bonenkai meeting which, as you know, is the Tomonokai New Year celebration."

"Look, here come Joan's parents with her grandparents!" Peter exclaimed excitedly. "Never thought I'd see all of them together again! What a day for me and my future wife, the mother of our children."

"Yes, a fine family," added Johnston. "For a few hours, she has to behave as 'oyakoko?"

"Yes, I know the term. She says she prefers being 'nonky', or 'laid-back', but relishes being a 'oyakoko', a child who takes care of her parents. 'Oy' means 'parents' and 'koko' means child. She calls her grandfather, 'oji-chan, and her grandmother, 'oba-chan'."

Peter was beyond himself with joy. Just watching her with Kimi and Sayu, the oldest sister who just joined them, relating with their parents and grandparents, almost overwhelmed him with warmth and good feeling.

"Anyone of that family can recognize me. I know them so well, and they seem to appreciate me, although I think down deep in their hearts, they wish she had fallen in love with a Nisei."

"But, the way I understand it, she isn't really a full-fledged Nisei, she is a Nisei-sansei, right?" asked Johnston.

"Yes, and our children would be Italian-American-Sansei-Yansei-human."

Johnston chuckled softly,

"How so? It certainly is complicated."

"Well, the way I understand it, Joan's father was born in Japan, which makes him Issei. Her mother was born in California, which makes her a Nisei. Joan, born to an Issei and Nisei is a Nisei-Sansei, a third-generation born. Our children, Sansei-Yonsei, will be fourth-generation. That's why I call them Italian-American-Sandei-Younsei-human."

"Look at Joan now, in between mom and grandmother, standing and greeting the first arrivals of the elderly with their sons and daughters. Wish I had photos of these moments."

"Cameras strictly forbidden," said Johnston, a touch of sternness in his voice.

"Mr. Ikeda had a camera at Tule Lake. Why not here?"

"The Ikeda family was interned there first, when the interment experience all began. Rules were lax. Later, when the family was transferred here, he was asked if he had one in his luggage, and, being the honest man he is, he said, 'Yes'. It was confiscated instantly, without a word or comment. He'll get it back at the end of the war. But I agree, watching her relating to everyone without being aware of it is truly a highlight, a peak life moment. You'll never forget it, lieutenant."

"I'm so glad I'm here. This was just wonderful, Mr. Johnston. Thank you. Thank you from the bottom of my heart. I will cherish the last half hour, candidly watching her go about her business without her knowing. I was observing every moment, has been very, very special.

So, now, let's walk into the patio and I will walk toward her and . . . Oh oh, who's that soldier crossing the picnic grass toward her . . . he's wounded, an arm in a sling . . . why, that's . . . that's Yoshi! He was in our high school classes. He always had a little crush on her . . . Yes, I think it is him . . . and he's headed straight for Joan's family table. Is that a Purple Heart on his chest?"

"No, lieutenant, I heard he arrived late last night from a ceremony with the President. He's wearing the Congressional Medal of Honor. I didn't know he knew your Joan."

CHAPTER TWENTY-THREE

-

"No! No! Pure Insanity! No! Impossible!"

hom'o-phon'ic adj. (Greek homophonos), French homes…the same pitch; unisonous. Of or pertaining to sounding alike; of the same letter or character expressing a homonym, a word or name with the same pronunciation as another by with a different meaning origin and spelling.

Invisible fingers seemed to suddenly emerge from an ethereal disbelieve to clutch his heart. Instinct forced him to instantly turn away, lest Mr. Johnston observe his initial vague alarm surge into a crippling shock and anxiety.

His mind in a devastating whirlwind, Peter, feeling the first tear reach his cheek, turned back to continue observing Joan and her irresistible charm, beautiful face, and pleasant soft voice in animated discussions with internees he didn't recognize. Joan, hearing quick steps on the picnic grass then the flagstones of the hospital courtyard behind her, turned, then allowed herself a joyous yelp.

It was indeed Yoshiaki Ito, one of Peter's several friends in the ninth and tenth grades at Edison High School on South Center Street in Stockton. In a virtual dash across the half-dozen steps toward him, Joan, with her singular mannerisms and enthusiasm, eagerly slid her hand into the palm of his free hand, her fingers grasping his fingers. Rivetted, Peter watched Joan inquisitively scrutinize his eyes, verifying he was well. Clasping his face with both her hands, she kissed him hard and long on the lips.

Then, smiling broadly, and with quivering lips, she bit his ear, and whispered something into it. Yoshi nodded eagerly, an obvious radiance gleaming from his eyes.

His mind a chaotic mess, Peter sagged. Backing away from the window, and leaning against a stack of linen boxes, Peter had seen enough. Cold, sick, and riddled with grief, he staggered as he began to walk out. His face ashen, his head slightly drooped, he turned to Johnston and whispered hoarsely,

"Mr. Johnston, thank you for your thoughtfulness in taking me under your wing here this morning. Truly, thank you, sir."

"I'm so sorry, lieutenant. Being an old southern romantic, and too old to serve, I was hoping to assist a damn good fighter, I've learned. Miss Ikeda is precious and all here, including the U.S. Army MPs, love her. It didn't take me long to see why she chose you. I'm so sorry. Usually my words come like rain-filled streams. No pauses between them. But now, there are no words to be said."

"Well, you good man, if my friends have to be rounded up like common criminals and sent thousands of miles away from their homes to so-called 'relocation' and 'internment' camps, I want them under your safety and security. No finer man would there be to watch over their health and well-being."

Peter paused, as he felt a single tear reach his upper lip, then added,

"Right now, for both of us, words are futile and unnecessary. I need time to staunch the flow of pain the only way I know how, being alone in a long walk. So, if you'll excuse me, I'll be walking and trotting back to the station in order to leave immediately for the California West Coast and my next assignment."

"Well, sir, again, I…"

"Oh, for goodness sake, it's all O.K. A broken heart isn't a life or death issue. My joy was to see Joan a few minutes ago with her heart beating high with delight when she saw the man she truly loved."

Johnston remained silent as he observed the activities in the courtyard.

"As I think about it, Yoshi always seemed a little keen on Joan. But, she wanted me, and the whole city of Stockton, California, knew I wanted her. We were both on strict college-bound academic course work. So, we were in the Latin Club, Honor Society, Student Council, etc. together. He wasn't. He was a team baseball and football star, and taking classes in the industrial arts. I dealt with words. He dealt with nuts and bolts. She chose to be at my side. That's not to put him down. I always liked him. He's honorable and courageous, like all the Nisei boys I know and respect. His personal qualities are sterling. I suppose Yoshi and his family arrived in camp about the same time as Joan and hers."

"Yes, Joan's a few weeks earlier than his. From California, they went to Tule Lake, then transferred here. Once here, they were inseparable in all events, activities, and volunteer services."

Peter, shaking visibly, turned for the final time to glance through the window. Joan and Yoshi were huddled on a bench at the near end of the courtyard within a dozen yards of where Peter was gazing upon them.

"Look at how ineffably tender her mannerism are around him. She is truly the 'hidden deer', now, the ultimate feminine, pure womanhood in love with a wonderful man."

"Last night, he arrived from Fort Shelby in Mississippi, and reported to the Rohwer camp acting director, Mr. Marvin Ziegler, the principal of our onsite school while the Director is away for a conference in Washington. After welcoming him 'home', he was led to the Community Council, which had been alerted the wounded hero was back. After Yoshiaki, described his fight with German machine-gunners in northern Italy, and how he was decorated with the Distinguished Service Cross and Silver Star, Mr. Hayashi, the block manager of his parents' apartment, led him there where he is now a resident. Not even his parents knew he was returning last night."

"Can you believe that? A genuine hero, severely wounded, having to return to his parents' 'apartment' separated from other 'apartments' by blankets, and given an old, used World War I cot to sleep on?" asked Peter angrily.

"He said that his Commander, Lieutenant Colonial Gordon Sinclair, chief of the 100th Battalion of the 442nd Regiment Combat Team, asked for a Congressional Medal of Honor, but the higher-ups discouraged it. They told him to rewrite the request for the Distinguished Service Cross with Silver Star."

"What action?"

"Serenity under fire, whatever that means," responded the Red Cross Director. "All I know is what he told us last night. With part of his shoulder shot off, he underwent intense German Wehrmacht fire, machine gun, mortar and artillery, to retrieve, one at a time, four, fellow wounded Nisei Troops. Before he went out to get them, he tried drawing fire away from them onto himself. Once he got the four back to safety, he quickly organized a standoff with those who could still fire. His standoff lasted more than an hour until rescue troops arrived. From Rohwer, Captain Darrell Nishikawa witnessed the whole three-hour episode, from beginning to end.

"Oh," smiled Peter, "Yoshi wouldn't quit. Not him. Just like him. A true hero. I always had enormous regard and admiration for him. But

I never once figured on that out there," Peter said calmly, standing straight and stiff, head down. Johnston noted the twinkle in Peter's eye he had admired earlier that morning had died. So had the red flush in his face.

"Naw, no matter how I try to cut it, they make together one heck of a team for human decency, propriety, Japanese-American culture, and love between a full man and a beautiful woman, and mother-to-be. How is one disappointed or depressed about that? I wanted the guy to be me, but...Well, Yoshi, that lucky guy, now holds a piece of the sun in his hands," he soliloquized more to himself than the Red Cross Director.

Unable to endure the scene, the linen closet, even the presence of the gentle, kind, Mr. Johnston any longer, Peter, with a pale, silent face, wheeled and hurried out of the small linen supply room and hospital for the street leading to camp's outer fence and exit. As he was waved out by the Military Police, he heard Ray Johnston shout, "Don't forget the radiograms I gave you!"

It was nearing 0100 that day as Peter walked across the tracks of the Missouri Pacific Railroad 71 to the nearby Highway Arkansas State Highway No. 1. Without a glance over at the Rohwer camp, which was parallel to the tracks and highway, he walked naturally, normally in the midday heat and mild humidity. He bit his lip, thinking he should have asked Mr. Johnston not to mention to anyone, especially Joan and Yoshi, that he had been present at the very moment they were reunited after Yoshi had enlisted.

No sooner than he had begun his journey back to the Southern Pacific Station down, walking neither hurriedly nor leisurely, when passing vehicles, automobiles, trucks, buses, vans, panels, lorries and virtually every four-wheeled motorized transportation in that part of

Arkansas stopped to offer him, one of America's finest in uniform a ride.

"Like a lift, soldier?"

"Thank you, citizen. No, I'm just fine. Need time to think and exercise. Appreciate your thoughtfulness," Peter responded, waving the drivers on. Scanning the horizon, relishing the rare views of the Mississippi from occasional rises in the road, Peter marveled over what everyone in the Armed Forces knew to be true: No military man on foot along any road in the nation was denied transportation lest the driver be subject to lifelong guilt. The American public was truly proud of its fighting forces.

For almost three hours, Peter walked in the glaring sun. Virtually every vehicle driving toward him honked, its driver waving. Every form of transportation that passed him headed in the same direction pulled over and offered a ride anywhere the lieutenant wanted to go in McGehee.

Floor-flat, but punctuated by native pines, the geography between Rohwer and the train station was uninspiring. A light breeze helped in cooling the landscape, but not in his feelings of rejection, betrayal and abandonment. Although he yearned for solitude to ponder his future without Joan at his side, he was, in all honesty, helpless, distraught, haunted and lonely, perhaps the loneliest of his entire life. He had never been so disturbed. His usually cool, easy, all-solving mind was gone. Whirling thoughts told him he would have to live with an oppressed, dead heart.

With the edge of McGehee in the distance, and the station a few blocks beyond, Peter's moist eyes began to dry and his mind cleared a bit. He paused, panting from the long exhaustive exertion in a small roundabout and gazed toward the Mississippi River. Temporary U.S.

Army wooden storage buildings lay between the river and himself, with all their natural work and activities encircling them. What was going on was so normal and wonderful to behold that he decided to resolve his despondency. He chose at that very moment, at that spot, not to live his future life in her memory. He would never bear any antipathy toward Joan and Yoshi. No consternation, resentment, or jealousy. He would never be sulky, sullen, or bitter. He would never again be consumed by her, her wide, oval amber-brown eyes and jet-black hair, or how cute and pert she looked in home-sewn pedal pushers.

No, he thought, as the weather in the late afternoon became more onerous.

Then, as Peter was to finalize the trek to the Southern Pacific Station less than 30 minutes away, he remembered the unopened confidential radiograms that had arrived in the Military Police Administrative section that morning.

The first radiogram he pulled from his pocket was from Captain Oscar Del Barbra. Expecting a terse congratulatory sentence about his successful arrival at Rohwer, he opened it by tearing the end off. His half-smile froze in disbelief as he read,

"McClellan M.P. has flight schedule for your immediate return."

"What?" he gasped. "What?", he almost yelled.

Peter instantly searched his pocket for the other radiogram, pulled it forth, ripped it open, and saw it was radioed from Major General Rupertus' Headquarters-office. To his utter shock and horror, he read,

"Ghoul struck again early this morning. Return this day."

Peter felt his knees buckle.

At first, the cogent radiograms were so overwhelming, so trenchant, he did not comprehend the meaning of the words. Slowly, ever so slowly, as he gazed up into the cloudless sky, he began to grasp the inevitableness of their meaning.

"A third murder-mad Marine is involved?"

To Peter, at that moment, all the love stories in the history of the world rolled into one was not as significant as finding the third, maybe fourth, even fifth murderers. The change of heart of a young woman, regardless of how devastating it was to her fiancée who was "moon burned" every time he spoke to or saw her, was nothing compared to more young Marines doomed to death.

As Peter again attempted to vocalize a sound of shock, the familiar twinge of that "something" that undefined annoyance again hit him. Suddenly, an outburst of questions deluged him. A copycat Ghoul at work? A killing of passion made to appear planned and systematic in order to blame the Ghoul? Was Pinoe a wanna-be mad-murderer? Or, did the real Ghoul finally show himself? Are there more than two Ghouls? Three? Maybe, four or five? Each a facsimile of the other? Using the same systematic methodology? Or, was this latest death blamed on the Ghoul's resurrection, nothing more than a typical grudge fight between two Marines, resulting in a death made to appear the Ghoul committed it?

Peter concluded that the answers were quintessentially innate, intrinsic, to Pinoe's utterances as he was fighting for his life.

"For God's sake," he thought to himself, "I simply couldn't grasp what Pinoe was desperately trying to utter with his lisp. Peter felt the overall answer was within his grasp! But how soon would the clue break through? First of all, was he attempting to say one or two names? All he heard was "silly-gun", "believe-in-your-gun","spider man," "billet-gun", "willowy-gun", "winning-gun", "wiggle-gun", "widow-gun", "billings-gate gun", etc. etc.

Did any combinations make sense? For example, "billet-gun", or "billet", was a note or short letter. "Billing-gate" was a former London-city gate fish market notorious for foul, abusive language. No combination made any sense. Peter was conscious SOMETHING was within those lisped-pronounced words. But what? And, the more he thought about the various combinations, and the scramblings, the lonelier he became.

As he entered McGehee, the traffic along the highway seemed to increase. In the town's outskirts, pedestrians waved, yelled or greeted him in some manner or other.Although always respectful in acknowledging a hail or salute with a smile and thumbs up, Peter hurried, the burden of anxious-confusion on his shoulder.

Pensively, Peter entered the lobby of the station, surprised by the traffic of passengers arriving and departing, carrying valises, grips, packages, bags, binders, satchels, and even picks and shovels and other equipment. Walking across the waiting room perusing the noisy activity, Timmy Timms was nowhere to be seen. Opening the ticket office door as ticket buyers waiting in line observed his brashness, Peter spotted the station master seated at the desk next to the cot he had slept on the night before. Inundated with paperwork that needed attention, Timmy paid little attention to the visitor. As the vendor continued selling tickets at his window stall, Peter asked,

"Tim, can I get a ticket on the first train to Northern California?"

Instantly, Timms turned, smiling,

"There you are! Been waiting for you all afternoon. Ray Johnston called after you left the camp and told me everything. I immediately booked you on the Southern Pacific bound for San Antonio where you'll change trains for Los Angeles, Oakland, and Portland."

In appreciative amazement, Peter, looking warmly into the eyes of the station master standing before him, pencil behind the ear, outstretched hand, and said,

"You really are a good friend, Mr. Timmy Timms."

Startled by the sound of his own voice saying "that another rush of jumbled images and thoughts" for some strange reason crossed his mind.

"Why this sudden onslaught?" he asked himself. There was absolute silence. Timmy's lips were moving, but there were no words. The moment was crazy. Joan's beautiful face seemed to permeate his entire vision. Yet Pinoe entered, followed by Ellen, clutching a shiny Ka-Bar, screaming for his death. Then, Yosh tried to push everyone aside, but Pinoe slapped him down as he again uttered, "Billet-gun", "wind-gun", "willing-gun", "bit-gun", "bin-gun", "bitter-gun". What code was that? And, why, near death, would he try to enunciate such words? Oh, for solitude just now, in some lonely, wild Southwest geography, some vastness in Arizona, New Mexico, and West Texas, to decipher and decode those words. To roam with his new friend Timmy Timms in a beautiful, quiet place to sort the bothersome, annoying puzzle out, to face the riddle. Timmy Timms would stare the conundrum down without bewilderment or confusion.

Yes, Timmy Timms. You, a McGehee, Arkansas stationmaster, honest and hardworking as all good men, would solve "brittle-gun", whatever that meant.

"Silly-gun," Timmy Timms, "bitter-gun", "bitumen-gun", Billy Lundigan.

Billy Lundigan?

William Lundigan?

Bill Lundigan? Pure insanity!

"No!" Peter screamed, "No!
No! No! No! Impossible!
Bill Lundigan?

CHAPTER TWENTY–FOUR

-

The Return

With the last subdued light of sunset fading in the cloudless sky over the Russell Islands, Peter opened his eyes to a cherry-red hue silhouetting Pavuvu and Banika.

Gazing out a small forward window of the twin-engine C-47 aircraft that transported both cargo and passengers, he was grim and desolate. After long naps across the Pacific toward the runway on Banika, Peter's mind began to stir, and scramble into a whirling kaleidoscope. Hours and hours of blue waters, endless white and gray clouds, and the steady churning propellers blending with mental pictures of the Ghoul's murdered dead, Joan's smiles, which always warmed him, and, above all, the eager eyes and handsome face of his best friend, Bill Lundigan, now incarcerated at Peter's request in the 1st Division stockade on Banika, forced him to fathom the full measure of his relationships between Pinoe, Ellen, Schneidermann and Bill. Dealing with Bill was brutal and self-tormenting enough, but repeatedly reimagining Ellen's death was inconsolable.

The 7,000-mile flight from McClellan near the San Francisco Bay Area to Honolulu, he flew on a Liberator of the Marine 494 Bombardment Group assigned to the Seventh Airforce. Then, within an hour, he was on the C-47 headed across the south for Banika-Pavuvu. Unlike the individual seats of the Liberator, the seats of the cargo plane ran along the side of the interior like a subway car. With indentations at intervals deep enough to hold a paratrooper's parachute, he leaned back and slept, dozed, or napped the rest of the way. Most of the other passengers slept sitting with their heads in cupped hands.

Now, in the cool starlit night, the C-47 began a graceful descent to the airfield from the minimum approach altitude. Gear up, flap's down, power maintained at the normal controllable speed, the cargo plane seemed to glide the last thousand yards onto the runway.Peter understood that like all planes of World War II, his C-47 was loaded for flight beyond the weight limit, which all aircraft manufactures wash their hands of. His C-47 was no exception.

With the dull sound of impact, Peter smiled slightly and soliloquized, "Perfect weather, wonderfully-built cargo transport, competent experienced pilots, successful flight, superb landing."

Safely on the ground, everything was quiet.

Awaiting permission to disembark the aircraft, Peter sat quietly, gazing at the dozen or so Corsairs lined up and being readied for takeoff. Suddenly, through the night mist, a familiar black Buick was noticed peeling toward the C-47. A knowing smile beamed across the lieutenant's face. Peter knew full-well it was the staff car assigned to Captain Oscar "Slim" Del Barbra, Chief, Military Police, USMC 1st Division.

Uneasily, he watched the Buick pull up to the airfield's movable ramp being rolled toward the C-47's exit door. Peter quivered. He looked forward to the warmth of welcome Captain Del Barbra and Second Lieutenant Guidi would give him. But, more than all else, he was riddled with the most puzzling question of all: Was his buddy a third party to murder, or, indeed, was he the primary Ghoul?

Anxiously, even apprehensively, Peter sat, feeling lonely, shadowed by doubt, and burden with uncertainties. Although he wanted to acknowledge and reciprocate the affectionate, intimate hugs of friendship from both Del Barbra and Guidi, he couldn't, as he stepped from the plane and down the ramp. These were Marine officers who liked and respected him, yet as he stood before them by the ramp in the cold, breezy night, he was preoccupied.

Searchingly, Peter's eyes met the captain's, hoping beyond hope and reality that Corporeal Lundigan had somehow exonerated himself.

"Well, prodigy, you've been gone less than a handful of days, ostensibly for a week or two vacation, and upon your return a new assignment. Well, you're 'back home', at least until you finally put the Ghoul in a coffin with rotting coconuts and land crabs."

"Huh?" asked Toscanini, in a soft, tormented voice. "Captain, as exhausted and hungry as I am, I must see Bill tonight. There's no rest until I do. Even if I have to awaken him and roll him off his stockade cot. He's my friend, and I must know if he's part of the Ghoul, or the Ghoul himself. Will you drive me over there, now?"

"Why, no need, lieutenant. The corporeal is gone. He scribbled you a note before he boarded."

"Huh?" Peter repeated, bewildered, his eyes wide, searching, demanding, burning intently, penetrating Del Barbra's.

"What?" he repeated, a smile beginning to creep across his lips. "How's that?"

"Here's the letter! He wrote it on the gangplank as he was boarding. You had me incarcerate him for reasons you didn't fully explain. I did. When he was still a free man, and you were gone, a Ghoul killing of a nurse occurred. Then, while I had him in a cell under guard, another nurse was killed in the same way. He couldn't be the Ghoul. Whatever reason you had to lock him up was off base. Still don't know what you were thinking. But we know that Corporeal Bill Lundigan, who saved your life by shooting that Ghoul woman who was going to Ka-Bar your face is not the Ghoul."

As Captain Del Barbra continued, Peter, stunned, but deliriously so, accepted the letter with a trembling hand.

"So, your friend is out there somewhere on his way to Honolulu and Stateside. I cut his orders yesterday, right after I released him. He followed me from his cell right back to my office. He's going to advance combat photography school. We're all happy Bill is innocent. Your job, after you read his confidential letter to you, is to find the real Ghoul."

In a virtual hallucinatory state, Peter, somewhat hesitantly, tore open Bill's letter. Would it be angry? Insulting? Mocking? If so, Peter told himself, "I sure as hell deserve it - - to put him in a brig cell, my best friend who shot and killed a woman he may have been in love with who was about to slaughter me…"

As the captain and second lieutenant stood by, Peter read,

"You worthless fart."

"Who knows if you'll ever read this scrawled note, but if so, I need you to know this--you are my friend in this life, and the next, and the one after that and, hell, Peter, through the infinity of infinites. Simply put, you are my friend, whether I am yours."

"I was jailed for more than seven days, apparently on your orders. No one will explain why. Pondering it, I can only surmise you consider me a part of the Ghoul, or even the Ghoul himself."

"Matters not. I am no Ghoul, or knew of his activities. He left clues all around us, and we couldn't see them. I was always on edge around Pinoe and a bit disquieted around Ellen who, I saw from the beginning loved you. But on the day of the big performance, I was for some reason more restless and fearful because sitting next to her I saw her so fidgety and jittery. Then Hope left to pee, you followed him, Pinoe followed you, and Ellen, without a glance or word to me who escorted her to the front row, jumped up after a moment and followed him. In a flash, I knew I had to be there for whatever was going on. As she entered the officers' toilet house, I saw her pull a Ka-Bar from the large bag she always carried. When I saw her running toward your back, her Marine fighting knife held high, I pulled my .45 and shot her dead. Later, when I wanted to talk, you and Hope had been pulled away."

Who knows if we'll ever meet again? But as you always believed, loyalty is everything, Peter, you have mine."

Peter handed the letter to Del Barbra who, with Guidi reading it over his captain's shoulder, began to slowly read and digest it. Meanwhile, Peter stepped away and gazed up at the gloriously, glistening white stars in the South Pacific night sky.

"I put him aboard the USS DuPage (APA-41), which set sail at 0200 this morning for Hawaii. From there, he's to board the USS Burleigh (APA-95) for San Diego and immediately report to the U.S. Naval Hospital for 'treatment', possibly surgery, of this spinal condition. You know as much as anyone about that injury from high school football which still has him limping slightly."

"Yeah, he's always been in pain from it. Glad he's finally getting it done. I'll reach him there," Peter said soberly, still looking skyward. "How did you classify him?"

"Combat photographer, 3rd Battalion, 1st Mariners, 1st Marine Division, Corporal. His orders indicate his destination is the Joint Combat Camera Center at Fort Meade in Maryland to be trained as a Cinematographer for Combat Footage, the cameraman who films the most costly, dangerous fighting and battles for military analyses. Then, he'll be attached to the 5th Division for our next operation, probably the invasion of Guam or Okinawa on our way to Tokyo. He'll be assigned to the 5th's Photographic Services Branch, which means he'll always be filming from the forward points. The survival rate of such photographers is less than 25%."

"I know. I know," Peter said pensively, while nodding more to himself than to Captain Del Barbra. Slowly, his grim, uncompromising body posture and facial expression began to metamorphize into a relaxed embarrassment and heartfelt guilt. Peter's softer side, sensitivity, kindness, and endearment, began to emanate.

As the Captain of the Military Police led Peter to the waiting Buick for transportation to his sleeping quarters, and Guidi assuming the wheel, Peter smilingly commented,

"The hero ham of an actor. I'm so, so relieved, although a nurse and sentry had to pay for the clarification with their lives. Bill is 'Semper Fi', thank God Almighty. Did you know that none other than Louie B. Mayer, boss of MGM, was furious with Bill for signing up to go to war after his studio spent so much money grooming him for the picture industry? Can you imagine that? Bill, like so many of our boys, felt it was his duty for his country to enlist and Hollywood was mad at him. How can a guy like that turn out to be a murder-mad murdering his own buddies? I should have known it couldn't be him. I'm so angry with myself…"

With Guidi driving, Del Barbra on the passenger side of the front seat turned to Peter in the back seat and said,

"He's such a popular radio and screen star, he'll return more famous than ever. The 'cheapies' and lesser-known studios like RKO and Republic can use him. He's better looking and a better actor than anything they have."

"I liked him in 'Salute to the Marines' with Walter Berry," interjected Second Lieutenant Guidi.

"Well, Bill's a good man. You solve these last two murders quickly, your next assignment according to the scuttlebutt will put you near San Diego to visit Bill, who'll probably still be in bed."

"Unless the 'one who acts in plays and movies' is off somewhere with his hand-cranked 16-milimeter Bell & Howell Eyemo camera shooting half-inch frames on celluloid of combat."

"Well, whatever pleases. We've got our own work to do. Just hope the Ghoul sleeps in tonight. It'll save a life and a whole lot of work for us. Meanwhile, just for tonight, you'll sleep in my office. Arrangements are being finalized for your own quarters with the general headquarters staff."

"Anything to eat there?"

"We'll stop at the officers' mess before I take you up to the cot. I have to go back to my office to make the calls to ensure the 0700 meeting in the morning. Dr. Schneidermann has been the lead investigator since you left."

Peter, leaning back on the soft cushioned seat of the Buick, continued looking out the window during the final minutes to Captain Del Barbra's office. Finally, after a long moment of silence, he said, "I never appreciated Schneidermann's snaky coldness. The new field of psychology and psychiatry is attracting the mentally ill. The sick of mind those on the borderline of insanity. Men become psychologists or psychiatrist for one of two reasons. Either they are fascinated, truly intrigued, by the depths of the unconscious, desiring to explore it in order to heal the ill. Or, struggling to grasp and know it so that he can understand and heal himself. Schneidermann, from the initial moment of meeting him, told me by his entire demeanor that he is among the latter group. I may be unfair, but my instinct, my intuition tells me he is little more than a fraud. I tell you both all this in absolute strict confidentiality. Not a hint from either of you that I don't want to deal with our Dr. Schneidermann."

As the Buick pulled up to general headquarters and Captain Del Barbra's office, Peter was heard mumbling in the backseat.

"Schneidermann, what a laugh! He's no Lundigan, this Schneidermann who always seemed brooding, rancorously ranking over some narcissistic hurt or injury from childhood. Compared to Lundigan; Schneidermann is... "son-of-a-gun," "sprit-of-the-gun," "I-need-a-gun," Bill Lundigun, Lundigan, Schneidermann, Schneidermann, Schneidermann, The lisp . . . Dr. Schneidermann???"

. . to be continued . . . .

"Evil is evil and must be consumed in the flames of Hell, for there can
be no reconciliation with it . . . Evil is the path by which we reach the
good, the experience of freedom of the spirit and an inner victory over
the temptation of non-being."

Nikolai Berdyaev,
"Freedom And the Spirit,"
1935, p184.

AFTERWORD

The War in the South Pacific is long over, and, except for a rare battle reminiscence and occasional island-hopping history, forgotten.

Apropos is George Howe's statement from his Christopher Award-Winning World War II novel, "Call It Treason" (1949), produced as the superb 20th Century-Fox feature film, "Decisions Before Dawn" (1951) when he wrote, "…a man is alive as long as he is remembered, and killed only by forgetfulness…"

In all probability, no one today, including the few remaining veterans of the 1st and 5th Divisions, remembers the Ghoul, and the commotions he caused, if he indeed even existed. Today, some 75 years later, uncertainty shrouds The Ghoul, or Charlie the Choker, like a heavy shadow. Should a vague recollection exist, it is certainly one as "bitter as despair."

For all the erasures of supposed Ghoul incidents, did he really exist? Was he invented? Divined? In that "Pavuvu Nocturne" article about the Mad Ghoul, or Charlie the Choker, which appeared in the August, 1947, issue of USMC "Leatherneck Magazine", Corpsman Donald H. Edgeman wrote,

"The entire First Division evacuated Pavuvu in 1945, leaving 'Charlie' behind. Perhaps even now, he is stalking the jungles in a vain search for Marine victims and relishing the memory of all the disturbances he caused. But whether man or beast, this strangler of the night who defied grenades, machine guns, pistols, and clubs, may still revel in the knowledge that his mystery remains unsolved.

Other than a full chapter in Russell Davis' 1961 book, "Marine At War," and a few paragraphs in Craig M. Cameron's 1994 epic, "American Samurai--Myth and Imagination In the Conduct of Battle in the First Marine Division, 1941-1951," nothing about the mystery has appeared in print.

Infantryman Davis wrote in Chapter 8, "Rumor and the Mad Ghoul," pages 167-168,

"The Ghoul did not last much longer. According to reports, there were guards on every company street (in Tent City), and the military police made patrols all through the night. The Ghoul was sighted a few times, but always from a distance, and he was always running - - perhaps from a guard. The report was that his hands almost touched the ground when he ran, and that he loped like an animal. Everyone knew it was only a matter of time before we got him. Even a Ghoul couldn't beat the First Division permanently."

Davis continued describing how a large dark, man, wet and plastered with mud and panting as an animal, broke out of the swamp and onto the road. A military policeman raised his .45 and commanded the dark man to halt. Instead, the man turned and charged the armed military officer. The military policeman shot him three times, close up, with a .45.

"The Ghoul was dead." Davis concluded, although there was no proof that such a creature, as the Ghoul ever existed. But I believed in him at the time, and so did most of the Marines. Loneliness and a life in which rumor served as a morning newspaper could have created the Ghoul, spread his fame, and killed him off. No one will ever really know."

When Bob Loring, the preeminent book reviewer of the USMC "Leatherneck Magazine", questioned fellow Marine Colonel Walter

Ford about the 75-year-old rumor, Ford, equally legendary and nonpareil as the editor of the distinguished military magazine for more than three decades, responded,

"Bob,

I had never heard of the Mad Ghoul, but I searched the Leatherneck online archives and found a few mentions of the Mad Ghoul, also referred to as 'Charlie the Choker'. I recommend you, as a member, access the free online archives and search for the Mad Ghoul and Charlie the Choker. You will find the few Sound Off letters and the 'We-The Marines' content on this subject.

In one Sound Off item, you will read how Karl Schuon wrote he 'placed a blank sheet of paper into the typewriter' and created the Mad Ghoul on Pavuvu. It is not a true story according to Schuon who was a Marine on the Leatherneck staff in 1947 and penned many fiction articles for the magazine. As well as the many fiction articles in Leatherneck, Karl also wrote a book on bowling and other books.

Search his name as author in the "Leatherneck Magazine" files, and you will see how prolific he was as a writer. He later became the managing editor and wrote the original 'Home of the Commandants' book that became a series published by the Leatherneck Association.

Pavuvu was well-known as a 'pit' and hated by the Marines, so Schuon's fiction was highly believable. In reading the old Leatherneck material, you will also note that the Mad Ghoul was left behind on Pavuvu."

Karl A. Schuon, a native of Allentown, PA, joined the Corps shortly before the end of World War II. In the years that followed, he authorized numerous articles for "Leatherneck Magazine", served as artist for the "Marine Corps Gazette", and eventually was named managing editor of the magazine and remained so until his retirement in 1977. In his later years, he served as managing editor of "Leatherneck". During those years, he authored some 10 books, including the biography of astronaut John Glenn, "Home of the Commandants", the "U.S. Marine Corps Biographical Dictionary", and numerous short stories and plays.

So, as for the Ghoul?

Charlie the Choker?

Who will solve the mystery?

THE END

MEET THE AUTHOR
Don DeNevi

Don DeNevi was born in Stockton, California, where his father ran a hardware store. Seeing the Stanley Kramer film "My Six Convicts" at the age of 14 incited a life-long fascination with the psychology of imprisonment and the viability of rehabilitation. In the late 1950s, he interned as a teacher at a prison near Stockton before graduating from College of the Pacific with a B.A. in History. He continued his education at U.C. Berkeley, from which he received his Ed. D in the early 1970s, and has since taught classes such as Criminal Profiling, Organized Crime in America, Classic Crime Cinema and Understanding the Criminal Mind at multiple colleges throughout the Bay Area. In addition, Don was Recreation Director at San Quentin State Prison for 15 years, where he introduced a comprehensive recreation program and built the prison's first tennis court. The author of dozens of books, Don is a prolific writer and a fan favorite for many readers.

THANK YOU FOR READING!

If you enjoyed this book, we would appreciate your customer review on your book seller's website or on Goodreads.

Also, we would like for you to know that you can find more great books like this one at
www.CreativeTexts.com